PENGUIN CLASSICS

SELECTED STORIES

Ringgold Wilmer Lardner was born in Niles, Michigan, in 1885. His family was prominent and conventional, but he chose to follow the raffish trade of sportswriting. After rising steadily through several jobs on various Chicago newspapers, he was appointed in 1913 to write the celebrated column "In the Wake of the News" for the *Chicago Tribune*. During the six years in which he held this assignment he also became a prolific writer of articles and short stories for national magazines; what remains his most famous book, *You Know Me Al*, published in 1916, was a collection of six of these stories, written in the first-person voice of a semiliterate baseball player, Jack Keefe. In 1919 Lardner moved to New York and began writing a freelance newspaper column as well as more stories, among them "Haircut," "I Can't Breathe," and "The Golden Honeymoon." In the 1920s he was perhaps the most famous newspaperman in the United States, read by millions each week. His stories and articles were regularly collected in books, including *How to Write Short Stories* and *Round Up*, but he never wrote a novel. Since early adulthood he had been an alcoholic, and eventually his hard drinking caught up with him. He died, in 1933, at the age of forty-eight.

Jonathan Yardley is the book critic of and a columnist for *The Washington Post*. He is the author of five books—*Ring: A Biography of Ring Lardner* (1977), *Our Kind of People: The Story of an American Family* (1989), *Out of Step: Notes from a Purple Decade* (1991), *States of Mind: A Personal Journey Through the Mid-Atlantic* (1993), and a biography of the novelist Frederick Exley (Random House, 1997). He is also the editor of H. L. Mencken's posthumous memoir, *My Life As Author and Editor* (1993). He was awarded a Nieman Fellowship in Journalism by Harvard University for the academic year 1968–69 and a Pulitzer Prize for Distinguished Criticism in 1981. He lives in Baltimore, Maryland.

D0071472

SELECTED STORIES

RING LARDNER

EDITED WITH
AN INTRODUCTION BY
JONATHAN YARDLEY

PENGUIN BOOKS

PENGUIN BOOKS
Published by the Penguin Group
Penguin Group (USA) Inc., 375 Hudson Street, New York, New York 10014, U.S.A.
Penguin Group (Canada), 90 Eglinton Avenue East, Suite 700, Toronto,
Ontario, Canada M4P 2Y3 (a division of Pearson Penguin Canada Inc.)
Penguin Books Ltd, 80 Strand, London WC2R 0RL, England
Penguin Ireland, 25 St Stephen's Green, Dublin 2, Ireland (a division of Penguin Books Ltd)
Penguin Group (Australia), 250 Camberwell Road, Camberwell,
Victoria 3124, Australia (a division of Pearson Australia Group Pty Ltd)
Penguin Books India Pvt Ltd, 11 Community Centre, Panchsheel Park, New Delhi – 110 017, India
Penguin Group (NZ), cnr Airborne and Rosedale Roads,
Albany, Auckland 1310, New Zealand (a division of Pearson New Zealand Ltd)
Penguin Books (South Africa) (Pty) Ltd, 24 Sturdee Avenue,
Rosebank, Johannesburg 2196, South Africa

Penguin Books Ltd, Registered Offices: 80 Strand, London WC2R 0RL, England

First published in Penguin Books 1997

7 9 10 8

Selection and introduction copyright © Jonathan Yardley, 1997
All rights reserved

LIBRARY OF CONGRESS CATALOGING IN PUBLICATION DATA
Lardner, Ring, 1885–1933.
[Short stories. Selections]
Selected stories / Ring Lardner ; edited with an introduction by
Jonathan Yardley.
p.   cm. — (Penguin twentieth-century classics)
Includes bibliographical references.
ISBN 0 14 11.8018 8
1. United States—Social life and customs—20th century—Fiction.
2. Baseball stories, American.   3. Humorous stories, American.
I. Yardley, Jonathan.   II. Title.   III. Series.
PS3523.A7A6   1997
813'.52—dc20   96-44827

Printed in the United States of America
Set in Sabon

CONTENTS

INTRODUCTION

In the best of circumstances literary reputation is difficult to track and almost impossible to explain. In the case of Ring Lardner, it is all of that and more. In part because he was not a literary writer but a sports-writer and a newspaper humorist; in part because he steadfastly declined to expand the relatively thin body of his fiction from the short story to the novel; in part because he was indifferent to if not contemptuous of critical opinion—for these and other reasons Lardner has been an elu-sive target for the few literary scholars who have chosen to study his work, and thus his standing among the masters and mistresses of the canon has never been secure.

This may be changing. To some extent that has little to do with Lardner and everything to do with contemporary realities. At a time when the pool of doctoral candidates is steadily growing and the pool of fresh subjects for specialization is steadily shrinking, many writers previously thought to have been at the margins are being rushed into a respectability they do not always deserve. To be sure, no academic cult has formed itself around Lardner as has, for example, gathered around Zora Neale Hurston or Sarah Orne Jewett, yet he has not suffered the total eclipse that was assumed to be his fate only a couple of decades ago. Fears that he would be seen as a mere period character who wrote mere period pieces now seem unfounded; some of his stories are still widely read in high schools and colleges, students and other readers still respond to them with laughter and pleasure, and the fashionable stand-ing that baseball now enjoys among the illuminati has further enhanced his status. It appears that he will be around for a while longer.

As one who has a small investment in and a large admiration for Lardner, I welcome this revival of interest in the man and his work, yet from time to time I worry that it may be happening for the wrong reasons. Writers, like all artists, should be recognized and honored for what they actually did rather than for what we wish, or imagine, they had done. Lardner's accomplishment is genuine and in certain respects important, yet it is decidedly minor when placed alongside the work of others—Faulkner, Dreiser, Cather, Wharton, Mencken—who were his approximate contemporaries. In my biography of Lardner, which was published in 1977, I argued that his keen ear for American speech was "the chief instrument of a revolution in American fiction," one that eventually was completed by others whose gifts and vision were greater than his own; nothing has persuaded me to alter that view, but by the same token nothing has diminished my conviction that his work deserves to be read for its own merits as much as for the doors it opened for those more celebrated others.

The most important thing to know about Ring Lardner is that he was a newspaperman who stumbled, almost accidentally, into short-story writing. On March 7, 1914, one day after his twenty-ninth birthday, Lardner published a story in the *Saturday Evening Post* called "A Busher's Letters Home," a first-person narrative in the American vernacular "by" a fictitious, semiliterate professional baseball player named Jack Keefe. It was the first of six stories that two years later were collected as *You Know Me Al*, the "novel" that secured Lardner's national reputation, but there is no reason to believe that Lardner had set out to write an extended work of fiction or, for that matter, that he had set out to write fiction at all, as the term was then understood.

For nearly a year before the appearance of that first story Lardner had written "In the Wake of the News," a popular feature of the *Chicago Tribune*'s sports pages. Up to then it had been a fairly conventional sports column, but Lardner's restless mind and quirky imagination quickly transformed it into something that was entirely *sui generis,* a grab bag into which he tossed any old thing that happened to pop into his head. This included stories—about baseball players, about his own small but growing family, about ordinary Chicagoans—that occupied a territory somewhere between fact and fiction. The editors of the *Tribune* apparently recognized Lardner's unique gifts and granted him considerable latitude to develop them. The result was that "In the Wake of the News" became the laboratory in which he tested and explored himself, and during the six years in which he wrote the column, as his reputation expanded far beyond Chicago, his editors granted him ever more freedom.

He always exercised that freedom within the boundaries of journalism, or newspapering as it was then commonly called. There is absolutely no reason to believe that he ever saw "In the Wake of the News" as a springboard into literary short stories or any other form of "serious" fiction, nor is there any reason to believe that he thought such writing was of greater consequence than the work he did every day for the *Tribune*. He wrote the first "Busher" story not because the siren song of fiction at last became irresistible but because an editor of the *Tribune* had offered $50 for a baseball story to be published in the feature section. Ring came up with "A Busher's Letters Home," which the editor rejected, apparently because he was uneasy about its unschooled prose. Precisely what happened thereafter is a matter of dispute, but the end result was that the story was bought for the *Saturday Evening Post* by its legendary editor, George Horace Lorimer.

Ring was paid $250 for the story, which is to say at least $2,500 in late-1990s dollars. That was a lot of money for a young newspaperman who doted on his family and wanted to provide it with all the amenities he could afford. After readers of the *Post* responded to the first Jack Keefe story with wild enthusiasm, the price soon jumped all the way to $1,500. Lardner, who was then and always would be a thoroughgoing professional, recognized the opportunity for what it was and seized it. He was on his way to becoming one of the most popular and successful writers in the country: In 1919 he left Chicago and the *Tribune* for New York and a nationally circulated column, and by the 1920s his short stories were bringing in fees in the neighborhood of $30,000 in late-1990s dollars. In 1921 he bought a small estate on Long Island, made friends with the famous, and became one of the famous himself.

The stories in this collection cover the period between the publication of "A Busher's Letters Home" and the arrival of the Lardner family at Great Neck—the period, that is, during which the transformation of Lardner from regional newspaper columnist to nationally celebrated writer was accomplished. What he did in these years cannot really be called an apprenticeship, for Lardner's training was in journalism rather than in literary fiction and had been completed long before 1914. Neither can it be called a period of mature achievement and self-fulfillment, for it was not until after 1921 that Lardner wrote most of the stories—"Haircut," "I Can't Breathe," "The Golden Honeymoon," "A Day with Conrad Green," "The Love Nest"—that made him a fixture in the American English class syllabus. Instead it was a period in which accomplishment and exploration were mixed, in which some of Lardner's finest work (*You Know Me Al*, "The Young Immigrunts," "Some Like Them Cold") stands alongside other work ("Alibi Ike," "The Facts," "Harmony") that anticipates but does not match his most famous stories.

Between 1914 and 1921 Lardner published about seventy stories in various national magazines, chiefly the *Saturday Evening Post*, so those in this volume represent about a third of the fiction he wrote during the period. These have been selected not as the most representative but as the best. They are arranged chronologically except that "Call for Mr. Keefe" (1918) and "Along Came Ruth" (1919) are placed immediately after *You Know Me Al* (1916) in order to maintain the continuity of Jack Keefe's story; there are many other Keefe stories in addition to these, but none comes close to the level of the eight published herein, indeed some are embarrassingly contrived and are best left undisturbed.

The transformation of Lardner's fiction during this period is self-evident. At the beginning he is limited to baseball and the men who played it. As his friend Scott Fitzgerald wrote after Lardner's death in 1933, during his newspaper apprenticeship "Ring moved in the company of a few dozen illiterates playing a boy's game. . . . with no more possibilities in it than a boy could master, a game bounded by walls which kept out novelty or danger, change or adventure." As a summary judgment of Lardner's career this is open to dispute, but as a characterization of that career's beginnings it is entirely true. Still, we can see Ring gradually widening his horizons, expanding them to include not merely the ballplayers whom he used as stand-ins for ordinary Americans but, in time, the ordinary people themselves. Over the years American manners became his true subject, and he came to depict them with utterly unsentimental clarity.

It has often been argued—and a story such as "Some Like Them Cold" lends weight to the argument—that Lardner was what Clifton Fadiman called "the police dog of American fiction, except that his hatred is not the product of mere crabbedness but of an eye that sees too deep." Lardner thought this was ludicrous, as indeed it is, but it is a common misapprehension: that because Lardner was a social critic who looked at his fellow Americans with a cold and penetrating eye, he therefore was a "hater" who held those Americans in contempt. The truth was that he possessed a remarkable ability to couch his criticism of American society, culture, and mores in terms that amused rather than gave offense; it is precisely this same ability that distinguishes the newspaper columns and personal memoirs of Russell Baker. Both of these writers, who in most other respects are dissimilar, temper their chilly view of the American landscape with an affection for the people who inhabit and shape it; this is why American readers—who are, after all, those selfsame people—respond to their work in kind, with affection and self-mocking laughter.

It is noteworthy that although Lardner was immensely popular in his own country from the mid-1910s to the early 1930s, the most trenchant early assessment of his work came from England. During the 1920s

American intellectuals still suffered from an inferiority complex and tended to believe that any writing or art that accurately reflected American reality was inherently unworthy of serious consideration; this was especially true of the literary community, which was beginning to feel the liberating effects of Menckenism but was still under the thumb of the old guard. Lardner was read by many American intellectuals but usually with reservations influenced by European standards, as we shall see when the subject of Lardner and the novel comes up; but two prominent English critics had no difficulty in looking past the superficial frivolity of Lardner's work and locating its fundamental depth.

The first of these, surprisingly, was Virginia Woolf. Writing in the mid-1920s about the Jack Keefe baseball stories, she readily admitted utter ignorance about their specific milieu but argued, correctly, that this was essentially beside the point. She said he wrote "the best prose that has come our way"—meaning, presumably, the best prose to cross the Atlantic from the United States to England—and she took note of "the quickest strokes, the surest touch, the sharpest insight" with which Lardner "lets Jack Keefe the baseball player cut out his own outline, fill in his own depths, until the figure of the foolish, boastful, innocent athlete lives before us." In words that both anticipated and disputed Scott Fitzgerald's posthumous assessment, she wrote:

> It is no coincidence that the best of Mr. Lardner's stories are about games, for one may guess that Mr. Lardner's interest in games has solved one of the most difficult problems of the American writer; it has given him a clue, a centre, a meeting place for the divers activities of people whom a vast continent isolates, whom no tradition controls. Games give him what society gives his English brother. Whatever the precise reason, Mr. Lardner at any rate provides something unique in its kind, something indigenous to the soil, which the traveler may carry off as a trophy to prove to the incredulous that he has actually been to America and found it a foreign land.

That uncommonly astute judgment stood for more than three decades as the definitive critical evaluation of Lardner—as, if you will, the literary argument on his behalf. Then, in 1959, V. S. Pritchett reviewed a collection of Lardner's work newly published in England. He said that the "specifically American contribution to literature" was "talk" and that Lardner was the principal agent of it. "Now," he wrote, "mainly under the double influence of Joyce and Lardner's American successors—the stream of consciousness being married to the stream of garrulity—we begin to have a talking prose and are likely to have more."

It is this that directs us toward Lardner's true place in American, and twentieth-century, literature. To say that a writer's influence is greater than his actual achievement may seem halfhearted praise, but in Lardner's case it is anything except belittling. As every story in this volume attests, Lardner had an ear for American speech that was astonishingly accurate; he also had a perfect ear for music, and there is ample reason to believe that the two are intimately connected. It is an ear that we have taken for granted for decades, because it is a commonplace in American fiction. But it was Lardner who made it so.

Until Lardner came along the talk in American fiction bore little resemblance to real American talk. Even language intended to be informal and colloquial emerged on the printed page as stilted and artificial. Mark Twain, by any other measure a far greater writer than Lardner, understood the rough essence of American life but was buffaloed by its speech, which he tried to capture with an excess of apostrophes and italics and clunky ruralisms, as suggested by a passage chosen entirely at random from *The Adventures of Huckleberry Finn*: " 'Dry up! I don't want to hear no more *out* of you!' says the duke. 'And *now* you see what you *got* by it. They've got all their own money back, and all of *ourn* but a shekel or two, *besides*. G'long to bed—and don't you deffersit *me* no more deffersits, long 's *you* live!' "

Small wonder that young Americans now have problems with *Huckleberry Finn* that have nothing to do with its antiquated use of racial epithets; it is hard to read because its dialogue is often strained and out of date. Consider by contrast this passage from "Gullible's Travels," also chosen entirely at random:

"I want a highball," I says to the boy.
"What's your number?" says he.
"It varies," I says. "Sometimes I can hold twenty and sometimes four or five makes me sing."
"I mean, have you got a locker here?" he says.
"No; but I want to get one," says I.
"The gent over there to the desk will fix you," says he.
So over to the desk I went and ast for a locker.
"What do you drink?" ast the gent.
"I'm from Chicago," I says. "I drink bourbon."

What a difference! Where Twain stumbles all over himself trying to capture the American language in fake folk speech, Lardner gets it exactly right by the simple expedient of setting down exactly what he hears. "The gent over there to the desk will fix you" is the essence of American speech, as are "ast" and "I says." To be sure our speech continues to evolve, so an heir to the Lardner tradition such as Elmore Leonard or George V. Higgins will use somewhat different colloquialisms, but the flavor is the same, which is why Lardner's language only occasionally seems faded or unfamiliar.

Because we now take colloquial language for granted, it may be difficult for us to venture backward to the early years of the twentieth century and to imagine the shock effect that work such as *You Know Me Al* or *The Big Town* must have had. Even in the mass-circulation magazines, which were to America then what television is to America now, people talked in an awkward pidgin English that readers could understand but with which they could not connect. My hunch is that the real reason so many thousands responded with such joy to the early Jack Keefe stories was that they heard their own voices therein and were transfixed by what they heard.

Others were reading those stories, and taking note. Ernest Hemingway—another writer, incidentally, more important for his influence than for his own work—was a boy in suburban Chicago who feasted on "In the Wake of the News." He wrote Lardner imitations for his high-school newspaper; this did not sit well with the school superintendent, who castigated the boy for lowering his standards to mere journalism, but it served Hemingway well in later years as he refined his own journalism into something at once smaller and larger. Others who read Lardner with more than casual interest included James T. Farrell, Will Rogers, Edward Streeter, Eudora Welty, Sherwood Anderson, Nathanael West, John O'Hara, and James Thurber. The reputations of some of these have faded, but all were regarded as major writers in their day, and their collective influence on American literature was substantial; it is no exaggeration to say that they would not have been the writers they were had it not been for the liberation that Lardner afforded them, the chance to write the real American language.

H. L. Mencken, who was Lardner's most fervent and perceptive American admirer, called such speech *sermo vulgus* and contended, in his magisterial *The American Language*, that "the business of reporting it with complete accuracy had to wait for Ring Lardner, a Chicago newspaper reporter, who began experimenting with it in 1908 or thereabout." He continued: "In his grotesque but searching tales of baseball players, pugilists, movie queens, song-writers and other such dismal persons he set down common American with the utmost precision, and yet with enough imagination to make his work a contribution of genuine and permanent value to the national literature. In any story of his taken at random it is possible to unearth almost every grammatical peculiarity of the vulgar speech, and he always resisted very stoutly the temptation to lay on its humors too thickly." In a footnote Mencken gilded the lily:

My own debt to him was very large. The first edition of the present work, published in 1919, brought me into contact with him, and for the second edition, published in 1921, he prepared two amusing specimens of the common speech in action. At that time, and almost until his death, he made penetrating and valuable suggestions. His ear for the minor peculiarities of vulgar American was extraordinarily keen. Once, sitting with him, I used the word *feller.* "Where and when," he demanded, "did you ever hear anyone say *feller?*" I had to admit, on reflection, that the true form was *fella,* though it is almost always written *feller* by authors. But never by Lardner. So far as I can make out, there is not a single error in the whole canon of his writings.

High praise indeed. It almost certainly would have pleased Lardner, who was not vain but did have a realistic and honest sense of the value of his own work. He admired Mencken, seems to have enjoyed his company, and surely would have treasured so generous an assessment from so trustworthy a source. What we have no way of knowing is whether he would have accepted that assessment as the most, and the best, that could have been said about him. One of the mysteries about this taciturn and inward man is what he thought about his life's work. Was he content with what he had done, or did he wish that there had been more of it? We know that he cherished dreams of success in the theater—dreams that came close to fruition with the play, *June Moon,* that he wrote in collaboration with George S. Kaufmann—but did he also have dreams of literary success as well, of writing books that would assure the perpetuation of his name?

Such evidence as he gave us suggests to the contrary. In the 1920s, when at Scott Fitzgerald's urging the firm of Scribner's began publishing collections of Lardner's stories, he made a great show of diffidence about them. The first was published (in 1924) under the self-mocking title *How to Write Short Stories.* He supplied an equally self-mocking preface in which he wrote: ". . . a little group of our deeper drinkers

INTRODUCTION   xv

has suggested that maybe boys and gals who wants to take up writing
as their life work would be benefited if some person like I was to give
them a few hints in regards to the technic of the short story, how to go
about planning it and writing it, when and where to plant the love
interest and climax, and finally how to market the finished product
without leaving no bad taste in the mouth." He proceeded to suggest
sample titles ("Basil Hargrave's Vermitage," or "Fun at the Incinerating
Plant") and to demonstrate "how an apparently trivial thing such as a
line of dialogue will upset an entire plot and lead an author far from
the path he had pointed for himself." The message was clear: Nothing
herein is to be taken seriously.

It was not received thus in all quarters. Edmund Wilson, another of
Lardner's admirers, praised the book but couched that praise in ad-
monitory terms. Wilson wrote: "Will Ring Lardner, then, go on to his
Huckleberry Finn or has he already told all he knows? It may be that
the mechanical repetition of a trick that one finds in such a story as
'Horseshoes' and the melodramatic exaggeration of 'Champion' indicate
limitations. But you never know: here is a man who has had the freedom
of the modern West no less than Mark Twain did of the old one, who
approaches it, as Mark Twain did, with a perceptive interest in human
beings instead of with the naturalist's formula—a man who lives at a
time when, if one be not sold irredeemably into bondage to the *Saturday
Evening Post*, it is far easier for a serious writer to get published and
find a hearing than it was in Mark Twain's day. If Ring Lardner has
anything more to give us, the time has now come to deliver it. He has
not even popular glory to gain by pursuing any other course. . . ." To
which Wilson pointedly added: "What bell might Lardner ring if he set
out to give us the works?"

It is a question that has no answer. Lardner never addressed it, at
least not in print. He was aware that Fitzgerald wanted him to hunt
bigger game, as did Maxwell Perkins, the editor at Scribner's who
worked with both of them, but there is no evidence that he took such
counsel seriously. He may well have thought that comments such as
Wilson's were gratuitous, that what he wrote was his own business and
no one else's. This is a view that I shared while writing Lardner's biography, but I am now less certain of it. We have no reason to believe
that Lardner ever tried his hand at a long work of fiction, and that
seems to me a pity: not because he somehow owed it to himself, or to
us, or to the Anglo-European literary tradition, to write a novel, but
because it would have been interesting to see if he could have brought
it off. He showed in the best of the short stories—as well as in his two

accidental "novels," *You Know Me Al* and *The Big Town*—that he could create characters and situations in "the quickest strokes" so admired by Virginia Woolf. Wouldn't it have been interesting to see how he would have handled those challenges over the long haul of a novel?

It would interest us, but as for Lardner himself, who knows? I think it would have pleased him had he been able to write a successful novel, but obviously the thought of such pleasure was not sufficiently compelling to push him into trying. For that matter there is reason to doubt that he could have written a work of long fiction that would have satisfied both his readers' expectations and his own exacting standards. To have a genuine gift for either the short story or the novel is a rare blessing; to have a genuine gift for both is rarer still. Lardner had the short-story writer's genius: to grasp the essentials of a situation and cut right through to them with those "quickest strokes" and "surest touch" and "sharpest insight." But in none of his stories can one sense a novel yearning to be born; indeed the best stories come closer to vignettes, brief episodes in which character is revealed and, quite often, hypocrisy is exposed. To write stories such as these is no small thing, but a writer needs to be able to do more than that in order to flesh out the length and breadth of a novel.

So when one looks at Ring Lardner's literary legacy, it's hard not to feel a sense of frustration and incompleteness. He did a great deal, but he could have done much more. It is worth bearing in mind, though, that there was much in his life besides a lack of literary ambition to prevent him from doing more than he did. The most important limitation upon him was not the outline of a baseball field—what Fitzgerald, evoking a celebrated player of Ring's day, called "the diameter of Frank Chance's diamond"—but the way of the newspaperman. It is true that a handful of writers have cut their eyeteeth on newspapers and then gone on to larger business, but they are exceptions to an inflexible rule. Not merely does newspaper writing sap one's energies and thus discourage one from pursuing other, more challenging work, but it encourages the habit of evanescence. Even the journalist who takes his work seriously understands that it is gone with the wind, and over the years acquires a diffidence if not outright flippancy that is the enemy of literature. I have no doubt that Lardner was afflicted by this, that he simply could not see the point of trying anything that could not be done quickly and that would not pay handsomely. The difference between the born writer and the professional writer is wide; Ring Lardner was always the efficient professional.

He was also, no matter his taciturnity, a convivial fellow. He enjoyed the company of baseball people, show-business people, and newspaper people. This company was often, indeed usually, mixed with alcoholic beverages of which Ring early in his life became a habitual and heavy consumer. He held his liquor well, which made it all the easier for him to hold a lot of it. By the mid-1920s, the time of his greatest fame and accomplishment, alcohol was beginning to exact its price, not merely upon his health but also upon his productivity. He wrote right up to the end, and some of that late work has the old spark, but the energy that had brought him to the top was gone; even if he had wanted to write for the ages, he was in no condition to do so.

All of which is too bad, but what life is without its shortcomings and disappointments? By contrast with what Lardner failed to do, what he did is substantial and is beginning to show staying power. His work remains in print and almost always can be found in bookstore shelves allocated to serious literature. He is still revered by sportswriters and other journalists, and his influence can still be seen in their work. Most of all he is still present in almost every line an American writes. He is the man who taught us how we talk, and that is achievement enough for any lifetime.

SUGGESTIONS FOR FURTHER READING

Berg, A. Scott. *Max Perkins, Editor of Genius*. New York: Dutton, 1978.

Bruccoli, Matthew J., and Layman, Richard. *Ring Lardner: A Descriptive Bibliography*. Pittsburgh: University of Pittsburgh Press, 1976.

Caruthers, Clifford, ed. *Ring Around Max: The Correspondence of Ring Lardner & Maxwell Perkins*. Dekalb, Ill.: Northern Illinois University Press, 1973.

Elder, Donald. *Ring Lardner*. New York: Doubleday, 1956.

Fitzgerald, F. Scott. *The Crack-Up*. Ed. Edmund Wilson. New York: New Directions, 1945.

Kuehl, John, and Bryer, Jackson, eds. *Dear Scott, Dear Max: The Fitzgerald-Perkins Correspondence*. New York: Scribner's, 1971.

Lardner, Ring. *The Annotated Baseball Stories of Ring W. Lardner*. Ed. George W. Hilton. Stanford, Calif.: Stanford University Press, 1995.

———. *First and Last*. Ed. Gilbert Seldes. New York: Scribner's, 1934.

———. *Haircut and Other Stories*. New York: Vintage, 1984.

———. *The Portable Ring Lardner*. Ed. Gilbert Seldes. New York: Viking, 1946.

———. *Some Champions*. Ed. Matthew J. Bruccoli and Richard Layman. New York: Scribner's, 1976.

Lardner, Ring Jr. *The Lardners: My Family Remembered*. New York: Harper & Row, 1976.

Mencken, Henry L. *The American Language*. 4th ed. New York: Knopf, 1962.

Rice, Grantland. *The Tumult and the Shouting: My Life in Sport*. New York: A. S. Barnes, 1954.

Ritter, Lawrence. *The Glory of Their Times: The Story of the Early Days of Baseball Told by the Men Who Played It*. New York: Macmillan, 1966.

Turnbull, Andrew. *The Letters of F. Scott Fitzgerald*. New York: Scribner's, 1963.

———. *Scott Fitzgerald: A Biography*. New York: Scribner's, 1962.

Wilson, Edmund. *The Shock of Recognition*. New York: Doubleday, 1943.

———. *The Shores of Light*. New York: Vintage, 1961.

———. *The Twenties*. New York: Farrar, Straus & Giroux, 1975.

Woolf, Virginia. *The Moment and Other Essays*. New York: Harcourt Brace, 1948.

Yardley, Jonathan. *Ring: A Biography of Ring Lardner*. New York: Random House, 1977.

A NOTE ON THE TEXT

The work of Ring Lardner remains untouched by textual scholarship. No original typescripts are known to exist. This book, like all other republications of Lardner material, is based on the texts as they originally appeared in book form, in *You Know Me Al, How to Write Short Stories, Gullible's Travels, The Young Immigrunts, The Big Town,* and *Some Champions.*

YOU KNOW ME AL

Terre Haute, Indiana, September 6

FRIEND AL: Well, Al old pal I suppose you seen in the paper where I been sold to the White Sox. Believe me Al it comes as a surprise to me and I bet it did to all you good old pals down home. You could of knocked me over with a feather when the old man come up to me and says Jack I've sold you to the Chicago Americans.

I didn't have no idea that anything like that was coming off. For five minutes I was just dum and couldn't say a word.

He says We aren't getting what you are worth but I want you to go up to that big league and show those birds that there is a Central League on the map. He says Go and pitch the ball you been pitching down here and there won't be nothing to it. He says All you need is the nerve and Walsh or no one else won't have nothing on you.

So I says I would do the best I could and I thanked him for the treatment I got in Terre Haute. They always was good to me here and though I did more than my share I always felt that my work was appresiated. We are finishing second and I done most of it. I can't help but be proud of my first year's record in professional baseball and you know I am not boasting when I say that Al.

Well Al it will seem funny to be up there in the big show when I never was really in a big city before. But I guess I seen enough of life not to be scared of the high buildings eh Al?

I will just give them what I got and if they don't like it they can send me back to the old Central and I will be perfectly satisfied.

I didn't know anybody was looking me over, but one of the boys told me that Jack Doyle the White Sox scout was down here looking at me when Grand Rapids was here. I beat them twice in that serious. You know Grand Rapids never had a chance with me when I was right. I shut them out in the first game and they got one run in the second on account of Flynn misjuging that fly ball. Anyway Doyle liked my work and he wired Comiskey to buy me. Comiskey come back with an offer and they excepted it. I don't know how much they got but anyway I am sold to the big league and believe me Al I will make good.

1

Well Al I will be home in a few days and we will have some of the
good old times. Regards to all the boys and tell them I am still their pal
and not all swelled up over this big league business.

Your pal,   JACK.

Chicago, Illinois, December 14

OLD PAL: Well Al I have not got much to tell you. As you know Comiskey wrote me that if I was up in Chi this month to drop in and see
him. So I got here Thursday morning and went to his office in the
afternoon. His office is out to the ball park and believe me its some
park and some office.

I went in and asked for Comiskey and a young fellow says He is not
here now but can I do anything for you? I told him who I am and says
I had an engagement to see Comiskey. He says The boss is out of town
hunting and did I have to see him personally?

I says I wanted to see about signing a contract. He told me I could
sign as well with him as Comiskey and he took me into another office.
He says What salary did you think you ought to get? and I says I
wouldn't think of playing ball in the big league for less than three thousand dollars per annum. He laughed and says You don't want much.
You better stick round town till the boss comes back. So here I am and
it is costing me a dollar a day to stay at the hotel on Cottage Grove
Avenue and that don't include my meals.

I generally eat at some of the cafes round the hotel but I had supper
downtown last night and it cost me fifty-five cents. If Comiskey don't
come back soon I won't have no more money left.

Speaking of money I won't sign no contract unless I get the salary
you and I talked of, three thousand dollars. You know what I was
getting in Terre Haute, a hundred and fifty a month, and I know it's
going to cost me a lot more to live here. I made inquiries round here
and find I can get board and room for eight dollar a week but I will be
out of town half the time and will have to pay for my room when I am
away or look up a new one when I come back. Then I will have to buy
cloths to wear on the road in places like New York. When Comiskey
comes back I will name him three thousand dollars as my lowest figure
and I guess he will come through when he sees I am in ernest. I heard
that Walsh was getting twice as much as that.

The papers says Comiskey will be back here sometime to-morrow.
He has been hunting with the president of the league so he ought to

feel pretty good. But I don't care how he feels. I am going to get a contract for three thousand and if he don't want to give it to me he can do the other thing. You know me Al.   Yours truly,   JACK.

Chicago, Illinois, December 16
DEAR FRIEND AL: Well I will be home in a couple of days now but I wanted to write you and let you know how I come out with Comiskey. I signed my contract yesterday afternoon. He is a great old fellow Al and no wonder everybody likes him. He says Young man will you have a drink? But I was to smart and wouldn't take nothing. He says You was with Terre Haute? I says Yes I was. He says Doyle tells me you were pretty wild. I says Oh no I got good control. He says Well do you want to sign? I says Yes if I get my figure. He asks What is my figure and I says three thousand dollars per annum. He says Don't you want the office furniture too? Then he says I thought you was a young ballplayer and I didn't know you wanted to buy my park.

We kidded each other back and forth like that a while and then he says You better go out and get the air and come back when you feel better. I says I feel O. K. now and I want to sign a contract because I have got to get back to Bedford. Then he calls the secretary and tells him to make out my contract. He give it to me and it calls for two hundred and fifty a month. He says You know we always have a city serious here in the fall where a fellow picks up a good bunch of money. I hadn't thought of that so I signed up. My yearly salary will be fifteen hundred dollars besides what the city serious brings me. And that is only for the first year. I will demand three thousand or four thousand dollars next year.

I would of started home on the evening train but I ordered a suit of cloths from a tailor over on Cottage Grove and it won't be done till tomorrow. It's going to cost me twenty bucks but it ought to last a long time. Regards to Frank and the bunch.   Your pal,   JACK.

Paso Robles, California, March 2
OLD PAL AL: Well Al we been in this little berg now a couple of days and its bright and warm all the time just like June. Seems funny to have it so warm this early in March but I guess this California climate is all they said about it and then some.

It would take me a week to tell you about our trip out here. We came on a Special Train De Lukes and it was some train. Every place we stopped there was crowds down to the station to see us go through and all the people looked me over like I was a actor or something. I guess my hight and shoulders attracted their attention. Well Al we finally got to Oakland which is across part of the ocean from Frisco. We will be back there later on for practice games.

We stayed in Oakland a few hours and then took a train for here. It was another night in a sleeper and believe me I was tired of sleepers before we got here. I have road one night at a time but this was four straight nights. You know Al I am not built right for a sleeping car birth.

The hotel here is a great big place and got good eats. We got in at breakfast time and I made a B line for the dining room. Kid Gleason who is a kind of asst. manager to Callahan come in and sat down with me. He says Leave something for the rest of the boys because they will be just as hungry as you. He says Ain't you afraid you will cut your throat with that knife. He says There ain't no extra charge for using the forks. He says You shouldn't ought to eat so much because you're overweight now. I says You may think I am fat, but it's all solid bone and muscle. He says Yes I suppose it's all solid bone from the neck up. I guess he thought I would get sore but I will let them kid me now because they will take off their hats to me when they see me work.

Manager Callahan called us all to his room after breakfast and give us a lecture. He says there would be no work for us the first day but that we must all take a long walk over the hills. He also says we must not take the training trip as a joke. Then the colored trainer give us our suits and I went to my room and tried mine on. I ain't a bad looking guy in the White Sox uniform Al. I will have my picture taken and send you boys some.

My roommate is Allen a lefthander from the Coast League. He don't look nothing like a pitcher but you can't never tell about them dam left handers. Well I didn't go on the long walk because I was tired out. Walsh stayed at the hotel too and when he seen me he says Why didn't you go with the bunch? I says I was too tired. He says Well when Callahan comes back you better keep out of sight or tell him you are sick. I says I don't care nothing for Callahan. He says No but Callahan is crazy about you. He says You better obey orders and you will git along better. I guess Walsh thinks I am some rube.

When the bunch come back Callahan never said a word to me but Gleason come up and says Where was you? I told him I was too tired to go walking. He says Well I will borrow a wheel-barrow some place and push you round. He says Do you sit down when you pitch? I let him kid me because he has not saw my stuff yet.

Next morning half the bunch mostly vetrans went to the ball park which isn't no better than the one we got at home. Most of them was vetrans as I say but I was in the bunch. That makes things look pretty good for me don't it Al? We tossed the ball round and hit fungos and run round and then Callahan asks Scott and Russell and I to warm up easy and pitch a few to the batters. It was warm and I felt pretty good so I warmed up pretty good. Scott pitched to them first and kept laying them right over with nothing on them. I don't believe a man gets any batting practice that way. So I went in and after I lobbed a few over I cut loose my fast one. Lord was to bat and he ducked out of the way and then throwed his bat to the bench. Callahan says What's the matter Harry? Lord says I forgot to pay up my life insurance. He says I ain't ready for Walter Johnson's July stuff.

Well Al I will make them think I am Walter Johnson before I get through with them. But Callahan come out to me and says What are you trying to do kill somebody? He says Save your smoke because you're going to need it later on. He says Go easy with the boys at first or I won't have no batters. But he was laughing and I guess he was pleased to see the stuff I had.

There is a dance in the hotel to-night and I am up in my room writing this in my underwear while I get my suit pressed. I got it all mussed up coming out here. I don't know what shoes to wear. I asked Gleason and he says Wear your baseball shoes and if any of the girls gets fresh with you spike them. I guess he was kidding me.

Write and tell me all the news about home. Yours truly,   JACK.

Paso Robles, California, March 7

FRIEND AL: I showed them something out there to-day Al. We had a game between two teams. One team was made up of most of the regulars and the other was made up of recruts. I pitched three innings for the recruts and shut the old birds out. I held them to one hit and that was a ground ball that the recrut shortstop Johnson ought to of ate up. I struck Collins out and he is one of the best batters in the bunch. I used my fast ball most of the while but showed them a few spitters and they missed them a foot. I guess I must of got Walsh's goat with my spitter because him and I walked back to the hotel together and he talked like he was kind of jealous. He says You will have to learn to cover up your spitter. He says I could stand a mile away and tell when you was going to throw it. He says Some of these days I will learn you how to cover it up. I guess Al I know how to cover it up all right without Walsh learning me.

I always sit at the same table in the dining room along with Gleason and Collins and Bodie and Fournier and Allen the young lefthander I told you about. I feel sorry for him because he never says a word. To-night at supper Bodie says How did I look to-day Kid? Gleason says Just like you always do in the spring. You looked like a cow. Gleason seems to have the whole bunch scared of him and they let him say anything he wants to. I let him kid me to but I ain't scared of him. Collins then says to me You got some fast ball there boy. I says I was not as fast to-day as I am when I am right. He says Well then I don't want to hit against you when you are right. Then Gleason says to Collins Cut that stuff out. Then he says to me Don't believe what he tells you boy. If the pitchers in this league weren't no faster than you I would still be playing ball and I would be the best hitter in the country.

After supper Gleason went out on the porch with me. He says Boy you have got a little stuff but you have got a lot to learn. He says You field your position like a wash woman and you don't hold the runners up. He says When Chase was on second base to-day he got such a lead on you that the little catcher couldn't of shot him out at third with a rifle. I says They all thought I fielded my position all right in the Central League. He says Well if you think you do it all right you better go back to the Central League where you are appresiated. I says You can't send me back there because you could not get wavers. He says Who would claim you? I says St. Louis and Boston and New York.

You know Al what Smith told me this winter. Gleason says Well if you're not willing to learn St. Louis and Boston and New York can have you and the first time you pitch against us we will steal fifty bases. Then he quit kidding and asked me to go to the field with him early to-morrow morning and he would learn me some things. I don't think he can learn me nothing but I promised I would go with him.

There is a little blonde kid in the hotel here who took a shine to me at the dance the other night but I am going to leave the skirts alone. She is real society and a swell dresser and she wants my picture. Regards to all the boys.   Your friend,   JACK.

P. S. The boys thought they would be smart to-night and put something over on me. A boy brought me a telegram and I opened it and it said You are sold to Jackson in the Cotton States League. For just a minute they had me going but then I happened to think that Jackson is in Michigan and there's no Cotton States League round there.

Paso Robles, California, March 9

DEAR FRIEND AL: You have no doubt read the good news in the papers before this reaches you. I have been picked to go to Frisco with the first team. We play practice games up there about two weeks while the second club plays in Los Angeles. Poor Allen had to go with the second club. There's two other recrut pitchers with our part of the team but my name was first on the list so it looks like I had made good. I knowed they would like my stuff when they seen it. We leave here to-night. You got the first team's address so you will know where to send my mail. Callahan goes with us and Gleason goes with the second club. Him and I have got to be pretty good pals and I wish he was going with us even if he don't let me eat like I want to. He told me this morning to remember all he had learned me and to keep working hard. He didn't learn me nothing I didn't know before but I let him think so.

The little blonde don't like to see me leave here. She lives in Detroit and I may see her when I go there. She wants me to write but I guess I better not give her no encouragement.

Well Al I will write you a long letter from Frisco.

Yours truly,   JACK.

Oakland, California, March 19

DEAR OLD PAL: They have gave me plenty of work here all right. I have pitched four times but have not went over five innings yet. I worked against Oakland two times and against Frisco two times and only three runs have been scored off me. They should only ought to of had one but Bodie misjuged a easy fly ball in Frisco and Weaver made a wild peg in Oakland that let in a run. I am not using much but my fast ball but I have got a world of speed and they can't foul me when I am right. I whiffed eight men in five innings in Frisco yesterday and could of did better than that if I had of cut loose.

Manager Callahan is a funny guy and I don't understand him sometimes. I can't figure out if he is kidding or in ernest. We road back to Oakland on the ferry together after yesterday's game and he says Don't you never throw a slow ball? I says I don't need no slow ball with my spitter and my fast one. He says No of course you don't need it but if I was you I would get one of the boys to learn it to me. He says And you better watch the way the boys fields their positions and holds up the runners. He says To see you work a man might think they had a rule in the Central League forbidding a pitcher from leaving the box or looking toward first base.

I told him the Central didn't have no rule like that. He says And I noticed you taking your wind up when What's His Name was on second base there to-day. I says Yes I got more stuff when I wind up. He says Of course you have but if you wind up like that with Cobb on base he will steal your watch and chain. I says Maybe Cobb can't get on base when I work against him. He says That's right and maybe San Francisco Bay is made of grapejuice. Then he walks away from me.

He give one of the youngsters a awful bawling out for something he done in the game at supper last night. If he ever talks to me like he done to him I will take a punch at him. You know me Al.

I come over to Frisco last night with some of the boys and we took in the sights. Frisco is some live town Al. We went all through China Town and the Barbers' Coast. Seen lots of swell dames but they was all painted up. They have beer out here that they call steam beer. I had a few glasses of it and it made me logey. A glass of that Terre Haute beer would go pretty good right now.

We leave here for Los Angeles in a few days and I will write you from there. This is some country Al and I would love to play ball round here.   Your Pal,   JACK.

P. S.—I got a letter from the little blonde and I suppose I got to answer it.

Los Angeles, California, March 26

FRIEND AL: Only four more days of sunny California and then we start back East. We got exhibition games in Yuma and El Paso, Texas, and Oklahoma City and then we stop over in St. Joe, Missouri, for three days before we go home. You know Al we open the season in Cleveland and we won't be in Chi no more than just passing through. We don't play there till April eighteenth and I guess I will work in that serious all right against Detroit. Then I will be glad to have you and the boys come up and watch me as you suggested in your last letter.

I got another letter from the little blonde. She has went back to Detroit but she give me her address and telephone number and believe me Al I am going to look her up when we get there the twenty-ninth of April.

She is a stenographer and was out here with her uncle and aunt.

I had a run in with Kelly last night and it looked like I would have to take a wallop at him but the other boys separated us. He is a bush outfielder from the New England League. We was playing poker. You know the boys plays poker a good deal but this was the first time I got in. I was having pretty good luck and was about four bucks to the good and I was thinking of quitting because I was tired and sleepy. Then Kelly opened the pot for fifty cents and I stayed. I had three sevens. No one else stayed. Kelly stood pat and I drawed two cards. And I catched my fourth seven. He bet fifty cents but I felt pretty safe even if he did have a pat hand. So I called him. I took the money and told them I was through.

Lord and some of the boys laughed but Kelly got nasty and begun to pan me for quitting and for the way I played. I says Well I won the pot didn't I? He says Yes and he called me something. I says I got a notion to take a punch at you.

He says Oh you have have you? And I come back at him. I says Yes I have have I? I would of busted his jaw if they hadn't stopped me. You know me Al.

I worked here two times once against Los Angeles and once against Venice. I went the full nine innings both times and Venice beat me four to two. I could of beat them easy with any kind of support. I walked a couple of guys in the forth and Chase drops a throw and Collins lets a fly ball get away from him. At that I would of shut them out if I had wanted to cut loose. After the game Callahan says You didn't look so good in there to-day. I says I didn't cut loose. He says Well you been working pretty near three weeks now and you ought to be in shape to cut loose. I says Oh I am in shape all right. He says Well don't work no harder than you have to or you might get hurt and then the league would blow up. I don't know if he was kidding me or not but I guess he thinks pretty well of me because he works me lots oftener than Walsh or Scott or Benz.

I will try to write you from Yuma, Texas, but we don't stay there only a day and I may not have time for a long letter.

Yours truly, JACK.

Yuma, Arizona, April 1

DEAR OLD AL: Just a line to let you know we are on our way back East. This place is in Arizona and it sure is sandy. They haven't got no regular ball club here and we play a pick-up team this afternoon. Callahan told me I would have to work. He says I am using you because we want to get through early and I know you can beat them quick. That is the first time he has said anything like that and I guess he is wiseing up that I got the goods.

We was talking about the Athaletics this morning and Callahan says None of you fellows pitch right to Baker. I was talking to Lord and

Scott afterward and I say to Scott How do you pitch to Baker? He says I use my fadeaway. I says How do you throw it? He says Just like you throw a fast ball to anybody else. I says Why do you call it a fadeaway then? He says Because when I throw it to Baker it fades away over the fence.

This place is full of Indians and I wish you could see them Al. They don't look nothing like the Indians we seen in that show last summer.

Your old pal,   JACK.

Oklahoma City, April 4

FRIEND AL: Coming out of Amarillo last night I and Lord and Weaver was sitting at a table in the dining car with a old lady. None of us were talking to her but she looked me over pretty careful and seemed to kind of like my looks. Finally she says Are you boys with some football club? Lord nor Weaver didn't say nothing so I thought it was up to me and I says No mam this is the Chicago White Sox Ball Club. She says I knew you were athaletes. I says Yes I guess you could spot us for athaletes. She says Yes indeed and specially you. You certainly look healthy. I says You ought to see me stripped. I didn't see nothing funny about that but I thought Lord and Weaver would die laughing. Lord had to get up and leave the table and he told everybody what I said.

All the boys wanted me to play poker on the way here but I told them I didn't feel good. I know enough to quit when I am ahead Al. Callahan and I sat down to breakfast all alone this morning. He says Boy why don't you get to work? I says What do you mean? Ain't I working? He says You ain't improving none. You have got the stuff to make a good pitcher but you don't go after bunts and you don't cover first base and you don't watch the baserunners. He made me kind of sore talking that way and I says Oh I guess I can get along all right.

He says Well I am going to put it up to you. I am going to start you over in St. Joe day after to-morrow and I want you to show me something. I want you to cut loose with all you've got and I want you to get round the infield a little and show them you aren't tied in that box. I says Oh I can field my position if I want to. He says Well you better want to or I will have to ship you back to the sticks. Then he got up and left. He didn't scare me none Al. They won't ship me to no sticks after the way I showed on this trip and even if they did they couldn't get no wavers on me.

Some of the boys have begun to call me Four Sevens but it don't bother me none.   Yours truly,   JACK.

St. Joe, Missouri, April 7

FRIEND AL: It rained yesterday so I worked to-day instead and St. Joe done well to get three hits. They couldn't of scored if we had played all week. I give a couple of passes but I catched a guy flatfooted off of first base and I come up with a couple of bunts and throwed guys out. When the game was over Callahan says That's the way I like to see you work. You looked better to-day than you looked on the whole trip. Just once you wound up with a man on but otherwise you was all O. K. So I guess my job is cinched Al and I won't have to go to New York or St. Louis. I would rather be in Chi anyway because it is near home. I wouldn't care though if they traded me to Detroit. I hear from Violet right along and she says she can't hardly wait till I come to Detroit. She says she is strong for the Tigers but she will pull for me when I work against them. She is nuts over me and I guess she has saw lots of guys to.

I sent her a stickpin from Oklahoma City but I can't spend no more dough on her till after our first payday the fifteenth of the month. I had thirty bucks on me when I left home and I only got about ten left including the five spot I won in the poker game. I have to tip the waiters about thirty cents a day and I seen about twenty picture shows on the coast besides getting my cloths pressed a couple of times.

We leave here to-morrow night and arrive in Chi the next morning. The second club joins us there and then that night we go to Cleveland to open up. I asked one of the reporters if he knowed who was going to pitch the opening game and he says it would be Scott or Walsh but I guess he don't know much about it.

These reporters travel all round the country with the team all season and send in telegrams about the game every night. I ain't seen no Chi papers so I don't know what they been saying about me. But I should worry eh Al? Some of them are pretty nice fellows and some of them got the swell head. They hang round with the old fellows and play poker most of the time.

Will write you from Cleveland. You will see in the paper if I pitch the opening game.   Your old pal,   JACK.

Cleveland, Ohio, April 10

OLD FRIEND AL: Well Al we are all set to open the season this after-noon. I have just ate breakfast and I am sitting in the lobby of the hotel. I eat at a little lunch counter about a block from here and I saved seventy cents on breakfast. You see Al they give us a dollar a meal and if we don't want to spend that much all right. Our rooms at the hotel are paid for.

The Cleveland papers says Walsh or Scott will work for us this afternoon. I asked Callahan if there was any chance of me getting into the first game and he says I hope not. I don't know what he meant but he may surprise these reporters and let me pitch. I will beat them Al. Lajoie and Jackson is supposed to be great batters but the bigger they are the harder they fall.

The second team joined us yesterday in Chi and we practiced a little. Poor Allen was left in Chi last night with four others of the recruit pitchers. Looks pretty good for me eh Al? I only seen Gleason for a few minutes on the train last night. He says, Well you ain't took off much weight. You're hog fat. I says Oh I ain't fat. I didn't need to take off no weight. He says One good thing about it the club don't have to engage no birth for you because you spend all your time in the dining car. We kidded along like that a while and then the trainer rubbed my arm and I went to bed. Well Al I just got time to have my suit pressed before noon.   Yours truly,   JACK.

Cleveland, Ohio, April 11

FRIEND AL: Well Al I suppose you know by this time that I did not pitch and that we got licked. Scott was in there and he didn't have nothing. When they had us beat four to one in the eighth inning Callahan told me to go out and warm up and he put a batter in for Scott in our ninth. But Cleveland didn't have to play their ninth so I got no chance to work. But it looks like he means to start me in one of the games here. We got three more to play. Maybe I will pitch this afternoon. I got a postcard from Violet. She says Beat them Naps. I will give them a battle Al if I get a chance.

Glad to hear you boys have fixed it up to come to Chi during the Detroit serious. I will ask Callahan when he is going to pitch me and let you know. Thanks Al for the papers.   Your friend,   JACK.

St. Louis, Missouri, April 15

FRIEND AL: Well Al I guess I showed them. I only worked one inning but I guess them Browns is glad I wasn't in there no longer than that. They had us beat seven to one in the sixth and Callahan pulls Benz out. I honestly felt sorry for him but he didn't have nothing, not a thing. They was hitting him so hard I thought they would score a hundred runs. A righthander named Bumgardner was pitching for them and he didn't look to have nothing either but we ain't got much of a batting team Al. I could hit better than some of them regulars. Anyway Callahan called Benz to the bench and sent for me. I was down in the corner warming up with Kuhn. I wasn't warmed up good but you know I got the nerve Al and I run right out there like I meant business. There was a man on second and nobody out when I come in. I didn't know who was up there but I found out afterward it was Shotten. He's the centerfielder. I was cold and I walked him. Then I got warmed up good and I made Johnston look like a boob. I give him three fast balls and he let two of them go by and missed the other one. I would of handed him a spitter but Schalk kept signing for fast ones and he knows more about them batters than me. Anyway I whiffed Johnston. Then up come Williams and I tried to make him hit at a couple of bad ones. I was in the hole with two balls and nothing and come right across the heart with my fast one. I wish you could of saw the hop on it. Williams hit it right straight up and Lord was camped under it. Then up come Pratt the best hitter on their club. You know what I done to him don't you Al? I give him one spitter and another he didn't strike at that was a ball. Then I come back with two fast ones and Mister Pratt was a dead baby. And you notice they didn't steal no bases neither.

In our half of the seventh inning Weaver and Schalk got on and I was going up there with a stick when Callahan calls me back and sends Easterly up. I don't know what kind of managing you call that. I hit good on the training trip and he must of knew they had no chance to score off me in the innings they had left while they were liable to murder his other pitchers. I come back to the bench pretty hot and I says You're making a mistake. He says If Comiskey had wanted you to manage this team he would of hired you.

Then Easterly pops out and I says Now I guess you're sorry you didn't let me hit. That sent him right up in the air and he bawled me awful. Honest Al I would of cracked him right in the jaw if we hadn't been right out where everybody could of saw us. Well he sent Cicotte in to finish and they didn't score no more and we didn't neither.

I road down in the car with Gleason. He says Boy you shouldn't ought to talk like that to Cal. Some day he will lose his temper and bust you one. I says He won't never bust me. I says He didn't have no right to talk like that to me. Gleason says I suppose you think he's going to laugh and smile when we lost four out of the first five games. He says Wait till to-night and then go up to him and let him know you are sorry you sassed him. I says I didn't sass him and ain't sorry.

So after supper I seen Callahan sitting in the lobby and I went over and sit down by him. I says When are you going to let me work? He says I wouldn't never let you work only my pitchers are all shot to pieces. Then I told him about you boys coming up from Bedford to watch me during the Detroit serious and he says Well I will start you in the second game against Detroit. He says But I wouldn't if I had any pitchers. He says A girl could get out there and pitch better than some of them have been doing.

So you see Al I am going to pitch on the nineteenth. I hope you guys can be up there and I will show you something. I know I can beat them Tigers and I will have to do it even if they are Violet's team.

I notice that New York and Boston got trimmed today so I suppose they wish Comiskey would ask for waivers on me. No chance Al.

Your old pal,   JACK.

P. S.—We play eleven games in Chi and then go to Detroit. So I will see the little girl on the twenty-ninth.

Oh you Violet.

Chicago, Illinois, April 19

DEAR OLD PAL: Well Al it's just as well you couldn't come. They beat me and I am writing you this so as you will know the truth about the game and not get a bum steer from what you read in the papers.

I had a sore arm when I was warming up and Callahan should never ought to of sent me in there. And Schalk kept signing for my fast ball and I kept giving it to him because I thought he ought to know something about the batters. Weaver and Lord and all of them kept kicking them round the infield and Collins and Bodie couldn't catch nothing.

Callahan ought never to of left me in there when he seen how sore my arm was. Why, I couldn't of threw hard enough to break a pain of glass my arm was so sore.

They sure did run wild on the bases. Cobb stole four and Bush and Crawford and Veach about two apiece. Schalk didn't even make a peg half the time. I guess he was trying to throw me down.

The score was sixteen to two when Callahan finally took me out in the eighth and I don't know how many more they got. I kept telling him to take me out when I seen how bad I was but he wouldn't do it. They started bunting in the fifth and Lord and Chase just stood there and didn't give me no help at all.

I was all O. K. till I had the first two men out in the first inning. Then Crawford come up. I wanted to give him a spitter but Schalk signs me for the fast one and I give it to him. The ball didn't hop much and Crawford happened to catch it just right. At that Collins ought to of catched the ball. Crawford made three bases and up come Cobb. It was the first time I ever seen him. He hollered at me right off the reel. He says You better walk me you busher. I says I will walk you back to the bench. Schalk signs for a spitter and I gives it to him and Cobb misses it.

Then instead of signing for another one Schalk asks for a fast one and I shook my head no but he signed for it again and yells Put something on it. So I throwed a fast one and Cobb hits it right over second base. I don't know what Weaver was doing but he never made a move for the ball. Crawford scored and Cobb was on first base. First thing I knowed he had stole second while I held the ball. Callahan yells Wake up out there and I says Why don't your catcher tell me when they are going to steal. Schalk says Get in there and pitch and shut your mouth. Then I got mad and walked Veach and Moriarty but before I walked Moriarty Cobb and Veach pulled a double steal on Schalk. Gainor lifts a fly and Lord drops it and two more come in. Then Stanage walks and I whiffs their pitcher.

I come in to the bench and Callahan says Are your friends from Bedford up here? I was pretty sore and I says Why don't you get a catcher? He says We don't need no catcher when you're pitching because you can't get nothing past their bats. Then he says You better leave your uniform in here when you go out next inning or Cobb will steal it off your back. I says My arm is sore. He says Use your other one and you'll do just as good.

Gleason says Who do you want to warm up? Callahan says Nobody. He says Cobb is going to lead the league in batting and basestealing anyway so we might as well give him a good start. I was mad enough to punch his jaw but the boys winked at me not to do nothing.

Well I got some support in the next inning and nobody got on. Between innings I says Well I guess I look better now don't I? Callahan says Yes but you wouldn't look so good if Collins hadn't jumped up on the fence and catched that one off Crawford. That's all the encouragement I got Al.

Cobb come up again to start the third and when Schalk signs me for a fast one I shakes my head. Then Schalk says All right pitch anything you want to. I pitched a spitter and Cobb bunts it right at me. I would of threw him out a block but I stubbed my toe in a rough place and fell down. This is the roughest ground I ever seen Al. Veach bunts and for a wonder Lord throws him out. Cobb goes to second and honest Al I forgot all about him being there and first thing I knowed he had stole third. Then Moriarty hits a fly ball to Bodie and Cobb scores though Bodie ought to of threw him out twenty feet.

They batted all round in the forth inning and scored four or five more. Crawford got the luckiest three-base hit I ever see. He popped one way up in the air and the wind blowed it against the fence. The wind is something fierce here Al. At that Collins ought to of got under it.

I was looking at the bench all the time expecting Callahan to call me in but he kept hollering Go on and pitch. Your friends want to see you pitch.

Well Al I don't know how they got the rest of their runs but they had more luck than any team I ever seen. And all the time Jennings was on the coaching line yelling like a Indian. Some day Al I'm going to punch his jaw.

After Veach had hit one in the eight Callahan calls me to the bench and says You're through for the day. I says It's about time you found out my arm was sore. He says I ain't worrying about your arm but I'm afraid some of our outfielders will run their legs off and some of them poor infielders will get killed. He says The reporters just sent me a message saying they had run out of paper. Then he says I wish some of the other clubs had pitchers like you so we could hit once in a while. He says Go in the clubhouse and get your arm rubbed off. That's the only way I can get Jennings sore he says.

Well Al that's about all there was to it. It will take two or three stamps to send this but I want you to know the truth about it. The way my arm was I ought never to of went in there.   Yours truly,   JACK.

Chicago, Illinois, April 25
FRIEND AL: Just a line to let you know I am still on earth. My arm feels pretty good again and I guess maybe I will work at Detroit. Violet writes that she can't hardly wait to see me. Looks like I got a regular girl now Al. We go up there the twenty-ninth and maybe I won't be glad to see her. I hope she will be out to the game the day I pitch. I will pitch the way I want to next time and them Tigers won't have such a picnic.

I suppose you seen what the Chicago reporters said about that game. I will punch a couple of their jaws when I see them.

Your pal,   JACK.

Chicago, Illinois, April 29
DEAR OLD AL: Well Al it's all over. The club went to Detroit last night and I didn't go along. Callahan told me to report to Comiskey this morning and I went up to the office at ten o'clock. He give me my pay to date and broke the news. I am sold to Frisco.

I asked him how they got wavers on me and he says Oh there was no trouble about that because they all heard how you tamed the Tigers. Then he patted me on the back and says Go out there and work hard boy and maybe you'll get another chance some day. I was kind of choked up so I walked out of the office.

I ain't had no fair deal Al and I ain't going to no Frisco. I will quit the game first and take that job Charley offered me at the billiard hall.

I expect to be in Bedford in a couple of days. I have got to pack up first and settle with my landlady about my room here which I engaged for all season thinking I would be treated square. I am going to rest and lay round home a while and try to forget this rotten game. Tell the boys about it Al and tell them I never would of got let out if I hadn't worked with a sore arm.

I feel sorry for that little girl up in Detroit Al. She expected me there today.   Your old pal,   JACK.

P. S. I suppose you seen where that lucky lefthander Allen shut out Cleveland with two hits yesterday. The lucky stiff.

THE BUSHER COMES BACK

San Francisco, California, May 13

FRIEND AL: I suppose you and the rest of the boys in Bedford will be supprised to learn that I am out here, because I remember telling you when I was sold to San Francisco by the White Sox that not under no circumstances would I report here. I was pretty mad when Comiskey give me my release, because I didn't think I had been given a fair show by Callahan. I don't think so yet Al and I never will but Bill Sullivan the old White Sox catcher talked to me and told me not to pull no boner by refuseing to go where they sent me. He says You're only hurting yourself. He says You must remember that this was your first time up in the big show and very few men no matter how much stuff they got can expect to make good right off the reel. He says All you need is experience and pitching out in the Coast League will be just the thing for you.

So I went in and asked Comiskey for my transportation and he says That's right Boy go out there and work hard and maybe I will want you back. I told him I hoped so but I don't hope nothing of the kind Al. I am going to see if I can't get Detroit to buy me, because I would rather live in Detroit than anywheres else. The little girl who got stuck on me this spring lives there. I guess I told you about her Al. Her name is Violet and she is some queen. And then if I got with the Tigers I wouldn't never have to pitch against Cobb and Crawford, though I believe I could show both of them up if I was right. They ain't got much of a ball club here and hardly any good pitchers outside of me. But I don't care.

I will win some games if they give me any support and I will get back in the big league and show them birds something. You know me, Al.   Your pal,   JACK.

Los Angeles, California, May 20

AL: Well old pal I don't suppose you can find much news of this league in the papers at home so you may not know that I have been standing this league on their heads. I pitched against Oakland up home and shut them out with two hits. I made them look like suckers Al. They hadn't never saw no speed like mine and they was scared to death the minute I cut loose. I could of pitched the last six innings with my foot and trimmed them they was so scared.

Well we come down here for a serious and I worked the second game. They got four hits and one run, and I just give them the one run. Their shortstop Johnson was on the training trip with the White Sox and of course I knowed him pretty well. So I eased up in the last inning and let him hit one. If I had of wanted to let myself out he couldn't of hit me with a board. So I am going along good and Howard our manager says he is going to use me regular. He's a pretty nice manager and not a bit sarcastic like some of them big leaguers. I am fielding my position good and watching the baserunners to. Thank goodness Al they ain't no Cobbs in this league and a man ain't scared of haveing his uniform stole off his back.

But listen Al I don't want to be bought by Detroit no more. It is all off between Violet and I. She wasn't the sort of girl I suspected. She is just like them all Al. No heart. I wrote her a letter from Chicago telling her I was sold to San Francisco and she wrote back a postcard saying something about not haveing no time to waste on bushers. What do you know about that Al? Calling me a busher. I will show them. She wasn't no good Al and I figure I am well rid of her. Good riddance is rubbish as they say.

I will let you know how I get along and if I hear anything about being sold or drafted.   Yours truly,   JACK.

San Francisco, California, July 20

FRIEND AL: You will forgive me for not writeing to you oftener when you hear the news I got for you. Old pal I am engaged to be married.

Her name is Hazel Carney and she is some queen, Al—a great big stropping girl that must weigh one hundred and sixty lbs. She is out to every game and she got stuck on me from watching me work.

Then she writes a note to me and makes a date and I meet her down on Market Street one night. We go to a nickel show together and have some time. Since then we been together pretty near every evening except when I was away on the road.

Night before last she asked me if I was married and I tells her No and she says a big handsome man like I ought not to have no trouble finding a wife. I tells her I ain't never looked for one and she says Well you wouldn't have to look very far. I asked her if she was married and she said No but she wouldn't mind it. She likes her beer pretty well and her and I had several and I guess I was feeling pretty good. Anyway I guess I asked her if she wouldn't marry me and she says it was O. K. I ain't a bit sorry Al because she is some doll and will make them all sit up back home. She wanted to get married right away but I said No wait till the season is over and maybe I will have more dough. She asked me what I was getting and I told her two hundred dollars a month. She says she didn't think I was getting enough and I don't neither but I will get the money when I get up in the big show again.

Anyway we are going to get married this fall and then I will bring her home and show her to you. She wants to live in Chi or New York but I guess she will like Bedford O. K. when she gets acquainted.

I have made good here all right Al. Up to a week ago Sunday I had won eleven straight. I have lost a couple since then, but one day I wasn't feeling good and the other time they kicked it away behind me.

I had a run in with Howard after Portland had beat me. He says Keep on running round with that skirt and you won't never win another game.

He says Go to bed nights and keep in shape or I will take your money. I told him to mind his own business and then he walked away from me. I guess he was scared I was going to smash him. No manager ain't going to bluff me Al. So I went to bed early last night and didn't keep my date with the kid. She was pretty sore about it but business before pleasure Al. Don't tell the boys nothing about me being engaged. I want to surprise them.   Your pal,   JACK.

Sacramento, California, August 16
FRIEND AL: Well Al I got the supprise of my life last night. Howard called me up after I got to my room and tells me I am going back to the White Sox. Come to find out, when they sold me out here they kept

a option on me and yesterday they exercised it. He told me I would have to report at once. So I packed up as quick as I could and then went down to say good-by to the kid. She was all broke up and wanted to go along with me but I told her I didn't have enough dough to get married. She said she would come anyway and we could get married in Chi but I told her she better wait. She cried all over my sleeve. She sure is gone on me Al and I couldn't help feeling sorry for her but I promised to send for her in October and then everything will be all O. K. She asked me how much I was going to get in the big league and I told her I would get a lot more money than out here because I wouldn't play if I didn't. You know me Al.

I come over here to Sacramento with the club this morning and I am leaveing to-night for Chi. I will get there next Tuesday and I guess Callahan will work me right away because he must of seen his mistake in letting me go by now. I will show them Al.

I looked up the skedule and I seen where we play in Detroit the fifth and sixth of September. I hope they will let me pitch there Al. Violet goes to the games and I will make her sorry she give me that kind of treatment. And I will make them Tigers sorry they kidded me last spring. I ain't afraid of Cobb or none of them now, Al.   Your pal,   JACK.

Chicago, Illinois, August 27

AL: Well old pal I guess I busted in right. Did you notice what I done to them Athaletics, the best ball club in the country? I bet Violet wishes she hadn't called me no busher.

I got here last Tuesday and set up in the stand and watched the game that afternoon. Washington was playing here and Johnson pitched. I was anxious to watch him because I had heard so much about him. Honest Al he ain't as fast as me. He shut them out, but they never was much of a hitting club. I went to the clubhouse after the game and shook hands with the bunch. Kid Gleason the assistant manager seemed pretty glad to see me and he says Well have you learned something? I says Yes I guess I have. He says Did you see the game this afternoon? I says I had and he asked me what I thought of Johnson. I says I don't think so much of him. He says Well I guess you ain't learned nothing then. He says What was the matter with Johnson's work? I says He ain't got nothing but a fast ball. Then he says Yes and Rockefeller ain't got nothing but a hundred million bucks.

Well I asked Callahan if he was going to give me a chance to work and he says he was. But I sat on the bench a couple of days and he didn't ask me to do nothing. Finally I asked him why not and he says I am saving you to work against a good club, the Athaletics. Well the Athaletics come and I guess you know by this time what I done to them. And I had to work against Bender at that but I ain't afraid of none of them now Al.

Baker didn't hit one hard all afternoon and I didn't have no trouble with Collins neither. I let them down with five blows all though the papers give them seven. Them reporters here don't no more about scoreing than some old woman. They give Barry a hit on a fly ball that Bodie ought to of eat up, only he stumbled or something and they handed Oldring a two base hit on a ball that Weaver had to duck to get out of the way from. But I don't care nothing about reporters. I beat them Athaletics and beat them good, five to one. Gleason slapped me on the back after the game and says Well you learned something after all. Rub some arnicky on your head to keep the swelling down and you may be a real pitcher yet. I says I ain't got no swell head. He says No. If I hated myself like you do I would be a moveing picture actor.

Well I asked Callahan would he let me pitch up to Detroit and he says Sure. He says Do you want to get revenge on them? I says, Yes I did. He says Well you have certainly got some comeing. He says I never seen no man get worse treatment than them Tigers give you last spring. I says Well they won't do it this time because I will know how to pitch to them. He says How are you going to pitch to Cobb? I says I am going to feed him on my slow one. He says Well Cobb had ought to make a good meal off of that. Then we quit jokeing and he says You have improved a hole lot and I am going to work you right along regular and if you can stand the gaff I may be able to use you in the city serious. You know Al the White Sox plays a city serious every fall with the Cubs and the players makes quite a lot of money. The winners get about eight hundred dollars a peace and the losers about five hundred. We will be the winners if I have anything to say about it.

I am tickled to death at the chance of working in Detroit and I can't hardly wait till we get there. Watch my smoke Al.

Your pal,   JACK.
P. S. I am going over to Allen's flat to play cards a while to-night. Allen is the left-hander that was on the training trip with us. He ain't got a thing, Al, and I don't see how he gets by. He is married and his wife's sister is visiting them. She wants to meet me but it won't do her much good. I seen her out to the game today and she ain't much for looks.

Detroit, Mich., September 6

FRIEND AL: I got a hole lot to write but I ain't got much time because we are going over to Cleveland on the boat at ten p.m. I made them Tigers like it Al just like I said I would. And what do you think, Al, Violet called me up after the game and wanted to see me but I will tell you about the game first.

They got one hit off of me and Cobb made it a scratch single that he beat out. If he hadn't of been so dam fast I would of had a no hit game. At that Weaver could of threw him out if he had of started after the ball in time. Crawford didn't get nothing like a hit and I whiffed him once. I give two walks both of them to Bush but he is such a little guy that you can't pitch to him.

When I was warming up before the game Callahan was standing beside me and pretty soon Jennings come over. Jennings says You ain't going to pitch that bird are you? And Callahan said Yes he was. Then Jennings says I wish you wouldn't because my boys is all tired out and can't run the bases. Callahan says They won't get no chance to-day. No, says Jennings I suppose not. I suppose he will walk them all and they won't have to run. Callahan says He won't give no bases on balls, he says. But you better tell your gang that he is liable to bean them and they better stay away from the plate. Jennings says He won't never hurt my boys by beaning them. Then I cut in. Nor you neither, I says. Callahan laughs at that so I guess I must of pulled a pretty good one. Jennings didn't have no comeback so he walks away.

Then Cobb come over and asked if I was going to work. Callahan told him Yes. Cobb says How many innings? Callahan says All the way. Then Cobb says Be a good fellow Cal and take him out early. I am lame and can't run. I butts in then and said Don't worry, Cobb. You won't have to run because we have got a catcher who can hold them third strikes. Callahan laughed again and says to me You sure did learn something out on that Coast.

Well I walked Bush right off the real and they all begun to holler on the Detroit bench There he goes again. Vitt come up and Jennings yells Leave your bat in the bag Osker. He can't get them over. But I got them over for that bird all O. K. and he pops out trying to bunt. And then I whiffed Crawford. He starts off with a foul that had me scared for a minute because it was pretty close to the foul line and it went clear out of the park. But he missed a spitter a foot and then I supprised them Al. I give him a slow ball and I honestly had to laugh to see him lunge for it. I bet he must of strained himself. He throwed his bat way like he was mad and I guess he was. Cobb came prancing up like he always does and yells Give me that slow one Boy. So I says All right. But I fooled him. Instead of giveing him a slow one like I said I was going I handed him a spitter. He hit it all right but it was a line drive right in Chase's hands. He says Pretty lucky Boy but I will get you next time. I come right back at him. I says Yes you will.

Well Al I had them going like that all through. About the sixth inning Callahan yells from the bench to Jennings What do you think of him now? And Jennings didn't say nothing. What could he of said?

Cobb makes their one hit in the eighth. He never would of made it if Schalk had of let me throw him spitters instead of fast ones. At that Weaver ought to of threw him out. Anyway they didn't score and we made a monkey out of Dubuque, or whatever his name is.

Well Al I got back to the hotel and snuck down the street a ways and had a couple of beers before supper. So I come to the supper table late and Walsh tells me they had been several phone calls for me. I go down to the desk and they tell me to call up a certain number. So I called up and they charged me a nickel for it. A girl's voice answers the phone and I says Was they some one there that wanted to talk to Jack Keefe? She says You bet they is. She says Don't you know me, Jack? This is Violet. Well, you could of knocked me down with a peace of bread. I says What do you want? She says Why I want to see you. I says Well you can't see me. She says Why what's the matter, Jack? What have I did that you should be sore at me? I says I guess you know all right. You called me a busher. She says Why I didn't do nothing of the kind. I says Yes you did on that postcard. She says I didn't write you no postcard.

Then we argued along for a while and she swore up and down that she didn't write me no postcard or call me no busher. I says Well then why didn't you write me a letter when I was in Frisco? She says she had lost my address. Well Al I don't know if she was telling me the truth or not but may be she didn't write that postcard after all. She was crying over the telephone so I says Well it is too late for I and you to get together because I am engaged to be married. Then she screamed and I hang up the receiver. She must of called back two or three times because they was calling my name round the hotel but I wouldn't go near the phone. You know me Al.

Well when I hang up and went back to finish my supper the dining room was locked. So I had to go out and buy myself a sandwich. They soaked me fifteen cents for a sandwich and a cup of coffee so with the nickel for the phone I am out twenty cents altogether for nothing. But then I would of had to tip the waiter in the hotel a dime.

Well Al I must close and catch the boat. I expect a letter from Hazel in Cleveland and maybe Violet will write to me too. She is stuck on me all right Al. I can see that. And I don't believe she could of wrote that postcard after all.   Yours truly,   JACK.

Boston, Massachusetts, September 12

OLD PAL: Well Al I got a letter from Hazel in Cleveland and she is comeing to Chi in October for the city serious. She asked me to send her a hundred dollars for her fare and to buy some cloths with. I sent her thirty dollars for the fare and told her she could wait till she got to Chi to buy her cloths. She said she would give me the money back as soon as she seen me but she is a little short now because one of her girl friends borrowed fifty off of her. I guess she must be pretty softhearted Al. I hope you and Bertha can come up for the wedding because I would like to have you stand up with me.

I all so got a letter from Violet and they was blots all over it like she had been crying. She swore she did not write that postcard and said she would die if I didn't believe her. She wants to know who the lucky girl is who I am engaged to be married to. I believe her Al when she says she did not write that postcard but it is too late now. I will let you know the date of my wedding as soon as I find out.

I guess you seen what I done in Cleveland and here. Allen was going awful bad in Cleveland and I relieved him in the eighth when we had a lead of two runs. I put them out in one-two-three order in the eighth but had hard work in the ninth due to rotten support. I walked Johnston and Chapman and Turner sacrificed them ahead. Jackson come up then and I had two strikes on him. I could of whiffed him but Schalk makes me give him a fast one when I wanted to give him a slow one. He hit it to Berger and Johnston ought to of been threw out at the plate but Berger fumbles and then has to make the play at first base. He got Jackson all O. K. but they was only one run behind then and Chapman was on third base. Lajoie was up next and Callahan sends out word for me to walk him. I thought that was rotten manageing because Lajoie or no one else can hit me when I want to cut loose. So after I give him two bad balls I tried to slip over a strike on him but the lucky stiff hit it on a line to Weaver. Anyway the game was over and I felt pretty good. But Callahan don't appresiate good work Al. He give me a call in the clubhouse and said if I ever disobeyed his orders again he would suspend me without no pay and lick me too. Honest Al it was all I could do to keep from wrapping his jaw but Gleason winks at me not to do nothing.

I worked the second game here and give them three hits two of which was bunts that Lord ought to of eat up. I got better support in Frisco than I been getting here Al. But I don't care. The Boston bunch couldn't of hit me with a shovvel and we beat them two to nothing. I worked against Wood at that. They call him Smoky Joe and they say he has got a lot of speed.

Boston is some town, Al, and I wish you and Bertha could come here sometime. I went down to the wharf this morning and seen them unload the fish. They must of been a million of them but I didn't have time to count them. Every one of them was five or six times as big as a blue gill.

Violet asked me what would be my address in New York City so I am dropping her a postcard to let her know all though I don't know what good it will do her. I certainly won't start no correspondents with her now that I am engaged to be married.   Yours truly,   JACK.

New York, New York, September 16

FRIEND AL: I opened the serious here and beat them easy but I know you must of saw about it in the Chi papers. At that they don't give me no fair show in the Chi papers. One of the boys bought one here and I seen in it where I was lucky to win that game in Cleveland. If I knowed which one of them reporters wrote that I would punch his jaw.

Al I told you Boston was some town but this is the real one. I never seen nothing like it and I been going some since we got here. I walked down Broadway the Main Street last night and I run into a couple of the ball players and they took me to what they call the Garden but it ain't like the gardens at home because this one is indoors. We sat down to a table and had several drinks. Pretty soon one of the boys asked me if I was broke and I says No, why? He says You better get some lubricateing oil and loosen up. I don't know what he meant but pretty soon when we had had a lot of drinks the waiter brings a check and hands it to me. It was for one dollar. I says Oh I ain't paying for all of them. The waiter says This is just for that last drink.

I thought the other boys would make a holler but they didn't say nothing. So I give him a dollar bill and even then he didn't act satisfied so I asked him what he was waiting for and he said Oh nothing, kind of sassy. I was going to bust him but the boys give me the sign to shut up and not to say nothing. I excused myself pretty soon because I wanted to get some air. I give my check for my hat to a boy and he brought my hat and I started going and he says Haven't you forgot something? I guess he must of thought I was wearing a overcoat.

Then I went down the Main Street again and some man stopped me and asked me did I want to go to the show. He said he had a ticket. I asked him what show and he said the Follies. I never heard of it but I told him I would go if he had a ticket to spare. He says I will spare you this one for three dollars. I says You must take me for some boob. He says No I wouldn't insult no boob. So I walks on but if he had of insulted me I would of busted him.

I went back to the hotel then and run into Kid Gleason. He asked me to take a walk with him so out I go again. We went to the corner and he bought me a beer. He don't drink nothing but pop himself. The two drinks was only ten cents so I says This is the place for me. He says Where have you been? and I told him about paying one dollar for three drinks. He says I see I will have to take charge of you. Don't go round with them ball players no more. When you want to go out and see the sights come to me and I will stear you. So to-night he is going to stear me. I will write to you from Philadelphia. Your pal,   JACK.

Philadelphia, Pa., September 19

FRIEND AL: They won't be no game here to-day because it is raining. We all been loafing round the hotel all day and I am glad of it because I got all tired out over in New York City. I and Kid Gleason went round together the last couple of nights over there and he wouldn't let me spend no money. I seen a lot of girls that I would of like to of got acquainted with but he wouldn't even let me answer them when they spoke to me. We run in to a couple of peaches last night and they had us spotted too. One of them says I'll bet you're a couple of ball players. But Kid says You lose your bet. I am a bellhop and the big rube with me is nothing but a pitcher.

One of them says What are you trying to do kid somebody? He says Go home and get some soap and remove your disguise from your face. I didn't think he ought to talk like that to them and I called him about it and said maybe they was lonesome and it wouldn't hurt none if we treated them to a soda or something. But he says Lonesome. If I don't get you away from here they will steal everything you got. They won't even leave you your fast ball. So we left them and he took me to a picture show. It was some California pictures and they made me think of Hazel so when I got back to the hotel I sent her three post-cards.

Gleason made me go to my room at ten oclock both nights but I was pretty tired anyway because he had walked me all over town. I guess we must of saw twenty shows. He says I would take you to the grand opera only it would be throwing money away because we can hear Ed Walsh for nothing. Walsh has got some voice Al a loud high tenor.

To-morrow is Sunday and we have a double header Monday on account of the rain to-day. I thought sure I would get another chance to beat the Athaletics and I asked Callahan if he was going to pitch me here but he said he thought he would save me to work against Johnson in Washington. So you see Al he must figure I am about the best he has got. I'll beat him Al if they get a couple of runs behind me.

Yours truly,   JACK.

P. S. They was a letter here from Violet and it pretty near made me feel like crying. I wish they was two of me so both them girls could be happy.

Washington, D. C., September 22

DEAR OLD AL: Well Al here I am in the capital of the United States. We got in last night and I been walking round town all morning. But I didn't tire myself out because I am going to pitch against Johnson this afternoon.

This is the prettiest town I ever seen but I believe they is more colored people here than they is in Evansville or Chi. I seen the White House and the Monumunt. They say that Bill Sullivan and Gabby St. once catched a baseball that was threw off of the top of the Monumunt but I bet they couldn't catch it if I threwed it.

I was in to breakfast this morning with Gleason and Bodie and Weaver and Fournier. Gleason says I'm supprised that you ain't sick in bed to-day. I says Why?

He says Most of our pitchers gets sick when Cal tells them they are going to work against Johnson. He says Here's these other fellows all feeling pretty sick this morning and they ain't even pitchers. All they have to do is hit against him but it looks like as if Cal would have to send substitutes in for them. Bodie is complaining of a sore arm which he must of strained drawing to two card flushes. Fournier and Weaver have strained their legs doing the tango dance. Nothing could cure them except to hear that big Walter had got throwed out of his machine and wouldn't be able to pitch against us in this serious.

I says I feel O. K. and I ain't afraid to pitch against Johnson and I ain't afraid to hit against him neither. Then Weaver says Have you ever saw him work? Yes, I says, I seen him in Chi. Then Weaver says Well if you have saw him work and ain't afraid to hit against him I'll bet you would go down to Wall Street and holler Hurrah for Roosevelt. I says No I wouldn't do that but I ain't afraid of no pitcher and what is

more if you get me a couple of runs I'll beat him. Then Fournier says
Oh we will get you a couple of runs all right. He says That's just as
easy as catching whales with a angleworm.

Well Al I must close and go in and get some lunch. My arm feels
great and they will have to go some to beat me Johnson or no Johnson.

Your pal,   JACK.

Washington, D. C., September 22

FRIEND AL: Well I guess you know by this time that they didn't get no
two runs for me, only one, but I beat him just the same. I beat him one
to nothing and Callahan was so pleased that he give me a ticket to the
theater. I just got back from there and it is pretty late and I already
have wrote you one letter to-day but I am going to sit up and tell you
about it.

It was cloudy before the game started and when I was warming up
I made the remark to Callahan that the dark day ought to make my
speed good. He says Yes and of course it will handicap Johnson.

While Washington was takeing their practice their two coachers
Schaefer and Altrock got out on the infield and cut up and I pretty near
busted laughing at them. They certainly is funny Al. Callahan asked me
what was I laughing at and I told him and he says That's the first time
I ever seen a pitcher laugh when he was going to work against Johnson.
He says Griffith is a pretty good fellow to give us something to laugh
at before he shoots that guy at us.

I warmed up good and told Schalk not to ask me for my spitter much
because my fast one looked faster than I ever seen it. He says It won't
make much difference what you pitch to-day. I says Oh, yes, it will
because Callahan thinks enough of me to work me against Johnson and
I want to show him he didn't make no mistake. Then Gleason says No
he didn't make no mistake. Wasteing Cicotte or Scotty would of been
a mistake in this game.

Well, Johnson whiffs Weaver and Chase and makes Lord pop out in
the first inning. I walked their first guy but I didn't give Milan nothing
to bunt and finally he flied out. And then I whiffed the next two. On
the bench Callahan says That's the way, boy. Keep that up and we got
a chance.

Johnson had fanned four of us when I come up with two out in the
third inning and he whiffed me to. I fouled one though that if I had
ever got a good hold of I would of knocked out of the park. In the first
seven innings we didn't have a hit off of him. They had got five or six
lucky ones off of me and I had walked two or three, but I cut loose

with all I had when they was men on and they couldn't do nothing with me. The only reason I walked so many was because my fast one was jumping so. Honest Al it was so fast that Evans the umpire couldn't see it half the time and he called a lot of balls that was right over the heart.

Well I come up in the eighth with two out and the score still nothing and nothing. I had whiffed the second time as well as the first but it was account of Evans missing one on me. The eighth started with Shanks muffing a fly ball off of Bodie. It was way out by the fence so he got two bases on it and he went to third while they was throwing Berger out. Then Schalk whiffed.

Callahan says Go up and try to meet one Jack. It might as well be you as anybody else. But your old pal didn't whiff this time Al. He gets two strikes on me with fast ones and then I passed up two bad ones. I took my healthy at the next one and slapped it over first base. I guess I could of made two bases on it but I didn't want to tire myself out. Anyway Bodie scored and I had them beat. And my hit was the only one we got off of him so I guess he is a pretty good pitcher after all Al.

They filled up the bases on me with one out in the ninth but it was pretty dark then and I made McBride and their catcher look like suckers with my speed.

I felt so good after the game that I drunk one of them pink cocktails. I don't know what their name is. And then I sent a postcard to poor little Violet. I don't care nothing about her but it don't hurt me none to try and cheer her up once in a while. We leave here Thursday night for home and they had ought to be two or three letters there for me from Hazel because I haven't heard from her lately. She must of lost my road addresses.

Your pal,   JACK.

P. S. I forgot to tell you what Callahan said after the game. He said I was a real pitcher now and he is going to use me in the city serious. If he does Al we will beat them Cubs sure.

Chicago, Illinois, September 27

FRIEND AL: They wasn't no letter here at all from Hazel and I guess she must of been sick. Or maybe she didn't think it was worth while writeing as long as she is comeing next week.

I want to ask you to do me a favor Al and that is to see if you can find me a house down there. I will want to move in with Mrs. Keefe, don't that sound funny Al? sometime in the week of October twelfth. Old man Cutting's house or that yellow house across from you would be O. K. I would rather have the yellow one so as to be near you. Find

out how much rent they want Al and if it is not no more than twelve
dollars a month get it for me. We will buy our furniture here in Chi
when Hazel comes.

We have a couple of days off now Al and then we play St. Louis two
games here. Then Detroit comes to finish the season the third and fourth
of October.   Your pal,   JACK.

                                        Chicago, Illinois, October 3
DEAR OLD AL: Thanks Al for getting the house. The one-year lease is
O. K. You and Bertha and me and Hazel can have all sorts of good
times together. I guess the walk needs repairs but I can fix that up when
I come. We can stay at the hotel when we first get there.

I wish you could of came up for the city serious Al but anyway I
want you and Bertha to be sure and come up for our wedding. I will
let you know the date as soon as Hazel gets here.

The serious starts Tuesday and this town is wild over it. The Cubs
finished second in their league and we was fifth in ours but that don't
scare me none. We would of finished right on top if I had of been here
all season.

Callahan pitched one of the bushers against Detroit this afternoon
and they beat him bad. Callahan is saveing up Scott and Allen and
Russell and Cicotte and I for the big show. Walsh isn't in no shape and
neither is Benz. It looks like I would have a good deal to do because
most of them others can't work no more than once in four days and
Allen ain't no good at all.

We have a day to rest after to-morrow's game with the Tigers and
then we go at them Cubs.   Your pal,   JACK.
P. S. I have got it figured that Hazel is fixing to surprise me by
dropping in on me because I haven't heard nothing yet.

                                        Chicago, Illinois, October 7
FRIEND AL: Well Al you know by this time that they beat me to-day
and tied up the serious. But I have still got plenty of time Al and I will
get them before it is over. My arm wasn't feeling good Al and my fast
ball didn't hop like it had ought to. But it was the rotten support I got
that beat me. That lucky stiff Zimmerman was the only guy that got a
real hit off of me and he must of shut his eyes and throwed his bat
because the ball he hit was a foot over his head. And if they hadn't been
makeing all them errors behind me they wouldn't of been nobody on
bases when Zimmerman got that lucky scratch. The serious now stands
one and one Al and it is a cinch we will beat them even if they are a

bunch of lucky stiffs. They has been great big crowds at both games and it looks like as if we should ought to get over eight hundred dollars a peace if we win and we will win sure because I will beat them three straight if necessary.

But Al I have got bigger news than that for you and I am the happyest man in the world. I told you I had not heard from Hazel for a long time. To-night when I got back to my room they was a letter waiting for me from her.

Al she is married. Maybe you don't know why that makes me happy but I will tell you. She is married to Kid Levy the middle weight. I guess my thirty dollars is gone because in her letter she called me a cheap skate and she inclosed one one-cent stamp and two twos and said she was paying me for the glass of beer I once bought her. I bought her more than that Al but I won't make no holler. She all so said not for me to never come near her or her husband would bust my jaw. I ain't afraid of him or no one else Al but they ain't no danger of me ever bothering them. She was no good and I was sorry the minute I agreed to marry her.

But I was going to tell you why I am happy or maybe you can guess. Now I can make Violet my wife and she's got Hazel beat forty ways. She ain't nowheres near as big as Hazel but she's classier Al and she will make me a good wife. She ain't never asked me for no money.

I wrote her a letter the minute I got the good news and told her to come on over here at once at my expense. We will be married right after the serious is over and I want you and Bertha to be sure and stand up with us. I will wire you at my own expence the exact date.

It all seems like a dream now about Violet and I haveing our mis-understanding Al and I don't see how I ever could of accused her of sending me that postcard. You and Bertha will be just as crazy about her as I am when you see her Al. Just think Al I will be married inside of a week and to the only girl I ever could of been happy with instead of the woman I never really cared for except as a passing fancy. My happyness would be complete Al if I had not of let that woman steal thirty dollars off of me.   Your happy pal,   JACK.

P. S. Hazel probibly would of insisted on us takeing a trip to Niagara falls or somewheres but I know Violet will be perfectly satisfied if I take her right down to Bedford. Oh you little yellow house.

Chicago, Illinois, October 9

FRIEND AL: Well Al we have got them beat three games to one now and will wind up the serious to-morrow sure. Callahan sent me in to save poor Allen yesterday and I stopped them dead. But I don't care now Al. I have lost all interest in the game and I don't care if Callahan pitches me to-morrow or not. My heart is just about broke Al and I wouldn't be able to do myself justice feeling the way I do.

I have lost Violet Al and just when I was figureing on being the happyest man in the world. We will get the big money but it won't do me no good. They can keep my share because I won't have no little girl to spend it on.

Her answer to my letter was waiting for me at home to-night. She is engaged to be married to Joe Hill the big lefthander Jennings got from Providence. Honest Al I don't see how he gets by. He ain't got no more curve ball than a rabbit and his fast one floats up there like a big balloon. He beat us the last game of the regular season here but it was because Callahan had a lot of bushers in the game.

I wish I had knew then that he was stealing my girl and I would of made Callahan pitch me against him. And when he come up to bat I would of beaned him. But I don't suppose you could hurt him by hitting him in the head. The big stiff. Their wedding ain't going to come off till next summer and by that time he will be pitching in the Southwestern Texas League for about fifty dollars a month.

Violet wrote that she wished me all the luck and happyness in the world but it is too late for me to be happy Al and I don't care what kind of luck I have now.

Al you will have to get rid of that lease for me. Fix it up the best way you can. Tell the old man I have changed my plans. I don't know just yet what I will do but maybe I will go to Australia with Mike Donlin's team. If I do I won't care if the boat goes down or not. I don't believe I will even come back to Bedford this winter. It would drive me wild to go past that little house every day and think how happy I might of been.

Maybe I will pitch to-morrow Al and if I do the serious will be over to-morrow night. I can beat them Cubs if I get any kind of decent support. But I don't care now Al. Yours truly, JACK.

Chicago, Illinois, October 12

AL: Your letter received. If the old man won't call it off I guess I will have to try and rent the house to some one else. Do you know of any couple that wants one Al? It looks like I would have to come down there myself and fix things up someway. He is just mean enough to stick me with the house on my hands when I won't have no use for it.

They beat us the day before yesterday as you probibly know and it rained yesterday and to-day. The papers says it will be all O. K. to-morrow and Callahan tells me I am going to work. The Cub pitchers was all shot to peaces and the bad weather is just nuts for them because it will give Cheney a good rest. But I will beat him Al if they don't kick it away behind me.

I must close because I promised Allen the little lefthander that I would come over to his flat and play cards a while to-night and I must wash up and change my collar. Allen's wife's sister is visiting them again and I would give anything not to have to go over there. I am through with girls and don't want nothing to do with them.

I guess it is maybe a good thing it rained to-day because I dreamt about Violet last night and went out and got a couple of high balls before breakfast this morning. I hadn't never drank nothing before breakfast before and it made me kind of sick. But I am all O. K. now.

Your pal,   JACK.

Chicago, Illinois, October 13

DEAR OLD AL: The serious is all over Al. We are the champions and I done it. I may be home the day after to-morrow or I may not come for a couple of days. I want to see Comiskey before I leave and fix up about my contract for next year. I won't sign for no less than five thousand and if he hands me a contract for less than that I will leave the White Sox flat on their back. I have got over fourteen hundred dollars now Al with the city serious money which was $814.30 and I don't have to worry.

Them reporters will have to give me a square deal this time Al. I had everything and the Cubs done well to score a run. I whiffed Zimmerman three times. Some of the boys say he ain't no hitter but he is a hitter and a good one Al only he could not touch the stuff I got. The umps give them their run because in the fourth inning I had Leach flatfooted off of second base and Weaver tagged him O. K. but the umps wouldn't call it. Then Schulte the lucky stiff happened to get a hold of one and pulled it past first base. I guess Chase must of been asleep. Anyway they scored but I don't care because we piled up six runs on Cheney and I drove in one of them myself with one of the prettiest singles you ever see. It was a spitter and I hit it like a shot. If I had hit it square it would of went out of the park.

Comiskey ought to feel pretty good about me winning and I guess he will give me a contract for anything I want. He will have to or I will go to the Federal League.

We are all invited to a show to-night and I am going with Allen and his wife and her sister Florence. She is O. K. Al and I guess she thinks the same about me. She must because she was out to the game to-day and seen me hand it to them. She maybe ain't as pretty as Violet and Hazel but as they say beauty isn't only so deep.

Well Al tell the boys I will be with them soon. I have gave up the idea of going to Australia because I would have to buy a evening full-dress suit and they tell me they cost pretty near fifty dollars.

Yours truly,   JACK.

Chicago, Illinois, October 14

FRIEND AL: Never mind about that lease. I want the house after all Al and I have got the supprise of your life for you.

When I come home to Bedford I will bring my wife with me. I and Florence fixed things all up after the show last night and we are going to be married to-morrow morning. I am a busy man to-day Al because I have got to get the license and look round for furniture. And I have also got to buy some new cloths but they are haveing a sale on Cottage ·Grove Avenue at Clark's store and I know one of the clerks there.

I am the happyest man in the world Al. You and Bertha and I and Florence will have all kinds of good times together this winter because I know Bertha and Florence will like each other. Florence looks something like Bertha at that. I am glad I didn't get tied up with Violet or Hazel even if they was a little bit prettier than Florence.

Florence knows a lot about baseball for a girl and you would be supprised to hear her talk. She says I am the best pitcher in the league and she has saw them all. She all so says I am the best looking ball player she ever seen but you know how girls will kid a guy Al. You will like her O. K. I fell for her the first time I seen her.

Your old pal,   JACK.

P. S. I signed up for next year. Comiskey slapped me on the back when I went in to see him and told me I would be a star next year if I took good care of myself. I guess I am a star without waiting for next year Al. My contract calls for twenty-eight hundred a year which is a thousand more than I was getting. And it is pretty near a cinch that I will be in on the World Serious money next season.

P. S. I certainly am relieved about that lease. It would of been fierce to of had that place on my hands all winter and not getting any use out of it. Everything is all O. K. now. Oh you little yellow house.

THE BUSHER'S HONEYMOON

Chicago, Illinois, October 17

FRIEND AL: Well Al it looks as if I would not be writeing so much to you now that I am a married man. Yes Al I and Florrie was married the day before yesterday just like I told you we was going to be and Al I am the happyest man in the world though I have spent $30 in the last 3 days incluseive. You was wise Al to get married in Bedford where not nothing is nearly half so dear. My expenses was as follows:

License	$2.00
Preist	3.50
Haircut and shave	.35
Shine	.05
Carfair	.45
New suit	14.50
Show tickets	3.00
Flowers	.50
Candy	.30
Hotel	4.50
Tobacco both kinds	.25

You see Al it costs a hole lot of money to get married here. The sum of what I have wrote down is $29.40 but as I told you I have spent $30 and I do not know what I have did with that other $0.60. My new brother-in-law Allen told me I should ought to give the preist $5 and I thought it should be about $2 the same as the license so I split the difference and give him $3.50. I never seen him before and probily won't never see him again so why should I give him anything at all when it is his business to marry couples? But I like to do the right thing. You know me Al.

I thought we would be in Bedford by this time but Florrie wants to stay here a few more days because she says she wants to be with her sister. Allen and his wife is thinking about takeing a flat for the winter instead of going down to Waco Texas where they live. I don't see no sense in that when it costs so much to live here but it is none of my business if they want to throw their money away. But I am glad I got a wife with some sense though she kicked because I did not get no room with a bath which would cost me $2 a day instead of $1.50. I says I guess the clubhouse is still open yet and if I want a bath I can go over there and take the shower. She says Yes and I suppose I can go and jump in the lake. But she would not do that Al because the lake here is cold at this time of the year.

When I told you about my expenses I did not include in it the meals because we would be eating them if I was getting married or not getting married only I have to pay for six meals a day now instead of three and I didn't used to eat no lunch in the playing season except once in a while when I knowed I was not going to work that afternoon. I had a meal ticket which had not quite ran out over to a resturunt on Indiana Ave and we eat there for the first day except at night when I took Allen and his wife to the show with us and then he took us to a chop suye resturunt. I guess you have not never had no chop suye Al and I am here to tell you you have not missed nothing but when Allen was going to buy the supper what could I say? I could not say nothing.

Well yesterday and to-day we been eating at a resturunt on Cottage Grove Ave near the hotel and at the resturunt on Indiana that I had the meal ticket at only I do not like to buy no new meal ticket when I am not going to be round here no more than a few days. Well Al I guess the meals has cost me all together about $1.50 and I have eat very little myself. Florrie always wants desert ice cream or something and that runs up into money faster than regular stuff like stake and ham and eggs.

Well Al Florrie says it is time for me to keep my promise and take her to the moveing pictures which is $0.20 more because the one she likes round here costs a dime apeace. So I must close for this time and will see you soon.   Your pal,   JACK.

Chicago, Illinois, October 22

AL: Just a note Al to tell you why I have not yet came to Bedford yet where I expected I would be long before this time. Allen and his wife have took a furnished flat for the winter and Allen's wife wants Florrie to stay here untill they get settled. Meentime it is costing me a hole lot of money at the hotel and for meals besides I am paying $10 a month rent for the house you got for me and what good am I getting out of it? But Florrie wants to help her sister and what can I say? Though I did make her promise she would not stay no longer than next Saturday at least. So I guess Al we will be home on the evening train Saturday and then may be I can save some money.

I know Al that you and Bertha will like Florrie when you get acquainted with her spesially Bertha though Florrie dresses pretty swell and spends a hole lot of time fusing with her face and her hair.

She says to me to-night Who are you writeing to and I told her Al

Blanchard who I have told you about a good many times. She says I
bet you are writeing to some girl and acted like as though she was kind
of jealous. So I thought I would tease her a little and I says I don't know
no girls except you and Violet and Hazel. Who is Violet and Hazel? she
says. I kind of laughed and says Oh I guess I better not tell you and
then she says I guess you will tell me. That made me kind of mad
because no girl can't tell me what to do. She says Are you going to tell
me? and I says No.

Then she says If you don't tell me I will go over to Marie's that is
her sister Allen's wife and stay all night. I says Go on and she went
downstairs but I guess she probily went to get a soda because she has
some money of her own that I give her. This was about two hours ago
and she is probily down in the hotel lobby now trying to scare me by
makeing me believe she has went to her sister's. But she can't fool me
Al and I am now going out to mail this letter and get a beer. I won't
never tell her about Violet and Hazel if she is going to act like that.

Yours truly,   JACK.

Chicago, Illinois, October 24
FRIEND AL: I guess I told you Al that we would be home Saturday
evening. I have changed my mind. Allen and his wife has a spair bedroom and wants us to come there and stay a week or two. It won't cost
nothing except they will probily want to go out to the moveing pictures
nights and we will probily have to go along with them and I am a man
Al that wants to pay his share and not be cheap.

I and Florrie had our first quarrle the other night. I guess I told you
the start of it but I don't remember. I made some crack about Violet
and Hazel just to tease Florrie and she wanted to know who they was
and I would not tell her. So she gets sore and goes over to Marie's to
stay all night. I was just kidding Al and was willing to tell her about
them two poor girls whatever she wanted to know except that I don't
like to brag about girls being stuck on me. So I goes over to Marie's
after her and tells her all about them except that I turned them down
cold at the last minute to marry her because I did not want her to get
all swelled up. She made me sware that I did not never care nothing
about them and that was easy because it was the truth. So she come
back to the hotel with me just like I knowed she would when I ordered
her to.

They must not be no mistake about who is the boss in my house.
Some men lets their wife run all over them but I am not that kind. You
know me Al.

I must get busy and pack my suitcase if I am going to move over to Allen's. I sent three collars and a shirt to the laundrey this morning so even if we go over there to-night I will have to take another trip back this way in a day or two. I won't mind Al because they sell my kind of beer down to the corner and I never seen it sold nowheres else in Chi. You know the kind it is, eh Al? I wish I was lifting a few with you to-night.   Your pal,   JACK.

Chicago, Illinois, October 28

DEAR OLD AL: Florrie and Marie has went downtown shopping because Florrie thinks she has got to have a new dress though she has got two changes of cloths now and I don't know what she can do with another one. I hope she don't find none to suit her though it would not hurt none if she got something for next spring at a reduckshon. I guess she must think I am Charles A. Comiskey or somebody. Allen has went to a colledge football game. One of the reporters give him a pass. I don't see nothing in football except a lot of scrapping between little slobs that I could lick the whole bunch of them so I did not care to go. The reporter is one of the guys that travled round with our club all summer. He called up and said he hadn't only the one pass but he was not hurting my feelings none because I would not go to no rotten football game if they payed me.

The flat across the hall from this here one is for rent furnished. They want $40 a month for it and I guess they think they must be lots of suckers running round loose. Marie was talking about it and says Why don't you and Florrie take it and then we can be right together all winter long and have some big times? Florrie says It would be all right with me. What about it Jack? I says What do you think I am? I don't have to live in no high price flat when I got a home in Bedford where they ain't no people trying to hold everybody up all the time. So they did not say no more about it when they seen I was in ernest. Nobody cannot tell me where I am going to live sister-in-law or no sister-in-law. If I was to rent the rotten old flat I would be paying $50 a month rent includeing the house down in Bedford. Fine chance Al.

Well Al I am lonesome and thirsty so more later.

Your pal,   JACK.

Chicago, Illinois, November 2

FRIEND AL: Well Al I got some big news for you. I am not comeing to Bedford this winter after all except to make a visit which I guess will be round Xmas. I changed my mind about that flat across the hall from the Allens and decided to take it after all. The people who was in it and owns the furniture says they would let us have it till the 1 of May if we would pay $42.50 a month which is only $2.50 a month more than they would of let us have it for a short time. So you see we got a bargain because it is all furnished and everything and we won't have to blow no money on furniture besides the club goes to California the middle of Febuery so Florrie would not have no place to stay while I am away.

The Allens only subleased their flat from some other people till the 2 of Febuery and when I and Allen goes West Marie can come over and stay with Florrie so you see it is best all round. If we should of boughten furniture it would cost us in the neighborhood of $100 even without no piano and they is a piano in this here flat which makes it nice because Florrie plays pretty good with one hand and we can have lots of good times at home without it costing us nothing except just the bear liveing expenses. I consider myself lucky to of found out about this before it was too late and somebody else had of gotten the tip.

Now Al old pal I want to ask a great favor of you Al. I all ready have payed one month rent $10 on the house in Bedford and I want you to see the old man and see if he won't call off that lease. Why should I be paying $10 a month rent down there and $42.50 up here when the house down there is not no good to me because I am liveing up here all winter? See Al? Tell him I will gladly give him another month rent to call off the lease but don't tell him that if you don't have to. I want to be fare with him.

If you will do this favor for me, Al, I won't never forget it. Give my kindest to Bertha and tell her I am sorry I and Florrie won't see her right away but you see how it is Al.   Yours,   JACK.

Chicago, Illinois, November 30

FRIEND AL: I have not wrote for a long time have I Al but I have been very busy. They was not enough furniture in the flat and we have been buying some more. They was enough for some people maybe but I and Florrie is the kind that won't have nothing but the best. The furniture them people had in the liveing room was oak but they had a bookcase bilt in in the flat that was mohoggeny and Florrie would not stand for no joke combination like that so she moved the oak chairs and table in to the spair bedroom and we went downtown to buy some mohoggeny. But it costs too much Al and we was feeling pretty bad about it when we seen some Sir Cashion walnut that was prettier even than the mohoggeny and not near so expensive. It is not no real Sir Cashion walnut but it is just as good and we got it reasonable. Then we got some mission chairs for the dining room because the old ones was just straw and was no good and we got a big lether couch for $9 that somebody can sleep on if we get to much company.

I hope you and Bertha can come up for the holidays and see how comfertible we are fixed. That is all the new furniture we have boughten but Florrie set her heart on some old Rose drapes and a red table lamp that is the biggest you ever seen Al and I did not have the heart to say no. The hole thing cost me in the neighborhood of $110 which is very little for what we got and then it will always be ourn even when we move away from this flat though we will have to leave the furniture that belongs to the other people but their part of it is not no good anyway.

I guess I told you Al how much money I had when the season ended. It was $1400 all told includeing the city serious money. Well Al I got in the neighborhood of $800 left because I give $200 to Florrie to send down to Texas to her other sister who had a bad egg for a husband that managed a club in the Texas Oklahoma League and this was the money she had to pay to get the divorce. I am glad Al that I was lucky enough to marry happy and get a good girl for my wife that has got some sense and besides if I have got $800 left I should not worry as they say.   Your pal,   JACK.

Chicago, Illinois, December 7

DEAR OLD AL: No I was in ernest Al when I says that I wanted you and Bertha to come up here for the holidays. I know I told you that I might come to Bedford for the holidays but that is all off. I have gave up the idea of comeing to Bedford for the holidays and I want you to be sure and come up here for the holidays and I will show you a good time. I would love to have Bertha come to and she can come if she wants to only Florrie don't know if she would have a good time or not and thinks maybe she would rather stay in Bedford and you came alone. But be sure and have Bertha come if she wants to come but maybe she would not injoy it. You know best Al.

I don't think the old man give me no square deal on that lease but if he wants to stick me all right. I am grateful to you Al for trying to fix it up but maybe you could of did better if you had of went at it in a different way. I am not finding no fault with my old pal though. Don't think that. When I have a pal I am the man to stick to him threw thick and thin. If the old man is going to hold me to that lease I guess I will have to stand it and I guess I won't starv to death for no $10 a month because I am going to get $2800 next year besides the city serious money and maybe we will get into the World Serious too. I know we will if Callahan will pitch me every 3d day like I wanted him to last season. But if you had of approached the old man in a different way maybe you could of fixed it up. I wish you would try it again Al if it is not no trouble.

We had Allen and his wife here for thanksgiveing dinner and the dinner cost me better than $5. I thought we had enough to eat to last a week but about six o'clock at night Florrie and Marie said they was hungry and we went downtown and had dinner all over again and I payed for it and it cost me $5 more. Allen was all ready to pay for it when Florrie said No this day's treat is on us so I had to pay for it but I don't see why she did not wait and let me do the talking. I was going to pay for it any way.

Be sure and come and visit us for the holidays Al and of coarse if Bertha wants to come bring her along. We will be glad to see you both. I won't never go back on a friend and pal. You know me Al.

Your old pal, JACK.

Chicago, Illinois, December 20

FRIEND AL: I don't see what can be the matter with Bertha because you know Al we would not care how she dressed and would not make no kick if she come up here in a night gown. She did not have no license to say we was to swell for her because we did not never think of nothing like that. I wish you would talk to her again Al and tell her she need not get sore on me and that both her and you is welcome at my house any time I ask you to come. See if you can't make her change her mind Al because I feel like as if she must of took offense at something I may of wrote you. I am sorry you and her are not comeing but I suppose you know best. Only we was getting all ready for you and Florrie said only the other day that she wished the holidays was over but that was before she knowed you was not comeing. I hope you can come Al.

Well Al I guess there is not no use talking to the old man no more. You have did the best you could but I wish I could of came down there and talked to him. I will pay him his rotten old $10 a month and the next time I come to Bedford and meet him on the street I will bust his jaw. I know he is a old man Al but I don't like to see nobody get the best of me and I am sorry I ever asked him to let me off. Some of them old skinflints has no heart Al but why should I fight with a old man over chicken feed like $10? Florrie says a star pitcher like I should not ought never to scrap about little things and I guess she is right Al so I will pay the old man his $10 a month if I have to.

Florrie says she is jealous of me writeing to you so much and she says she would like to meet this great old pal of mine. I would like to have her meet you to Al and I would like to have you change your mind and come and visit us and I am sorry you can't come Al.

Yours truly,   JACK.

Chicago, Illinois, December 27

OLD PAL: I guess all these lefthanders is alike though I thought this Allen had some sense. I thought he was different from the most and was not no rummy but they are all alike Al and they are all lucky that somebody don't hit them over the head with a ax and kill them but I guess at that you could not hurt no lefthanders by hitting them over the head. We was all down on State St. the day before Xmas and the girls was all tired out and ready to go home but Allen says No I guess we better stick down a while because now the crowds is out and it will be fun to watch them. So we walked up and down State St. about a hour longer and finally we come in front of a big jewlry store window and in it was a swell dimond ring that was marked $100. It was a ladies' ring so Marie says to Allen Why don't you buy that for me? And Allen says Do you really want it? And she says she did.

So we tells the girls to wait and we goes over to a salloon where Allen has got a friend and gets a check cashed and we come back and he bought the ring. Then Florrie looks like as though she was getting all ready to cry and I asked her what was the matter and she says I had not boughten her no ring not even when we was engaged. So I and Allen goes back to the salloon and I gets a check cashed and we come back and bought another ring but I did not think the ring Allen had boughten was worth no $100 so I gets one for $75. Now Al you know I am not makeing no kick on spending a little money for a present for my own wife but I had allready boughten her a rist watch for $15 and a rist watch was just what she had wanted. I was willing to give her the ring if she had not of wanted the rist watch more than the ring but when I give her the ring I kept the rist watch and did not tell her nothing about it.

Well I come downtown alone the day after Xmas and they would not take the rist watch back in the store where I got it. So I am going to give it to her for a New Year's present and I guess that will make Allen feel like a dirty doose. But I guess you cannot hurt no lefthander's feelings at that. They are all alike. But Allen has not got nothing but a dinky curve ball and a fast ball that looks like my slow one. If Comiskey was not good hearted he would of sold him long ago.

I sent you and Bertha a cut glass dish Al which was the best I could get for the money and it was pretty high pricet at that. We was glad to get the pretty pincushions from you and Bertha and Florrie says to tell you that we are well supplied with pincushions now because the ones you sent makes a even half dozen. Thanks Al for remembering us and thank Bertha too though I guess you paid for them.

Your pal,   JACK.

Chicago, Illinois, Januery 3

OLD PAL: Al I been pretty sick ever since New Year's eve. We had a table at 1 of the swell resturunts downtown and I never seen so much wine drank in my life. I would rather of had beer but they would not sell us none so I found out that they was a certain kind that you can get for $1 a bottle and it is just as good as the kind that has got all them fancy names but this lefthander starts ordering some other kind about 11 oclock and it was $5 a bottle and the girls both says they liked it better. I could not see a hole lot of difference myself and I would of gave $0.20 for a big stine of my kind of beer. You know me Al. Well Al you know they is not nobody than can drink more than your old pal and I was all O. K. at one oclock but I seen the girls was getting kind of sleepy so I says we better go home.

Then Marie says Oh, shut up and don't be no quiter. I says You better shut up yourself and not be telling me to shut up, and she says What will you do if I don't shut up? And I says I would bust her in the jaw. But you know Al I would not think of busting no girl. Then Florrie says You better not start nothing because you had to much to drink or you would not be talking about busting girls in the jaw. Then I says I don't care if it is a girl I bust or a lefthander. I did not mean nothing at all Al but Marie says I had insulted Allen and he gets up and slaps my face. Well Al I am not going to stand that from nobody not even if he is my brother-in-law and a lefthander that has not got enough speed to brake a pain of glass.

So I give him a good beating and the waiters butts in and puts us all out for fighting and I and Florrie comes home in a taxi and Allen and his wife don't get in till about 5 oclock so I guess she must of had to of took him to a doctor to get fixed up. I been in bed ever since till just this morning kind of sick to my stumach. I guess I must of eat something that did not agree with me. Allen come over after breakfast this morning and asked me was I all right so I guess he is not sore over the beating I give him or else he wants to make friends because he has saw that I am a bad guy to monkey with.

Florrie tells me a little while ago that she paid the hole bill at the resturunt with my money because Allen was broke so you see what kind of a cheap skate he is Al and some day I am going to bust his jaw. She won't tell me how much the bill was and I won't ask her to no more because we had a good time outside of the fight and what do I care if we spent a little money?   Yours truly,   JACK.

Chicago, Illinois, Januery 20

FRIEND AL: Allen and his wife have gave up the flat across the hall from us and come over to live with us because we got a spair bedroom and why should they not have the bennifit of it? But it is pretty hard for the girls to have to cook and do the work when they is four of us so I have a hired girl who does it all for $7 a week. It is great stuff Al because now we can go round as we please and don't have to wait for no dishes to be washed or nothing. We generally almost always has dinner downtown in the evening so it is pretty soft for the girl too. She don't generally have no more than one meal to get because we generally run round downtown till late and don't get up till about noon.

That sounds funny don't it Al, when I used to get up at 5 every morning down home. Well Al I can tell you something else that may sound funny and that is that I lost my taste for beer. I don't seem to care for it no more and I found I can stand allmost as many drinks of other stuff as I could of beer. I guess Al they is not nobody ever lived can drink more and stand up better under it than me. I make the girls and Allen quit every night.

I only got just time to write you this short note because Florrie and Marie is giving a big party to-night and I and Allen have got to beat it out of the house and stay out of the way till they get things ready. It is Marie's berthday and she says she is 22 but say Al if she is 22 Kid Gleason is 30. Well Al the girls says we must blow so I will run out and mail this letter.   Yours truly,   JACK.

Chicago, Illinois, Januery 31

AL: Allen is going to take Marie with him on the training trip to California and of course Florrie has been at me to take her along. I told her postivly that she can't go. I can't afford no stunt like that but still I am up against it to know what to do with her while we are on the trip because Marie won't be here to stay with her. I don't like to leave her here all alone but they is nothing to it Al I can't afford to take her along. She says I don't see why you can't take me if Allen takes Marie. And I says That stuff is all O. K. for Allen because him and Marie has

YOU KNOW ME AL 45

been grafting off of us all winter. And then she gets mad and tells me I should not ought to say her sister was no grafter. I did not mean nothing like that Al but you don't never know when a woman is going to take offense.

If our furniture was down in Bedford everything would be all O. K. because I could leave her there and I would feel all O. K. because I would know that you and Bertha would see that she was getting along O. K. But they would not be no sense in sending her down to a house that has not no furniture in it. I wish I knowed somewheres where she could visit Al. I would be willing to pay her bord even.

Well Al enough for this time.   Your old pal,   JACK.

Chicago, Illinois, Febuery 4

FRIEND AL: You are a real old pal Al and I certainly am greatful to you for the invatation. I have not told Florrie about it yet but I am sure she will be tickled to death and it is certainly kind of you old pal. I did not never dream of nothing like that. I note what you say Al about not excepting no bord but I think it would be better and I would feel better if you would take something say about $2 a week.

I know Bertha will like Florrie and that they will get along O. K. together because Florrie can learn her how to make her cloths look good and fix her hair and fix up her face. I feel like as if you had took a big load off of me Al and I won't never forget it.

If you don't think I should pay no bord for Florrie all right. Suit yourself about that old pal.

We are leaveing here the 20 of Febuery and if you don't mind I will bring Florrie down to you about the 18. I would like to see the old bunch again and spesially you and Bertha.   Yours,   JACK.

P. S. We will only be away till April 14 and that is just a nice visit. I wish we did not have no flat on our hands.

Chicago, Illinois, Febuery 9

OLD PAL: I want to thank you for asking Florrie to come down there and visit you Al but I find she can't get away. I did not know she had no engagements but she says she may go down to her folks in Texas and she don't want to say that she will come to visit you when it is so indefanate. So thank you just the same Al and thank Bertha too.

Florrie is still at me to take her along to California but honest Al I can't do it. I am right down to my last $50 and I have not payed no rent for this month. I owe the hired girl 2 weeks' salary and both I and Florrie needs some new cloths.

Florrie has just came in since I started writeing this letter and we
have been talking some more about California and she says maybe if I
would ask Comiskey he would take her along as the club's guest. I had
not never thought of that Al and maybe he would because he is a pretty
good scout and I guess I will go and see him about it. The league has
its skedule meeting here tomorrow and may be I can see him down to
the hotel where they meet at. I am so worried Al that I can't write no
more but I will tell you how I come out with Comiskey.

                                           Your pal,   JACK.

                                 Chicago, Illinois, Febuery 11
FRIEND AL: I am up against it right Al and I don't know where I am
going to head in at. I went down to the hotel where the league was
holding its skedule meeting at and I seen Comiskey and got some money
off of the club but I owe all the money I got off of them and I am still
wondering what to do about Florrie.

Comiskey was busy in the meeting when I went down there and they
was not no chance to see him for a while so I and Allen and some of
the boys hung round and had a few drinks and fanned. This here Joe
Hill the busher that Detroit has got that Violet is hooked up to was
round the hotel. I don't know what for but I felt like busting his jaw
only the boys told me I had better not do nothing because I might kill
him and any way he probily won't be in the league much longer. Well
finally Comiskey got threw the meeting and I seen him and he says Hello
young man what can I do for you? And I says I would like to get $100
advance money. He says Have you been takeing care of yourself down
in Bedford? And I told him I had been liveing here all winter and it did
not seem to make no hit with him though I don't see what business it
is of hisn where I live.

So I says I had been takeing good care of myself. And I have Al. You
know that. So he says I should come to the ball park the next day which
is to-day and he would have the secretary take care of me but I says I
could not wait and so he give me $100 out of his pocket and says he
would have it charged against my salery. I was just going to brace him
about the California trip when he got away and went back to the
meeting.

Well Al I hung around with the bunch waiting for him to get threw
again and we had some more drinks and finally Comiskey was threw
again and I braced him in the lobby and asked him if it was all right to
take my wife along to California. He says Sure they would be glad to

have her along. And then I says Would the club pay her fair? He says
I guess you must of spent that $100 buying some nerve. He says Have
you not got no sisters that would like to go along to? He says Does
your wife insist on the drawing room or will she take a lower birth? He
says Is my special train good enough for her?

Then he turns away from me and I guess some of the boys must of
heard the stuff he pulled because they was laughing when he went away
but I did not see nothing to laugh at. But I guess he ment that I would
have to pay her fair if she goes along and that is out of the question Al.
I am up against it and I don't know where I am going to head in at.

Your pal, JACK.

Chicago, Illinois, Febuery 12

DEAR OLD AL: I guess everything will be all O. K. now at least I am
hopeing it will. When I told Florrie about how I come out with Comiskey she bawled her head off and I thought for a while I was going
to have to call a doctor or something but pretty soon she cut it out and
we sat there a while without saying nothing. Then she says If you could
get your salery razed a couple of hundred dollars a year would you
borrow the money ahead somewheres and take me along to California?
I says Yes I would if I could get a couple hundred dollars more salery
but how could I do that when I had signed a contract for $2800 last
fall allready? She says Don't you think you are worth more than $2800?
And I says Yes of coarse I was worth more than $2800. She says Well
if you will go and talk the right way to Comiskey I believe he will give
you $3000 but you must be sure you go at it the right way and don't
go and ball it all up.

Well we argude about it a while because I don't want to hold nobody
up Al but finally I says I would. It would not be holding nobody up
anyway because I am worth $3000 to the club if I am worth a nichol.
The papers is all saying that the club has got a good chance to win the
pennant this year and talking about the pitching staff and I guess they
would not be no pitching staff much if it was not for I and one or two
others—about one other I guess.

So it looks like as if everything will be all O. K. now Al. I am going
to the office over to the park to see him the first thing in the morning
and I am pretty sure that I will get what I am after because if I do not
he will see that I am going to quit and then he will see what he is up
against and not let me get away.

I will let you know how I come out. Your pal, JACK.

Chicago, Illinois, Febuery 14

FRIEND AL: Al old pal I have got a big supprise for you. I am going to
the Federal League. I had a run in with Comiskey yesterday and I guess
I told him a thing or 2. I guess he would of been glad to sign me at my
own figure before I got threw but I was so mad I would not give him
no chance to offer me another contract.

I got out to the park at 9 oclock yesterday morning and it was a
hour before he showed up and then he kept me waiting another hour
so I was pretty sore when I finally went in to see him. He says Well
young man what can I do for you? I says I come to see about my
contract. He says Do you want to sign up for next year all ready? I says
No I am talking about this year. He says I thought I and you talked
business last fall. And I says Yes but now I think I am worth more
money and I want to sign a contract for $3000. He says If you behave
yourself and work good this year I will see that you are took care of.
But I says That won't do because I have got to be sure I am going to
get $3000.

Then he says I am not sure you are going to get anything. I says
What do you mean? And he says I have gave you a very fare contract
and if you don't want to live up to it that is your own business. So I
give him a awful call Al and told him I would jump to the Federal
League. He says Oh, I would not do that if I was you. They are haveing
a hard enough time as it is. So I says something back to him and he did
not say nothing to me and I beat it out of the office.

I have not told Florrie about the Federal League business yet as I am
going to give her a big supprise. I bet they will take her along with me
on the training trip and pay her fair but even if they don't I should not
worry because I will make them give me a contract for $4000 a year
and then I can afford to take her with me on all the trips.

I will go down and see Tinker to-morrow morning and I will write
you to-morrow night Al how much salery they are going to give me.
But I won't sign for no less than $4000. You know me Al.

Yours,   JACK.

Chicago, Illinois, Febuery 15

OLD PAL: It is pretty near midnight Al but I been to bed a couple of
times and I can't get no sleep. I am worried to death Al and I don't
know where I am going to head in at. Maybe I will go out and buy a
gun Al and end it all and I guess it would be better for everybody. But
I cannot do that Al because I have not got the money to buy a gun
with.

I went down to see Tinker about signing up with the Federal League and he was busy in the office when I come in. Pretty soon Buck Perry the pitcher that was with Boston last year come out and seen me and as Tinker was still busy we went out and had a drink together. Buck shows me a contract for $5000 a year and Tinker had allso gave him a $500 bonus. So pretty soon I went up to the office and pretty soon Tinker seen me and called me into his private office and asked what did I want. I says I was ready to jump for $4000 and a bonus. He says I thought you was signed up with the White Sox. I says Yes I was but I was not satisfied. He says That does not make no difference to me if you are satisfied or not. You ought to of came to me before you signed a contract. I says I did not know enough but I know better now. He says Well it is to late now. We cannot have nothing to do with you because you have went and signed a contract with the White Sox. I argude with him a while and asked him to come out and have a drink so we could talk it over but he said he was busy so they was nothing for me to do but blow.

So I am not going to the Federal League Al and I will not go with the White Sox because I have got a raw deal. Comiskey will be sorry for what he done when his team starts the season and is up against it for good pitchers and then he will probily be willing to give me anything I ask for but that don't do me no good now Al. I am way in debt and no chance to get no money from nobody. I wish I had of stayed with Terre Haute Al and never saw this league.   Your pal,   JACK.

Chicago, Illinois, Febuery 17

FRIEND AL: Al don't never let anybody tell you that these here lefthanders is right. This Allen my own brother-in-law who married sisters has been grafting and spongeing on me all winter Al. Look what he done to me now Al. You know how hard I been up against it for money and I know he has got plenty of it because I seen it on him. Well Al I was scared to tell Florrie I was cleaned out and so I went to Allen yesterday and says I had to have $100 right away because I owèd the rent and owed the hired girl's salery and could not even pay no grocery bill. And he says No he could not let me have none because he has got to save all his money to take his wife on the trip to California. And here he has been liveing on me all winter and maybe I could of took my wife to California if I had not of spent all my money takeing care of this no good lefthander and his wife. And Al honest he has not got a thing and ought not to be in the league. He gets by with a dinky curve ball and has not got no more smoke than a rabbit or something.

Well Al I felt like busting him in the jaw but then I thought No I might kill him and then I would have Marie and Florrie both to take care of and God knows one of them is enough besides paying his funeral expenses. So I walked away from him without takeing a crack at him and went into the other room where Florrie and Marie was at. I says to Marie I says Marie I wish you would go in the other room a minute because I want to talk to Florrie. So Marie beats it into the other room and then I tells Florrie all about what Comiskey and the Federal League done to me. She bawled something awful and then she says I was no good and she wished she had not never married me. I says I wisht it too and then she says Do you mean that and starts to cry.

I told her I was sorry I says that because they is not no use fusing with girls Al specially when they is your wife. She says No California trip for me and then she says What are you going to do? And I says I did not know. She says Well if I was a man I would do something. So then I got mad and I says I will do something. So I went down to the corner salloon and started in to get good and drunk but I could not do it Al because I did not have the money.

Well old pal I am going to ask you a big favor and it is this I want you to send me $100 Al for just a few days till I can get on my feet. I do not know when I can pay it back Al but I guess you know the money is good and I know you have got it. Who would not have it when they live in Bedford? And besides I let you take $20 in June 4 years ago Al and you give it back but I would not have said nothing to you if you had of kept it. Let me hear from you right away old pal.

                                        Yours truly,   JACK.

                                        Chicago, Illinois, Febuery 19
AL: I am certainly greatful to you Al for the $100 which come just a little while ago. I will pay the rent with it and part of the grocery bill and I guess the hired girl will have to wait a while for hern but she is sure to get it because I don't never forget my debts. I have changed my mind about the White Sox and I am going to go on the trip and take Florrie along because I don't think it would not be right to leave her here alone in Chi when her sister and all of us is going.

I am going over to the ball park and up in the office pretty soon to see about it. I will tell Comiskey I changed my mind and he will be glad to get me back because the club has not got no chance to finish nowheres without me. But I won't go on no trip or give the club my services without them giveing me some more advance money so as I can take Florrie along with me because Al I would not go without her.

Maybe Comiskey will make my salery $3000 like I wanted him to when he sees I am willing to be a good fellow and go along with him and when he knows that the Federal League would of gladly gave me $4000 if I had not of signed no contract with the White Sox.

I think I will ask him for $200 advance money Al and if I get it may be I can send part of your $100 back to you but I know you cannot be in no hurry Al though you says you wanted it back as soon as possible. You could not be very hard up Al because it don't cost near so much to live in Bedford as it does up here.

Anyway I will let you know how I come out with Comiskey and I will write you as soon as I get out to Paso Robles if I don't get no time to write you before I leave.   Your pal,   JACK.

P. S. I have took good care of myself all winter Al and I guess I ought to have a great season.

P. S. Florrie is tickled to death about going along and her and I will have some time together out there on the Coast if I can get some money somewheres.

Chicago, Illinois, Febuery 21

FRIEND AL: I have not got the heart to write this letter to you Al. I am up here in my $42.50 a month flat and the club has went to California and Florrie has went too. I am flat broke Al and all I am asking you is to send me enough money to pay my fair to Bedford and they and all their leagues can go to hell Al.

I was out to the ball park early yesterday morning and some of the boys was there allready fanning and kidding each other. They tried to kid me to when I come in but I guess I give them as good as they give me. I was not in no mind for kidding Al because I was there on business and I wanted to see Comiskey and get it done with.

Well the secretary come in finally and I went up to him and says I wanted to see Comiskey right away. He says The boss was busy and what did I want to see him about and I says I wanted to get some advance money because I was going to take my wife on the trip. He says This would be a fine time to be telling us about it even if you was going on the trip.

And I says What do you mean? And he says You are not going on no trip with us because we have got wavers on you and you are sold to Milwaukee.

Honest Al I thought he was kidding at first and I was waiting for him to laugh but he did not laugh and finally I says What do you mean? And he says Cannot you understand no English? You are sold to Milwaukee. Then I says I want to see the boss. He says It won't do you no good to see the boss and he is to busy to see you. I says I want to get some money. And he says You cannot get no money from this club and all you get is your fair to Milwaukee. I says I am not going to no Milwaukee anyway and he says I should not worry about that. Suit yourself.

Well Al I told some of the boys about it and they was pretty sore and says I ought to bust the secretary in the jaw and I was going to do it when I thought No I better not because he is a little guy and I might kill him.

I looked all over for Kid Gleason but he was not nowheres round and they told me he would not get into town till late in the afternoon. If I could of saw him Al he would of fixed me all up. I asked 3 or 4 of the boys for some money but they says they was all broke.

But I have not told you the worst of it yet Al. When I come back to the flat Allen and Marie and Florrie was busy packing up and they asked me how I come out. I told them and Allen just stood there stareing like a big rummy but Marie and Florrie both begin to cry and I almost felt like as if I would like to cry to only I am not no baby Al.

Well Al I told Florrie she might just is well quit packing and make up her mind that she was not going nowheres till I got money enough to go to Bedford where I belong. She kept right on crying and it got so I could not stand it no more so I went out to get a drink because I still had just about a dollar left yet.

It was about 2 oclock when I left the flat and pretty near 5 when I come back because I had ran in to some fans that knowed who I was and would not let me get away and besides I did not want to see no more of Allen and Marie till they was out of the house and on their way.

But when I come in Al they was nobody there. They was not nothing there except the furniture and a few of my things scattered round. I sit down for a few minutes because I guess I must of had to much to drink but finally I seen a note on the table addressed to me and I seen it was Florrie's writeing.

I do not remember just what was there in the note Al because I tore it up the minute I read it but it was something about I could not support no wife and Allen had gave her enough money to go back to Texas and she was going on the 6 oclock train and it would not do me no good to try and stop her.

Well Al they was not no danger of me trying to stop her. She was

not no good and I wisht I had not of never saw either she or her sister
or my brother-in-law.

For a minute I thought I would follow Allen and his wife down to
the deepo where the special train was to pull out of and wait till I see
him and punch his jaw but I seen that would not get me nothing.

So here I am all alone Al and I will have to stay here till you send
me the money to come home. You better send me $25 because I have
got a few little debts I should ought to pay before I leave town. I am
not going to Milwaukee Al because I did not get no decent deal and
nobody cannot make no sucker out of me.

Please hurry up with the $25 Al old friend because I am sick and
tired of Chi and want to get back there with my old pal.

Yours,   JACK.

P. S. Al I wish I had of took poor little Violet when she was so stuck
on me.

A NEW BUSHER BREAKS IN

Chicago, Illinois, March 2

FRIEND AL: Al that peace in the paper was all O. K. and the right dope
just like you said. I seen president Johnson the president of the league
to-day and he told me the peace in the papers was the right dope and
Comiskey did not have no right to sell me to Milwaukee because the
Detroit Club had never gave no wavers on me. He says the Detroit Club
was late in fileing their claim and Comiskey must of tooken it for
granted that they was going to wave but president Johnson was pretty
sore about it at that and says Comiskey did not have no right to sell
me till he was positive that they was not no team that wanted me.

It will probily cost Comiskey some money for acting like he done
and not paying no attention to the rules and I would not be supprised
if president Johnson had him throwed out of the league.

Well I asked president Johnson should I report at once to the Detroit
Club down south and he says No you better wait till you hear from
Comiskey and I says What has Comiskey got to do with it now? And
he says Comiskey will own you till he sells you to Detroit or somewheres
else. So I will have to go out to the ball park to-morrow and see is they
any mail for me there because I probily will get a letter from Comiskey
telling me I am sold to Detroit.

If I had of thought at the time I would of knew that Detroit never
would give no wavers on me after the way I showed Cobb and Craw-

ford up last fall and I might of knew too that Detroit is in the market for good pitchers because they got a rotten pitching staff but they won't have no rotten staff when I get with them.

If necessary I will pitch every other day for Jennings and if I do we will win the pennant sure because Detroit has got a club that can get 2 or 3 runs every day and all as I need to win most of my games is 1 run. I can't hardly wait till Jennings works me against the White Sox and what I will do to them will be a plenty. It don't take no pitching to beat them anyway and when they get up against a pitcher like I they might as well leave their bats in the bag for all the good their bats will do them.

I guess Cobb and Crawford will be glad to have me on the Detroit Club because then they won't never have to hit against me except in practice and I won't pitch my best in practice because they will be teammates of mine and I don't never like to show none of my teammates up. At that though I don't suppose Jennings will let me do much pitching in practice because when he gets a hold of a good pitcher he won't want me to take no chances of throwing my arm away in practice.

Al just think how funny it will be to have me pitching for the Tigers in the same town where Violet lives and pitching on the same club with her husband. It will not be so funny for Violet and her husband though because when she has a chance to see me work regular she will find out what a mistake she made takeing that lefthander instead of a man that has got some future and soon will be makeing 5 or $6000 a year because I won't sign with Detroit for no less than $5000 at most. Of coarse I could of had her if I had of wanted to but still and all it will make her feel pretty sick to see me winning games for Detroit while her husband is batting fungos and getting splinters in his unie from slideing up and down the bench.

As for her husband the first time he opens his clam to me I will haul off and bust him one in the jaw but I guess he will know more than to start trouble with a man of my size and who is going to be one of their stars while he is just holding down a job because they feel sorry for him. I wish he could of got the girl I married instead of the one he got and I bet she would of drove him crazy. But I guess you can't drive a lefthander crazyer than he is to begin with.

I have not heard nothing from Florrie Al and I don't want to hear nothing. I and her is better apart and I wish she would sew me for a bill of divorce so she could not go round claiming she is my wife and disgraceing my name. If she would consent to sew me for a bill of divorce I would gladly pay all the expenses and settle with her for any sum of money she wants say about $75.00 or $100.00 and they is no reason I should give her a nichol after the way her and her sister Marie and her brother-in-law Allen grafted off of me. Probily I could sew her for a bill of divorce but they tell me it costs money to sew and if you just lay low and let the other side do the sewing it don't cost you a nichol.

It is pretty late Al and I have got to get up early to-morrow and go to the ball park and see is they any mail for me. I will let you know what I hear old pal.   Your old pal,   JACK.

Chicago, Illinois, March 4

AL: I am up against it again. I went out to the ball park office yesterday and they was nobody there except John somebody who is asst secretary and all the rest of them is out on the Coast with the team. Maybe this here John was trying to kid me but this is what he told me. First I says Is they a letter here for me? And he says No. And I says I was expecting word from Comiskey that I should join the Detroit Club and he says What makes you think you are going to Detroit? I says Comiskey asked wavers on me and Detroit did not give no wavers. He says Well that is not no sign that you are going to Detroit. If Comiskey can't get you out of the league he will probily keep you himself and it is a cinch he is not going to give no pitcher to Detroit no matter how rotten he is.

I says What do you mean? And he says You just stick round town till you hear from Comiskey and I guess you will hear pretty soon because he is comeing back from the Coast next Saturday. I says Well the only thing he can tell me is to report to Detroit because I won't never pitch again for the White Sox. Then John gets fresh and says I suppose you will quit the game and live on your saveings and then I blowed out of the office because I was scared I would loose my temper and break something.

So you see Al what I am up against. I won't never pitch for the White Sox again and I want to get with the Detroit Club but how can I if Comiskey won't let me go? All I can do is stick round till next Saturday and then I will see Comiskey and I guess when I tell him what I think of him he will be glad to let me go to Detroit or anywheres else. I will have something on him this time because I know that he did not pay no attention to the rules when he told me I was sold to Milwaukee and if he tries to slip something over on me I will tell president Johnson of the league all about it and then you will see where Comiskey heads in at.

Al old pal that $25.00 you give me at the station the other day is all shot to peaces and I must ask you to let me have $25.00 more which will make $75.00 all together includeing the $25.00 you sent me before I come home. I hate to ask you this favor old pal but I know you have got the money. If I am sold to Detroit I will get some advance money and pay up all my dedts incluseive.

If he don't let me go to Detroit I will make him come across with part of my salery for this year even if I don't pitch for him because I signed a contract and was ready to do my end of it and would of if he had not of been nasty and tried to slip something over on me. If he refuses to come across I will hire a attorney at law and he will get it all. So Al you see you have got a cinch on getting back what you lone me but I guess you know that Al without all this talk because you have been my old pal for a good many years and I have allways treated you square and tried to make you feel that I and you was equals and that my success was not going to make me forget my old friends.

Wherever I pitch this year I will insist on a salary of 5 or $6000 a year. So you see on my first pay day I will have enough to pay you up and settle the rest of my dedts but I am not going to pay no more rent for this rotten flat because they tell me if a man don't pay no rent for a while they will put him out. Let them put me out. I should not worry but will go and rent my old room that I had before I met Florrie and got into all this trouble.

The sooner you can send me that $35.00 the better and then I will owe you $85.00 incluseive and I will write and let you know how I come out with Comiskey.   Your pal,   JACK.

Chicago, Illinois, March 12

FRIEND AL: I got another big supprise for you and this is it I am going to pitch for the White Sox after all. If Comiskey was not a old man I guess I would of lost my temper and beat him up but I am glad now that I kept my temper and did not loose it because I forced him to make a lot of consessions and now it looks like as though I would have a big year both pitching and money.

He got back to town yesterday morning and showed up to his office in the afternoon and I was there waiting for him. He would not see me for a while but finally I acted like as though I was getting tired of waiting and I guess the secretary got scared that I would beat it out of the office and leave them all in the lerch. Anyway he went in and spoke to Comiskey and then come out and says the boss was ready to see me. When I went into the office where he was at he says Well young man what can I do for you? And I says I want you to give me my release so as I

can join the Detroit Club down South and get in shape. Then he says
What makes you think you are going to join the Detroit Club? Because
we need you here. I says Then why did you try to sell me to Milwaukee?
But you could not because you could not get no wavers.

Then he says I thought I was doing you a favor by sending you to
Milwaukee because they make a lot of beer up there. I says What do
you mean? He says You been keeping in shape all this winter by trying
to drink this town dry and besides that you tried to hold me up for
more money when you allready had signed a contract allready and so
I was going to send you to Milwaukee and learn you something and
besides you tried to go with the Federal League but they would not take
you because they was scared to.

I don't know where he found out all that stuff at Al and besides he
was wrong when he says I was drinking to much because they is not
nobody that can drink more than me and not be effected. But I did not
say nothing because I was scared I would forget myself and call him
some name and he is a old man. Yes I did say something. I says Well I
guess you found out that you could not get me out of the league and
then he says Don't never think I could not get you out of the league. If
you think I can't send you to Milwaukee I will prove it to you that I
can. I says You can't because Detroit won't give no wavers on me. He
says Detroit will give wavers on you quick enough if I ask them.

Then he says Now you can take your choice you can stay here and
pitch for me at the salery you signed up for and you can cut out the
monkey business and drink water when you are thirsty or else you can
go up to Milwaukee and drownd yourself in one of them brewrys.
Which shall it be? I says How can you keep me or send me to Milwaukee when Detroit has allready claimed my services? He says Detroit has
claimed a lot of things and they have even claimed the pennant but that
is not no sign they will win it. He says And besides you would not want
to pitch for Detroit because then you would not never have no chance
to pitch against Cobb and show him up.

Well Al when he says that I knowed he appresiated what a pitcher I
am even if he did try to sell me to Milwaukee or he would not of made
that remark about the way I can show Cobb and Crawford up. So I
says Well if you need me that bad I will pitch for you but I must have
a new contract. He says Oh I guess we can fix that up O. K. and he
steps out in the next room a while and then he comes back with a new
contract. And what do you think it was Al? It was a contract for 3 years
so you can see I am sure of my job here for 3 years and everything is
all O. K.

The contract calls for the same salery a year for 3 years that I was going to get before for only 1 year which is $2800.00 a year and then I will get in on the city serious money too and the Detroit Club don't have no city serious and have no chance to get into the World Serious with the rotten pitching staff they got. So you see Al he fixed me up good and that shows that he must think a hole lot of me or he would of sent me to Detroit or maybe to Milwaukee but I don't see how he could of did that without no wavers.

Well Al I allmost forgot to tell you that he has gave me a ticket to Los Angeles where the 2d team are practicing at now but where the 1st team will be at in about a week. I am leaveing to-night and I guess before I go I will go down to president Johnson and tell him that I am fixed up all O. K. and have not got no kick comeing so that president Johnson will not fine Comiskey for not paying no attention to the rules or get him fired out of the league because I guess Comiskey must be all O. K. and good hearted after all.

I won't pay no attention to what he says about me drinking this town dry because he is all wrong in regards to that. He must of been jokeing I guess because nobody but some boob would think he could drink this town dry but at that I guess I can hold more than anybody and not be effected. But I guess I will cut it out for a while at that because I don't want to get them sore at me after the contract they give me.

I will write to you from Los Angeles Al and let you know what the boys says when they see me an I will bet that they will be tickled to death. The rent man was round to-day but I seen him comeing and he did not find me. I am going to leave the furniture that belongs in the flat in the flat and allso the furniture I bought which don't amount to much because it was not no real Sir Cashion walnut and besides I don't want nothing round me to remind me of Florrie because the sooner her and I forget each other the better.

Tell the boys about my good luck Al but it is not no luck neither because it was comeing to me.   Yours truly,   JACK.

Los Angeles, California, March 16
AL: Here I am back with the White Sox again and it seems to good to be true because just like I told you they are all tickled to death to see me. Kid Gleason is here in charge of the 2d team and when he seen me come into the hotel he jumped up and hit me in the stumach but he

acts like that whenever he feels good so I could not get sore at him though he had no right to hit me in the stumach. If he had of did it in ernest I would of walloped him in the jaw.

He says Well if here ain't the old lady killer. He ment Al that I am strong with the girls but I am all threw with them now but he don't know nothing about the troubles I had. He says Are you in shape? And I told him Yes I am. He says Yes you look in shape like a barrel. I says They is not no fat on me and if I am a little bit bigger than last year it is because my mussels is bigger. He says Yes your stumach mussels is emense and you must of gave them plenty of exercise. Wait till Bodie sees you and he will want to stick round you all the time because you make him look like a broom straw or something. I let him kid me along because what is the use of getting mad at him? And besides he is all O. K. even if he is a little rough.

I says to him A little work will fix me up all O. K. and he says You bet you are going to get some work because I am going to see to it myself. I says You will have to hurry because you will be going up to Frisco in a few days and I am going to stay here and join the 1st club. Then he says You are not going to do no such a thing. You are going right along with me. I knowed he was kidding me then because Callahan would not never leave me with the 2d team no more after what I done for him last year and besides most of the stars generally allways goes with the 1st team on the training trip.

Well I seen all the rest of the boys that is here with the 2d team and they all acted like as if they was glad to see me and why should not they be when they know that me being here with the White Sox and not with Detroit means that Callahan won't have to do no worrying about his pitching staff? But they is four or 5 young recrut pitchers with the team here and I bet they is not so glad to see me because what chance have they got?

If I was Comiskey and Callahan I would not spend no money on new pitchers because with me and 1 or 2 of the other boys we got the best pitching staff in the league. And instead of spending the money for new pitching recruts I would put it all in a lump and buy Ty Cobb or Sam Crawford off of Detroit or somebody else who can hit and Cobb and Crawford is both real hitters Al even if I did make them look like suckers. Who wouldn't?

Well Al to-morrow a.m. I am going out and work a little and in the p.m. I will watch the game between we and the Venice Club but I won't pitch none because Gleason would not dare take no chances of me hurting my arm. I will write to you in a few days from here because no matter what Gleason says I am going to stick here with the 1st team because I know Callahan will want me along with him for a attraction.

Your pal,   JACK.

San Francisco, California, March 20

FRIEND AL: Well Al here I am back in old Frisco with the 2d team but I will tell you how it happened Al. Yesterday Gleason told me to pack up and get ready to leave Los Angeles with him and I says No I am going to stick here and wait for the 1st team and then he says I guess I must of overlooked something in the papers because I did not see nothing about you being appointed manager of the club. I says No I am not manager but Callahan is manager and he will want to keep me with him. He says I got a wire from Callahan telling me to keep you with my club but of coarse if you know what Callahan wants better than he knows it himself why then go ahead and stay here or go jump in the Pacific Ocean.

Then he says I know why you don't want to go with me and I says Why? And he says Because you know I will make you work and won't let you eat everything on the bill of fair includeing the name of the hotel at which we are stopping at. That made me sore and I was just going to call him when he says Did not you marry Mrs. Allen's sister? And I says Yes but that is not none of your business. Then he says Well I don't want to butt into your business but I heard you and your wife had some kind of a argument and she beat it. I says Yes, she give me a rotten deal. He says Well then I don't see where it is going to be very pleasant for you traveling round with the 1st club because Allen and his wife is both with that club and what do you want to be mixed up with them for? I says I am not scared of Allen or his wife or no other old hen.

So here I am Al with the 2d team but it is only for a while till Callahan gets sick of some of them pitchers he has got and sends for me so as he can see some real pitching. And besides I am glad to be here in Frisco where I made so many friends when I was pitching here for a short time till Callahan heard about my work and called me back to the big show where I belong at and nowheres else.

Yours truly,   JACK.

San Francisco, California, March 25

OLD PAL: Al I got a supprise for you. Who do you think I seen last night? Nobody but Hazel. Her name now is Hazel Levy because you know Al she married Kid Levy the middleweight and I wish he was champion of the world Al because then it would not take me more than about a minute to be champion of the world myself. I have not got nothing against him though because he married her and if he had not of I probily would of married her myself but at that she could not of treated me no worse than Florrie. Well they was setting at a table in the cafe where her and I use to go pretty near every night. She spotted me when I first come in and sends a waiter over to ask me to come and have a drink with them. I went over because they was no use being nasty and let bygones be bygones.

She interduced me to her husband and he asked me what I was drinking. Then she butts in and says Oh you must let Mr. Keefe buy the drinks because it hurts his feelings to have somebody else buy the drinks. Then Levy says Oh he is one of these here spendrifts is he? and she says Yes he don't care no more about a nichol than his right eye does. I says I guess you have got no holler comeing on the way I spend my money. I don't steal no money anyway. She says What do you mean? and I says I guess you know what I mean. How about that $30.00 that you borrowed off of me and never give it back? Then her husband cuts in and says You cut that line of talk out or I will bust you. I says Yes you will. And he says Yes I will.

Well Al what was the use of me starting trouble with him when he has got enough trouble right to home and besides as I say I have not got nothing against him. So I got up and blowed away from the table and I bet he was relieved when he seen I was not going to start nothing. I beat it out of there a while afterward because I was not drinking nothing and I don't have no fun setting round a place and lapping up ginger ail or something. And besides the music was rotten.

Al I am certainly glad I throwed Hazel over because she has grew to be as big as a horse and is all painted up. I don't care nothing about them big dolls no more or about no other kind neither. I am off of them all. They can all of them die and I should not worry.

Well Al I done my first pitching of the year this p.m. and I guess I showed them that I was in just as good a shape as some of them birds that has been working a month. I worked 4 innings against my old team the San Francisco Club and I give them nothing but fast ones but they sure was fast ones and you could hear them zip. Charlie O'Leary was trying to get out of the way of one of them and it hit his bat and went over first base for a base hit but at that Fournier would of eat it up if it had of been Chase playing first instead of Fournier.

That was the only hit they got off of me and they ought to of been ashamed to of tooken that one. But Gleason don't appresiate my work and him and I allmost come to blows at supper. I was pretty hungry and I ordered some stake and some eggs and some pie and some ice cream and some coffee and a glass of milk but Gleason would not let me have the pie or the milk and would not let me eat more than ½ the stake. And it is a wonder I did not bust him and tell him to mind his own business. I says What right have you got to tell me what to eat? And he says You don't need nobody to tell you what to eat you need somebody to keep you from floundering yourself. I says Why can't I eat what I want to when I have worked good?

He says Who told you you worked good and I says I did not need nobody to tell me. I know I worked good because they could not do nothing with me. He says Well it is a good thing for you that they did not start bunting because if you had of went to stoop over and pick up the ball you would of busted wide open. I says Why? and he says because you are hog fat and if you don't let up on the stable and fancy groceries we will have to pay 2 fairs to get you back to Chi. I don't remember now what I says to him but I says something you can bet on that. You know me Al.

I wish Al that Callahan would hurry up and order me to join the 1st team. If he don't Al I believe Gleason will starve me to death. A little slob like him don't realize that a big man like I needs good food and plenty of it.   Your pal,   JACK.

Salt Lake City, Utah, April 1
AL: Well Al we are on our way East and I am still with the 2d team and I don't understand why Callahan don't order me to join the 1st team but maybe it is because he knows that I am all right and have got the stuff and he wants to keep them other guys round where he can see if they have got anything.

The recrut pitchers that is along with our club have not got nothing and the scout that reckommended them must of been full of hops or something. It is not no common thing for a club to pick up a man that has got the stuff to make him a star up here and the White Sox was pretty lucky to land me but I don't understand why they throw their money away on new pitchers when none of them is no good and besides who would want a better pitching staff than we got right now without no raw recruts and bushers.

I worked in Oakland the day before yesterday but he only let me go the 1st 4 innings. I bet them Oakland birds was glad when he took me out. When I was in that league I use to just throw my glove in the box and them Oakland birds was licked and honest Al some of them turned white when they seen I was going to pitch the other day.

I felt kind of sorry for them and I did not give them all I had so they got 5 or 6 hits and scored a couple of runs. I was not feeling very good at that and besides we got some awful excuses for a ball player on this club and the support they give me was the rottenest I ever seen gave anybody. But some of them won't be in this league more than about 10 minutes more so I should not fret as they say.

We play here this afternoon and I don't believe I will work because the team they got here is not worth wasteing nobody on. They must be a lot of boobs in this town Al because they tell me that some of them has got ½ a dozen wives or so. And what a man wants with 1 wife is a misery to me let alone a ½ dozen.

I will probily work against Denver because they got a good club and was champions of the Western League last year. I will make them think they are champions of the Epworth League or something.

Yours truly,   JACK.

Des Moines, Iowa, April 10

FRIEND AL: We got here this a.m. and this is our last stop and we will be in old Chi to-morrow to open the season. The 1st team gets home to-day and I would be there with them if Callahan was a real manager who knowed something about manageing because if I am going to open the season I should ought to have 1 day of rest at home so I would have all my strength to open the season. The Cleveland Club will be there to open against us and Callahan must know that I have got them licked any time I start against them.

As soon as my name is announced to pitch the Cleveland Club is licked or any other club when I am right and they don't kick the game away behind me.

Gleason told me on the train last night that I was going to pitch here to-day but I bet by this time he has got orders from Callahan to let me rest and to not give me no more work because suppose even if I did not start the game to-morrow I probily will have to finish it.

Gleason has been sticking round me like as if I had a million bucks or something. I can't even sit down and smoke a cigar but what he is there to knock the ashes off of it. He is O. K. and good-hearted if he is a little rough and keeps hitting me in the stumach but I wish he would leave me alone sometimes espesially at meals. He was in to breakfast with me this a.m. and after I got threw I snuck off down the street and got something to eat. That is not right because it costs me money when I have to go away from the ho- tel and eat and what right has he got to try and help me order my meals? Be- cause he don't know what I want and what my stumach wants.

My stumach don't want to have him punching it all the time but he keeps on doing it. So that shows he don't know what is good for me. But he is a old man Al otherwise I would not stand for the stuff he pulls. The 1st thing I am going to do when we get to Chi is I am going to a resturunt somewheres and get a good meal where Gleason or no one else can't get at me. I know allready what I am going to eat and that is a big stake and a apple pie and that is not all.

Well Al watch the papers and you will see what I done to that Cleveland Club and I hope Lajoie and Jackson is both in good shape because I don't want to pick on no cripples.   Your pal,   JACK.

Chicago, Illinois, April 16

OLD PAL: Yesterday was the 1st pay day old pal and I know I promised to pay you what I owe you and it is $75.00 because when I asked you for $35.00 before I went West you only sent me $25.00 which makes the hole sum $75.00. Well Al I can't pay you now because the pay we drawed was only for 4 days and did not amount to nothing and I had to buy a meal ticket and fix up about my room rent.

And then they is another thing Al which I will tell you about. I come into the clubhouse the day the season opened and the 1st guy I seen was Allen. I was going up to bust him but he come up and held his hand out and what was they for me to do but shake hands with him if he is going to be yellow like that? He says Well Jack I am glad they did not send you to Milwaukee and I bet you will have a big year. I says Yes I will have a big year O. K. if you don't sick another 1 of your sister-in-laws on to me. He says Oh don't let they be no hard feelings about that. You know it was not no fault of mine and I bet if you was to write to Florrie everything could be fixed up O. K.

I says I don't want to write to no Florrie but I will get a attorney at law to write to her. He says You don't even know where she is at and I says I don't care where she is at. Where is she? He says She is down to her home in Waco, Texas, and if I was you I would write to her myself and not let no attorney at law write to her because that would get her mad and besides what do you want a attorney at law to write to her about? I says I am going to sew her for a bill of divorce.

Then he says On what grounds? and I says Dessertion. He says You better not do no such thing or she will sew you for a bill of divorce for none support and then you will look like a cheap guy. I says I don't care what I look like. So you see Al I had to send Florrie $10.00 or maybe she would be mean enough to sew me for a bill of divorce on the ground of none support and that would make me look bad.

Well Al, Allen told me his wife wanted to talk to me and try and fix things up between I and Florrie but I give him to understand that I would not stand for no meeting with his wife and he says Well suit yourself about that but they is no reason you and I should quarrel.

You see Al he don't want no mix-up with me because he knows he could get nothing but the worst of it. I will be friends with him but I won't have nothing to do with Marie because if it had not of been for she and Florrie I would have money in the bank besides not being in no danger of getting sewed for none support.

I guess you must of read about Joe Benz getting married and I guess he must of got a good wife and 1 that don't bother him all the time because he pitched the opening game and shut Cleveland out with 2 hits. He was pretty good Al, better than I ever seen him and they was a couple of times when his fast ball was pretty near as fast as mine.

I have not worked yet Al and I asked Callahan to-day what was the matter and he says I was waiting for you to get in shape. I says I am in shape now and I notice that when I was pitching in practice this a.m. they did not hit nothing out of the infield. He says That was because you are so spread out that they could not get nothing past you. He says The way you are now you cover more ground than the grandstand. I says Is that so? And he walked away.

We got out on a trip to Cleveland and Detroit and St. Louis in a few days and maybe I will take my regular turn then because the other pitchers has been getting away lucky because most of the hitters has not got their batting eye as yet but wait till they begin hitting and then it will take a man like I to stop them.

The 1st of May is our next pay day Al and then I will have enough money so as I can send you the $75.00.   Your pal,   JACK.

Detroit, Michigan, April 28

FRIEND AL: What do you think of a rotten manager that bawls me out and fines me $50.00 for losing a 1 to 0 game in 10 innings when it was my 1st start this season? And no wonder I was a little wild in the 10th when I had not had no chance to work and get control. I got a good notion to quit this rotten club and jump to the Federals where a man gets some kind of treatment. Callahan says I throwed the game away on purpose but I did not do no such a thing Al because when I throwed that ball at Joe Hill's head I forgot that the bases was full and besides if Gleason had not of starved me to death the ball that hit him in the head would of killed him.

And how could a man go to 1st base and the winning run be forced in if he was dead which he should ought to of been the lucky left handed stiff if I had of had my full strenth to put on my fast one instead of being ½ starved to death and weak. But I guess I better tell you how it come off. The papers will get it all wrong like they generally allways does.

Callahan asked me this a.m. if I thought I was hard enough to work and I was tickled to death, because I seen he was going to give me a chance. I told him Sure I was in good shape and if them Tigers scored a run off me he could keep me setting on the bench the rest of the summer. So he says All right I am going to start you and if you go good maybe Gleason will let you eat some supper.

Well Al when I begin warming up I happened to look up in the grand stand and who do you think I seen? Nobody but Violet. She smiled when she seen me but I bet she felt more like crying. Well I smiled back at her because she probily would of broke down and made a seen or something if I had not of. They was not nobody warming up for Detroit when I begin warming up but pretty soon I looked over to their bench and Joe Hill Violet's husband was warming up. I says to myself Well here is where I show that bird up if they got nerve enough to start him against me but probily Jennings don't want to waste no real pitcher on this game which he knows we got cinched and we would of had it cinched Al if they had of got a couple of runs or even 1 run for me.

Well, Jennings come passed our bench just like he allways does and tried to pull some of his funny stuff. He says Hello are you still in the league? I says Yes but I come pretty near not being. I came pretty near being with Detroit. I wish you could of heard Gleason and Callahan laugh when I pulled that one on him. He says something back but it was not no hot comeback like mine.

Well Al if I had of had any work and my regular control I guess I would of pitched a 0 hit game because the only time they could touch me was when I had to ease up to get them over. Cobb was out of the game and they told me he was sick but I guess the truth is that he knowed I was going to pitch. Crawford got a couple of lucky scratch hits off of me because I got in the hole to him and had to let up. But the way that lucky left handed Hill got by was something awful and if I was as lucky as him I would quit pitching and shoot craps or something.

Our club can't hit nothing anyway. But batting against this bird was just like hitting fungos. His curve ball broke about ½ a inch and you could of wrote your name and address on his fast one while it was comeing up there. He had good control but who would not when they put nothing on the ball?

Well Al we could not get started against the lucky stiff and they could not do nothing with me even if my suport was rotten and I give a couple or 3 or 4 bases on balls but when they was men waiting to score I zipped them threw there so as they could not see them let alone hit them. Every time I come to the bench between innings I looked up to where Violet was setting and give her a smile and she smiled back and once I seen her clapping her hands at me after I had made Moriarty pop up in the pinch.

Well we come along to the 10th inning, 0 and 0, and all of a sudden we got after him. Bodie hits one and Schalk gets 2 strikes and 2 balls and then singles. Callahan tells Alcock to bunt and he does it but Hill sprawls all over himself like the big boob he is and the bases is full with nobody down. Well Gleason and Callahan argude about should they send somebody up for me or let me go up there and I says Let me go up there because I can murder this bird and Callahan says Well they is nobody out so go up and take a wallop.

Honest Al if this guy had of had anything at all I would of hit 1 out of the park, but he did not have even a glove. And how can a man hit pitching which is not no pitching at all but just slopping them up? When I went up there I hollered to him and says Stick 1 over here now you yellow stiff. And he says Yes I can stick them over allright and that is where I got something on you.

Well Al I hit a foul off of him that would of been a fare ball and broke up the game if the wind had not of been against it. Then I swung and missed a curve that I don't see how I missed it. The next 1 was a yard outside and this Evans calls it a strike. He has had it in for me ever since last year when he tried to get funny with me and I says something back to him that stung him. So he calls this 3d strike on me and I felt like murdering him. But what is the use?

I throwed down my bat and come back to the bench and I was glad Callahan and Gleason was out on the coaching line or they probily would of said something to me and I would of cut loose and beat them up. Well Al Weaver and Blackburne looked like a couple of rums up there and we don't score where we ought to of had 3 or 4 runs with any kind of hitting.

I would of been all O. K. in spite of that peace of rotten luck if this big Hill had of walked to the bench and not said nothing like a real pitcher. But what does he do but wait out there till I start for the box and I says Get on to the bench you lucky stiff or do you want me to hand you something? He says I don't want nothing more of yourn. I allready got your girl and your goat.

Well Al what do you think of a man that would say a thing like that? And nobody but a lefthander could of. If I had of had a gun I would of killed him deader than a doornail or something. He starts for the bench and I hollered at him Wait till you get up to that plate and then I am going to bean you. Honest Al I was so mad I could not see the plate or nothing. I don't even know who it was come up to bat 1st but whoever it was I hit him in the arm and he walks to first base. The next guy bunts and Chase tries to pull off 1 of them plays of hisn instead of playing safe and he don't get nobody. Well I kept getting madder and madder and I walks Stanage who if I had of been myself would not foul me.

Callahan has Scotty warming up and Gleason runs out from the bench and tells me I am threw but Callahan says Wait a minute he is going to let Hill hit and this big stiff ought to be able to get him out of the way and that will give Scotty a chance to get warm. Gleason says You better not take a chance because the big busher is hogwild, and they kept argueing till I got sick of listening to them and I went back to the box and got ready to pitch. But when I seen this Hill up there I forgot all about the ball game and I cut loose at his bean.

Well Al my control was all O. K. this time and I catched him square on the fourhead and he dropped like as if he had been shot. But pretty soon he gets up and gives me the laugh and runs to first base. I did not know the game was over till Weaver come up and pulled me off the field. But if I had not of been ½ starved to death and weak so as I could not put all my stuff on the ball you can bet that Hill never would of ran to first base and Violet would of been a widow and probily a lot better off than she is now. At that I never should ought to of tried to kill a lefthander by hitting him in the head.

Well Al they jumped all over me in the clubhouse and I had to hold myself back or I would of gave somebody the beating of their life. Callahan tells me I am fined $50.00 and suspended without no pay. I asked him What for and he says They would not be no use in telling you because you have not got no brains. I says Yes I have to got some brains and he says Yes but they is in your stumach. And then he says I wish we had of sent you to Milwaukee and I come back at him. I says I wish you had of.

Well Al I guess they is no chance of getting square treatment on this club and you won't be supprised if you hear of me jumping to the Federals where a man is treated like a man and not like no white slave.

Yours truly,   JACK.

Chicago, Illinois, May 2

AL: I have got to disappoint you again Al. When I got up to get my pay yesterday they held out $150.00 on me. $50.00 of it is what I was fined for loosing a 1 to 0 10-inning game in Detroit when I was so weak that I should ought never to of been sent in there and the $100.00 is the advance money that I drawed last winter and which I had forgot all about and the club would of forgot about it to if they was not so tight fisted.

So you see all I get for 2 weeks' pay is about $80.00 and I sent $25.00 to Florrie so she can't come no none support business on me.

I am still suspended Al and not drawing no pay now and I got a notion to hire a attorney at law and force them to pay my salary or else jump to the Federals where a man gets good treatment.

Allen is still after me to come over to his flat some night and see his wife and let her talk to me about Florrie but what do I want to talk about Florrie for or talk about nothing to a nut lefthander's wife?

The Detroit Club is here and Cobb is playing because he knows I am suspended but I wish Callahan would call it off and let me work against them and I would certainly love to work against this Joe Hill again and I bet they would be a different story this time because I been getting something to eat since we been home and I got back most of my strenth.

Your old pal,   JACK.

Chicago, Illinois, May 5

FRIEND AL: Well Al if you been reading the papers you will know before this letter is received what I done. Before the Detroit Club come here Joe Hill had win 4 strate but he has not win no 5 strate or won't neither Al because I put a crimp in his winning streek just like I knowed I would do if I got a chance when I was feeling good and had all my strenth. Callahan asked me yesterday a.m. if I thought I had enough rest and I says Sure because I did not need no rest in the 1st place. Well, he says, I thought maybe if I layed you off a few days you would do some thinking and if you done some thinking once in a while you would be a better pitcher.

Well anyway I worked and I wish you could of saw them Tigers trying to hit me Cobb and Crawford incluseive. The 1st time Cobb come

up Weaver catched a lucky line drive off of him and the next time I
eased up a little and Collins run back and took a fly ball off of the
fence. But the other times he come up he looked like a sucker except
when he come up in the 8th and then he beat out a bunt but allmost
anybody is liable to do that once in a while.

Crawford got a scratch hit between Chase and Blackburne in the 2d
inning and in the 4th he was gave a three-base hit by this Evans who
should ought to be writeing for the papers instead of trying to umpire.
The ball was 2 feet foul and I bet Crawford will tell you the same thing
if you ask him. But what I done to this Hill was awful. I give him my
curve twice when he was up there in the 3d and he missed it a foot.
Then I come with my fast ball right past his nose and I bet if he had
not of ducked it would of drove that big horn of hisn clear up in the
press box where them rotten reporters sits and smokes their hops. Then
when he was looking for another fast one I slopped up my slow one
and he is still swinging at it yet.

But the best of it was that I practally won my own game. Bodie and
Schalk was on when I come up in the 5th and Hill hollers to me and
says I guess this is where I shoot one of them bean balls. I says Go
ahead and shoot and if you hit me in the head and I ever find it out I
will write and tell your wife what happened to you. You see what I was
getting at Al. I was insinuateing that if he beaned me with his fast one
I would not never know nothing about it if somebody did not tell me
because his fast one is not fast enough to hurt nobody even if it should
hit them in the head. So I says to him Go ahead and shoot and if you
hit me in the head and I ever find it out I will write and tell your wife
what happened to you. See, Al?

Of coarse you could not hire me to write to Violet but I did not
mean that part of it in ernest. Well sure enough he shot at my bean and
I ducked out of the way though if it had of hit me it could not of did
no more than tickle. He takes 2 more shots and misses me and then
Jennings hollers from the bench What are you doing pitching or trying
to win a cigar? So then Hill sees what a monkey he is makeing out of
himself and tries to get one over, but I have him 3 balls and nothing
and what I done to that groover was a plenty. She went over Bush's
head like a bullet and got between Cobb and Veach and goes clear to
the fence. Bodie and Schalk scores and I would of scored to if anybody
else beside Cobb had of been chaseing the ball. I got 2 bases and Weaver
scores me with another wallop.

Say, I wish I could of heard what they said to that baby on the bench.
Callahan was tickled to death and he says Maybe I will give you back

that $50.00 if you keep that stuff up. I guess I will get that $50.00 back next pay day and if I do Al I will pay you the hole $75.00.

Well Al I beat them 5 to 4 and with good support I would of held them to 1 run but what do I care as long as I beat them? I wish though that Violet could of been there and saw it.   Yours truly,   JACK.

Chicago, Illinois, May 29

OLD PAL: Well Al I have not wrote to you for a long while but it is not because I have forgot you and to show I have not forgot you I am incloseing the $75.00 which I owe you. It is a money order Al and you can get it cashed by takeing it to Joe Higgins at the P. O.

Since I wrote to you Al I been East with the club and I guess you know what I done in the East. The Athaletics did not have no right to win that 1 game off of me and I will get them when they come here the week after next. I beat Boston and just as good as beat New York twice because I beat them 1 game all alone and then saved the other for Eddie Cicotte in the 9th inning and shut out the Washington Club and would of did the same thing if Johnson had of been working against me instead of this left handed stiff Boehling.

Speaking of lefthanders Allen has been going rotten and I would not be supprised if they sent him to Milwaukee or Frisco or somewheres.

But I got bigger news than that for you Al. Florrie is back and we are liveing together in the spair room at Allen's flat so I hope they don't send him to Milwaukee or nowheres else because it is not costing us nothing for room rent and this is no more than right after the way the Allens grafted off of us all last winter.

I bet you will be supprised to know that I and Florrie has made it up and they is a secret about it Al which I can't tell you now but maybe next month I will tell you and then you will be more supprised than ever. It is about I and Florrie and somebody else. But that is all I can tell you now.

We got in this a.m. Al and when I got to my room they was a slip of paper there telling me to call up a phone number so I called it up and it was Allen's flat and Marie answered the phone. And when I reckonized her voice I was going to hang up the phone but she says Wait a minute somebody wants to talk to you. And then Florrie come to the phone and I was going to hang up the phone again when she pulled this secret on me that I was telling you about.

So it is all fixed up between us Al and I wish I could tell you the secret but that will come later. I have tooken my baggage over to Allen's and I am there now writeing to you while Florrie is asleep. And after a while I am going out and mail this letter and get a glass of beer because I think I have got 1 comeing now on account of this secret. Florrie says she is sorry for the way she treated me and she cried when she seen me. So what is the use of me being nasty Al? And let bygones be bygones.

Your pal,   JACK.

Chicago, Illinois, June 16

FRIEND AL: Al I beat the Athaletics 2 to 1 to-day but I am writeing to you to give you the supprise of your life. Old pal I got a baby and he is a boy and we are going to name him Allen which Florrie thinks is after his uncle and aunt Allen but which is after you old pal. And she can call him Allen but I will call him Al because I don't never go back on my old pals. The baby was born over to the hospital and it is going to cost me a bunch of money but I should not worry. This is the secret I was going to tell you Al and I am the happyest man in the world and I bet you are most as tickled to death to hear about it as I am.

The baby was born just about the time I was makeing McInnis look like a sucker in the pinch but they did not tell me nothing about it till after the game and then they give me a phone message in the clubhouse. I went right over there and everything was all O. K. Little Al is a homely little skate but I guess all babys is homely and don't have no looks till they get older and maybe he will look like Florrie or I then I won't have no kick comeing.

Be sure and tell Bertha the good news and tell her everything has came out all right except that the rent man is still after me about that flat I had last winter. And I am still paying the old man $10.00 a month for that house you got for me and which has not never done me no good. But I should not worry about money when I got a real family. Do you get that Al, a real family?

Well Al I am to happy to do no more writeing to-night but I wanted you to be the 1st to get the news and I would of sent you a telegram only I did not want to scare you.   Your pal,   JACK.

Chicago, Illinois, July 2

OLD PAL: Well old pal I just come back from St. Louis this a.m. and found things in pretty fare shape. Florrie and the baby is out to Allen's and we will stay there till I can find another place. The Dr. was out to look at the baby this a.m. and the baby was waveing his arm round in the air. And Florrie asked was they something the matter with him that he kept waveing his arm. And the Dr. says No he was just getting his exercise.

Well Al I noticed that he never waved his right arm but kept waveing his left arm and I asked the Dr. why was that. Then the Dr. says I guess he must be left handed. That made me sore and I says I guess you doctors don't know it all. And then I turned round and beat it out of the room.

Well Al it would be just my luck to have him left handed and Florrie should ought to of knew better than to name him after Allen. I am going to hire another Dr. and see what he has to say because they must be some way of fixing babys so as they won't be left handed. And if necessary I will cut his left arm off of him. Of coarse I would not do that Al. But how would I feel if a boy of mine turned out like Allen and Joe Hill and some of them other nuts?

We have a game with St. Louis to-morrow and a double header on the 4th of July. I guess probily Callahan will work me in one of the 4th of July games on account of the holiday crowd.

Your pal,   JACK.

P. S. Maybe I should ought to leave the kid left handed so as he can have some of their luck. The lucky stiffs.

THE BUSHER'S KID

Chicago, Illinois, July 31

FRIEND AL: Well Al what do you think of little Al now? But I guess I better tell you first what he done. Maybe you won't believe what I am telling you but did you ever catch me telling you a lie? I guess you know you did not Al. Well we got back from the East this a.m. and I don't have to tell you we had a rotten trip and if it had not of been for me beating Boston once and the Athaletics two times we would of been ashamed to come home.

I guess these here other pitchers thought we was haveing a vacation and when they go up in the office to-morrow to get there checks they should ought to be arrested if they take them. I would not go nowheres near Comiskey if I had not of did better than them others but I can go and get my pay and feel all O. K. about it because I done something to ern it.

Me loseing that game in Washington was a crime and Callahan says so himself. This here Weaver throwed it away for me and I would not be surprised if he done it from spitework because him and Scott is pals and probily he did not want to see me winning all them games when Scott was getting knocked out of the box. And no wonder when he has not got no stuff. I wish I knowed for sure that Weaver was throwing me down and if I knowed for sure I would put him in a hospital or somewheres.

But I was going to tell you what the kid done Al. So here goes. We are still liveing at Allen's and his wife. So I and him come home together from the train. Well Florrie and Marie was both up and the baby was up too—that is he was not up but he was woke up. I beat it right into the room where he was at and Florrie come in with me. I says Hello Al and what do you suppose he done. Well Al he did not say Hello pa or nothing like that because he is not only one month old. But he smiled at me just like as if he was glad to see me and I guess maybe he was at that.

I was tickled to death and I says to Florrie Did you see that. And she says See what. I says The baby smiled at me. Then she says They is something the matter with his stumach. I says I suppose because a baby smiles that is a sign they is something the matter with his stumach and if he had the toothache he would laugh. She says You think your smart but I am telling you that he was not smileing at all but he was makeing a face because they is something the matter with his stumach. I says I guess I know the difference if somebody is smileing or makeing a face. And she says I guess you don't know nothing about babys because you never had none before. I says How many have you had. And then she got sore and beat it out of the room.

I did not care because I wanted to be in there alone with him and see would he smile at me again. And sure enough Al he did. Then I called Allen in and when the baby seen him he begin to cry. So you see I was right and Florrie was wrong. It don't take a man no time at all to get wise to these babys and it don't take them long to know if a man is there father or there uncle.

When he begin to cry I chased Allen out of the room and called Florrie because she should ought to know by this time how to make him stop crying. But she was still sore and she says Let him cry or if you know so much about babys make him stop yourself. I says Maybe he is sick. And she says I was just telling you that he had a pane in his stumach or he would not of made that face that you said was smileing at you.

I says Do you think we should ought to call the doctor but she says No if you call the doctor every time he has the stumach acke you might just as well tell him he should bring his trunk along and stay here. She says All babys have collect and they is not no use fusing about it but come and get your breakfast.

Well Al I did not injoy my breakfast because the baby was crying all the time and I knowed he probily wanted I should come in and visit with him. So I just eat the prunes and drunk a little coffee and did not wait for the rest of it and sure enough when I went back in our room and started talking to him he started smileing again and pretty soon he went to sleep so you see Al he was smileing and not makeing no face and that was a hole lot of bunk about him haveing the collect. But I don't suppose I should ought to find fault with Florrie for not knowing no better because she has not never had no babys before but still and all I should think she should ought to of learned something about them by this time or ask somebody.

Well Al little Al is woke up again and is crying and I just about got time to fix him up and get him asleep again and then I will have to go to the ball park because we got a poseponed game to play with Detroit and Callahan will probily want me to work though I pitched the next to the last game in New York and would of gave them a good beating except for Schalk dropping that ball at the plate but I got it on these Detroit babys and when my name is announced to pitch they feel like forfiting the game. I won't try for no strike out record because I want them to hit the first ball and get the game over with quick so as I can get back here and take care of little Al.   Your pal,   JACK.

P. S. Babys is great stuff Al and if I was you I would not wait no longer but would hurry up and adopt 1 somewheres.

Chicago, Illinois, August 15

OLD PAL: What do you think Al. Kid Gleason is comeing over to the flat and look at the baby the day after to-morrow when we don't have no game skeduled but we have to practice in the a.m. because we been going so rotten. I had a hard time makeing him promise to come but he is comeing and I bet he will be glad he come when he has came. I says to him in the clubhouse Do you want to see a real baby? And he says You're real enough for me Boy.

I says No I am talking about babys. He says Oh I thought you was talking about ice cream soda or something. I says No I want you to come over to the flat to-morrow and take a look at my kid and tell me what you think of him. He says I can tell you what I think of him without takeing no look at him. I think he is out of luck. I says What do you mean out of luck. But he just laughed and would not say no more.

I asked him again would he come over to the flat and look at the baby and he says he had troubles enough without that and kidded along for a while but finally he seen I was in ernest and then he says he would come if I would keep the missus out of the room while he was there because he says if she seen him she would probily be sorry she married me.

He was just jokeing and I did not take no excepshun to his remarks because Florrie could not never fall for him after seeing me because he is not no big stropping man like I am but a little runt and look at how old he is. But I am glad he is comeing because he will think more of me when he sees what a fine baby I got though he thinks a hole lot of me now because look what I done for the club and where would they be at if I had jumped to the Federal like I once thought I would. I will tell you what he says about little Al and I bet he will say he never seen no prettyer baby but even if he don't say nothing at all I will know he is kidding.

The Boston Club comes here to-morrow and plays 4 days includeing the day after to-morrow when they is not no game. So on account of the off day maybe I will work twice against them and if I do they will wish the grounds had of burned down.   Yours truly,   JACK.

Chicago, Illinois, August 17

AL: Well old pal what did I tell you about what I would do to that Boston Club? And now Al I have beat every club in the league this year because yesterday was the first time I beat the Boston Club this year but now I have beat all of them and most of them severel times.

This should ought to of gave me a record of 16 wins and 0 defeats because the only game I lost was throwed away behind me but instead of that my record is 10 games win and 6 defeats and that don't include the games I finished up and helped the other boys win which is about 6 more alltogether but what do I care about my record Al? because I am not the kind of man that is allways thinking about there record and playing for there record while I am satisfied if I give the club the best I got and if I win all O. K. And if I lose who's fault is it. Not mine Al.

I asked Callahan would he let me work against the Boston Club again before they go away and he says I guess I will have to because you are going better than anybody else on the club. So you see Al he is beginning to appresiate my work and from now on I will pitch in my regular turn and a hole lot offtener then that and probily Comiskey will see the stuff I am made from and will raise my salery next year even if he has got me signed for 3 years and for the same salery I am getting now.

But all that is not what I was going to tell you Al and what I was going to tell you was about Gleason comeing to see the baby and what he thought about him. I sent Florrie and Marie downtown and says I would take care of little Al and they was glad to go because Florrie says she should ought to buy some new shoes though I don't see what she wants of no new shoes when she is going to be tied up in the flat for a long time yet on account of the baby and nobody cares if she wears shoes in the flat or goes round in her bear feet. But I was glad to get rid of the both of them for a while because little Al acts better when they is not no women round and you can't blame him.

The baby was woke up when Gleason come in and I and him went right in the room where he was laying. Gleason takes a look at him and says Well that is a mighty fine baby and you must of boughten him. I says What do you mean? And he says I don't believe he is your own baby because he looks humaner than most babys. And I says Why should not he look human. And he says Why should he.

Then he goes to work and picks the baby right up and I was a-scared he would drop him because even I have not never picked him up though I am his father and would be a-scared of hurting him. I says Here, don't pick him up and he says Why not? He says Are you going to leave him on that there bed the rest of his life? I says No but you don't know how to handle him. He says I have handled a hole lot bigger babys than him or else Callahan would not keep me.

Then he starts patting the baby's head and I says Here, don't do that because he has got a soft spot in his head and you might hit it. He says I thought he was your baby and I says Well he is my baby and he says Well then they can't be no soft spot in his head. Then he lays little Al down because he seen I was in ernest and as soon as he lays him down the baby begins to cry. Then Gleason says See he don't want me to lay him down and I says Maybe he has got a pane in his stumach and he says I would not be supprised because he just took a good look at his father.

But little Al did not act like as if he had a pane in his stumach and he kept sticking his finger in his mouth and crying. And Gleason says He acts like as if he had a toothacke. I says How could he have a toothacke when he has not got no teeth? He says That is easy. I have saw a lot of pitchers complane that there arm was sore when they did not have no arm.

Then he asked me what was the baby's name and I told him Allen but that he was not named after my brother-in-law Allen. And Gleason says I should hope not. I should hope you would have better sense than to name him after a lefthander. So you see Al he don't like them no better then I do even if he does jolly Allen and Russell along and make them think they can pitch.

Pretty soon he says What are you going to make out of him, a ball-player? I says Yes I am going to make a hitter out of him so as he can join the White Sox and then maybe they will get a couple of runs once in a while. He says If I was you I would let him pitch and then you won't have to give him no educasion. Besides, he says, he looks now like he would divellop into a grate spitter.

Well I happened to look out of the window and seen Florrie and Marie comeing acrost Indiana Avenue and I told Gleason about it. And you ought to of seen him run. I asked him what was his hurry and he says it was in his contract that he was not to talk to no women but I knowed he was kidding because I allready seen him talking to severel of the players' wifes when they was on trips with us and they acted like as if they thought he was a regular comeedion though they really is not nothing funny about what he says only it is easy to make women laugh when they have not got no grouch on about something.

Well Al I am glad Gleason has saw the baby and maybe he will fix it with Callahan so as I won't have to go to morning practice every a.m. because I should ought to be home takeing care of little Al when Florrie is washing the dishs or helping Marie round the house. And besides why should I wear myself all out in practice because I don't need to practice pitching and I could hit as well as the rest of the men on our club if I never seen no practice.

After we get threw with Boston, Washington comes here and then we go to St. Louis and Cleveland and then come home and then go East again. And after that we are pretty near threw except the city serious. Callahan is not going to work me no more after I beat Boston again till it is this here Johnson's turn to pitch for Washington. And I hope it is not his turn to work the 1st game of the serious because then I would not have no rest between the last game against Boston and the 1st game against Washington.

But rest or no rest I will work against this here Johnson and show him up for giveing me that trimming in Washington, the lucky stiff. I wish I had a team like the Athaletics behind me and I would loose about 1 game every 6 years and then they would have to get all the best of it from these rotten umpires.   Your pal,   JACK.

New York, New York, September 16
FRIEND AL: Al it is not no fun running round the country no more and I wish this dam trip was over so as I could go home and see how little Al is getting along because Florrie has not wrote since we was in Philly which was the first stop on this trip. I am a-scared they is something

the matter with the little fellow or else she would of wrote but then if they was something the matter with him she would of sent me a telegram or something and let me know.

So I guess they can't be nothing the matter with him. Still and all I don't see why she has not wrote when she knows or should ought to know that I would be worrying about the baby. If I don't get no letter to-morrow I am going to send her a telegram and ask her what is the matter with him because I am positive she would of wrote if they was not something the matter with him.

The boys has been trying to get me to go out nights and see a show or something but I have not got no heart to go to shows. And besides Callahan has not gave us no pass to no show on this trip. I guess probily he is sore on account of the rotten way the club has been going but still he should ought not to be sore on me because I have win 3 out of my last 4 games and would of win the other if he had not of started me against them with only 1 day's rest and the Athaletics at that, who a man should ought not to pitch against if he don't feel good.

I asked Allen if he had heard from Marie and he says Yes he did but she did not say nothing about little Al except that he was keeping her awake nights balling. So maybe Al if little Al is balling they is something wrong with him. I am going to send Florrie a telegram to-morrow— that is if I don't get no letter.

If they is something the matter with him I will ask Callahan to send me home and he won't want to do it neither because who else has he got that is a regular winner. But if little Al is sick and Callahan won't let me go home I will go home anyway. You know me Al.

Yours truly,   JACK.

Boston, Massachusetts, September 24

AL: I bet if Florrie was a man she would be a lefthander. What do you think she done now Al? I sent her a telegram from New York when I did not get no letter from her and she did not pay no atension to the telegram. Then when we got up here I sent her another telegram and it was not more than five minutes after I sent the 2d telegram till I got a letter from her. And it said the baby was all O. K. but she had been so busy takeing care of him that she had not had no time to write.

Well when I got the letter I chased out to see if I could catch the boy who had took my telegram but he had went allready so I was spending $.60 for nothing. Then what does Florrie do but send me a telegram after she got my second telegram and tell me that little Al is all O. K., which I knowed all about then because I had just got her letter. And

she sent her telegram c.o.d. and I had to pay for it at this end because
she had not paid for it and that was $.60 more but I bet if I had of
knew what was in the telegram before I read it I would of told the boy
to keep it and would not of gave him no $.60 but how did I know if
little Al might not of tooken sick after Florrie had wrote the letter?

I am going to write and ask her if she is trying to send us both to
the Poor House or somewheres with her telegrams. I don't care nothing
about the $.60 but I like to see a woman use a little judgement though
I guess that is impossable.

It is my turn to work to-day and to-night we start West but we have
got to stop off at Cleveland on the way. I have got a nosion to ask
Callahan to let me go right on threw to Chi if I win to-day and not
stop off at no Cleveland but I guess they would not be no use because
I have got that Cleveland Club licked the minute I put on my glove. So
probily Callahan will want me with him though it don't make no difference if we win or lose now because we have not got no chance for
the pennant. One man can't win no pennant Al I don't care who he is.

Your pal,   JACK.

Chicago, Illinois, October 2

FRIEND AL: Well old pal I am all threw till the city serious and it is all
fixed up that I am going to open the serious and pitch 3 of the games
if nessary. The club has went to Detroit to wind up the season and
Callahan did not take me along but left me here with a couple other
pitchers and Billy Sullivan and told me all as I would have to do was
go over to the park the next 3 days and warm up a little so as to keep
in shape. But I don't need to be in no shape to beat them Cubs Al. But
it is a good thing Al that Allen was tooken on the trip to Detroit or I
guess I would of killed him. He has not been going good and he has
been acting and talking nasty to everybody because he can't win no
games.

Well the 1st night we was home after the trip little Al was haveing
a bad night and was balling pretty hard and they could not nobody in
the flat get no sleep. Florrie says he was haveing the collect and I says
Why should he have the collect all the time when he did not drink
nothing but milk? She says she guessed the milk did not agree with him
and upsetted his stumach. I says Well he must take after his mother if
his stumach gets upsetted every time he takes a drink because if he took
after his father he could drink a hole lot and not never be effected. She
says You should ought to remember he has only got a little stumach
and not a great big resservoire. I says Well if the milk don't agree with

him why don't you give him something else? She says Yes I suppose I
should ought to give him weeny worst or something.

Allen must of heard us talking because he hollered something and I
did not hear what it was so I told him to say it over and he says Give
the little X-eyed brat poison and we would all be better off. I says You
better take poison yourself because maybe a rotten pitcher like you
could get by in the league where you're going when you die. Then I
says Besides I would rather my baby was X-eyed then to have him left
handed. He says It is better for him that he is X-eyed or else he might
get a good look at you and then he would shoot himself. I says Is that
so? and he shut up. Little Al is not no more X-eyed than you or I are
Al and that was what made me sore because what right did Allen have
to talk like that when he knowed he was lying?

Well the next morning Allen nor I did not speak to each other and
I seen he was sorry for the way he had talked and I was willing to fix
things up because what is the use of staying sore at a man that don't
know no better.

But all of a sudden he says When are you going to pay me what you
owe me? I says What do you mean? And he says You been liveing here
all summer and I been paying all the bills. I says Did not you and Marie
ask us to come here and stay with you and it would not cost us nothing.
He says Yes but we did not mean it was a life sentence. You are getting
more money than me and you don't never spend a nichol. All I have to
do is pay the rent and buy your food and it would take a millionare or
something to feed you.

Then he says I would not make no holler about you grafting off of
me if that brat would shut up nights and give somebody a chance to
sleep. I says You should ought to get all the sleep you need on the bench.
Besides, I says, who done the grafting all last winter and without no
invatation? If he had of said another word I was going to bust him but
just then Marie come in and he shut up.

The more I thought about what he said and him a rotten lefthander
that should ought to be hussling freiht the more madder I got and if he
had of opened his head to me the last day or 2 before he went to Detroit
I guess I would of finished him. But Marie stuck pretty close to the both
of us when we was together and I guess she knowed they was something
in the air and did not want to see her husband get the worst of it though
if he was my husband and I was a woman I would push him under a
st. car.

But Al I won't even stand for him saying that I am grafting off of
him and I and Florrie will get away from here and get a flat of our own

as soon as the city serious is over. I would like to bring her and the kid down to Bedford for the winter but she wont listen to that.

I allmost forgot Al to tell you to be sure and thank Bertha for the little dress she made for little Al. I don't know if it will fit him or not because Florrie has not yet tried it on him yet and she says she is going to use it for a dishrag but I guess she is just kidding.

I suppose you seen where Callahan took me out of that game down to Cleveland but it was not because I was not going good Al but it was because Callahan seen he was makeing a mistake wasteing me on that bunch who allmost any pitcher could beat. They beat us that game at that but only by one run and it was not no fault of mine because I was tooken out before they got the run that give them the game.

Your old pal,   JACK.

Chicago, Illinois, October 4
FRIEND AL: Well Al the club winds up the season at Detroit to-morrow and the serious starts the day after to-morrow and I will be in there giveing them a battle. I wish I did not have nobody but the Cubs to pitch against all season and you bet I would have a record that would make Johnson and Mathewson and some of them other swell heads look like a dirty doose.

I and Florrie and Marie has been haveing a argument about how could Florrie go and see the city serious games when they is not nobody here that can take care of the baby because Marie wants to go and see the games to even though they is not no more chance of Callahan starting Allen than a rabbit or something.

Florrie and Marie says I should ought to hire a nurse to take care of little Al and Florrie got pretty sore when I told her nothing doing because in the first place I can't afford to pay no nurse a salery and in the second place I would not trust no nurse to take care of the baby because how do I know the nurse is not nothing but a grafter or a dope fiend maybe and should ought not to be left with the baby?

Of coarse Florrie wants to see me pitch and a man can't blame her for that but I won't leave my baby with no nurse Al and Florrie will have to stay home and I will tell her what I done when I get there. I might of gave my consent to haveing a nurse at that if it had not of been for the baby getting so sick last night when I was takeing care of him while Florrie and Marie and Allen was out to a show and if I had not of been home they is no telling what would of happened. It is a cinch that none of them bonehead nurses would of knew what to do.

Allen must of been out of his head because right after supper he says he would take the 2 girls to a show. I says All right go on and I will take care of the baby. Then Florrie says Do you think you can take care of him all O. K.? And I says Have not I tooken care of him before allready? Well, she says, I will leave him with you only don't run in to him every time he cries. I says Why not? And she says Because it is good for him to cry. I says You have not got no heart or you would not talk that way.

They all give me the laugh but I let them get away with it because I am not picking no fights with girls and why should I bust this Allen when he don't know no better and has not got no baby himself. And I did not want to do nothing that would stop him takeing the girls to a show because it is time he spent a peace of money on somebody.

Well they all went out and I went in on the bed and played with the baby. I wish you could of saw him Al because he is old enough now to do stunts and he smiled up at me and waved his arms and legs round and made a noise like as if he was trying to say Pa. I did not think Florrie had gave him enough covers so I rapped him up in some more and took a blanket off of the big bed and stuck it round him so as he could not kick his feet out and catch cold.

I thought once or twice he was going off to sleep but all of a sudden he begin to cry and I seen they was something wrong with him. I give him some hot water but that made him cry again and I thought maybe he was to cold yet so I took another blanket off of Allen's bed and wrapped that round him but he kept on crying and trying to kick inside the blankets. And I seen then that he must have collect or something.

So pretty soon I went to the phone and called up our regular Dr. and it took him pretty near a hour to get there and the baby balling all the time. And when he come he says they was nothing the matter except that the baby was to hot and told me to take all them blankets off of him and then soaked me 2 dollars. I had a nosion to bust his jaw. Well pretty soon he beat it and then little Al begin crying again and kept getting worse and worse so finally I got a-scared and run down to the corner where another Dr. is at and I brung him up to see what was the matter but he said he could not see nothing the matter but he did not charge me a cent so I thought he was not no robber like our regular doctor even if he was just as much of a boob.

The baby did not cry none while he was there but the minute he had went he started crying and balling again and I seen they was not no use of fooling no longer so I looked around the house and found the medicine the doctor left for Allen when he had a stumach acke once and I give the baby a little of it in a spoon but I guess he did not like the taste because he hollered like a Indian and finally I could not stand it no longer so I called that second Dr. back again and this time he seen that the baby was sick and asked me what I had gave it and I told him some stumach medicine and he says I was a fool and should ought not to of gave the baby nothing. But while he was talking the baby stopped crying and went off to sleep so you see what I done for him was the right thing to do and them doctors was both off of there nut.

This second Dr. soaked me 2 dollars the 2d time though he had not did no more than when he was there the 1st time and charged me nothing but they is all a bunch of robbers Al and I would just as leave trust a policeman.

Right after the baby went to sleep Florrie and Marie and Allen come home and I told Florrie what had came off but instead of giveing me credit she says If you want to kill him why don't you take a ax? Then Allen butts in and says Why don't you take a ball and throw it at him? Then I got sore and I says Well if I did hit him with a ball I would kill him while if you was to throw that fast ball of yours at him and hit him in the head he would think the musketoes was biteing him and brush them off. But at that, I says, you could not hit him with a ball except you was aiming at something else.

I guess they was no comeback to that so him and Marie went to there room. Allen should ought to know better than to try and get the best of me by this time and I would shut up anyway if I was him after getting sent home from Detroit with some of the rest of them when he only worked 3 innings up there and they had to take him out or play the rest of the game by electrick lights.

I wish you could be here for the serious Al but you would have to stay at a hotel because we have not got no spair room and it would cost you a hole lot of money. But you can watch the papers and you will see what I done.   Yours truly,   JACK.

Chicago, Illinois, October 6

DEAR OLD PAL: Probily before you get this letter you will of saw by the paper that we was licked in the first game and that I was tooken out but the papers don't know what really come off so I am going to tell you and you can see for yourself if it was my fault.

I did not never have no more stuff in my life then when I was warming up and I seen the Cubs looking over to our bench and shakeing there heads like they knowed they did not have no chance. O'Day was going to start Cheney who is there best bet and had him warming up but when he seen the smoke I had when I and Schalk was warming up he changed his mind because what was the use of useing his best pitcher when I had all that stuff and it was a cinch that no club in the world could score a run off of me when I had all that stuff?

So he told a couple others to warm up to and when my name was announced to pitch Cheney went and set on the bench and this here lefthander Pierce was announced for them.

Well Al you will see by the paper where I sent there 1st 3 batters back to the bench to get a drink of water and all 3 of them good hitters Leach and Good and this here Saier that hits a hole lot of home runs but would not never hit one off of me if I was O. K. Well we scored a couple in our half and the boys on the bench all says Now you got enough to win easy because they won't never score none off of you.

And they was right to because what chance did they have if this thing that I am going to tell you about had not of happened? We goes along seven innings and only 2 of there men had got to 1st base one of them on a bad peg of Weaver's and the other one I walked because this blind Evans don't know a ball from a strike. We had not did no more scoreing off of Pierce not because he had no stuff but because our club could not take a ball in there hands and hit it out of the infield.

Well Al I did not tell you that before I come out to the park I kissed little Al and Florrie good by and Marie says she was going to stay home to and keep Florrie Co. and they was not no reason for Marie to come to the game anyway because they was not a chance in the world for Allen to do nothing but hit fungos. Well while I was doing all this here swell pitching and makeing them Cubs look like a lot of rummys I was thinking about little Al and Florrie and how glad they would be when I come home and told them what I done though of coarse little Al is not only a little over 3 months of age and how could he appresiate what I done? But Florrie would.

Well Al when I come in to the bench after there ½ of the 7th I happened to look up to the press box to see if the reporters had gave Schulte a hit on that one Weaver throwed away and who do you think I seen in a box right alongside of the press box? It was Florrie and Marie and both of them claping there hands and hollering with the rest of the bugs.

Well old pal I was never so supprised in my life and it just took all the heart out of me. What was they doing there and what had they did with the baby? How did I know that little Al was not sick or maybe dead and balling his head off and nobody round to hear him?

I tried to catch Florrie's eyes but she would not look at me. I hollered her name and the bugs looked at me like as if I was crazy and I was to

Al. Well I seen they was not no use of standing out there in front of the stand so I come into the bench and Allen was setting there and I says Did you know your wife and Florrie was up there in the stand? He says No and I says What are they doing here? And he says What would they be doing here—mending there stockings? I felt like busting him and I guess he seen I was mad because he got up off of the bench and beat it down to the corner of the field where some of the others was getting warmed up though why should they have anybody warming up when I was going so good?

Well Al I made up my mind that ball game or no ball game I was not going to have little Al left alone no longer and I seen they was not no use of sending word to Florrie to go home because they was a big crowd and it would take maybe 15 or 20 minutes for somebody to get up to where she was at. So I says to Callahan You have got to take me out. He says What is the matter? Is your arm gone? I says No my arm is not gone but my baby is sick and home all alone. He says Where is your wife? And I says She is setting up there in the stand.

Then he says How do you know your baby is sick? And I says I don't know if he is sick or not but he is left home all alone. He says Why don't you send your wife home? And I says I could not get word to her in time. He says Well you have only got two innings to go and the way your going the game will be over in 10 minutes. I says Yes and before 10 minutes is up my baby might die and are you going to take me out or not? He says Get in there and pitch you yellow dog and if you don't I will take your share of the serious money away from you.

By this time our part of the inning was over and I had to go out there and pitch some more because he would not take me out and he has not got no heart Al. Well Al how could I pitch when I kept thinking maybe the baby was dying right now and maybe if I was home I could do something? And instead of paying attension to what I was doing I was thinking about little Al and looking up there to where Florrie and Marie was setting and before I knowed what come off they had the bases full and Callahan took me out.

Well Al I run to the clubhouse and changed my cloths and beat it for home and I did not even hear what Callahan and Gleason says to me when I went by them but I found out after the game that Scott went in and finished up and they batted him pretty hard and we was licked 3 and 2.

When I got home the baby was crying but he was not all alone after all Al because they was a little girl about 14 years of age there watching him and Florrie had hired her to take care of him so as her and Marie could go and see the game. But just think Al of leaveing little Al with a girl 14 years of age that did not never have no babys of her own! And what did she know about takeing care of him? Nothing Al.

You should ought to of heard me ball Florrie out when she got home and I bet she cried pretty near enough to flood the basemunt. We had it hot and heavy and the Allens butted in but I soon showed them where they was at and made them shut there mouth.

I had a good nosion to go out and get a hole lot of drinks and was just going to put on my hat when the doorbell rung and there was Kid Gleason. I thought he would be sore and probily try to ball me out and I was not going to stand for nothing but instead of balling me out he come and shook hands with me and interduced himself to Florrie and asked how was little Al.

Well we all set down and Gleason says the club was depending on me to win the serious because I was in the best shape of all the pitchers. And besides the Cubs could not never hit me when I was right and he was telling the truth to.

So he asked me if I would stand for the club hireing a train nurse to stay with the baby the rest of the serious so as Florrie could go and see her husband win the serious but I says No I would not stand for that and Florrie's place was with the baby.

So Gleason and Florrie goes out in the other room and talks a while and I guess he was persuadeing her to stay home because pretty soon they come back in the room and says it was all fixed up and I would not have to worry about little Al the rest of the serious but could give the club the best I got. Gleason just left here a little while ago and I won't work to-morrow Al but I will work the day after and you will see what I can do when I don't have nothing to worry me.

Your pal,   JACK.

Chicago, Illinois, October 8

OLD PAL: Well old pal we got them 2 games to one now and the serious is sure to be over in three more days because I can pitch 2 games in that time if nessary. I shut them out to-day and they should ought not to of had four hits but should ought to of had only 2 but Bodie don't cover no ground and 2 fly balls that he should ought to of eat up fell safe.

But I beat them anyway and Benz beat them yesterday but why should he not beat them when the club made 6 runs for him? All they made for me was three but all I needed was one because they could not hit me with a shuvvel. When I come to the bench after the 5th inning they was a note there for me from the boy that answers the phone at the ball park and it says that somebody just called up from the flat and says the baby was asleep and getting along fine. So I felt good Al and I was better than ever in the 6th.

When I got home Florrie and Marie was both there and asked me how did the game come out because I beat Allen home and I told them all about what I done and I bet Florrie was proud of me but I supose Marie is a little jellus because how could she help it when Callahan is depending on me to win the serious and her husband is wearing out the wood on the bench? But why should she be sore when it is me that is winning the serious for them? And if it was not for me Allen and all the rest of them would get about $500.00 apeace instead of the winner's share which is about $750.00 apeace.

Cicotte is going to work to-morrow and if he is lucky maybe he can get away with the game and that will leave me to finish up the day after to-morrow but if nessary I can go in to-morrow when they get to hitting Cicotte and stop them and then come back the following day and beat them again. Where would this club be at Al if I had of jumped to the Federal?   Yours truly,   JACK.

Chicago, Illinois, October 11

FRIEND AL: We done it again Al and I guess the Cubs won't never want to play us again not so long as I am with the club. Before you get this letter you will know what we done and who done it but probily you could of guessed that Al without seeing no paper.

I got 2 more of them phone messiges about the baby dureing the game and I guess that was what made me so good because I knowed then that Florrie was takeing care of him but I could not help feeling sorry for Florrie because she is a bug herself and it must of been pretty hard for her to stay away from the game espesially when she knowed I was going to pitch and she has been pretty good to sacrifice her own plesure for little Al.

Cicotte was knocked out of the box the day before yesterday and then they give this here Faber a good beating but I wish you could of saw what they done to Allen when Callahan sent him in after the game was gone allready. Honest Al if he had not of been my brother in law I would of felt like laughing at him because it looked like as if they would have to call the fire department to put the side out. They had Bodie and Collins hollering for help and with there tongue hanging out from running back to the fence.

Anyway the serious is all over and I won't have nothing to do but

stay home and play with little Al but I don't know yet where my home
is going to be at because it is a cinch I won't stay with Allen no longer.
He has not came home since the game and I suppose he is out somewheres lapping up some beer and spending some of the winner's share
of the money which he would not of had no chance to get in on if it
had not of been for me.

I will write and let you know my plans for the winter and I wish
Florrie would agree to come to Bedford but nothing doing Al and after
her staying home and takeing care of the baby instead of watching me
pitch I can't be too hard on her but must leave her have her own way
about something.   Your pal,   JACK.

Chicago, Illinois, October 13

AL: I am all threw with Florrie Al and I bet when you hear about It
you won't say it was not no fault of mine but no man liveing who is
any kind of a man would act different from how I am acting if he had
of been decieved like I been.

Al Florrie and Marie was out to all them games and was not home
takeing care of the baby at all and it is not her fault that little Al is not
dead and that he was not killed by the nurse they hired to take care of
him while they went to the games when I thought they was home takeing care of the baby. And all them phone messiges was just fakes and
maybe the baby was sick all the time I was winning them games and
balling his head off instead of being asleep like they said he was.

Allen did not never come home at all the night before last and when
he come in yesterday he was a sight and I says to him Where have you
been? And he says I have been down to the Y. M. C. A. but that is not
none of your business. I says Yes you look like as if you had been to
the Y. M. C. A. and I know where you have been and you have been
out lushing beer. And he says Suppose I have and what are you going
to do about it? And I says Nothing but you should ought to be ashamed
of yourself and leaveing Marie here while you was out lapping up beer.

Then he says Did you not leave Florrie home while you was getting
away with them games, you lucky stiff? And I says Yes but Florrie had
to stay home and take care of the baby but Marie don't never have to
stay home because where is your baby? You have not got no baby. He
says I would not want no X-eyed baby like yourn. Then he says So you
think Florrie stayed to home and took care of the baby do you? And I
says What do you mean? And he says You better ask her.

So when Florrie come in and heard us talking she busted out crying
and then I found out what they put over on me. It is a wonder Al that

I did not take some of that cheap furniture them Allens got and bust it over there heads, Allen and Florrie. This is what they done Al. The club give Florrie $50.00 to stay home and take care of the baby and she said she would and she was to call up every so often and tell me the baby was all O. K. But this here Marie told her she was a sucker so she hired a nurse for part of the $50.00 and then her and Marie went to the games and beat it out quick after the games was over and come home in a taxicab and chased the nurse out before I got home.

Well Al when I found out what they done I grabbed my hat and goes out and got some drinks and I was so mad I did not know where I was at or what come off and I did not get home till this a.m. And they was all asleep and I been asleep all day and when I woke up Marie and Allen was out but Florrie and I have not spoke to each other and I won't never speak to her again.

But I know now what I am going to do Al and I am going to take little Al and beat it out of here and she can sew me for a bill of divorce and I should not worry because I will have little Al and I will see that he is tooken care of because I guess I can hire a nurse as well as they can and I will pick out a train nurse that knows something. Maybe I and him and the nurse will come to Bedford Al but I don't know yet and I will write and tell you as soon as I make up my mind. Did you ever hear of a man getting a rottener deal Al? And after what I done in the serious too.   Your pal,   JACK.

Chicago, Illinois, October 17

OLD PAL: I and Florrie has made it up Al but we are threw with Marie and Allen and I and Florrie and the baby is staying at a hotel here on Cottage Grove Avenue the same hotel we was at when we got married only of coarse they was only the 2 of us then.

And now Al I want to ask you a favor and that is for you to go and see old man Cutting and tell him I want to ree-new the lease on that house for another year because I and Florrie has decided to spend the winter in Bedford and she will want to stay there and take care of little Al while I am away on trips next summer and not stay in no high-price flat up here. And may be you and Bertha can help her round the house when I am not there.

I will tell you how we come to fix things up Al and you will see that I made her apollojize to me and after this she will do what I tell her to and won't never try to put nothing over. We was eating breakfast—I and Florrie and Marie. Allen was still asleep yet because I guess he must of had a bad night and he was snoreing so as you could hear him in the next st. I was not saying nothing to nobody but pretty soon Florrie says to Marie I don't think you and Allen should ought to kick on the baby crying when Allen's snoreing makes more noise than a hole wagonlode of babys. And Marie got sore and says I guess a man has got a right to snore in his own house and you and Jack has been grafting off of us long enough.

Then Florrie says What did Allen do to help win the serious and get that $750.00? Nothing but set on the bench except when they was makeing him look like a sucker the 1 inning he pitched. The trouble with you and Allen is you are jellous of what Jack has did and you know he will be a star up here in the big league when Allen is tending bar which is what he should ought to be doing because then he could get stewed for nothing.

Marie says Take your brat and get out of the house. And Florrie says Don't you worry because we would not stay here no longer if you hired us. So Florrie went in her room and I followed her in and she says Let's pack up and get out.

Then I says Yes but we won't go nowheres together after what you done to me but you can go where you dam please and I and little Al will go to Bedford. Then she says You can't take the baby because he is mine and if you was to take him I would have you arrested for kidnaping. Besides, she says, what would you feed him and who would take care of him?

I says I would find somebody to take care of him and I would get him food from a resturunt. She says He can't eat nothing but milk and I says Well he has the collect all the time when he is eating milk and he would not be no worse off if he was eating watermelon. Well, she says, if you take him I will have you arrested and sew you for a bill of divorce for dessertion.

Then she says Jack you should not ought to find no fault with me for going to them games because when a woman has a husband that can pitch like you can do you think she wants to stay home and not see her husband pitch when a lot of other women is cheering him and makeing her feel proud because she is his wife?

Well Al as I said right along it was pretty hard on Florrie to have to stay home and I could not hardly blame her for wanting to be out there where she could see what I done so what was the use of argueing?

So I told her I would think it over and then I went out and I went and seen a attorney at law and asked him could I take little Al away and he says No I did not have no right to take him away from his mother and besides it would probily kill him to be tooken away from her and then he soaked me $10.00 the robber.

Then I went back and told Florrie I would give her another chance and then her and I packed up and took little Al in a taxicab over to this hotel. We are threw with the Allens Al and let me know right away if I can get that lease for another year because Florrie has gave up and will go to Bedford or anywheres else with me now.

                                                    Yours truly,   JACK.

                                          Chicago, Illinois, October 18
FRIEND AL: Old pal I won't never forget your kindnus and this is to tell you that I and Florrie except your kind invatation to come and stay with you till we can find a house and I guess you won't regret it none because Florrie will livun things up for Bertha and Bertha will be crazy about the baby because you should ought to see how cute he is now Al and not yet four months old. But I bet he will be talking before we know it.

We are comeing on the train that leaves here at noon Saturday Al and the train leaves here about 12 oclock and I don't know what time it gets to Bedford but it leaves here at noon so we shall be there probily in time for supper.

I wish you would ask Ben Smith will he have a hack down to the deepo to meet us but I won't pay no more than $.25 and I should think he should ought to be glad to take us from the deepo to your house for nothing.   Your pal,   JACK.

P. S. The train we are comeing on leaves here at noon Al and will probily get us there in time for a late supper and I wonder if Bertha would have spair ribs and crout for supper. You know me Al.

THE BUSHER BEATS IT HENCE

                                          Chicago, Ill., Oct. 20
FRIEND AL: I guess may be you will begin to think I dont never do what I am going to do and that I change my mind a hole lot because I wrote and told you that I and Florrie and little Al would be in Bedford to-day and here we are in Chi yet on the day when I told you we would get to Bedford and I bet Bertha and you and the rest of the boys will be dissapointed but Al I dont feel like as if I should ought to leave the White Sox in a hole and that is why I am here yet and I will tell you

how it come off but in the 1st place I want to tell you that it wont
make a diffrence of more than 5 or 6 or may be 7 days at least and we
will be down there and see you and Bertha and the rest of the boys just
as soon as the N. Y. giants and the White Sox leaves here and starts a
round the world. All so I remember I told you to fix it up so as a hack
would be down to the deepo to meet us to-night and you wont get this
letter in time to tell them not to send no hack so I supose the hack will
be there but may be they will be somebody else that gets off of the train
that will want the hack and then every thing will be all O. K. but
if they is not nobody else that wants the hack I will pay them ½ of
what they was going to charge me if I had of came and road in the hack
though I dont have to pay them nothing because I am not going to ride
in the hack but I want to do the right thing and besides I will want a
hack at the deepo when I do come so they will get a peace of money
out of me any way so I dont see where they got no kick comeing even
if I dont give them a nichol now.

I will tell you why I am still here and you will see where I am trying
to do the right thing. You knowed of coarse that the White Sox and
the N. Y. giants was going to make a trip a round the world and they
been after me for a long time to go a long with them but I says No I
would not leave Florrie and the kid because that would not be fare and
besides I would be paying rent and grocerys for them some wheres and
me not getting nothing out of it and besides I would probily be spending
a hole lot of money on the trip because though the club pays all of our
regular expences they would be a hole lot of times when I felt like
blowing my self and buying some thing to send home to the Mrs and
to good old friends of mine like you and Bertha so I turned them down
and Callahan acted like he was sore at me but I dont care nothing for
that because I got other people to think a bout and not Callahan and
besides if I was to go a long the fans in the towns where we play at
would want to see me work and I would have to do a hole lot of
pitching which I would not be getting nothing for it and it would not
count in no standing because the games is to be just for fun and what
good would it do me and besides Florrie says I was not under no cir-
cumstance to go and of coarse I would go if I wanted to go no matter
what ever she says but all and all I turned them down and says I would
stay here all winter or rather I would not stay here but in Bedford. Then
Callahan says All right but you know before we start on the trip the
giants and us is going to play a game right here in Chi next Sunday and
after what you done in the city serious the fans would be sore if they
did not get no more chance to look at you so will you stay and pitch

part of the game here and I says I would think it over and I come home
to the hotel where we are staying at and asked Florrie did she care if
we did not go to Bedford for an other week and she says No she did
not care if we dont go for 6 years so I called Callahan up and says I
would stay and he says Thats the boy and now the fans will have an
other treat so you see Al he appresiates what I done and wants to give
the fans fare treatment because this town is nuts over me after what I
done to them Cubs but I could do it just the same to the Athaletics or
any body else if it would of been them in stead of the Cubs. May be
we will leave here the a.m. after the game that is Monday and I will let
you know so as you can order an other hack and tell Bertha I hope she
did not go to no extra trouble a bout getting ready for us and did not
order no spair ribs and crout but you can eat them up if she all ready
got them and may be she can order some more for us when we come
but tell her it dont make no diffrence and not to go to no trouble
because most anything she has is O. K. for I and Florrie accept of coarse
we would not want to make no meal off of sardeens or something.

Well Al I bet them N. Y. giants will wish I would of went home
before they come for this here exibishun game because my arm feels
grate and I will show them where they would be at if they had to play
ball in our league all the time though I suppose they is some pitchers in
our league that they would hit good against them if they can hit at all
but not me. You see in the papers how I come out and I will write and
tell you a bout it. Your pal, JACK.

Chicago, Ill., Oct. 25

OLD PAL: I have not only got a little time but I have got some news
for you and I knowed you would want to hear all a bout it so I am
writeing this letter and then I am going to catch the train. I would be
saying good by to little Al instead of writeing this letter only Florrie
wont let me wake him up and he is a sleep but may be by the time I
get this letter wrote he will be a wake again and I can say good by to
him. I am going with the White Sox and giants as far as San Francisco
or may be Van Coover where they take the boat at but I am not going
a round the world with them but only just out to the coast to help them
out because they is a couple of men going to join them out there and
untill them men join them they will be short of men and they got a hole
lot of exibishun games to play before they get out there so I am going
to help them out. It all come off in the club house after the game to-
day and I will tell you how it come off but 1st I want to tell you a bout
the game and honest Al them giants is the luckyest team in the world

and it is not no wonder they keep wining the penant in that league because a club that has got there luck could win ball games with out sending no team on the field at all but staying down to the hotel.

They was a big crowd out to the park so Callahan says to me I did not know if I was going to pitch you or not but the crowd is out here to see you so I will have to let you work so I warmed up but I knowed the minute I throwed the 1st ball warming up that I was not right and I says to Callahan I did not feel good but he says You wont need to feel good to beat this bunch because they heard a hole lot a bout you and you would have them beat if you just throwed your glove out there in the box. So I went in and tried to pitch but my arm was so lame it pretty near killed me every ball I throwed and I bet if I was some other pitchers they would not never of tried to work with my arm so sore but I am not like some of them yellow dogs and quit because I would not dissapoint the crowd or throw Callahan down when he wanted me to pitch and was depending on me. You know me Al. So I went in there but I did not have nothing and if them giants could of hit at all in stead of like a lot of girls they would of knock down the fence because I was not my self. At that they should not ought to of had only the 1 run off of me if Weaver and them had not of begin kicking the ball a round like it was a foot ball or something. Well Al what with dropping fly balls and booting them a round and this in that the giants was gave 5 runs in the 1st 3 innings and they should ought to of had just the 1 run or may be not that and that ball Merkle hit in to the seats I was trying to waist it and a man that is a good hitter would not never of hit at it and if I was right this here Merkle could not foul me in 9 years. When I was comeing into the bench after the 3th inning this here smart alex Mcgraw came passed me from the 3 base coaching line and he says Are you going on the trip and I says No I am not going on no trip and he says That is to bad because if you was going we would win a hole lot of games and I give him a hot come back and he did not say nothing so I went in to the bench and Callahan says Them giants is not such rotten hitters is they and I says No they hit pretty good when a man has got a sore arm against them and he says Why did not you tell me your arm was sore and I says I did not want to dissapoint no crowd that come out here to see me and he says Well I guess you need not pitch no more because if I left you in there the crowd might begin to get tired of watching you a bout 10 oclock to-night and I says What do you mean and he did not say nothing more so I set there a while and then went to the club house. Well Al after the game Callahan come in to the club house and I was still in there yet talking to the trainer and getting my arm rubbed and Callahan says Are you getting your arm in shape for next year and I says No but it give me so much pane I could not stand it and he says I bet if you was feeling good you could make them giants look like a sucker and I says You know I could make them look like a sucker and he says Well why dont you come a long with us and you will get an other chance at them when you feel good and I says I would like to get an other crack at them but I could not go a way on no trip and leave the Mrs and the baby and then he says he would not ask me to make the hole trip a round the world but he wisht I would go out to the coast with them because they was hard up for pitchers and he says Mathewson of the giants was not only going as far as the coast so if the giants had there star pitcher that far the White Sox should ought to have theren and then some of the other boys coaxed me would I go so finely I says I would think it over and I went home and seen Florrie and she says How long would it be for and I says a bout 3 or 4 weeks and she says If you dont go will we start for Bedford right a way and I says Yes and then she says All right go a head and go but if they was any thing should happen to the baby while I was gone what would they do if I was not a round to tell them what to do and I says Call a Dr. in but dont call no Dr. if you dont have to and besides you should ought to know by this time what to do for the baby when he got sick and she says Of coarse I know a little but not as much as you do because you know it all. Then I says No I dont know it all but I will tell you some things before I go and you should not ought to have no trouble so we fixed it up and her and little Al is to stay here in the hotel untill I come back which will be a bout the 20 of Nov. and then we will come down home and tell Bertha not to get to in patient and we will get there some time. It is going to cost me $6.00 a week at the hotel for a room for she and the baby besides there meals but the babys meals dont cost nothing yet and Florrie should not ought to be very hungry because we been liveing good and besides she will get all she can eat when we come to Bedford and it wont cost me nothing for meals on the trip out to the coast because Comiskey and Mcgraw pays for that.

I have not even had no time to look up where we play at but we stop off at a hole lot of places on the way and I will get a chance to make them giants look like a sucker before I get threw and Mcgraw wont be so sorry I am not going to make the hole trip. You will see by the papers what I done to them before we get threw and I will write as soon as we stop some wheres long enough so as I can write and now I am going to say good by to little Al if he is a wake or not a wake and wake him up and say good by to him because even if he is not only 5 months old he is old enough to think a hole lot of me and why not. I all so got to say good by to Florrie and fix it up with the hotel clerk a bout she and the baby staying here a while and catch the train. You will hear from me soon old pal.   Your pal,   JACK.

St. Joe, Miss., Oct. 29

FRIEND AL: Well Al we are on our way to the coast and they is quite a party of us though it is not no real White Sox and giants at all but some players from off of both clubs and then some others that is from other clubs a round the 2 leagues to fill up. We got Speaker from the Boston club and Crawford from the Detroit club and if we had them with us all the time Al I would not never loose a game because one or the other of them 2 is good for a couple of runs every game and that is all I need to win my games is a couple of runs or only 1 run and I would win all my games and would not never loose a game.

I did not pitch to-day and I guess the giants was glad of it because no matter what Mcgraw says he must of saw from watching me Sunday that I was a real pitcher though my arm was so sore I could not hardly raze it over my sholder so no wonder I did not have no stuff but at that I could of beat his gang with out no stuff if I had of had some kind of decent suport. I will pitch against them may be to-morrow or may be some day soon and my arm is all O. K. again now so I will show them up and make them wish Callahan had of left me to home. Some of the men has brung there wife a long and besides that there is some other men and there wife that is not no ball players but are going a long for the trip and some more will join the party out the coast before they get a bord the boat but of coarse I and Mathewson will drop out of the party then because why should I or him go a round the world and throw our arms out pitching games that dont count in no standing and that we dont get no money for pitching them out side of just our bare expences. The people in the towns we played at so far has all wanted to shake hands with Mathewson and I so I guess they know who is the real pitchers on these here 2 clubs no matter what them reporters says and the stars is all ways the men that the people wants to shake there hands with and make friends with them but Al this here Mathewson pitched to-day and honest Al I dont see how he gets by and either the batters in the National league dont know nothing a bout hitting or else he is such a old man that they feel sorry for him and may be when he was a bout 10 years younger then he is may be then he had some thing and was a pretty fare pitcher but all as he does now is stick the 1st ball

right over with 0 on it and pray that they dont hit it out of the park.
If a pitcher like he can get by in the National league and fool them
batters they is not nothing I would like better then to pitch in the National league and I bet I would not get scored on in 2 to 3 years. I heard
a hole lot a bout this here fade away that he is supposed to pitch and
it is a ball that is throwed out between 2 fingers and falls in at a right
hand batter and they is not no body cant hit it but if he throwed 1 of
them things to-day he done it while I was a sleep and they was not no
time when I was not wide a wake and looking right at him and after
the game was over I says to him Where is that there fade a way I heard
so much a bout and he says O I did not have to use none of my regular
stuff against your club and I says Well you would have to use all you
got if I was working against you and he says Yes if you worked like
you done Sunday I would have to do some pitching or they would not
never finish the game. Then I says a bout me haveing a sore arm Sunday
and he says I wisht I had a sore arm like yourn and a little sence with
it and was your age and I would not never loose a game so you see Al
he has heard a bout me and is jellus because he has not got my stuff
but they cant every body expect to have the stuff that I got or ½ as
much stuff. This smart alex Mcgraw was trying to kid me to-day and
says Why did not I make friends with Mathewson and let him learn me
some thing a bout pitching and I says Mathewson could not learn me
nothing and he says I guess thats right and I guess they is not nobody
could learn you nothing a bout nothing and if you was to stay in the
league 20 years probily you would not be no better then you are now
so you see he had to add mit that I am good Al even if he has not saw
me work when my arm was O. K.

Mcgraw says to me to-night he says I wisht you was going all the
way and I says Yes you do. I says Your club would look like a sucker
after I had worked against them a few times and he says May be thats
right to because they would not know how to hit against a regular
pitcher after that. Then he says But I dont care nothing a bout that but
I wisht you was going to make the hole trip so as we could have a good
time. He says We got Steve Evans and Dutch Schaefer going a long and
they is both of them funny but I like to be a round with boys that is
funny and dont know nothing a bout it. I says Well I would go a long
only for my wife and baby and he says Yes it would be pretty tough
on your wife to have you a way that long but still and all think how
glad she would be to see you when you come back again and besides
them dolls acrost the ocean will be pretty sore at I and Callahan if we
tell them we left you to home. I says Do you suppose the people over

there has heard a bout me and he says Sure because they have wrote a lot of letters asking me to be sure and bring you and Mathewson a long. Then he says I guess Mathewson is not going so if you was to go and him left here to home they would not be nothing to it. You could have things all your own way and probily could marry the Queen of europe if you was not all ready married. He was giveing me the strate dope this time Al because he did not crack a smile and I wisht I could go a long but it would not be fare to Florrie but still and all did not she leave me and beat it for Texas last winter and why should not I do the same thing to her only I am not that kind of a man. You know me Al.

We play in Kansas city to-morrow and may be I will work there because it is a big town and I have got to close now and write to Florrie.

Your old pal,　　Jack.

Abilene, Texas, Nov. 4

Al: Well Al I guess you know by this time that I have worked against them 2 times since I wrote to you last time and I beat them both times and Mcgraw knows now what kind of a pitcher I am and I will tell you how I know because after the game yesterday he road down to the place we dressed at a long with me and all the way in the automobile he was after me to say I would go all the way a round the world and finely it come out that he wants I should go a long and pitch for his club and not pitch for the White Sox. He says his club is up against it for pitchers because Mathewson is not going and all they got left is a man named Hern that is a young man and not got no experiense and Wiltse that is a lefthander. So he says I have talked it over with Callahan and he says if I could get you to go a long it was all O. K. with him and you could pitch for us only I must not work you to hard because he is depending on you to win the penant for him next year. I says Did not none of the other White Sox made no holler because may be they might have to bat against me and he says Yes Crawford and Speaker says they would not make the trip if you was a long and pitching against them but Callahan showed them where it would be good for them next year because if they hit against you all winter the pitchers they hit against next year will look easy to them. He was crazy to have me go a long on the hole trip but of coarse Al they is not no chance of me going on acct. of Florrie and little Al but you see Mcgraw has cut out his trying to kid me and is treating me now like a man should ought to be treated that has did what I done.

They was not no game here to-day on acct. of it raining and the people here was sore because they did not see no game but they all come a round to look at us and says they must have some speechs from the most prommerent men in the party so I and Comiskey and Mcgraw and Callahan and Mathewson and Ted Sullivan that I guess is putting up the money for the trip made speechs and they clapped there hands harder when I was makeing my speech then when any 1 of the others was makeing there speech. You did not know I was a speech maker did you Al and I did not know it neither untill to-day but I guess they is not nothing I cant do if I make up my mind and 1 of the boys says that I done just as well as Dummy Taylor could of.

I have not heard nothing from Florrie but I guess may be she is to busy takeing care of little Al to write no letters and I am not worring none because she give me her word she would let me know was they some thing the matter.   Yours truly,   JACK.

San Dago, Cal., Nov. 9

FRIEND AL: Al some times I wisht I was not married at all and if it was not for Florrie and little Al I would go a round the world on this here trip and I guess the boys in Bedford would not be jellus if I was to go a round the world and see everything they is to be saw and some of the boys down home has not never been no futher a way then Terre Haute and I dont mean you Al but some of the other boys. But of coarse Al when a man has got a wife and a baby they is not no chance for him to go a way on 1 of these here trips and leave them a lone so they is not no use I should even think a bout it but I can't help thinking a bout it because the boys keeps after me all the time to go. Callahan was talking a bout it to me to-day and he says he knowed that if I was to pitch for the giants on the trip his club would not have no chance of wining the most of the games on the trip but still and all he wisht I would go a long because he was a scared the people over in Rome and Paris and Africa and them other countrys would be awful sore if the 2 clubs come over there with out bringing none of there star pitchers along. He says We got Speaker and Crawford and Doyle and Thorp and some of them other real stars in all the positions accept pitcher and it will make us look bad if you and Mathewson don't neither 1 of you come a long. I says What is the matter with Scott and Benz and this here lefthander Wiltse and he says They is not nothing the matter with none of them accept they is not no real stars like you and Mathewson and if we cant show them forreners 1 of you 2 we will feel like as if we was cheating them. I says You would not want me to pitch my best against your club would you and he says O no I would not want you to pitch your best or get your self all wore out for next year but I would want you to let up enough so as we could make a run oncet in a while so the games would not be to 1 sided. I says Well they is not no use talking a bout it because I could not leave my wife and baby and he says Why dont you write and ask your wife and tell her how it is and can you go. I says No because she would make a big holler and besides of coarse I would go any way if I wanted to go with out no yes or no from her only I am not the kind of a man that runs off and leaves his family and besides they is not nobody to leave her with because her and her sister Allens wife has had a quarrle. Then Callahan says Where is Allen at now is he still in Chi. I says I dont know where is he at and I dont care where he is at because I am threw with him. Then Callahan says I asked him would he go on the trip before the season was over but he says he could not and if I knowed where was he I would wire a telegram to him and ask him again. I says What would you want him a long for and he says Because Mcgraw is shy of pitchers and I says I would try and help him find 1. I says Well you should ought not to have no trouble finding a man like Allen to go along because his wife probily would be glad to get rid of him. Then Callahan says Well I wisht you would get a hold of where Allen is at and let me know so as I can wire him a telegram. Well Al I know where Allen is at all O. K. but I am not going to give his adress to Callahan because Mcgraw has treated me all O. K. and why should I wish a man like Allen on to him and besides I am not going to give Allen no chance to go a round the world or no wheres else after the way he acted a bout I and Florrie haveing a room in his flat and asking me to pay for it when he give me a invatation to come there and stay. Well Al it is to late now to cry in the sour milk but I wisht I had not never saw Florrie untill next year and then I and her could get married just like we done last year only I dont know would I do it again or not but I guess I would on acct. of little Al.   Your pal,   JACK.

San Francisco, Cal., Nov. 14

OLD PAL: Well old pal what do you know a bout me being back here in San Francisco where I give the fans such a treat 2 years ago and then I was not nothing but a busher and now I am with a team that is going a round the world and are crazy to have me go a long only I cant because of my wife and baby. Callahan wired a telegram to the reporters here from Los Angeles telling them I would pitch here and I guess they is going to be 20 or 25000 out to the park and I will give them the best I got.

But what do you think Florrie has did Al. Her and the Allens has

made it up there quarrle and is friends again and Marie told Florrie to
write and tell me she was sorry we had that there argument and let by
gones be by gones. Well Al it is all O. K. with me because I cant help
not feeling sorry for Allen because I dont beleive he will be in the league
next year and I feel sorry for Marie to because it must be pretty tough
on her to see how well her sister done and what a misstake she made
when she went and fell for a lefthander that could not fool a blind man
with his curve ball and if he was to hit a man in the head with his fast
ball they would think there nose iched. In Florries letter she says she
thinks us and the Allens could find an other flat like the 1 we had last
winter and all live in it to gether in stead of going to Bedford but I have
wrote to her before I started writeing this letter all ready and told her
that her and I is going to Bedford and the Allens can go where they feel
like and they can go and stay on a boat on Michigan lake all winter if
they want to but I and Florrie is comeing to Bedford. Down to the
bottom of her letter she says Allen wants to know if Callahan or
Mcgraw is shy of pitchers and may be he would change his mind and
go a long on the trip. Well Al I did not ask either Callahan nor Mcgraw
nothing a bout it because I knowed they was looking for a star and not
for no lefthander that could not brake a pane of glass with his fast 1
so I wrote and told Florrie to tell Allen they was all filled up and would
not have no room for no more men.

It is pretty near time to go out to the ball park and I wisht you could
be here Al and hear them San Francisco fans go crazy when they hear
my name announced to pitch. I bet they wish they had of had me here
this last year.   Yours truly,   JACK.

Medford, Organ, Nov. 16
FRIEND AL: Well Al you know by this time that I did not pitch the hole
game in San Francisco but I was not tooken out because they was hitting
me Al but because my arm went back on me all of a sudden and it was
the change in the clime it that done it to me and they could not hire me
to try and pitch another game in San Francisco. They was the biggest
crowd there that I ever seen in San Francisco and I guess they must of
been 40000 people there and I wisht you could of heard them yell when
my name was announced to pitch. But Al I would not never of went in
there but for the crowd. My arm felt like a wet rag or some thing and
I knowed I would not have nothing and besides the people was packed
in a round the field and they had to have ground rules so when a man
hit a pop fly it went in to the crowd some wheres and was a 2 bagger
and all them giants could do against me was pop my fast ball up in the

YOU KNOW ME AL 103

air and then the wind took a hold of it and dropped it in to the crowd
the lucky stiffs. Doyle hit 3 of them pop ups in to the crowd so when
you see them 3 2 base hits oposit his name in the score you will know
they was not no real 2 base hits and the infielders would of catched
them had it not of been for the wind. This here Doyle takes a awful
wallop at a ball but if I was right and he swang at a ball the way he
done in San Francisco the catcher would all ready be throwing me back
the ball a bout the time this here Doyle was swinging at it. I can make
him look like a sucker and I done it both in Kansas city and Bonham
and if he will get up there and bat against me when I feel good and
when they is not no wind blowing I will bet him a $25.00 suit of cloths
that he cant foul 1 off of me. Well when Callahan seen how bad my
arm was he says I guess I should ought to take you out and not run no
chance of you getting killed in there and so I quit and Faber went in to
finnish it up because it dont make no diffrence if he hurts his arm or
dont. But I guess Mcgraw knowed my arm was sore to because he did
not try and kid me like he done that day in Chi because he has saw
enough of me since then to know I can make his club look rotten when
I am O.K. and my arm is good. On the train that night he come up and
says to me Well Jack we catched you off your strid to-day or you would
of gave us a beating and then he says What your arm needs is more
work and you should ought to make the hole trip with us and then you
would be in fine shape for next year but I says You cant get me to make
no trip so you might is well not do no more talking a bout it and then
he says Well I am sorry and the girls over to Paris will be sorry to but
I guess he was just jokeing a bout the last part of it.

Well Al we go to 1 more town in Organ and then to Washington
but of coarse it is not the same Washington we play at in the summer
but this is the state Washington and have not got no big league club
and the boys gets there boat in 4 more days and I will quit them and
then I will come strate back to Chi and from there to Bedford.

Your pal,   JACK.

Portland, Organ, Nov. 17
FRIEND AL: I have just wrote a long letter to Florrie but I feel like as if
I should ought to write to you because I wont have no more chance for
a long while that is I wont have no more chance to male a letter because
I will be on the pacific Ocean and un less we should run passed a boat
that was comeing the other way they would not be no chance of getting
no letter maled. Old pal I am going to make the hole trip clear a round
the world and back and so I wont see you this winter after all but when

I do see you Al I will have a lot to tell you a bout my trip and besides I will write you a letter a bout it from every place we head in at.

I guess you will be surprised a bout me changeing my mind and makeing the hole trip but they was not no way for me to get out of it and I will tell you how it all come off. While we was still in that there Medford yesterday Mcgraw and Callahan come up to me and says was they not no chance of me changeing my mind a bout makeing the hole trip. I says No they was not. Then Callahan says Well I dont know what we are going to do then and I says Why and he says Comiskey just got a letter from president Wilson the President of the united states and in the letter president Wilson says he had got an other letter from the king of Japan who says that they would not stand for the White Sox and giants comeing to Japan un less they brought all there stars a long and president Wilson says they would have to take there stars a long because he was a scared if they did not take there stars a long Japan would get mad at the united states and start a war and then where would we be at. So Comiskey wired a telegram to president Wilson and says Mathewson could not make the trip because he was so old but would everything be all O. K. if I was to go a long and president Wilson wired a telegram back and says Yes he had been talking to the priest from Japan and he says Yes it would be all O. K. I asked them would they show me the letter from president Wilson because I thought may be they might be kiding me and they says they could not show me no letter because when Comiskey got the letter he got so mad that he tore it up. Well Al I finely says I did not want to brake up there trip but I knowed Florrie would not stand for letting me go so Callahan says All right I will wire a telegram to a friend of mine in Chi and have him get a hold of Allen and send him out here and we will take him a long and I says It is to late for Allen to get here in time and Mcgraw says No they was a train that only took 2 days from Chi to where ever it was the boat is going to sale from because the train come a round threw canada and it was down hill all the way. Then I says Well if you will wire a telegram to my wife and fix things up with her I will go a long with you but if she is going to make a holler it is all off. So we all 3 went to the telegram office to gether and we wired Florrie a telegram that must of cost $2.00 but Callahan and Mcgraw payed for it out of there own pocket and then we waited a round a long time and the anser come back and the anser was longer than the telegram we wired and it says it would not make no difference to her but she did not know if the baby would make a holler but he was hollering most of the time any

way so that would not make no diffrence but if she let me go it was on
condishon that her and the Allens could get a flat to gether and stay in
Chi all winter and not go to no Bedford and hire a nurse to take care
of the baby and if I would send her a check for the money I had in the
bank so as she could put it in her name and draw it out when she need
it. Well I says at 1st I would not stand for nothing like that but Callahan
and Mcgraw showed me where I was makeing a mistake not going when
I could see all them diffrent countrys and tell Florrie all a bout the trip
when I come back and then in a year or 2 when the baby was a little
older I could make an other trip and take little Al and Florrie a long so
I finely says O. K. I would go and we wires still an other telegram to
Florrie and told her O. K. and then I set down and wrote her a check
for ½ the money I got in the bank and I got $500.00 all together there
so I wrote the check for ½ of that or $250.00 and maled it to her and
if she cant get a long on that she would be a awful spendrift because I
am not only going to be a way untill March. You should ought to of
heard the boys cheer when Callahan tells them I am going to make the
hole trip but when he tells them I am going to pitch for the giants and
not for the White Sox I bet Crawford and Speaker and them wisht I
was going to stay to home but it is just like Callahan says if they bat
against me all winter the pitchers they bat against next season will look
easy to them and you wont be supprised Al if Crawford and Speaker
hits a bout 500 next year and if they hit good you will know why it is.
Steve Evans asked me was I all fixed up with cloths and I says No but
I was going out and buy some cloths includeing a full dress suit of
evening cloths and he says You dont need no full dress suit of evening
cloths because you look funny enough with out them. This Evans is a
great kidder Al and no body never gets sore at the stuff he pulls some
thing like Kid Gleason. I wisht Kid Gleason was going on the trip Al
but I will tell him all a bout it when I come back.

Well Al old pal I wisht you was going a long to and I bet we could
have the time of our life but I will write to you right a long Al and I
will send Bertha some post cards from the different places we head in
at. I will try and write you a letter on the boat and male it as soon as
we get to the 1st station which is either Japan or Yokohama I forgot
which. Good by Al and say good by to Bertha for me and tell her how
sorry I and Florrie is that we cant come to Bedford this winter but we
will spend all the rest of the winters there and her and Florrie will have
a plenty of time to get acquainted. Good by old pal.

Your pal,   JACK.

Seattle, Wash., Nov. 18

AL: Well Al it is all off and I am not going on no trip a round the world
and back and I been looking for Callahan or Mcgraw for the last ½
hour to tell them I have changed my mind and am not going to make
no trip because it would not be fare to Florrie and besides that I think
I should ought to stay home and take care of little Al and not leave him
to be tooken care of by no train nurse because how do I know what
would she do to him and I am not going to tell Florrie nothing a bout
it but I am going to take the train to-morrow night right back to Chi
and supprise her when I get there and I bet both her and little Al will
be tickled to death to see me. I supose Mcgraw and Callahan will be
sore at me for a while but when I tell them I want to do the right thing
and not give my famly no raw deal I guess they will see where I am
right.

We was to play 2 games here and was to play 1 of them in Tacoma
and the other here but it rained and so we did not play neither 1 and
the people was pretty mad a bout it because I was announced to pitch
and they figured probily this would be there only chance to see me in
axion and they made a awful holler but Comiskey says No they would
not be no game because the field neither here or in Tacoma was in no
shape for a game and he would not take no chance of me pitching and
may be slipping in the mud and straneing myself and then where would
the White Sox be at next season. So we been laying a round all the p.m.
and I and Dutch Schaefer had a long talk to gether while some of the
rest of the boys was out buying some cloths to take on the trip and Al
I bought a full dress suit of evening cloths at Portland yesterday and
now I owe Callahan the money for them and am not going on no trip
so probily I wont never get to ware them and it is just $45.00 throwed
a way but I would rather throw $45.00 a way then go on a trip a round
the world and leave my family all winter.

Well Al I and Schaefer was talking to gether and he says Well may
be this is the last time we will ever see the good old US and I says What
do you mean and he says People that gos acrost the pacific Ocean most
generally all ways has there ship recked and then they is not no more
never heard from them. Then he asked me was I a good swimmer and
I says Yes I had swam a good deal in the river and he says Yes you
have swam in the river but that is not nothing like swimming in the
pacific Ocean because when you swim in the pacific Ocean you cant
move your feet because if you move your feet the sharks comes up to
the top of the water and bites at them and even if they did not bite your
feet clean off there bite is poison and gives you the hiderofobeya and

when you get that you start barking like a dog and the water runs in to your mouth and chokes you to death. Then he says Of coarse if you can swim with out useing your feet you are all O. K. but they is very few can do that and espesially in the pacific Ocean because they got to keep useing there hands all the time to scare the sord fish a way so when you dont dare use your feet and your hands is busy you got nothing left to swim with but your stumach mussles. Then he says You should ought to get a long all O. K. because your stumach muscles should ought to be strong from the exercise they get so I guess they is not no danger from a man like you but men like Wiltse and Mike Donlin that is not hog fat like you has not got no chance. Then he says Of coarse they have been times when the boats got acrost all O. K. and only a few lives lost but it dont offten happen and the time the old Minneapolis club made the trip the boat went down and the only thing that was saved was the catchers protector that was full of air and could not do nothing else but flote. Then he says May be you would flote to if you did not say nothing for a few days.

I asked him how far would a man got to swim if some thing went wrong with the boat and he says O not far because they is a hole lot of ilands a long the way that a man could swim to but it would not do a man no good to swim to these here ilands because they dont have nothing to eat on them and a man would probily starve to death un less he happened to swim to the sandwich ilands. Then he says But by the time you been out on the pacific Ocean a few months you wont care if you get any thing to eat or not. I says Why not and he says the pacific Ocean is so ruff that not nothing can set still not even the stuff you eat. I asked him how long did it take to make the trip acrost if they was not no ship reck and he says they should ought to get acrost a long in febuery if the weather was good. I says Well if we dont get there until febuery we won't have no time to train for next season and he says You wont need to do no training because this trip will take all the weight off of you and every thing else you got. Then he says But you should not ought to be scared of getting sea sick because they is 1 way you can get a way from it and that is to not eat nothing at all while you are on the boat and they tell me you dont eat hardly nothing any way so you wont miss it. Then he says Of coarse if we should have good luck and not get in to no ship reck and not get shot by 1 of them war ships we will have a grate time when we get acrost because all the girls in europe and them places is nuts over ballplayers and espesially stars. I asked what did he mean saying we might get shot by 1 of them war ships and he says we would have to pass by Swittserland and the

Swittserland war ships was all the time shooting all over the ocean and
of coarse they was not trying to hit no body but they was as wild as
most of them lefthanders and how could you tell what was they going
to do next.

Well Al after I got threw talking to Schaefer I run in to Jack Sheridan
the umpire and I says I did not think I would go on no trip and I told
him some of the things Schaefer was telling me and Sheridan says Schaefer was kidding me and they was not no danger at all and of coarse Al
I did not believe ½ of what Schaefer was telling me and that has not
got nothing to do with me changeing my mind but I dont think it is not
hardly fare for me to go a way on a trip like that and leave Florrie and
the baby and suppose some of them things really did happen like Schaefer said though of coarse he was kidding me but if 1 of them was to
happen they would not be no body left to take care of Florrie and little
Al and I got a $1000.00 insurence policy but how do I know after I am
dead if the insurence co. comes acrost and gives my famly the money.

Well Al I will male this letter and then try again and find Mcgraw
and Callahan and then I will look up a time table and see what train
can I get to Chi. I don't know yet when I will be in Bedford and maybe
Florrie has hired a flat all ready but the Allens can live in it by them
self and if Allen says any thing a bout I paying for ½ of the rent I will
bust his jaw.   Your pal,   JACK.

                                      Victoria, Can., Nov. 19
DEAR OLD AL: Well old pal the boat gos to-night I am going a long
and I would not be takeing no time to write this letter only I wrote to
you yesterday and says I was not going and you probily would be expecting to see me blow in to Bedford in a few days and besides Al I got
a hole lot of things to ask you to do for me if any thing happens and I
want to tell you how it come a bout that I changed my mind and am
going on the trip. I am glad now that I did not write Florrie no letter
yesterday and tell her I was not going because now I would have to
write her an other letter and tell her I was going and she would be
expecting to see me the day after she got the 1st letter and in stead of
seeing me she would get this 2nd. letter and not me at all. I have all
ready wrote her a good by letter to-day though and while I was writeing
it Al I all most broke down and cried and espesially when I thought a
bout leaveing little Al so long and may be when I see him again he wont
be no baby no more or may be some thing will of happened to him or
that train nurse did some thing to him or may be I wont never see him
again no more because it is pretty near a cinch that some thing will

either happen to I or him. I would give all most any thing I got Al to be back in Chi with little Al and Florrie and I wisht she had not of never wired that telegram telling me I could make the trip and if some thing happens to me think how she will feel when ever she thinks a bout wireing me that telegram and she will feel all most like as if she was a murder.

Well Al after I had wrote you that letter yesterday I found Callahan and Mcgraw and I tell them I have changed my mind and am not going on no trip. Callahan says Whats the matter and I says I dont think it would be fare to my wife and baby and Callahan says Your wife says it would be all O. K. because I seen the telegram my self. I says Yes but she dont know how dangerus the trip is and he says Whos been kiding you and I says They has not no body been kiding me. I says Dutch Schaefer told me a hole lot of stuff but I did not believe none of it and that has not got nothing to do with it. I says I am not a scared of nothing but supose some thing should happen and then where would my wife and my baby be at. Then Callahan says Schaefer has been giveing you a lot of hot air and they is not no more danger on this trip then they is in bed. You been in a hole lot more danger when you was pitching some of them days when you had a sore arm and you would be takeing more chances of getting killed in Chi by 1 of them taxi cabs or the dog catcher then on the Ocean. This here boat we are going on is the Umpires of Japan and it has went acrost the Ocean a million times with out nothing happening and they could not nothing happen to a boat that the N. Y. giants was rideing on because they is to lucky. Then I says Well I have made up my mind to not go on no trip and he says All right then I guess we might is well call the trip off and I says Why and he says You know what president Wilson says a bout Japan and they wont stand for us comeing over there with out you a long and then Mcgraw says Yes it looks like as if the trip was off because we dont want to take no chance of starting no war between Japan and the united states. Then Callahan says You will be in fine with Comiskey if he has to call the trip off because you are a scared of getting hit by a fish. Well Al we talked and argude for a hour or a hour and ½ and some of the rest of the boys come a round and took Callahan and Mcgraw side and finely Callahan says it looked like as if they would have to posepone the trip a few days untill he could get a hold of Allen or some body and get them to take my place so finely I says I would go because I would not want to brake up no trip after they had made all there plans and some of the players wifes was all ready to go and would be dissapointed if they was not no trip. So Mcgraw and Callahan says Thats the way to talk and so I am going Al and we are leaveing to-night and may be this is the last letter you will ever get from me but if they does not nothing happen Al I will write to you a lot of letters and tell you all a bout the trip but you must not be looking for no more letters for a while untill we get to Japan where I can male a letter and may be its likely as not we wont never get to Japan.

Here is the things I want to ask you to try and do Al and I am not asking you to do nothing if we get threw the trip all right but if some thing happens and I should be drowned here is what I am asking you to do for me and that is to see that the insurence co. dont skin Florrie out of that $1000.00 policy and see that she all so gets that other $250.00 out of the bank and find her some place down in Bedford to live if she is willing to live down there because she can live there a hole lot cheaper then she can live in Chi and besides I know Bertha would treat her right and help her out all she could. All so Al I want you and Bertha to help take care of little Al untill he grows up big enough to take care of him self and if he looks like as if he was going to be left handed dont let him Al but make him use his right hand for every thing. Well Al they is 1 good thing and that is if I get drowned Florrie wont have to buy no lot in no cemetary and hire no herse.

Well Al old pal you all ways been a good friend of mine and I all ways tried to be a good friend of yourn and if they was ever any thing I done to you that was not O. K. remember by gones is by gones. I want you to all ways think of me as your best old pal. Good by old pal.   Your old pal,   JACK.

P.S. Al if they should not nothing happen and if we was to get acrost the Ocean all O. K. I am going to ask Mcgraw to let me work the 1st game against the White Sox in Japan because I should certainly ought to be right after giveing my arm a rest and not doing nothing at all on the trip acrost and I bet if Mcgraw lets me work Crawford and Speaker will wisht the boat had of sank. You know me Al.

CALL FOR MR. KEEFE!

FRIEND AL: Well Al the training trips over and we open up the season here tomorrow and I suppose the boys back home is all anxious to know about our chances and what shape the boys is in. Well old pal you can tell them we are out after that old flag this year and the club that beats us will know they have been in a battle. I'll say they will.

Speaking for myself personly I never felt better in my life and you know what that means Al. It means I will make a monkey out of this league and not only that but the boys will all have more confidence in themself and play better baseball when they know my arms right and that I can give them the best I got and if Rowland handles the club right and don't play no favorites like last season we will be so far out in front by the middle of July that Boston and the rest of them will think we have jumped to some other league.

Well I suppose the old towns all excited about Uncle Sam declairing war on Germany. Personly I am glad we are in it but between you and I Al I figure we ought to of been in it a long time ago right after the Louisiana was sank. I often say alls fair in love and war but that don't mean the Germans or no one else has got a right to murder American citizens but thats about all you can expect from a German and anybody that expects a square deal from them is a sucker. You don't see none of them umpireing in our league but at that they couldn't be no worse than the ones we got. Some of ours is so crooked they can't lay in a birth only when the trains making a curve.

But speaking about the war Al you couldn't keep me out of it only for Florrie and little Al depending on me for sport and of course theys the ball club to and I would feel like a trader if I quit them now when it looks like this is our year. So I might just as well make up my mind to whats got to be and not mop over it but I like to kid the rest of the boys and make them think I'm going to enlist to see their face fall and tonight at supper I told Gleason I thought I would quit the club and join the army. He tried to laugh it off with some of his funny stuff. He says "They wouldn't take you." "No," I said. "I suppose Uncle Sam is turning down men with a perfect physic." So he says "They don't want a man that if a shell would hit him in the head it would explode all over the trench and raise havioc." I forget what I said back to him.

Well Al I don't know if I will pitch in this serious or not but if I do I will give them a touch of high life but maybe Rowland will save me to open up at Detroit where a mans got to have something besides their glove. It takes more than camel flags to beat that bunch. I'll say it does.

Your pal, JACK.

Chicago, April 15

FRIEND AL: Well Al here I am home again and Rowland sent some of us home from St. Louis instead of takeing us along to Detroit and I suppose he is figureing on saveing me to open up the home season next Thursday against St. Louis because they always want a big crowd on opening day and St. Louis don't draw very good unless theys some extra attraction to bring the crowd out. But anyway I was glad to get home and see Florrie and little Al and honest Al he is cuter than ever and when he seen me he says "Who are you?" Hows that for a 3 year old?

Well things has been going along pretty good at home while I was away only it will take me all summer to pay the bills Florrie has ran up on me and you ought to be thankfull that Bertha aint 1 of these Apollos thats got to keep everybody looking at them or they can't eat. Honest Al to look at the clothes Florrie has boughten you would think we was planning to spend the summer at Newport News or somewhere. And she went and got herself a hired girl that sticks us for $8.00 per week and all as she does is cook up the meals and take care of little Al and run wild with a carpet sweeper and dust rag every time you set down to read the paper. I says to Florrie "What is the idea? The 3 of us use to get along O. K. without no help from Norway." So she says "I got sick in tired of staying home all the time or dragging the baby along with me when I went out." So I said I remembered when she wouldn't leave no one else take care of the kid only herself and she says "Yes but that was when I didn't know nothing about babys and every time he cried I thought he had lumbago or something but now I know he has got no intentions of dying so I quit worring about him."

So I said "Yes but I can't afford no high price servants to say nothing about dressing you like an actor and if you think I am going to spend all my salary on silks and satans and etc. you will get a big surprise." So she says "You might as well spend your money on me as leave the ball players take it away from you in the poker game and show their own wives a good time with it. But if you don't want me to spend your money I will go out and get some of my own to spend." Then I said

"What will you do teach school?" And she says "No and I won't teach school either." So I said "No I guess you won't. But if you think you want to try standing up behind a cigar counter or something all day why go ahead and try it and we'll see how long you will last." So she says "I don't have to stand behind no counter but I can go in business for myself and make more then you do." So I said "Yes you can" and she didn't have no come back.

Imagine Al a girl saying she could make more money then a big league pitcher. Probably theys a few of them that does but they are movie actors or something and I would like to see Florrie try to be a movie actor because they got to look pleasant all the time and Florrie would strain herself.

Well Al the ski jumper has got dinner pretty near ready and after dinner I am going over North and see what the Cubs look like and I wish I pitched in that league Al and the only trouble is that I would feel ashamed when I went after my pay check. Your old pal,   JACK.

Chicago, May 19

DEAR FRIEND AL: Well old pal if we wasn't married we would all have to go to war now and I mean all of us thats between 21 and 30. I suppose you seen about the Govt. passing the draft law and a whole lot of the baseball players will have to go but our club won't loose nobody except 1 or 2 bushers that don't count because all as they do any way is take up room on the bench and laugh when Rowland springs a joke.

When I first seen it in the paper this morning I thought it meant everybody that wasn't crippled up or something but Gleason explained it to me that if you got somebody to sport they leave you home and thats fair enough but he also says they won't take no lefthanders on acct. of the guns all being made for right handed men and thats just like the lucky stiffs to set in a rocking chair and take it easy while the regular fellows has got to go over there and get shot up but anyway the yellow stiffs would make a fine lot of soldiers because the first time a German looked X eyed at them they would wave a flag of truants.

But I can't help from wishing this thing had of come off before I seen Florrie or little Al and if I had money enough saved up so as they wouldn't have to worry I would go any way but I wouldn't wait for no draft. Gleason says I will have to register family or no family when the time comes but as soon as I tell them about Florrie they will give me an excuse. I asked him what they would do with the boys that wasn't excused and if they would send them right over to France and he says No they would keep them here till they learned to talk German. He says "You can't fight nobody without a quarrel and you can't quarrel with a man unless they can understand what you are calling them." So I asked him how about the aviators because their machines would be makeing so much noise that they couldn't tell if the other one was talking German or rag time and he said "Well if you are in an areoplane and you see a German areoplane coming tords you you can pretty near guess that he don't want to spoon with you."

Thats what I would like to be Al is an aviator and I think Gleasons afraid I'm going to bust into that end of the game though he pretends like he don't take me in ernest. "Why don't you?" he said "You could make good there all right because the less sense they got the better. But I wish you would quit practiceing till you get away from here." I asked him what he meant quit practiceing. "Well" he said "you was up in the air all last Tuesday afternoon."

He was refering to that game I worked against the Phila. club but honest Al my old souper was so sore I couldn't cut loose. Well Al a mans got a fine chance to save money when they are married to a girl like Florrie. When I got paid Tuesday the first thing when I come home she wanted to borrow $200.00 and that was all I had comeing so I said "What am I going to do the next 2 weeks walk back and forth to the ball park and back?" I said "What and the hell do you want with $200.00?" So then she begin to cry so I split it with her and give her a $100.00 and she wouldn't tell me what she wanted it for but she says she was going to supprise me. Well Al I will be supprised if she don't land us all out to the county farm but you can't do nothing with them when they cry.   Your pal,   JACK.

Chicago, May 24

FRIEND AL: What do you think Florrie has pulled off now? I told you she was fixing to land us in the poor house and I had the right dope. With the money I give her and some she got somewheres else she has opened up a beauty parlor on 43th St. right off of Michigan. Her and a girl that worked in a place like it down town.

Well Al when she sprung it on me you couldn't of knocked me down with a feather. I always figured girls was kind of crazy but I never seen one loose her mind as quick as that and I don't know if I ought to have them take her to some home or leave her learn her lesson and get over it.

I know you ain't got no beauty parlor in Bedford so I might as well tell you what they are. They are for women only and the women goes to them when they need something done to their hair or their face or their nails before a wedding or a eucher party or something. For inst. you and Bertha was up here and you wanted to take her to a show and she would have to get fixed up so she would go to this place and tell them to give her the whole treatment and first they would wash the grime out of her hair and then comb it up fluffy and then they would clean up her complexion with buttermilk and either get rid of the moles or else paint them white and then they would put some eyebrows on her with a pencil and red up her lips and polish her teeth and pair her finger nails and etc. till she looked as good as she could and it would cost her $5.00 or $10.00 according to what they do to her and if they would give her a bath and a massage I suppose its extra.

Well theys plenty of high class beauty parlors down town where women can go and know they will get good service but Florrie thinks she can make it pay out here with women that maybe haven't time to go clear down town because their husband or their friend might loose his mind in the middle of the afternoon and phone home that he had tickets for the Majestic or something and then of course they would have to rush over to some place in the neighborhood for repairs.

I didn't know Florrie was wise to the game but it seems she has been takeing some lessons down town without telling me nothing about it and this Miss Nevins thats in partners with her says Florrie is a darb. Well I wouldn't have no objections if I thought they was a chance for them to make good because she acts like she liked the work and its right close to where we live but it looks to me like their expenses would eat them up. I was in the joint this morning and the different smells alone must of cost them $100.00 to say nothing about all the bottles and cans and tools and brushs and the rent and furniture besides. I told Florrie I said "You got everything here but patients." She says "Don't worry about them. They will come when they find out about us." She says they have sent their cards to all the South Side 400.

"Well" I said "if they don't none of them show up in a couple of months I suppose you will call on the old meal ticket." So she says "You should worry." So I come away and went over to the ball park.

When I seen Kid Gleason I told him about it and he asked me where Florrie got the money to start up so I told him I give it to her. "You" he says "Where did you get it?" So just jokeing I said "Where do you suppose I got it? I stole it." So he says "You did if you got it from this ball club." But he was kidding Al because of course he knows I'm no thief. But I got the laugh on him this afternoon when Silk O'Loughlin chased him out of the ball park. Johnson was working against us and they was two out and Collins on second base and Silk called a third strike on Gandil that was down by his corns. So Gleason hollered "All right Silk you won't have to go to war. You couldn't pass the eye test." So Silk told him to get off the field. So then I hollered something at Silk and he hollered back at me "That will be all from you you big busher." So I said "You are a busher yourself you busher." So he said:

"Get off the bench and let one of the ball players set down."

So I and Gleason stalled a while and finely come into the club house and I said "Well Kid I guess we told him something that time." "Yes" says Gleason "you certainly burned him up but the trouble with me is I can't never think of nothing to say till it's too late." So I said "When a man gets past sixty you can't expect their brain to act quick." And he didn't say nothing back.

Well we win the ball game any way because Cicotte shut them out. The way some of the ball players was patting him on the back afterwards you would have thought it was the 1st. time anybody had ever pitched a shut out against the Washington club but I don't see no reason to swell a man up over it. If you shut out Detroit or Cleveland you are doing something but this here Washington club gets a bonus every time they score a run.

But it does look like we was going to cop that old flag and play the Giants for the big dough and it will sure be the Giants we will have to play against though some of the boys seem to think the Cubs have got a chance on acct. of them just winning 10 straight on their eastren trip but as Gleason says how can a club help from winning 10 straight in that league?   Your pal,   JACK.

Chicago, June 6

FRIEND AL: Well Al the clubs east and Rowland left me home because my old souper is sore again and besides I had to register yesterday for the draft. They was a big crowd down to the place we registered and you ought to seen them when I come in. They was all trying to get up close to me and I was afraid some of them would get hurt in the jam. All of them says "Hello Jack" and I give them a smile and shook hands with about a dozen of them. A man hates to have everybody stareing at you but you got to be pleasant or they will think you are swelled up and besides a man can afford to put themself out a little if its going to give the boys any pleasure.

I don't know how they done with you Al but up here they give us a card to fill out and then they give us another one to carry around with us to show that we been registered and what our number is. I had to put down my name on the first card and my age and where I live and the day I was born and what month and etc. Some of the questions was crazy like "Was I a natural born citizen?" I wonder what they think I am. Maybe they think I fell out of a tree or something. Then I had to tell them I was born in Bedford, Ind. and it asked what I done for a liveing and I put down that I was a pitcher but the man made me change it to ball player and then I had to give Comiskey's name and address and then name the people that was dependent on me so I put down a wife and one child.

And the next question was if I was married or single. I supposed they would know enough to know that a man with a wife dependent on him was probably married. Then it says what race and I had a notion to put down "pennant" for a joke but the man says to put down white. Then it asked what military service had I had and of course I says none and then come the last question Did I claim exemption and what grounds so the man told me to write down married with dependents.

Then the man turned over to the back of the card and wrote down about my looks. Just that I was tall and medium build and brown eyes and brown hair. And the last question was if I had lost an arm or leg or hand or foot or both eyes or was I other wise disabled so I told him about my arm being sore and thats why I wasn't east with the club but he didn't put it down. So thats all they was to it except the card he give me with my number which is 3403.

It looks to me like it was waisting a mans time to make you go down there and wait for your turn when they know you are married and got a kid or if they don't know it they could call up your home or the ball park and find it out but of course if they called up my flat when I or Florrie wasn't there they wouldn't get nothing but a bunch of Swede talk that they couldn't nobody understand and I don't believe the girl knows herself what she is talking about over the phone. She can talk english pretty good when shes just talking to you but she must think all the phone calls is long distance from Norway because the minute she gets that receiver up to her ear you can't hardly tell the difference between she and Hughey Jennings on the coaching line.

I told Florrie I said "This girl could make more then $8.00 per week if she would get a job out to some ball park as announcer and announce the batterys and etc. She has got the voice for it and she would be right in a class with the rest of them because nobody could make heads or tales out of what she was trying to get at."

Speaking about Florrie what do you think Al? They have had enough suckers to pay expenses and also pay up some of the money they borrowed and Florrie says if their business gets much bigger they will have to hire more help. How would you like a job Al white washing some dames nose or levelling off their face with a steam roller? Of course I am just jokeing Al because they won't allow no men around the joint but wouldn't it be some job Al? I'll say so.   Your old pal,   JACK.

Chicago, June 21

DEAR AL: Well Al I suppose you read in the paper the kind of luck I had yesterday but of course you can't tell nothing from what them dam reporters write and if they know how to play ball why aint they playing it instead of trying to write funny stuff about the ball game but at that some of it is funny Al because its so rotten its good. For inst. one of them had it in the paper this morning that I flied out to Speaker in that seventh inning. Well listen Al I hit that ball right on the pick and it went past that shortstop so fast that he didn't even have time to wave at it and if Speaker had of been playing where he belongs that ball would of went between he and Graney and bumped against the wall. But no. Speakers laying about ten feet back of second base and over to the left and of course the ball rides right to him and there was the whole ball game because that would of drove in 2 runs and made them play different then they did in the eigth. If a man is supposed to be playing center field why don't he play center field and of course I thought he was where he ought to been or I would of swung different.

Well the eigth opened up with the score 1 and 1 and I get 2 of them out but I got so much stuff I can't stick it just where I want to and I give Chapman a base on balls. At that the last one cut the heart of the plate but Evans called it a ball. Evans lives in Cleveland. Well I said "All right Bill you won't have to go to war. You couldn't pass the eye test." So he says "You must of read that one in a book." "No" I said "I didn't read it in no book either."

So up comes this Speaker and I says "What do you think you are going to do you lucky stiff?" So he says "I'm going to hit one where theys nobody standing in the way of it." I said "Yes you are." But I had to hold Chapman up at first base and Schalk made me waist 2 thinking Chapman was going and then of course I had to ease up and Speaker cracked one down the first base line but Gandil got his glove on it and if he hadn't of messed it all up he could of beat Speaker to the bag himself but instead of that they all started to ball me out for not covering. I told them to shut their mouth. Then Roth come up and I took a half wind up because of course I didn't think Chapman would be enough of a bone head to steal third with 2 out but him and Speaker pulled a double steal and then Rowland and all of them begin to yell at me and they got my mind off of what I was doing and then Schalk asked for a fast one though he said afterwards he didn't but I would of made him let me curve the ball if they hadn't got me all nervous yelling at me. So Roth hit one to left field that Jackson could of caught in his hip pocket if he had been playing right. So 2 runs come in and then Rowland takes me out and I would of busted him only for makeing a seen on the field.

I said to him "How can you expect a man to be at his best when I have not worked for a month?" So he said "Well it will be more than a month before you will work for me again." "Yes" I said "because I am going to work for Uncle Sam and join the army." "Well," he says "you won't need no steel helmet." "No" I said "and you wouldn't either." Then he says "I'm afraid you won't last long over there because the first time they give you a hand grenade to throw you will take your wind up and loose a hand." So I said "If Chapman is a smart ball player why and the hell did he steal third base with 2 out?" He couldn't answer that but he says "What was you doing all alone out in No Mans Land on that ball of Speakers to Gandil?" So I told him to shut up and I went in the club house and when he come in I didn't speak to him or to none of the rest of them either.

Well Al I would quit right now and go up to Fort Sheridan and try for a captain only for Florrie and little Al and of course if it come to a show down Comiskey would ask me to stick on acct. of the club being in the race and it wouldn't be the square thing for me to walk out on him when he has got his heart set on the pennant. Your pal,   JACK.

Chicago, July 5

FRIEND AL: Just a few lines Al to tell you how Florrie is getting along and I bet you will be surprised to hear about it. Well Al she paid me back my $100.00 day before yesterday and she showed me their figures for the month of June and I don't know if you will beleive it or not but she and Miss Nevins cleared $400.00 for the month or $200.00 a peace over and above all expenses and she says the business will be even better in the fall and winter time on acct. of more people going to partys and theaters then. How is that for the kind of a wife to have Al and the best part of it is that she is stuck on the work and a whole lot happier then when she wasn't doing nothing. They got 2 girls working besides themself and they are talking about moveing into a bigger store somewheres and she says we will have to find a bigger flat so as we can have a nurse and a hired girl instead of just the one.

Tell Bertha about it Al and tell her that when she comes up to Chi

she can get all prettied up and I will see they don't charge her nothing
for it.

The clubs over in Detroit but it was only a 5 day trip so Rowland
left me home to rest up my arm for the eastren clubs and Phila. is due
here the day after tomorrow and all as I ask is a chance at them. My
arm don't feel just exactly right but I could roll the ball up to the plate
and beat that club.

Its a cinch now that the Giants is comeing through in the other league
and if we can keep going it will be some worlds serious between the 2
biggest towns in the country and the club that wins ought to grab off
about $4500.00 a peace per man. Is that worth going after Al? I'll
say so.   Your old pal,   JACK.

                                                      Chicago, July 20
FRIEND AL: Well Al I don't suppose you remember my draft number
and I don't remember if I told it to you or not. It was 3403 Al. And it
was the 5th number drawed at Washington.

Well old pal they can wipe the town of Washington off of the map
and you won't hear no holler from me. The day before yesterday Rowland sends me in against the Washington club and of course it had to
be Johnson for them. And I get beat 3 and 2 and I guess its the only
time this season that Washington scored 3 runs in 1 day. And the next
thing they announce the way the draft come out and I'm No. 5 and its
a misery to me why my number wasn't the 1st. they drawed out instead
of the 5th.

Well Al of course it don't mean I got to go if I don't want to. I can
get out of it easy enough by telling them about Florrie and little Al and
besides Gleason says they have promised Ban Johnson that they won't
take no baseball stars till the seasons over and maybe not then and
besides theys probably some White Sox fans that will go to the front
for me and get me off on acct. of the club being in the fight for the
pennant and they can't nobody say I'm trying to get excused because I
said all season that I would go in a minute if it wasn't for my family
and the club being in the race and I give $50.00 last week for a liberty
bond that will only bring me in $1.75 per annum which is nothing you
might say. You couldn't sport a flee on $1.75 per annum.

Florrie wanted I should go right down to the City Hall or where ever
it is you go and get myself excused but Gleason says the only thing to
do is just wait till they call me and then claim exemptions. I read somewheres a while ago that President Wilson wanted baseball kept up be-

cause the people would need amusement and I asked Gleason if he had read about that and he says "Yes but that won't get you nothing because the rest of the soldiers will need amusement even more than the people."

Well Al I don't know what your number was or how you come out but I hope you had better luck but if you did get drawed you will probably have a hard time getting out of it because you don't make no big salary and you got no children and Bertha could live with your mother and pick up a few dollars sowing. Enough to pay for her board and clothes. Of course they might excuse you for flat feet which they say you can't get in if you have them. But if I was you Al I would be tickled to death to get in because it would give you a chance to see something outside of Bedford and if your feet gets by you ought to be O. K.

I guess they won't find fault with my feet or anything about me as far physical goes. Hey Al?

I will write as soon as I learn anything.　　　　Your pal,　　JACK.

Chicago, Aug. 6

FRIEND AL: Well Al I got notice last Friday that I was to show up right away over to Wendell Phillips high school where No. 5 board of exemptions was setting but when I got over there it was jamed so I went back there today and I have just come home from there now.

The 1st. man I seen was the doctor and he took my name and number and then he asked me if my health was O. K. and I told him it was only I don't feel good after meals. Then he asked me if I was all sound and well right now so I told him my pitching arm was awful lame and that was the reason I hadn't went east with the club. Then he says "Do you understand that if a man don't tell the truth about themself here they are libel to prison?" So I said he didn't have to worry about that.

So then he made me strip bear and I wish you had seen his eyes pop out when he got a look at my shoulders and chest I stepped on the scales and tipped the bean at 194 and he measured me at 6 ft. 1 and a half. Then he went all over me and poked me with his finger and counted my teeth and finely he made me tell him what different letters was that he held up like I didn't know the alphabet or something. So when he was through he says "Well I guess you ain't going to die right away." He signed the paper and sent me to the room where the rest of the board was setting.

Well 1 of them looked up my number and then asked me did I claim exemptions. I told him yes and he asked me what grounds so I said "I sport a wife and baby and besides I don't feel like it would be a square deal to Comiskey for me to walk out on him now." So he says "Have you got an affidavit from your wife that you sport her?" So I told him no and he says "Go and get one and bring it back here tomorrow but you don't need to bring none from Comiskey." So you see Comiskey must stand pretty good with them.

So he give me a blank for Florrie to fill out and when she gets home we will go to a notary and tend to it and tomorrow they will fix up my excuse and then I won't have nothing to think about only to get the old souper in shape for the big finish.   Your pal,   JACK.

Chicago, Aug. 8

DEAR OLD PAL: Well old pal it would seem like the best way to get along in this world is to not try and get nowheres because the minute a man gets somewheres they's people that can't hardly wait to bite your back.

The 1st. thing yesterday I went over to No. 5 board and was going to show them Florrie's affidavit but while I was pulling it out of my pocket the man I seen the day before called me over to 1 side and says "Listen Keefe I am a White Sox fan and don't want to see you get none the worst of it and if I was you I would keep a hold of that paper." So I asked him what for and he says "Do you know what the law is about telling the truth and not telling the truth and if you turn in an affidavit thats false and we find it out you and who ever made the affidavit is both libel to prison?" So I said what was he trying to get at and he says "We got informations that your wife is in business for herself and making as high as $250.00 per month which is plenty for she and your boy to get along on." "Yes" I said "but who pays for the rent of our flat and the hired girl and what we eat?" So he says "That don't make no difference. Your wife could pay for them and that settles it."

Well Al I didn't know what to say for a minute but finely I asked him where the informations come from and he says he was tipped off in a letter that who ever wrote it didn't sign their name the sneaks and I asked him how he knowed that they was telling the truth. So he says "Its our business to look them things up. If I was you I wouldn't make no claim for exemptions but just lay quiet and take a chance."

Then all of a sudden I had an idea Al and I will tell you about it but 1st. as soon as it come to me I asked the man if this here board was all the board they was and he says no that if they would not excuse me I could appeal to the Dist. board but if he was me he wouldn't do it because it wouldn't do no good and might get me in trouble. So I said "I won't get in no trouble" and he says "All right suit yourself." So I said I would take the affadavit and go to the Dist. board but he says no that I would have to get passed on 1st. by his board and then I could appeal if I wanted to.

So I left the affadavit and he says they would notify me how I come out so then I beat it home and called up Florrie and told her they was something important and for her to come up to the flat.

Well Al here was the idea. I had been thinking for a long time that while it was all O. K. for Florrie to earn a little money in the summer when I was tied up with the club it would be a whole lot better if we was both free after the season so as we could take little Al and go on a trip somewheres or maybe spend the winter in the south but of course if she kept a hold of her share in the business she couldn't get away so the best thing would be to sell out to Miss Nevins for a good peace of money and we could maybe buy us a winter home somewheres with what she got and whats comeing to me in the worlds serious.

So when Florrie got home I put it up to her. I said "Florrie I'm sick in tired of haveing you tied up in business because it don't seem right for a married woman to be in business when their husbands in the big league and besides a womans place is home especially when they got a baby so I want you to sell out and when I get my split of the worlds serious we will go south somewheres and buy a home."

Well she asked me how did I come out with the affadavit. So I said "The affadavit is either here nor there. I am talking about something else" and she says "Yes you are." And she says "I been worring all day about that affadavit because if they find out about it what will they do to us." So I said "You should worry because if this board won't excuse me I will go to the Dist. board and mean while you won't be earning nothing because you will be out of business." Well Al she had a better idea then that. She says "No I will hold on to the business till you go to the Dist. board and then if they act like they wouldn't excuse you you can tell them I am going to sell out. And if they say all right I will sell out. But if they say its to late why then I will still have something to live on if you have to go."

So when she said that about me haveing to go we both choked up a little but pretty soon I was O. K. and now Al it looks like a cinch I would get my exemptions from the Dist. board because if Florrie says she wants to sell out they can't stop her.   Your pal,   JACK.

Chicago, Aug. 22

FRIEND AL: Well Al its all over. The Dist. board won't let me off and between you and I Al I am glad of it and I only hope I won't have to go before I have had a chance at the worlds serious.

My case come up about noon. One of the men asked me my name and then looked over what they had wrote down about me. Then he says "Theys an affadavit here that says your wife and child depends on you. Is that true?" So I said yes it was and he asked me if my wife was in business and I said yes but she was thinking about selling out. So he asked me how much money she made in her business. I said "You can't never tell. Some times its so much and other times different." So he asked me what the average was and I said it was about $250.00 per month. Then he says "Why is she going to sell out?" I said "Because we don't want to live in Chi all winter" and he said "You needn't to worry." Then he said "If she makes $250.00 per month how do you figure she is dependent on you?" So I said "Because she is because I pay for the rent and everything." And he asked me what she done with the $250.00 and I told him she spent it on clothes.

So he says "$250.00 per month on clothes. How does she keep warm this weather?" I said "I guess they don't nobody have no trouble keeping warm in August." Then he says "Look here Keefe this affadavit mitigates against you. We will have to turn down your appeal and I guess your wife can take care of herself and the boy." I said "She can't when she sells out." "Well" he said "you tell her not to sell out. It may be hard for her at first to sport herself and the boy on $250.00 but if the worst comes to the worst she can wear the same shoes twice and she will find them a whole lot more comfortable the second time." So I said "She don't never have no trouble with her feet and if she did I guess she knows how to fix them."

Florrie was waiting for me when I got home. "Well" I said "now you see what your dam beauty parlor has done for us." And then she seen what had happened and begin to cry and of course I couldn't find no more fault with her and I called up the ball park and told them I was sick and wouldn't show up this P. M. and I and Florrie and little Al stayed home together and talked. That is little Al done all the talking. I and Florrie didn't seem to have nothing to say.

Tomorrow I am going to tell them about it over to the ball park. If they can get me off till after the worlds serious all right. And if they can't all right to.   Your old pal,   JACK.

P. S. Washington comes tomorrow and I am going to ask Rowland to leave me pitch. The worst I can get is a tie. They scored a run in St. Louis yesterday and that means they are through for the week.

DEAR AL: Well Al the one that laughs last gets all the best of it. Wait
till you hear what come off today.

When I come in the club house Rowland and Gleason was there all
alone. I told them hello and was going to spring the news on them but
when Rowland seen me he says "Jack I got some bad news for you."
So I said what was it. So he says "The boss sold you to Washington
this morning."

Well Al at first I couldn't say nothing and I forgot all about that I
wanted to tell them. But then I remembered it again and here is what I
pulled. I said "Listen Manager I beat the boss to it." "What do you
mean?" he said so I said "I'm signed up with Washington all ready only
I ain't signed with Griffith but with Uncle Sam." Thats what I pulled
on them Al and they both got it right away. Gleason jumped up and
shook hands with me and so did Rowland and then Rowland said he
would have to hurry up in the office and tell the Old Man. "But wait
a minute" I said. "I am going to quit you after this game because I don't
know when I will be called and theys lots of things I got to fix up." So
I stopped and Rowland asked me what I wanted and I said "Let me
pitch this game and I will give them the beating of their life."

So him and Gleason looked at each other and then Rowland says
"You know we can't afford to loose no ball games now. But if you
think you can beat them I will start you."

So then he blowed and I and Gleason was alone.

"Well kid" he says "you make the rest of us look like a monkey.
This game ain't nothing compared to what you are going to do. And
when you come back they won't be nothing to good for you and your
kid will be proud of you because you went while a whole lot of other
kids dads stayed home."

So he patted me on the back and I kind of choked up and then the
trainer come in and I had him do a little work on my arm.

Well Al you will see in the paper what I done to them. Before the
game the boss had told Griffith about me and called the deal off. So
while I was warming up Griffith come over and shook hands. He says
"I would of like to had you but I am a good looser." So I says "You
ought to be." So he couldn't help from laughing but he says "When you
come back I will go after you again." I said "Well if you don't get
somebody on the club between now and then that can hit something
besides fouls I won't come back." So he kind of laughed again and
walked away and then it was time for the game.

Well Al the official scorer give them 3 hits but he must be McMullins brother in law or something because McMullin ought to of throwed Milan out from here to Berlin on that bunt. But any way 3 hits and no runs is pretty good for a finish and between you and I Al I feel like I got the last laugh on Washington and Rowland to.

Your pal,   JACK.

Chicago, Sept. 18

FRIEND AL: Just time for a few lines while Florrie finishs packing up my stuff. I leave with the bunch tomorrow A.M. for Camp Grant at Rockford. I don't know how long we will stay there but I suppose long enough to learn to talk German and shoot and etc.

We just put little Al to bed and tonight was the first time we told him I was going to war. He says "Can I go to daddy?" Hows that for a 3 year old Al?

Well he will be proud of me when I come back and he will be proud of me if I don't come back and when he gets older he can go up to the kids that belong to some of these lefthanders and say "Where and the hell was your father when the war come off?"

Good by Al and say good by to Bertha for me.

Your Pal,   JACK.

P. S. I won't be in the serious against New York but how about the real worlds serious Al? Won't I be in that? I'll say so.

ALONG CAME RUTH

FRIEND AL: Well Al this is our last day here and we win the 1st. 2 games and lose yesterday and have got one more game to play and tonight we leave for Detroit. Well if we lose today we will have a even break on the serious and a club that can't do no better then break even with this St. Louis club better take up some other line of business but Gleason instead of useing a little judgement sent a lefthander in against them yesterday and they certainly give him a welcome and the more I see of lefthanders I am certainly glad I pitch with my right arm the way God intended for a man.

Well the boys on our club was feeling pretty cocky the 1st. 2 days about how they could hit but yesterday they could of played in a 16 ft. ring without no ground rules as the most of the time they was missing the ball all together and when they did hit it it acted like a geyser and it was Bert Gallia pitching against us and they all kept saying he didn't have nothing but when he got through with us we didn't have nothing either and that's the way it always goes when a pitcher makes a sucker out of a club he didn't have nothing but when they knock him out of the park he's pretty good.

Well any way I told Gleason last night that it looked like we wouldn't get no better then a even break here unless he stuck me in there to pitch the last game today. So he says "No I was figureing on you to open up in Detroit Sunday but of course if you are afraid of Detroit I can make different plans." So I said "I am not afraid of Detroit or nobody else and you know yourself that they can't no club beat me the way I am going whether its Detroit or no matter who it is." So he said "All right then keep your mouth shut about who is going to pitch because if you are going to manage the club I won't have no job left." Well let him try and run the ball club the way he wants to but if I was running the ball club and had a pitcher that is going the way I am going I would work him every other day and get a start on the other clubs as the games we win now counts just as much as the games we win in Sept.

Well Al Florrie went back to Chi last night though I wanted her to stick with the club and go on to Detroit with us but she said she had to get back, and tend to business at the beauty parlor so I told Gleason

that and he said he was sorry she was going to leave us as it was a releif
for him to look at something pretty once in a wile when most of the
time he had to watch ball players but he admired her for tending to
business and he wished it run in the family. He says "You should ought
to be thankfull that your Mrs. is what she is as most wifes is a drug on
their husband but your Mrs. makes more jack then you and if she give
up her business it would keep you hustleing to make both ends meet
the other, where if you missed a meal some time and died from it your
family would be that much ahead." So I said "Yes and that is because
your cheapskate ball club is only paying me a salary of $2400.00 per
annum instead of somewheres near what I am worth." So he said "I
have all ready told you that if you keep working hard and show me
something I will tear up your contract and give you a good one but
before I do it I will half to find out if you are going to win ball games
for me or just use up 1 lower birth like in old times." So I told him to
shut his mouth.

Well Al I thought the war with Germany was all over but Joe Jenkins
joined the club here and now the whole war is being played over again.
He is 1 of the catchers on the club and he was in France and if they
was any battles he wasn't in its because he can't pronounce them but
anybody that thinks the U.S. troop movements was slow over there
ought to listen to some of these birds that's came back and some of
them was at Verdun 1 evening and Flanders the next A. M. then down
to Nice the next day for a couple hours rest and up in the Oregon forest
the folling afternoon and etc. till its no wonder the Germans was dazzled. If some of these birds that was in the war could get around the
bases like they did around the western front all as the catchers would
dast do when they started to steal second base would be walk up the
base line towards third with the ball in their hand and try to scare them
from comeing all the way home.

Well its Detroit tomorrow and 3 more days after that and then home
and I haven't been there since the middle of March and I guess they's
2 kids that won't be tickled to death to see somebody eh Al?

Your pal,   JACK.

Detroit, April 28
FRIEND AL: Well old pal I suppose you read in the papers what come
off here yesterday and I guess Gleason won't have no more to say after
this about me being afraid of Detroit. The shoe points the other way
now and Detroit is the one that's afraid of me and no wonder.

I didn't have the stuff that I had down to St. Louis for the opening but I had enough to make a monkey out of Cobb and Veach and I couldn't help from feeling sorry for this new outfielder they have got name Flagstaff or something and I guess he was about half mast before I got through with him.

Well its a cinch now that I will open in Chi Thursday and I will give St. Louis another spanking and then I will make Gleason come acrost with that contract he has been promiseing me and if he trys to stall I will tell him he must either give me the jack or trade me to some other club and he has got good sence even if he don't act like it sometimes and they's a fine chance of him tradeing me though they's 7 other clubs in this league that would jump at it and Detroit is 1 of them though the Detroit club would be takeing a big chance if they got a hold of somebody that could realy pitch as the fans up here would die from surprise.

Well I had a letter from Florrie today and it was just like the most of her letters when you got through reading it you wondered what she had in mind and about all as she said was that she had a surprise to tell me when I got home and I use to get all excited when she wrote about them surprises but now I can guess what it is. She probably seen a roach in the apartment or something and any way I guess I can wait till I get home and not burn up the wires trying to find out before hand.

Your pal,   JACK.

Detroit, April 30

FRIEND AL: Well Al we leave for home tonight and open up the season in Chi tomorrow but I won't be out there pitching unless Gleason apologizes for what he pulled on me last night. It was more rotten weather yesterday just like we been haveing ever since the 1st. day in St. Louis and I near froze to death setting out there on the bench so when we come back to the hotel they was a friend of mine here in Detroit waiting for me here in the lobby and he come up in the room with me and I was still shivering yet with the cold and he said how would I like something to warm me up. So I said "That's a fine line of talk to hand out in a dry town." So he said I could easy get a hold of some refreshments if I realy wanted some and all as I would half to do would be call a bell hop and tell him what I wanted.

Well I felt like a good shot would just about save my life so I called a boy and told him to go fetch me some bourbon and he said O. K. and he went out and come back in about a half hr. and he had a qt. with him and I asked him how much did we owe him and he said $15.00. How is that for reasonable Al and I guess it was the liquor men

themselfs that voted Michigan dry and you can't blame them. Well my
friend seemed to of had a stroke in his arm so as he couldn't even begin
to reach in his pocket so I dug down and got 15 berrys and handed it
to the kid and he still stood there yet like he expected a tip so I told
him to beat it or I would tip him 1 in the jaw.

Well I asked my friend would he have a shot and his arm was O. K.
again and he took the bottle and went to it without waiting for no glass
or nothing but he got the neck of the bottle caught in his teeth and
before he could pry it loose they was about a quarter of the bourbon
gone.

Well I was just going to pore some of it out for myself and all of a
sudden they come a rap at the door and I said come in and who walked
in but Gleason. So I asked him what did he want.

So he said "Well you wasn't the 1st. one in the dinning rm. so I
thought you must be pretty sick so I come up to see what was the
matter." Well it was to late to hide the bottle and he come over to the
table where I was setting and picked it up and looked at it and then he
pored out a couple drops in the glass and tasted it and said it tastes like
pretty good stuff. So I said it ought to be pretty good stuff as it cost
enough jack so he asked me how much and I told him $15.00.

So he said "Well they's some of the newspaper boys has been asking
me to try and get a hold of some stuff for them so I will just take this
along."

So I said I guest the newspaper boys could write crazy enough without no help from the Michigan boot legs and besides the bottle belongs
to me as I payed good money for it. So Gleason said "Oh I wouldn't
think of stealing it off of you but I will take it and pay you for it. You
say it cost $15.00 but they's only about $11.00 and a half worth of it
left so I will settle with you for $11.00 and a half." Well I didn't want
to quarrel with him in the front of a outsider so I didn't say nothing
and he took the bottle and started out of the rm. and I said hold on a
minute where is my $11.00 and a half? So he said "Oh I am going to
fine you $11.00 and a half for haveing liquor in your rm. but instead
of takeing the fine out of your check I will take what's left in the bottle
and that makes us even." So he walked out.

Well Al only for my friend being here in the rm. I would of took the
bottle away from Gleason and cracked his head open with it but I didn't
want to make no seen before a outsider as he might tell it around and
people would say the White Sox players was fighting with their mgr. So
I left Gleason get away with $11.00 and a half worth of bourbon that

I payed $15.00 for it and never tasted it and don't know now if it was bourbon or cat nip.

Well my friend said "What kind of a bird are you to let a little scrimp like that make a monkey out of you?" So I said I didn't want to make no seen in the hotel. So he said "Well if it had of been me I would of made a seen even if it was in church." So I says "Well they's no danger of you ever haveing a chance to make a seen in church and a specialy with Gleason but if you did make a seen with Gleason you would be in church 3 days later and have a box right up close to the front."

Well Al I have told Gleason before this all ready that I would stand for him manageing me out on the old ball field but I wouldn't stand for him trying to run my private affairs and this time I mean it and if he don't apologize this P. M. or tonight on the train he will be shy of a pitcher tomorrow and will half to open up the home season with 1 of them other 4 flushers that claims they are pitchers but if Jackson and Collins didn't hit in 7 or 8 runs every day they would be beating rugs in the stead of ball clubs.

Well any way we go home tonight and tomorrow I will be where it don't cost no $15.00 per qt. and if Gleason walks in on me he can't only rob me of $.20 worth at a time unless he operates.

Your pal,   JACK.

Chi., May 3

FRIEND AL: Well Al I have just now came back from the ball pk. and will set down and write you a few lines before supper. I give the St. Louis club another good trimming today Al and that is 3 games I have pitched and win them all and only 1 run scored off of me in all 3 games together and that was the 1 the St. Louis club got today and they wouldn't of never had that if Felsch had of been playing right for Tobin. But 1 run off of me in 3 games is going some and I should worry how many runs they scratch in as long as I win the ball game.

Well you know we was to open up here Thursday and it rained and we opened yesterday and I was waiting for Gleason to tell me I was going to pitch and then I was going to tell him I would pitch if he would apologize to me for what he done in Detroit but instead of picking me to pitch he picked Lefty Williams and the crowd was sore at him for not picking me and before the 1st inning was over he was sore at himself and Lefty was enjoying the shower bath. Gallia give us another beating and after it was over Gleason come up to me in the club house and said he was going to start me today. So I said "How about what you pulled on me in Detroit?" So he says "Do you mean about grabbing that bottle off of you?" So I said yes and he says "Look at here Jack you have got a great chance to get somewheres this yr. and if you keep on pitching like the way you started you will make a name for yourself and I will see that you get the jack. But you can't do it and be stewed all the wile so that is the reason I took that bottle off of you." So I said "They's no danger of me being stewed all the wile or any part of the wile when bourbon is $15.00 per qt. and me getting a bat boy's salery." So he said "Well you lay off the old burb and pitch baseball and you won't be getting no bat boy's salary. And besides I have told the newspaper boys that you are going to pitch and it will be in the morning papers and if you don't pitch the bugs will jump out of the stand and knock me for a gool." So as long as he put it up to me that way I couldn't do nothing only say all right.

So sure enough it come out in the papers this A. M. that I was going to pitch and you ought to seen the crowd out there today Al and you ought to heard them when my name was gave out to pitch and when I walked out there on the field. Well I got away to a bad start you might say as Felsch wasn't laying right for Tobin and he got a two base hit on a ball that Felsch ought to of caught in his eye and then after I got rid of Gedeon this Sisler hit at a ball he couldn't hardly reach and it dropped over third base and Tobin scored and after that I made a monkey out of them and the 1st. time I come up to bat the fans give me a traveling bag and I suppose they think I have been running around the country all these yrs. with my night gown in a peach basket but I suppose we can give it to 1 of Florrie's friends next xmas and besides it shows the fans of old Chi have got a warm spot for old Jack.

Speaking about Florrie Al when we was in Detroit she wrote and said she had a surprise for me and I thought little Al had picked up a couple hives or something but no it seems like wile I was on the road she met some partys that runs a beauty parlor down town and they wanted she should sell her interest in the one out south and go in pardners with them and they would give her a third interest for $3000.00 and pay her a salery of $300.00 per mo. and a share of the receits and she could pay for her interest on payments. So she asked me what I thought about it and I said if I was her I would stick to what she had where she was makeing so good but no matter what I thought she would do like she felt like so what was the use of asking me so she said she didn't like to make a move without consulting me. That's a good one Al as the only move she ever made and did consult me about it was when we got married and then it wouldn't of made no differents to her what I said.

Well she will do as she pleases and if she goes into this here down town parlor and gets stung we should worry as I will soon be getting real jack and it looks like a cinch we would be in the world serious besides, and besides that the kids would be better off if she was out of business and could be home with them more as the way it is now they don't hardly ever see anybody only the Swede nurse and 1st. thing as we know they will be saying I ban this and I ban that and staying away from the bldg. all the wile like the janitor.   Your pal,   JACK.

Chi, May 6

FRIEND AL: 4 straight now Al. How is that for a way to start out the season? It was Detroit again today and that is twice I have beat them and twice I have beat St. Louis and it don't look like I was never going to stop. They got 2 runs off of me today but it was after we had 7 and had them licked and I kind of eased up to save the old souper for the Cleveland serious. But I wished you could of heard the 1 I pulled on Cobb. You know I have always kind of had him on the run ever since I come in the league and he would as leaf have falling archs as see me walk out there to pitch.

Well the 1st. time he come up they was 2 out and no one on and I had him 2 strikes and nothing and in place of monking with him I stuck a fast one right through the groove and he took it for a third strike. Well he come up again in the 4th. inning and little Bush was on third base and 1 out and Cobb hit the 1st. ball and hit it pretty good towards left field but Weaver jumped up and stabbed it with his glove hand and then stepped on third base and the side was out. Well Cobb hollered at me and said "You didn't put that strike acrost on me." So I said "No why should I put strikes acrost on you when I can hit your bat and get 2 out at a time?" You ought to of heard the boys give him the laugh.

Well he hit one for 3 bases in the 7th. inning with Bush and Ellison both on and that's how they got their 2 runs but he wouldn't of never hit the ball only I eased up on acct. of the lead we had and besides I felt sorry for him on acct. of the way the crowd was rideing him. So wile he was standing over there on third base I said "You wouldn't of hit that one Ty only I eased up." So he said "Yes I knew you was easing up and I wouldn't take advantage of you so that's why I bunted."

Well 1 more game with Detroit and then we go down to Cleveland and visit Mr. Speaker and the rest of the boys and Speaker hasn't been going any to good against them barbers that's supposed to pitch for Detroit and St. Louis so God help him when he runs up against Williams and Cicotte and I.   Your pal,   JACK.

Cleveland, May 9
FRIEND AL: Well Gleason told me today he wasn't going to pitch me here till the Sunday game to get the crowd. We have broke even on the 2 games so far and ought to of win them both only for bad pitching but we can't expect to win them all and you really can't blame the boys for not pitching baseball when we run into weather like we have got down here and it seems like every place we go its colder then where we just come from and I have heard about people going crazy with the heat but we will all be crazy with the cold if it keeps up like this way and Speaker was down to our hotel last night and said the Cleveland club had a couple of bushers from the Southern league that's all ready lost their mind and he told us what they pulled off wile the St. Louis club was here.

Well it seems like Cleveland was beat to death 1 day and they thought they would give some of the regulars a rest and they put in a young catcher name Drew and the 1st. time he come up to bat they was men on first and second and 1 out and Sothoron was pitching for St. Louis and 1 of the St. Louis infielders yelled at him "Don't worry about this bird as he will hit into a double play." Well Drew stood up there and took 3 strikes without never takeing the bat off his shoulder so then he come back to the bench and said "Well I crossed them on their double play."

Well in another game Bagby was pitching and he had them licked 8 to 1 in the 7th inning and he had a bad finger so they took him out and sent in a busher name Francis to finish the game. Well he got through 1 inning and when he come up to hit they was a man on 3d. base and 2 out and Davenport was pitching for St. Louis and he was kind of wild and he throwed 3 balls to Francis. So then he throwed a strike and Francis took it and then he throwed one that was over the kid's head but he took a cut at it and hit it over Tobin's head and made 3 bases on it. So when the inning was over Larry Gardner heard him calling himself names and balling himself out and Larry asked him what was the matter and he said he was just thinking that if he had of left that ball go by he would of had a base on balls.

Well I had a letter from Florrie today and she has closed up that deal and sold out her interest in the place out near home and went in pardners in that place down town and she said she thought it was a wise move and she would clean up a big bunch of jack and it won't only take her a little wile to pay for her interest in the new parlor as with what she had saved up and what she got out of the other joint she had over $2000.00 cash to start in with.

Well I don't know who her new pardners is but between you and I it looks to me like she was pulling a boner to leave a place where she knew her pardners was friends and go into pardners with a couple women that's probably old hands at the game and maybe wanted some new capital or something and are libel to get her role and then can her out of the firm but as I say they's no use me trying to tell her what to do and I might just is well tell Gleason to take Collins off of second base and send for Jakey Atz.

Well Al nothing to do till Sunday and if I beat them it will make me 5 straight and you can bet I will beat them Al as I am going like a crazy man and they can't no club stop me.   Your pal,   JACK.

                                                        Chi, May 12
FRIEND AL: Well old pal its kind of late to be setting up writeing a letter but I had a little run in with Florrie tonight and I don't feel like I could go to sleep and besides I don't half to work tomorrow as I win yesterday's game in Cleveland and Gleason is saveing me for the Boston serious.

Well we got in from Cleveland early this A. M. and of course I hurried right home and I was here before 8 o'clock but the Swede said Florrie had left home before 7 as she didn't want to be late on the new job and she would call me up dureing the forenoon. Well it got pretty near time to start over to the ball pk. before the phone rung and it was Florrie and I asked her if she wasn't going to congratulate me and she says what for and I said for what I done in Cleveland yesterday and she said she hadn't had time to look at the paper. So I told her I had win my 5th straight game and she acted about as interested as if I said we had a new mail man so I got kind of sore and told her I would half to hang up and go over to the ball pk. She said she would see me at supper and we hung up.

Well we had a long game this P. M. and it seemed longer on acct. of how anxious I was to get back home and when I finely got here it was half past 6 and no Florrie. Well the Swede said she had called up and said she had to stay down town and have supper with some business friends and she would try and be home early this evening.

Well the kids was put in bed and I tried to set down and eat supper alone and they didn't nothing taste right and finaly I give it up and put on my hat and went out and went in a picture show but it was as old as Pat and Mike so I blew it and went in Kramer's to get a couple drinks but I had kind of promised Gleason to lay off of the hard stuff and you take the beer you get now days and its cheaper to stay home and draw it out of the sink so I come back here and it was 8 bells and. still no Florrie.

Well I set down and picked up the evening paper and all of a sudden the phone rung and it was a man's voice and he wanted to know if Mrs. Keefe had got home. So I done some quick thinking and I said "Yes she is here who wants her?" So he said "That's all right. I just wanted to know if she got home O. K." So I said who is it but he had hung up. Well I rung central right back and asked her where that party had called from and she said she didn't know and I asked her what and the he—ll she did know and she begun to play some jazz on my ear drum so I hung up.

Well in about 10 minutes more Florrie come in and come running over to give me a smack like usual when I get back off a trip. But she didn't get by with it. So she asked what was the matter. So I said "They's nothing the matter only they was a bird called up here a wile ago and wanted to know if you was home." So she says "Well what of it?" So I said "I suppose he was 1 of them business friends that you had to stay down town to supper with them." So she said "Maybe he was." So I said "Well you ought to know if he was or not." So she says "Do you think I can tell you who all the people are that calls me up when I haven't even heard their voice? I don't even know a one of the girls that keeps calling up and asking for you." So I said "They don't no gals call up here and ask for me because they have got better sence but even if they did I couldn't help it as they see me out there on the ball field and want to get aquainted."

Then she swelled up and says "It may be hard for you to believe but there is actually men that want to get aquainted with me even if they never did see me out there on the ball field." So I said "You tell me who this bird is that called up on the phone." So she said "I thought they was only the 2 babys in this apartment but it seems like there is 3." So then she went in her rm. and shut the door.

Well Al that's the way it stands and if it wasn't for the kiddies I would pack up and move somewheres else but kiddies or no kiddies she has got to explain herself tomorrow morning and meanwile Al you should ought to thank God that you married a woman that isn't flighty and what if a wife ain't the best looker in the world if she has got something under her hat besides marcel wavers?   Your pal,   JACK.

Chi, May 14

FRIEND AL: Well old pal it looks like your old pal was through working
for nothing you might say and by tomorrow night I will be signed up
to a new contract calling for a $600.00 raise or $3000.00 per annum.
I guess I have all ready told you that Gleason promised to see that I got
real jack provide it I showed I wasn't no flash out of the pan and this
noon we come to a definite understanding.

We was to open against the Boston club and I called him to 1 side
in the club house and asked him if I was to pitch the game. So he says
you can suit yourself. So I asked him what he meant and he said "I am
going to give you a chance to get real money. If you win your game
against the Boston club I will tear up your old contract and give you a
contract for $3000.00. And you can pick your own spot. You can work
against them today or you can work against them tomorrow just as you
feel like. They will probably pitch Mays against us today and Ruth
tomorrow and you can take your choice." Well Al Mays has always
been good against our club and besides my old souper is better this kind
of weather the longer I give it a rest so after I though it over I said I
would wait and pitch against Ruth tomorrow. So tomorrow is my big
day and you know what I will do to them old pal and if the boys only
gets 1 run behind me that is all as I ask.

That's all we got today Al was 1 run but Eddie Cicotte was in there
with everything and the 1 run was a plenty. They was only 1 time when
they had a chance and it looked that time like they couldn't hardly help
from scoreing but Eddie hates to beat this Boston club on acct. they
canned him once and he certainly give a exhibition in there that I would
of been proud of myself. This inning I am speaking of Scott got on and
Schang layed down a bunt and Eddie tried to force Scott at second base
but he throwed bad and the ball went to center field and Scott got
around to third and Schang to second and they wasn't nobody out. Well
Mays hit a fly ball to Jackson but it was so short that Scott didn't dast
go in. Then Hooper popped up to Collins and Barry hit the 1st. ball
and fouled out to Schalkie. Some pitching eh Al and that is the kind I
will show them tomorrow. And another thing Eddie done was make a
monkey out of Ruth and struck him out twice and they claim he is a
great hitter Al but all you half to do is pitch right to him and pitch the
ball anywheres but where he can get a good cut at it.

Well they never had another look in against Eddie and we got a run
when Barry booted one on Collins and Jackson plastered one out between Ruth and Strunk for 2 bases.

Well Al I am feeling pretty good again as I and Florrie kind of made up our quarrel last night. She come home to supper and I was still acting kind of cross and she asked me if I was still mopping over that bird that called her up and I didn't say nothing so she said "Well that was a man that was the husband of 1 of the girls I had supper with and he was there to and him and his wife wanted to bring me home but I told them I didn't want nobody to bring me home so his wife probably told him to call up and see if I got home all right as they was worried." So she asked me if I was satisfied and I said I guessed I was but why couldn't she of told me that in the 1st. place and she said because she liked to see me jealous. Well I left her think I was jealous but between you and I it was just a kind of a kid on my part as of course I knew all the wile that she was O. K. only I wanted to make her give in and I knew she would if I just held out and pretended like I was sore. Make them come to you Al is the way to get along with them.

I haven't told Florrie what this game tomorrow means to us as I want to surprise her and if I win I will take her out somewheres on a party tomorrow night. And now old pal I must get to bed as I want to get a good rest before I tackle those birds. Oh you $600.00 baseball game.   Your pal,   JACK.

Chi, May 16

FRIEND AL: Well Al I don't care if school keeps or not and all as I wish is that I could get the flu or something and make a end out of it. I have quit the ball club Al and I have quit home and if I ever go back again to baseball it depends on whether I will have my kiddies to work for or whether they will be warded to her.

It all happened yesterday Al and I better start at the start and tell you what come off. Florrie had eat her breakfast and went down town before I got up but she left word with the ski jumper that she was going to try and get out to the ball game and maybe bring the rest of her pardners with her and show me off to them.

Well to make it a short story I was out to the pk. early and Gleason asked me how I felt and I told him fine and I certainly did Al and Danforth was working against us in batting practice to get us use to a lefthander and I was certainly slapping the ball on the pick and Gleason said it looked like I was figureing on winning my own game. Well we got through our batting practice and I looked up to where Florrie usualy sets right in back of our bench but she wasn't there but after a wile it come time for me to warm up and I looked over and Ruth was warming up for them so then I looked up in the stand again and there was Florrie. She was just setting down Al and she wasn't alone.

Well Al I had to look up there twice to make sure I wasn't looking cock eyed. But no I was seeing just what was there and what I seen was she and a man with her if that's what you want to call him.

Well I guess I couldn't of throwed more than 4 or 5 balls when I couldn't stand it no more so I told Lynn to wait a minute and Gleason was busy hitting to the infield so I snuck out under the bench and under the stand and I seen 1 of the ushers and sent word up to Florrie to come down a minute as I wanted to see her. Well I waited and finely she come down and we come to the pt. without waisting no time. I asked her to explain herself and do it quick. So she said "You needn't act so crazy as they's nothing to explain. I said I was going to bring my pardner out here and the gentleman with me is him." "Your pardner" I said "What does a man do in a beauty parlor?" "Well" she said "This man happens to do a whole lot.

"Besides owning two thirds of the business he is 1 of the best artists in the world on quaffs." Well I asked her what and the he—ll was quaffs and she said it meant fixing lady's hair.

Well by this time Gleason had found out I wasn't warming up and sent out to find me. So all as I had time to say was to tell her she better get that bird out of the stand before I come up there and quaffed him in the jaw. Then I had to leave her and go back on the field.

Well I throwed about a dozen more balls to Lynn and then I couldn't throw no more and Gleason come over and asked me what was the matter and I told him nothing so he said "Are you warmed up enough?" and I said "I should say I am."

Well Al to make it a short story pretty soon our names was announced to pitch and I walked out there on the field.

Well when I was throwing them practice balls to Schalk I didn't know if he was behind the plate or up in Comiskey's office and when Hooper stepped in the batters box I seen a dozen of him. Well I don't know what was signed for but I throwed something up there and Hooper hit it to right field for 2 bases. Then I throwed something else to Barry and he cracked it out to Jackson on the 1st. hop so fast that Hooper couldn't only get to third base. Well wile Strunk was up there I guess I must of looked up in the stand again and any way the ball I pitched come closer to the barber then it did to Strunk and before they got it back in the game Hooper had scored and Barry was on third base.

Then Schalkie come running out and asked me what was the matter so I said I didn't know but I thought they was getting our signs. "Well" he said "you certainly crossed them on that one as I didn't sign you for no bench ball." Then he looked over at Gleason to have me took out but Gleason hollered "Let him stay in there and see what kind of a money pitcher he is."

Well Al I didn't get one anywheres near close for Strunk and walked him and it was Ruth's turn. The next thing I seen of the ball it was sailing into the right field bleachers where the black birds sets. And that's all I seen of the ball game.

Well old pal I didn't stop to look up in the stand on the way out and I don't remember changing clothes or nothing but I know I must of rode straight down town and when I woke up this A. M. I was still down town and I haven't called up home or the ball pk. or nowheres else and as far as I am concerned I am through with the both of them as a man can't pitch baseball and have any home life and a man can't have the kind of home life I have got and pitch baseball.

All that worrys me is the kiddies and what will become of them if they don't ward them to me. And another thing I would like to know is who put me to bed in this hotel last night as who ever undressed me forgot to take off my clothes.   Your pal,   JACK.

                                                          Chi, May 20
FRIEND AL: Well Al I am writeing this from home and that means that everything is O. K. again as I decided to give in and let bygones be bygones for the kiddies sake and besides I found out that this bird that Florrie is pardners with him is O. K. and got a Mrs. of his own and she works down there with him and Florrie is cleaning up more jack then she could of ever made in the old parlor out south so as long as she is makeing good and everything is O. K. why they would be no sence in me makeing things unpleasant.

Well I told you about me staying down town 1 night and I stayed down till late the next P. M and finely I called up the Swede and told her to pack up my things as I was comeing out there the next day and get them. Well the Swede said that Gleason had been there the night before looking for me and he left word that I was to call him up at the ball pk. So I thought maybe he might have a letter out there for me or something or maybe I could persuade him to trade me to some other club so I called him up and just got him before he left the pk. and he asked me where I was at and said he wanted to see me so I give him the name of the hotel where I was stopping and he come down and met me there at 6 o'clock that night.

"Well" he says "I was over to see your little wife last night and I have got a notion to bust you in the jaw." So I asked him what he meant and he said "She sported your kids wile you was in the war and she is doing more than you to sport them now and she goes in pardners with a man that's O. K. and has got a wife of his own that works with him and you act like a big sap and make her cry and pretty near force her out of a good business and all for nothing except that you was born a busher and can't get over it."

So I said to him "You mind your own business and keep out of my business and trade me to some ball club where I can get a square deal and we will all get along a hole lot better." So he said where did I want to be traded and I said Boston. "Oh no" he said. "I would trade you to Boston in a minute only Babe Ruth wouldn't stand for it as he likes to have you on our club." But he said "The 1st. thing is what are you going to do about your family?" So I said I would go back to my family if Florrie would get out of that down town barber shop. So Gleason said "Now listen you are going back home right now tonight and your Mrs. isn't going to sacrifice her business neither." So I said "You can't make me do nothing I don't want to do." So he says "No I can't make you but I can tell your Mrs. about that St. Louis janitor's daughter that was down in Texas and then if she wants to get rid of you she can do it and be better off."

Well Al I thought as long as Florrie was all rapped up in this new business it wasn't right to make her drop it and pull out and besides there was the kiddies to be considered so I decided to not make no trouble. So I promised Gleason to go home that night.

So then I asked him about the ball club. "Well," he said "you still belong to us." "Yes" I said "but I can't work for no $2400.00."

"Well" he said "we are scheduled against a club now that hasn't no Ruths on it and its a club that even you should ought to beat and if you want to try it again why I will leave you pick your day to work against the Philadelphia club and the same bet goes."

So yesterday was the day I picked Al and Roth got a base hit and Burns got a base hit and that's all the base hits they got and the only 2 runs we got I drove in myself. But they was worth $600.00 to me Al and I guess Gleason knows now what kind of a money pitcher I am.

Your pal,   JACK.

ALIBI IKE

I

His right name was Frank X. Farrell, and I guess the X stood for "Excuse me." Because he never pulled a play, good or bad, on or off the field, without apologizin' for it.

"Alibi Ike" was the name Carey wished on him the first day he reported down South. O' course we all cut out the "Alibi" part of it right away for the fear he would overhear it and bust somebody. But we called him "Ike" right to his face and the rest of it was understood by everybody on the club except Ike himself.

He ast me one time, he says:

"What do you all call me Ike for? I ain't no Yid."

"Carey give you the name," I says. "It's his nickname for everybody he takes a likin' to."

"He mustn't have only a few friends then," says Ike. "I never heard him say 'Ike' to nobody else."

But I was goin' to tell you about Carey namin' him. We'd been workin' out two weeks and the pitchers was showin' somethin' when this bird joined us. His first day out he stood up there so good and took such a reef at the old pill that he had everyone lookin'. Then him and Carey was together in left field, catchin' fungoes, and it was after we was through for the day that Carey told me about him.

"What do you think of Alibi Ike?" ast Carey.

"Who's that?" I says.

"This here Farrell in the outfield," says Carey.

"He looks like he could hit," I says.

"Yes," says Carey, "but he can't hit near as good as he can apologize."

Then Carey went on to tell me what Ike had been pullin' out there. He'd dropped the first fly ball that was hit to him and told Carey his glove wasn't broke in good yet, and Carey says the glove could easy of been Kid Gleason's gran'father. He made a whale of a catch out o' the next one and Carey says "Nice work!" or somethin' like that, but Ike says he could of caught the ball with his back turned only he slipped when he started after it and, besides that, the air currents fooled him.

142

"I thought you done well to get to the ball," says Carey.

"I ought to been settin' under it," says Ike.

"What did you hit last year?" Carey ast him.

"I had malaria most o' the season," says Ike. "I wound up with .356."

"Where would I have to go to get malaria?" says Carey, but Ike didn't wise up.

I and Carey and him set at the same table together for supper. It took him half an hour longer'n us to eat because he had to excuse himself every time he lifted his fork.

"Doctor told me I needed starch," he'd say, and then toss a shoveful o' potatoes into him. Or, "They ain't much meat on one o' these chops," he'd tell us, and grab another one. Or he'd say: "Nothin' like onions for a cold," and then he'd dip into the perfumery.

"Better try that apple sauce," says Carey. "It'll help your malaria."

"Whose malaria?" says Ike. He'd forgot already why he didn't only hit .356 last year.

I and Carey begin to lead him on.

"Whereabouts did you say your home was?" I ast him.

"I live with my folks," he says. "We live in Kansas City—not right down in the business part—outside a ways."

"How's that come?" says Carey. "I should think you'd get rooms in the post office."

But Ike was too busy curin' his cold to get that one.

"Are you married?" I ast him.

"No," he says. "I never run round much with girls, except to shows onct in a wile and parties and dances and roller skatin'."

"Never take 'em to the prize fights, eh?" says Carey.

"We don't have no real good bouts," says Ike. "Just bush stuff. And I never figured a boxin' match was a place for the ladies."

Well, after supper he pulled a cigar out and lit it. I was just goin' to ask him what he done it for, but he beat me to it.

"Kind o' rests a man to smoke after a good workout," he says. "Kind o' settles a man's supper, too."

"Looks like a pretty good cigar," says Carey.

"Yes," says Ike. "A friend o' mine give it to me—a fella in Kansas City that runs a billiard room."

"Do you play billiards?" I ast him.

"I used to play a fair game," he says. "I'm all out o' practice now—can't hardly make a shot."

We coaxed him into a four-handed battle, him and Carey against

Jack Mack and I. Say, he couldn't play billiards as good as Willie Hoppe; not quite. But to hear him tell it, he didn't make a good shot all evenin'. I'd leave him an awful-lookin' layout and he'd gather 'em up in one try and then run a couple o' hundred, and between every carom he'd say he'd put too much stuff on the ball, or the English didn't take, or the table wasn't true, or his stick was crooked, or somethin'. And all the time he had the balls actin' like they was Dutch soldiers and him Kaiser William. We started out to play fifty points, but we had to make it a thousand so as I and Jack and Carey could try the table.

The four of us set round the lobby a wile after we was through playin', and when it got along toward bedtime Carey whispered to me and says:

"Ike'd like to go to bed, but he can't think up no excuse."

Carey hadn't hardly finished whisperin' when Ike got up and pulled it:

"Well, good night, boys," he says. "I ain't sleepy, but I got some gravel in my shoes and it's killin' my feet."

We knowed he hadn't never left the hotel since we'd came in from the grounds and changed our clo'es. So Carey says:

"I should think they'd take them gravel pits out o' the billiard room."

But Ike was already on his way to the elevator, limpin'.

"He's got the world beat," says Carey to Jack and I. "I've knew lots o' guys that had an alibi for every mistake they made; I've heard pitchers say that the ball slipped when somebody cracked one off'n 'em; I've heard infielders complain of a sore arm after heavin' one into the stand, and I've saw outfielders tooken sick with a dizzy spell when they've misjudged a fly ball. But this baby can't even go to bed without apologizin', and I bet he excuses himself to the razor when he gets ready to shave."

"And at that," says Jack, "he's goin' to make us a good man."

"Yes," says Carey, "unless rheumatism keeps his battin' average down to .400."

Well, sir, Ike kept whalin' away at the ball all through the trip till everybody knowed he'd won a job. Cap had him in there regular the last few exhibition games and told the newspaper boys a week before the season opened that he was goin' to start him in Kane's place.

"You're there, kid," says Carey to Ike, the night Cap made the 'nnouncement. "They ain't many boys that wins a big league berth their third year out."

"I'd of been up here a year ago," says Ike, "only I was bent over all season with lumbago."

II

It rained down in Cincinnati one day and somebody organized a little game o' cards. They was shy two men to make six and ast I and Carey to play.

"I'm with you if you get Ike and make it seven-handed," says Carey.

So they got a hold of Ike and we went up to Smitty's room.

"I pretty near forgot how many you deal," says Ike. "It's been a long wile since I played."

I and Carey give each other the wink, and sure enough, he was just as ig'orant about poker as billiards. About the second hand, the pot was opened two or three ahead of him, and they was three in when it come his turn. It cost a buck, and he throwed in two.

"It's raised, boys," somebody says.

"Gosh, that's right, I did raise it," says Ike.

"Take out a buck if you didn't meant to tilt her," says Carey.

"No," says Ike, "I'll leave it go."

Well, it was raised back at him and then he made another mistake and raised again. They was only three left in when the draw come. Smitty'd opened with a pair o' kings and he didn't help 'em. Ike stood pat. The guy that'd raised him back was flushin' and he didn't fill. So Smitty checked and Ike bet and didn't get no call. He tossed his hand away, but I grabbed it and give it a look. He had king, queen, jack and two tens. Alibi Ike he must have seen me peekin', for he leaned over and whispered to me.

"I overlooked my hand," he says. "I thought all the wile it was a straight."

"Yes," I says, "that's why you raised twice by mistake."

They was another pot that he come into with tens and fours. It was tilted a couple o' times and two o' the strong fellas drawed ahead of Ike. They each drawed one. So Ike throwed away his little pair and come out with four tens. And they was four treys against him. Carey'd looked at Ike's discards and then he says:

"This lucky bum busted two pair."

"No, no, I didn't," says Ike.

"Yes, yes, you did," says Carey, and showed us the two fours.

"What do you know about that?" says Ike. "I'd of swore one was a five spot."

Well, we hadn't had no pay day yet, and after a wile everybody except Ike was goin' shy. I could see him gettin' restless and I was wonderin' how he'd make the get-away. He tried two or three times. "I got to buy some collars before supper," he says.

"No hurry," says Smitty. "The stores here keeps open all night in April."

After a minute he opened up again.

"My uncle out in Nebraska ain't expected to live," he says. "I ought to send a telegram."

"Would that save him?" says Carey.

"No, it sure wouldn't," says Ike, "but I ought to leave my old man know where I'm at."

"When did you hear about your uncle?" says Carey.

"Just this mornin'," says Ike.

"Who told you?" ast Carey.

"I got a wire from my old man," says Ike.

"Well," says Carey, "your old man knows you're still here yet this afternoon if you was here this mornin'. Trains leavin' Cincinnati in the middle o' the day don't carry no ball clubs."

"Yes," says Ike, "that's true. But he don't know where I'm goin' to be next week."

"Ain't he got no schedule?" ast Carey.

"I sent him one openin' day," says Ike, "but it takes mail a long time to get to Idaho."

"I thought your old man lived in Kansas City," says Carey.

"He does when he's home," says Ike.

"But now," says Carey, "I s'pose he's went to Idaho so as he can be near your sick uncle in Nebraska."

"He's visitin' my other uncle in Idaho."

"Then how does he keep posted about your sick uncle?" ast Carey.

"He don't," says Ike. "He don't even know my other uncle's sick. That's why I ought to wire and tell him."

"Good night!" says Carey.

"What town in Idaho is your old man at?" I says.

Ike thought it over.

"No town at all," he says. "But he's near a town."

"Near what town?" I says.

"Yuma," says Ike.

Well, by this time he'd lost two or three pots and he was desperate. We was playin' just as fast as we could, because we seen we couldn't hold him much longer. But he was tryin' so hard to frame an escape that he couldn't pay no attention to the cards, and it looked like we'd get his whole pile away from him if we could make him stick.

The telephone saved him. The minute it begun to ring, five of us jumped for it. But Ike was there first.

"Yes," he says, answerin' it. "This is him. I'll come right down."

And he slammed up the receiver and beat it out o' the door without even sayin' good-by.

"Smitty'd ought to locked the door," says Carey.

"What did he win?" ast Carey.

We figured it up—sixty-odd bucks.

"And the next time we ask him to play," says Carey, "his fingers will be so stiff he can't hold the cards."

Well, we set round a wile talkin' it over, and pretty soon the telephone rung again. Smitty answered it. It was a friend of his'n from Hamilton and he wanted to know why Smitty didn't hurry down. He was the one that had called before and Ike had told him he was Smitty.

"Ike'd ought to split with Smitty's friend," says Carey.

"No," I says, "he'll need all he won. It costs money to buy collars and to send telegrams from Cincinnati to your old man in Texas and keep him posted on the health o' your uncle in Cedar Rapids, D. C."

III

And you ought to heard him out there on that field! They wasn't a day when he didn't pull six or seven, and it didn't make no difference whether he was goin' good or bad. If he popped up in the pinch he should of made a base hit and the reason he didn't was so-and-so. And if he cracked one for three bases he ought to had a home run, only the ball wasn't lively, or the wind brought it back, or he tripped on a lump o' dirt, roundin' first base.

They was one afternoon in New York when he beat all records. Big Marquard was workin' against us and he was good.

In the first innin' Ike hit one clear over that right field stand, but it was a few feet foul. Then he got another foul and then the count come to two and two. Then Rube slipped one acrost on him and he was called out.

"What do you know about that!" he says afterward on the bench. "I lost count. I thought it was three and one, and I took a strike."

"You took a strike all right," says Carey. "Even the umps knowed it was a strike."

"Yes," says Ike, "but you can bet I wouldn't of took it if I'd knew it was the third one. The score board had it wrong."

"That score board ain't for you to look at," says Cap. "It's for you to hit that old pill against."

"Well," says Ike, "I could of hit that one over the score board if I'd knew it was the third."

"Was it a good ball?" I says.

"Well, no, it wasn't," says Ike. "It was inside."

"How far inside?" says Carey.

"Oh, two or three inches or half a foot," says Ike.

"I guess you wouldn't of threatened the score board with it then," says Cap.

"I'd of pulled it down the right foul line if I hadn't thought he'd call it a ball," says Ike.

Well, in New York's part o' the innin' Doyle cracked one and Ike run back a mile and a half and caught it with one hand. We was all sayin' what a whale of a play it was, but he had to apologize just the same as for gettin' struck out.

"That stand's so high," he says, "that a man don't never see a ball till it's right on top o' you."

"Didn't you see that one?" ast Cap.

"Not at first," says Ike; "not till it raised up above the roof o' the stand."

"Then why did you start back as soon as the ball was hit?" says Cap.

"I knowed by the sound that he'd got a good hold of it," says Ike.

"Yes," says Cap, "but how'd you know what direction to run in?"

"Doyle usually hits 'em that way, the way I run," says Ike.

"Why don't you play blindfolded?" says Carey.

"Might as well, with that big high stand to bother a man," says Ike. "If I could of saw the ball all the time I'd of got it in my hip pocket."

Along in the fifth we was one run to the bad and Ike got on with one out. On the first ball throwed to Smitty, Ike went down. The ball was outside and Meyers throwed Ike out by ten feet.

You could see Ike's lips movin' all the way to the bench and when he got there he had his piece learned.

"Why didn't he swing?" he says.

"Why didn't you wait for his sign?" says Cap.

"He give me his sign," says Ike.

"What is his sign with you?" says Cap.

"Pickin' up some dirt with his right hand," says Ike.

"Well, I didn't see him do it," Cap says.

"He done it all right," says Ike.

Well, Smitty went out and they wasn't no more argument till they come in for the next innin'. Then Cap opened it up.

"You fellas better get your signs straight," he says.

"Do you mean me?" says Smitty.

"Yes," Cap says. "What's your sign with Ike?"

"Slidin' my left hand up to the end o' the bat and back," says Smitty.

"Do you hear that, Ike?" ast Cap.

"What of it?" says Ike.

"You says his sign was pickin' up dirt and he says it's slidin' his hand. Which is right?"

"I'm right," says Smitty. "But if you're arguin' about him goin' last innin', I didn't give him no sign."

"You pulled your cap down with your right hand, didn't you?" ast Ike.

"Well, s'pose I did," says Smitty. "That don't mean nothin'. I never told you to take that for a sign, did I?"

"I thought maybe you meant to tell me and forgot," says Ike.

They couldn't none of us answer that and they wouldn't of been no more said if Ike had of shut up. But wile we was settin' there Carey got on with two out and stole second clean.

"There!" says Ike. "That's what I was tryin' to do and I'd of got away with it if Smitty'd swang and bothered the Indian."

"Oh!" says Smitty. "You was tryin' to steal then, was you? I thought you claimed I give you the hit and run."

"I didn't claim no such a thing," says Ike. "I thought maybe you might of gave me a sign, but I was goin' anyway because I thought I had a good start."

Cap prob'ly would of hit him with a bat, only just about that time Doyle booted one on Hayes and Carey come acrost with the run that tied.

Well, we go into the ninth finally, one and one, and Marquard walks McDonald with nobody out.

"Lay it down," says Cap to Ike.

And Ike goes up there with orders to bunt and cracks the first ball into that right-field stand! It was fair this time, and we're two ahead, but I didn't think about that at the time. I was too busy watchin' Cap's face. First he turned pale and then he got red as fire and then he got blue and purple, and finally he just laid back and busted out laughin'. So we wasn't afraid to laugh ourselfs when we seen him doin' it, and when Ike come in everybody on the bench was in hysterics.

But instead o' takin' advantage, Ike had to try and excuse himself. His play was to shut up and he didn't know how to make it.

"Well," he says, "if I hadn't hit quite so quick at that one I bet it'd of cleared the center-field fence."

Cap stopped laughin'.

"It'll cost you plain fifty," he says.

"What for?" says Ike.

"When I say 'bunt' I mean 'bunt,' " says Cap.

"You didn't say 'bunt,' " says Ike.

"I says 'Lay it down,' " says Cap. "If that don't mean 'bunt,' what does it mean?"

" 'Lay it down' means 'bunt' all right," says Ike, "but I understood you to say 'Lay on it.' "

"All right," says Cap, "and the little misunderstandin' will cost you fifty."

Ike didn't say nothin' for a few minutes. Then he had another bright idear.

"I was just kiddin' about misunderstandin' you," he says. "I knowed you wanted me to bunt."

"Well, then, why didn't you bunt?" ast Cap.

"I was goin' to on the next ball," says Ike. "But I thought if I took a good wallop I'd have 'em all fooled. So I walloped at the first one to fool 'em, and I didn't have no intention o' hittin' it."

"You tried to miss it, did you?" says Cap.

"Yes," says Ike.

"How'd you happen to hit it?" ast Cap.

"Well," Ike says, "I was lookin' for him to throw me a fast one and I was goin' to swing under it. But he come with a hook and I met it right square where I was swingin' to go under the fast one."

"Great!" says Cap. "Boys," he says, "Ike's learned how to hit Marquard's curve. Pretend a fast one's comin' and then try to miss it. It's a good thing to know and Ike'd ought to be willin' to pay for the lesson. So I'm goin' to make it a hundred instead o' fifty."

The game wound up 3 to 1. The fine didn't go, because Ike hit like a wild man all through that trip and we made pretty near a clean-up. The night we went to Philly I got him cornered in the car and I says to him:

"Forget them alibis for a wile and tell me somethin'. What'd you do that for, swing that time against Marquard when you was told to bunt?"

"I'll tell you," he says. "That ball he throwed me looked just like the

one I struck out in the first innin' and I wanted to show Cap what I
could of done to that other one if I'd knew it was the third strike."

"But," I says, "the one you struck out on in the first innin' was a
fast ball."

"So was the one I cracked in the ninth," says Ike.

IV

You've saw Cap's wife, o' course. Well, her sister's about twict as good-
lookin' as her, and that's goin' some.

Cap took his missus down to St. Louis the second trip and the other
one come down from St. Joe to visit her. Her name is Dolly, and some
doll is right.

Well, Cap was goin' to take the two sisters to a show and he wanted
a beau for Dolly. He left it to her and she picked Ike. He'd hit three on
the nose that afternoon—off'n Sallee, too.

They fell for each other that first evenin'. Cap told us how it come
off. She begin flatterin' Ike for the star game he'd played and o' course
he begin excusin' himself for not doin' better. So she thought he was
modest and it went strong with her. And she believed everything he said
and that made her solid with him—that and her make-up. They was
together every mornin' and evenin' for the five days we was there. In
the afternoons Ike played the grandest ball you ever see, hittin' and
runnin' the bases like a fool and catchin' everything that stayed in the
park.

I told Cap, I says: "You'd ought to keep the doll with us and he'd
make Cobb's figures look sick."

But Dolly had to go back to St. Joe and we come home for a long
serious.

Well, for the next three weeks Ike had a letter to read every day and
he'd set in the clubhouse readin' it till mornin' practice was half over.
Cap didn't say nothin' to him, because he was goin' so good. But I and
Carey wasted a lot of our time tryin' to get him to own up who the
letters was from. Fine chanct!

"What are you readin'?" Carey'd say. "A bill?"

"No," Ike'd say, "not exactly a bill. It's a letter from a fella I used
to go to school with."

"High school or college?" I'd ask him.

"College," he'd say.

"What college?" I'd say.

Then he'd stall a wile and then he'd say:

"I didn't go to the college myself, but my friend went there."

"How did it happen you didn't go?" Carey'd ask him.

"Well," he'd say, "they wasn't no colleges near where I lived."

"Didn't you live in Kansas City?" I'd say to him.

One time he'd say he did and another time he didn't. One time he says he lived in Michigan.

"Where at?" says Carey.

"Near Detroit," he says.

"Well," I says, "Detroit's near Ann Arbor and that's where they got the university."

"Yes," says Ike, "they got it there now, but they didn't have it there then."

"I come pretty near goin' to Syracuse," I says, "only they wasn't no railroads runnin' through there in them days."

"Where'd this friend o' yours go to college?" says Carey.

"I forget now," says Ike.

"Was it Carlisle?" ast Carey.

"No," says Ike, "his folks wasn't very well off."

"That's what barred me from Smith," I says.

"I was goin' to tackle Cornell's," says Carey, "but the doctor told me I'd have hay fever if I didn't stay up North."

"Your friend writes long letters," I says.

"Yes," says Ike; "he's tellin' me about a ball player."

"Where does he play?" ast Carey.

"Down in the Texas League—Fort Wayne," says Ike.

"It looks like a girl's writin'," Carey says.

"A girl wrote it," says Ike. "That's my friend's sister, writin' for him."

"Didn't they teach writin' at this here college where he went?" says Carey.

"Sure," Ike says, "they taught writin', but he got his hand cut off in a railroad wreck."

"How long ago?" I says.

"Right after he got out o' college," says Ike.

"Well," I says, "I should think he'd of learned to write with his left hand by this time."

"It's his left hand that was cut off," says Ike; "and he was left-handed."

"You get a letter every day," says Carey. "They're all the same writin'. Is he tellin' you about a different ball player every time he writes?"

"No," Ike says. "It's the same ball player. He just tells me what he does every day."

"From the size o' the letters, they don't play nothin' but double-headers down there," says Carey.

We figured that Ike spent most of his evenin's answerin' the letters from his "friend's sister," so we kept tryin' to date him up for shows and parties to see how he'd duck out of 'em. He was bugs over spaghetti, so we told him one day that they was goin' to be a big feed of it over to Joe's that night and he was invited.

"How long'll it last?" he says.

"Well," we says, "we're goin' right over there after the game and stay till they close up."

"I can't go," he says, "unless they leave me come home at eight bells."

"Nothin' doin'," says Carey. "Joe'd get sore."

"I can't go then," says Ike.

"Why not?" I ast him.

"Well," he says, "my landlady locks up the house at eight and I left my key home."

"You can come and stay with me," says Carey.

"No," he says, "I can't sleep in a strange bed."

"How do you get along when we're on the road?" says I.

"I don't never sleep the first night anywheres," he says. "After that I'm all right."

"You'll have time to chase home and get your key right after the game," I told him.

"The key ain't home," says Ike. "I lent it to one o' the other fellas and he's went out o' town and took it with him."

"Couldn't you borry another key off'n the landlady?" Carey ast him.

"No," he says, "that's the only one they is."

Well, the day before we started East again, Ike come into the clubhouse all smiles.

"Your birthday?" I ast him.

"No," he says.

"What do you feel so good about?" I says.

"Got a letter from my old man," he says. "My uncle's goin' to get well."

"Is that the one in Nebraska?" says I.

"Not right in Nebraska," says Ike. "Near there."

But afterwards we got the right dope from Cap. Dolly'd blew in from Missouri and was going to make the trip with her sister.

V

Well, I want to alibi Carey and I for what come off in Boston. If we'd of had any idear what we was doin', we'd never did it. They wasn't nobody outside o' maybe Ike and the dame that felt worse over it than I and Carey.

The first two days we didn't see nothin' of Ike and her except out to the park. The rest o' the time they was sight-seein' over to Cambridge and down to Revere and out to Brook-a-line and all the other places where the rubes go.

But when we come into the beanery after the third game Cap's wife called us over.

"If you want to see somethin' pretty," she says, "look at the third finger on Sis's left hand."

Well, o' course we knowed before we looked that it wasn't goin' to be no hangnail. Nobody was su'prised when Dolly blew into the dinin' room with it—a rock that Ike'd bought off'n Diamond Joe the first trip to New York. Only o' course it'd been set into a lady's-size ring instead o' the automobile tire he'd been wearin'.

Cap and his missus and Ike and Dolly ett supper together, only Ike didn't eat nothin', but just set there blushin' and spillin' things on the table-cloth. I heard him excusin' himself for not havin' no appetite. He says he couldn't never eat when he was clost to the ocean. He'd forgot about them sixty-five oysters he destroyed the first night o' the trip before.

He was goin' to take her to a show, so after supper he went upstairs to change his collar. She had to doll up, too, and o' course Ike was through long before her.

If you remember the hotel in Boston, they's a little parlor where the piano's at and then they's another little parlor openin' off o' that. Well, when Ike come down Smitty was playin' a few chords and I and Carey was harmonizin'. We seen Ike go up to the desk to leave his key and we called him in. He tried to duck away, but we wouldn't stand for it.

We ast him what he was all duded up for and he says he was goin' to the theayter.

"Goin' alone?" says Carey.

"No," he says, "a friend o' mine's goin' with me."

"What do you say if we go along?" says Carey.

"I ain't only got two tickets," he says.

"Well," says Carey, "we can go down there with you and buy our own seats; maybe we can all get together."

"No," says Ike. "They ain't no more seats. They're all sold out."

"We can buy some off'n the scalpers," says Carey.

"I wouldn't if I was you," says Ike. "They say the show's rotten."

"What are you goin' for, then?" I ast.

"I didn't hear about it bein' rotten till I got the tickets," he says.

"Well," I says, "if you don't want to go I'll buy the tickets from you."

"No," says Ike, "I wouldn't want to cheat you. I'm stung and I'll just have to stand for it."

"What are you goin' to do with the girl, leave her here at the hotel?" I says.

"What girl?" says Ike.

"The girl you ett supper with," I says.

"Oh," he says, "we just happened to go into the dinin' room together, that's all. Cap wanted I should set down with 'em."

"I noticed," says Carey, "that she happened to be wearin' that rock you bought off'n Diamond Joe."

"Yes," says Ike. "I lent it to her for a wile."

"Did you lend her the new ring that goes with it?" I says.

"She had that already," says Ike. "She lost the set out of it."

"I wouldn't trust no strange girl with a rock o' mine," says Carey.

"Oh, I guess she's all right," Ike says. "Besides, I was tired o' the stone. When a girl asks you for somethin', what are you goin' to do?"

He started out toward the desk, but we flagged him.

"Wait a minute!" Carey says. "I got a bet with Sam here, and it's up to you to settle it."

"Well," says Ike, "make it snappy. My friend'll be here any minute."

"I bet," says Carey, "that you and that girl was engaged to be married."

"Nothin' to it," says Ike.

"Now look here," says Carey, "this is goin' to cost me real money if I lose. Cut out the alibi stuff and give it to us straight. Cap's wife just as good as told us you was roped."

Ike blushed like a kid.

"Well, boys," he says, "I may as well own up. You win, Carey."

"Yatta boy!" says Carey. "Congratulations!"

"You got a swell girl, Ike," I says.

"She's a peach," says Smitty.

"Well, I guess she's O. K.," says Ike. "I don't know much about girls."

"Didn't you never run round with 'em?" I says.

"Oh, yes, plenty of 'em," says Ike. "But I never seen none I'd fall for."

"That is, till you seen this one," says Carey.

"Well," says Ike, "this one's O. K., but I wasn't thinkin' about gettin' married yet a wile."

"Who done the askin'—her?" says Carey.

"Oh, no," says Ike, "but sometimes a man don't know what he's gettin' into. Take a good-lookin' girl, and a man gen'ally almost always does about what she wants him to."

"They couldn't no girl lasso me unless I wanted to be lassoed," says Smitty.

"Oh, I don't know," says Ike. "When a fella gets to feelin' sorry for one of 'em it's all off."

Well, we left him go after shakin' hands all round. But he didn't take Dolly to no show that night. Some time wile we was talkin' she'd come into that other parlor and she'd stood there and heard us. I don't know how much she heard. But it was enough. Dolly and Cap's missus took the midnight train for New York. And from there Cap's wife sent her on her way back to Missouri.

She'd left the ring and a note for Ike with the clerk. But we didn't ask Ike if the note was from his friend in Fort Wayne, Texas.

VI

When we'd came to Boston Ike was hittin' plain .397. When we got back home he'd fell off to pretty near nothin'. He hadn't drove one out o' the infield in any o' them other Eastern parks, and he didn't even give no excuse for it.

To show you how bad he was, he struck out three times in Brooklyn one day and never opened his trap when Cap ast him what was the matter. Before, if he'd whiffed oncet in a game he'd of wrote a book tellin' why.

Well, we dropped from first place to fifth in four weeks and we was still goin' down. I and Carey was about the only ones in the club that spoke to each other, and all as we did was remind ourself o' what a boner we'd pulled.

"It's goin' to beat us out o' the big money," says Carey.

"Yes," I says. "I don't want to knock my own ball club, but it looks like a one-man team, and when that one man's dauber's down we couldn't trim our whiskers."

"We ought to knew better," says Carey.

"Yes," I says, "but why should a man pull an alibi for bein' engaged to such a bearcat as she was?"

"He shouldn't," says Carey. "But I and you knowed he would or we'd never started talkin' to him about it. He wasn't no more ashamed o' the girl than I am of a regular base hit. But he just can't come clean on no subjec'."

Cap had the whole story, and I and Carey was as pop'lar with him as an umpire.

"What do you want me to do, Cap?" Carey'd say to him before goin' up to hit.

"Use your own judgment," Cap'd tell him. "We want to lose another game."

But finally, one night in Pittsburgh, Cap had a letter from his missus and he come to us with it.

"You fellas," he says, "is the ones that put us on the bum, and if you're sorry I think they's a chancet for you to make good. The old lady's out to St. Joe and she's been tryin' her hardest to fix things up. She's explained that Ike don't mean nothin' with his talk; I've wrote and explained that to Dolly, too. But the old lady says that Dolly says that she can't believe it. But Dolly's still stuck on this baby, and she's pinin' away just the same as Ike. And the old lady says she thinks if you two fellas would write to the girl and explain how you was always kiddin' with Ike and leadin' him on, and how the ball club was all shot to pieces since Ike quit hittin', and how he acted like he was goin' to kill himself, and this and that, she'd fall for it and maybe soften down. Dolly, the old lady says, would believe you before she'd believe I and the old lady, because she thinks it's her we're sorry for, and not him."

Well, I and Carey was only too glad to try and see what we could do. But it wasn't no snap. We wrote about eight letters before we got one that looked good. Then we give it to the stenographer and had it wrote out on a typewriter and both of us signed it.

It was Carey's idear that made the letter good. He stuck in somethin' about the world's serious money that our wives wasn't goin' to spend unless she took pity on a "boy who was so shy and modest that he was afraid to come right out and say that he had asked such a beautiful and handsome girl to become his bride."

That's prob'ly what got her, or maybe she couldn't of held out much longer anyway. It was four days after we sent the letter that Cap heard from his missus again. We was in Cincinnati.

"We've won," he says to us. "The old lady says that Dolly says she'll give him another chance. But the old lady says it won't do no good for Ike to write a letter. He'll have to go out there."

"Send him to-night," says Carey.

"I'll pay half his fare," I says.

"I'll pay the other half," says Carey.

"No," says Cap, "the club'll pay his expenses. I'll send him scoutin'."

"Are you goin' to send him to-night?"

"Sure," says Cap. "But I'm goin' to break the news to him right now. It's time we win a ball game."

So in the clubhouse, just before the game, Cap told him. And I certainly felt sorry for Rube Benton and Red Ames that afternoon! I and Carey was standin' in front o' the hotel that night when Ike come out with his suitcase.

"Sent home?" I says to him.

"No," he says, "I'm goin' scoutin'."

"Where to?" I says. "Fort Wayne?"

"No, not exactly," he says.

"Well," says Carey, "have a good time."

"I ain't lookin' for no good time," says Ike. "I says I was goin' scoutin'."

"Well, then," says Carey, "I hope you see somebody you like."

"And you better have a drink before you go," I says.

"Well," says Ike, "they claim it helps a cold."

GULLIBLE'S TRAVELS

I

I promised the Wife that if anybody ast me what kind of a time did I
have at Palm Beach I'd say I had a swell time. And if they ast me who
did we meet I'd tell 'em everybody that was worth meetin'. And if they
ast me didn't the trip cost a lot I'd say Yes; but it was worth the money.
I promised her I wouldn't spill none o' the real details. But if you can't
break a promise you made to your own wife what kind of a promise
can you break? Answer me that, Edgar.

I'm not one o' these kind o' people that'd keep a joke to themself
just because the joke was on them. But they's plenty of our friends that
I wouldn't have 'em hear about it for the world. I wouldn't tell you,
only I know you're not the village gossip and won't crack it to anybody.
Not even to your own Missus, see? I don't trust no women.

It was along last January when I and the Wife was both hit by the
society bacillus. I think it was at the opera. You remember me tellin'
you about us and the Hatches goin' to *Carmen* and then me takin' my
Missus and her sister, Bess, and four of one suit named Bishop to see
The Three Kings? Well, I'll own up that I enjoyed wearin' the soup and
fish and minglin' amongst the high polloi and pretendin' we really was
somebody. And I know my wife enjoyed it, too, though they was nothin'
said between us at the time.

The next stage was where our friends wasn't good enough for us no
more. We used to be tickled to death to spend an evenin' playin' rummy
with the Hatches. But all of a sudden they didn't seem to be no fun in
it and when Hatch'd call up we'd stall out of it. From the number o'
times I told him that I or the Missus was tired out and goin' right to
bed, he must of thought we'd got jobs as telephone linemen.

We quit attendin' pitcher shows because the rest o' the audience
wasn't the kind o' people you'd care to mix with. We didn't go over to
Ben's and dance because they wasn't no class to the crowd there. About
once a week we'd beat it to one o' the good hotels down-town, all
dressed up like a horse, and have our dinner with the rest o' the E-light.
They wasn't nobody talked to us only the waiters, but we could look

as much as we liked and it was sport tryin' to guess the names o' the gang at the next table.

Then we took to readin' the society news at breakfast. It used to be that I didn't waste time on nothin' but the market and sportin' pages, but now I pass 'em up and listen w'ile the Missus rattled off what was doin' on the Lake Shore Drive.

Every little w'ile we'd see where So-and-So was at Palm Beach or just goin' there or just comin' back. We got to kiddin' about it.

"Well," I'd say, "we'd better be startin' pretty soon or we'll miss the best part o' the season."

"Yes," the Wife'd say back, "we'd go right now if it wasn't for all them engagements next week."

We kidded and kidded till finally, one night, she forgot we was just kiddin'.

"You didn't take no vacation last summer," she says.

"No," says I. "They wasn't no chance to get away."

"But you promised me," she says, "that you'd take one this winter to make up for it."

"I know I did," I says; "but it'd be a sucker play to take a vacation in weather like this."

"The weather ain't like this everywheres," she says.

"You must of been goin' to night school," I says.

"Another thing you promised me," says she, "was that when you could afford it you'd take me on a real honeymoon trip to make up for the dinky one we had."

"That still goes," I says, "when I can afford it."

"You can afford it now," says she. "We don't owe nothin' and we got money in the bank."

"Yes," I says. "Pretty close to three hundred bucks."

"You forgot somethin'," she says. "You forgot them war babies."

Did I tell you about that? Last fall I done a little dabblin' in Crucial Steel and at this time I'm tellin' you about I still had a hold of it, but stood to pull down six hundred. Not bad, eh?

"It'd be a mistake to let loose now," I says.

"All right," she says. "Hold on, and I hope you lose every cent. You never did care nothin' for me."

Then we done a little spoonin' and then I ast her what was the big idear.

"We ain't swelled on ourself," she says; "but I know and you know that the friends we been associatin' with ain't in our class. They don't know how to dress and they can't talk about nothin' but their goldfish and their meat bills. They don't try to get nowheres, but all they do is play rummy and take in the Majestic. I and you like nice people and good music and things that's worth w'ile. It's a crime for us to be wastin' our time with riff and raff that'd run round barefooted if it wasn't for the police."

"I wouldn't say we'd wasted much time on 'em lately," I says.

"No," says she, "and I've had a better time these last three weeks than I ever had in my life."

"And you can keep right on havin' it," I says.

"I could have a whole lot better time, and you could, too," she says, "if we could get acquainted with some congenial people to go round with; people that's tastes is the same as ourn."

"If any o' them people calls up on the phone," I says, "I'll be as pleasant to 'em as I can."

"You're always too smart," says the Wife. "You don't never pay attention to no schemes o' mine."

"What's the scheme now?"

"You'll find fault with it because I thought it up," she says. "If it was your scheme you'd think it was grand."

"If it really was good you wouldn't be scared to spring it," I says.

"Will you promise to go through with it?" says she.

"If it ain't too ridic'lous," I told her.

"See! I knowed that'd be the way," she says.

"Don't talk crazy," I says. "Where'd we be if we'd went through with every plan you ever sprang?"

"Will you promise to listen to my side of it without actin' cute?" she says.

So I didn't see no harm in goin' that far.

"I want you to take me to Palm Beach," says she. "I want you to take a vacation, and that's where we'll spend it."

"And that ain't all we'd spend," I says.

"Remember your promise," says she.

So I shut up and listened.

The dope she give me was along these lines: We could get special round-trip rates on any o' the railroads and that part of it wouldn't cost nowheres near as much as a man'd naturally think. The hotel rates was pretty steep, but the meals was throwed in, and just imagine what them meals would be! And we'd be stayin' under the same roof with the Vanderbilts and Goulds, and eatin' at the same table, and probably, before we was there a week, callin' 'em Steve and Gus. They was dancin' every night and all the guests danced with each other, and how would it feel fox-trottin' with the president o' the B. & O., or the Delmonico girls from New York! And all Chicago society was down there, and when we met 'em we'd know 'em for life and have some real friends amongst 'em when we got back home.

That's how she had it figured and she must of been practisin' her speech, because it certainly did sound good to me. To make it short, I fell, and dated her up to meet me down-town the next day and call on the railroad bandits. The first one we seen admitted that his was the best route and that he wouldn't only soak us one hundred and forty-seven dollars and seventy cents to and from Palm Beach and back, includin' an apartment from here to Jacksonville and as many stop-overs as we wanted to make. He told us we wouldn't have to write for no hotel accommodations because the hotels had an agent right over on Madison Street that'd be glad to do everything to us.

So we says we'd be back later and then we beat it over to the Florida East Coast's local studio.

"How much for a double room by the week?" I ast the man.

"They ain't no weekly rates," he says. "By the day it'd be twelve dollars and up for two at the Breakers, and fourteen dollars and up at the Poinciana."

"I like the Breakers better," says I.

"You can't get in there," he says. "They're full for the season."

"That's a long spree," I says.

"Can we get in the other hotel?" ast the Wife.

"I can find out," says the man.

"We want a room with bath," says she.

"That'd be more," says he. "That'd be fifteen dollars or sixteen dollars and up."

"What do we want of a bath," I says, "with the whole Atlantic Ocean in the front yard?"

"I'm afraid you'd have trouble gettin' a bath," says the man. "The hotels is both o' them pretty well filled up on account o' the war in Europe."

"What's that got to do with it?" I ast him.

"A whole lot," he says. "The people that usually goes abroad is all down to Palm Beach this winter."

"I don't see why," I says. "If one o' them U-boats hit 'em they'd at least be gettin' their bath for nothin'."

We left him with the understandin' that he was to wire down there and find out what was the best they could give us. We called him up in a couple o' days and he told us we could have a double room, without no bath, at the *Poinciana*, beginnin' the fifteenth o' February. He didn't know just what the price would be.

Well, I fixed it up to take my vacation startin' the tenth, and sold out my Crucial Steel, and divided the spoils with the railroad company. We decided we'd stop off in St. Augustine two days, because the Missus found out somewheres that they might be two or three o' the Four Hundred lingerin' there, and we didn't want to miss nobody.

"Now," I says, "all we got to do is set round and wait for the tenth o' the month."

"Is that so!" says the Wife. "I suppose you're perfectly satisfied with your clo'es."

"I've got to be," I says, "unless the Salvation Army has somethin' that'll fit me."

"What's the matter with our charge account?" she says.

"I don't like to charge nothin'," I says, "when I know they ain't no chance of ever payin' for it."

"All right," she says, "then we're not goin' to Palm Beach. I'd rather stay home than go down there lookin' like general housework."

"Do you need clo'es yourself?" I ast her.

"I certainly do," she says. "About two hundred dollars' worth. But I got one hundred and fifty dollars o' my own."

"All right," I says. "I'll stand for the other fifty and then we're all set."

"No, we're not," she says. "That just fixes me. But I want you to look as good as I do."

"Nature'll see to that," I says.

But they was no arguin' with her. Our trip, she says, was an invest-ment; it was goin' to get us in right with people worth w'ile. And we wouldn't have a chance in the world unless we looked the part.

So before the tenth come round, we was long two new evenin' gowns, two female sport suits, four or five pairs o' shoes, all colors, one Tuxedo dinner coat, three dress shirts, half a dozen other kinds o' shirts, two pairs o' transparent white trousers, one new business suit and Lord knows how much underwear and how many hats and stockin's. And I had till the fifteenth o' March to pay off the mortgage on the old homestead.

Just as we was gettin' ready to leave for the train the phone rung. It was Mrs. Hatch and she wanted us to come over for a little rummy. I was shavin' and the Missus done the talkin'.

"What did you tell her?" I ast.

"I told her we was goin' away," says the Wife.

"I bet you forgot to mention where we was goin'," I says.

"Pay me," says she.

II

I thought we was in Venice when we woke up next mornin', but the porter says it was just Cairo, Illinois. The river'd went crazy and I bet they wasn't a room without a bath in that old burg.

As we set down in the diner for breakfast the train was goin' acrost the longest bridge I ever seen, and it looked like we was so near the water that you could reach right out and grab a handful. The Wife was a little wabbly.

"I wonder if it's really safe," she says.

"If the bridge stays up we're all right," says I.

"But the question is, Will it stay up?" she says.

"I wouldn't bet a nickel either way on a bridge," I says. "They're treacherous little devils. They'd cross you as quick as they'd cross this river."

"The trainmen must be nervous," she says. "Just see how we're draggin' along."

"They're givin' the fish a chance to get offen the track," I says. "It's against the law to spear fish with a cowcatcher this time o' year."

Well, the Wife was so nervous she couldn't eat nothin' but toast and coffee, so I figured I was justified in goin' to the prunes and steak and eggs.

After breakfast we went out in what they call the sun parlor. It was a glassed-in room on the tail-end o' the rear coach and it must of been a pleasant place to set and watch the scenery. But they was a gang o' missionaries or somethin' had all the seats and they never budged out o' them all day. Every time they'd come to a crossroads they'd toss a stack o' Bible studies out o' the back window for the southern heathen to pick up and read. I suppose they thought they was doin' a lot o' good for their fellow men, but their fellow passengers meanw'ile was gettin' the worst of it.

Speakin' o' the scenery, it certainly was somethin' grand. First we'd pass a few pine trees with fuzz on 'em and then a couple o' acres o' yellow mud. Then they'd be more pine trees and more fuzz and then more yellow mud. And after a w'ile we'd come to some pine trees with fuzz on 'em and then, if we watched close, we'd see some yellow mud.

Every few minutes the train'd stop and then start up again on low. That meant the engineer suspected he was comin' to a station and was scared that if he run too fast he wouldn't see it, and if he run past it without stoppin' the inhabitants wouldn't never forgive him. You see, they's a regular schedule o' duties that's followed out by the more prominent citizens down those parts. After their wife's attended to the chores and got the breakfast they roll out o' bed and put on their overalls and eat. Then they get on their horse or mule or cow or dog and ride down to the station and wait for the next train. When it comes they have a contest to see which can count the passengers first. The losers has to promise to work one day the followin' month. If one fella loses three times in the same month he generally always kills himself.

All the towns has got five or six private residences and seven or eight two-apartment buildin's and a grocery and a post-office. They told me that somebody in one o' them burgs, I forget which one, got a letter the day before we come through. It was misdirected, I guess.

The two-apartment buildin's is constructed on the ground floor, with a porch to divide one flat from the other. One's the housekeepin' side and the other's just a place for the husband and father to lay round in so's they won't be disturbed by watchin' the women work.

It was a blessin' to them boys when their states went dry. Just think what a strain it must of been to keep liftin' glasses and huntin' in their overalls for a dime!

In the afternoon the Missus went into our apartment and took a nap and I moseyed into the readin'-room and looked over some o' the comical magazines. They was a fat guy come in and set next to me. I'd heard him, in at lunch, tellin' the dinin'-car conductor what Wilson should of done, so I wasn't su'prised when he opened up on me.

"Tiresome trip," he says.

I didn't think it was worth w'ile arguin' with him.

"Must of been a lot o' rain through here," he says.

"Either that," says I, "or else the sprinklin' wagon run shy o' streets." He laughed as much as it was worth.

"Where do you come from?" he ast me.

"Dear old Chicago," I says.

"I'm from St. Louis," he says.

"You're frank," says I.

"I'm really as much at home one place as another," he says. "The Wife likes to travel and why shouldn't I humor her?"

"I don't know," I says. "I haven't the pleasure."

"Seems like we're goin' all the w'ile," says he. "It's Hot Springs or New Orleans or Florida or Atlantic City or California or somewheres."

"Do you get passes?" I ast him.

"I guess I could if I wanted to," he says. "Some o' my best friends is way up in the railroad business."

"I got one like that," I says. "He generally stands on the fourth or fifth car behind the engine."

"Do you travel much?" he ast me.

"I don't live in St. Louis," says I.

"Is this your first trip south?" he ast.

"Oh, no," I says. "I live on Sixty-fifth Street."

"I meant, have you ever been down this way before?"

"Oh, yes," says I. "I come down every winter."

"Where do you go?" he ast.

That's what I was layin' for.

"Palm Beach," says I.

"I used to go there," he says. "But I've cut it out. It ain't like it used to be. They leave everybody in now."

"Yes," I says; "but a man don't have to mix up with 'em."

"You can't just ignore people that comes up and talks to you," he says.

"Are you bothered that way much?" I ast.

"It's what drove me away from Palm Beach," he says.

"How long since you been there?" I ast him.

"How long you been goin' there?" he says.

"Me?" says I. "Five years."

"We just missed each other," says he. "I quit six years ago this winter."

"Then it couldn't of been there I seen you," says I. "But I know I seen you somewheres before."

"It might of been most anywheres," he says. "They's few places I haven't been at."

"Maybe it was acrost the pond," says I.

"Very likely," he says. "But not since the war started. I been steerin' clear of Europe for two years."

"So have I, for longer'n that," I says.

"It's certainly an awful thing, this war," says he.

"I believe you're right," says I; "but I haven't heard nobody express it just that way before."

"I only hope," he says, "that we succeed in keepin' out of it."

"If we got in, would you go?" I ast him.

"Yes, sir," he says.

"You wouldn't beat me," says I. "I bet I'd reach Brazil as quick as you."

"Oh, I don't think they'd be any action in South America," he says. "We'd fight defensive at first and most of it would be along the Atlantic Coast."

"Then maybe we could get accommodations in Yellowstone Park," says I.

"They's no sense in this country gettin' involved," he says. "Wilson hasn't handled it right. He either ought to of went stronger or not so strong. He's wrote too many notes."

"You certainly get right to the root of a thing," says I. "You must of thought a good deal about it."

"I know the conditions pretty well," he says. "I know how far you can go with them people over there. I been amongst 'em a good part o' the time."

"I suppose," says I, "that a fella just naturally don't like to butt in. But if I was you I'd consider it my duty to romp down to Washington and give 'em all the information I had."

"Wilson picked his own advisers," says he. "Let him learn his lesson."

"That ain't hardly fair," I says. "Maybe you was out o' town, or your phone was busy or somethin'."

"I don't know Wilson nor he don't know me," he says.

"That oughtn't to stop you from helpin' him out," says I. "If you seen a man drownin' would you wait for some friend o' the both o' you to come along and make the introduction?"

"They ain't no comparison in them two cases," he says. "Wilson ain't never called on me for help."

"You don't know if he has or not," I says. "You don't stick in one place long enough for a man to reach you."

"My office in St. Louis always knows where I'm at," says he. "My stenographer can reach me any time within ten to twelve hours."

"I don't think it's right to have this country's whole future dependin' on a St. Louis stenographer," I says.

"That's nonsense!" says he. "I ain't makin' no claim that I could save or not save this country. But if I and Wilson was acquainted I might tell him some facts that'd help him out in his foreign policy."

"Well, then," I says, "it's up to you to get acquainted. I'd introduce you myself only I don't know your name."

"My name's Gould," says he; "but you're not acquainted with Wilson."

"I could be, easy," says I. "I could get on a train he was goin' somewheres on and then go and set beside him and begin to talk. Lots o' people make friends that way."

It was gettin' along to'rd supper-time, so I excused myself and went back to the apartment. The Missus had woke up and wasn't feelin' good.

"What's the matter?" I ast her.

"This old train," she says. "I'll die if it don't stop goin' round them curves."

"As long as the track curves, the best thing the train can do is curve with it," I says. "You may die if it keeps curvin', but you'd die a whole lot sooner if it left the rails and went straight ahead."

"What you been doin'?" she ast me.

"Just talkin' to one o' the Goulds," I says.

"Gould!" she says. "What Gould?"

"Well," I says, "I didn't ask him his first name, but he's from St. Louis, so I suppose it's Ludwig or Heinie."

"Oh," she says, disgusted. "I thought you meant one o' the real ones."

"He's a real one, all right," says I. "He's so classy that he's passed up Palm Beach. He says it's gettin' too common."

"I don't believe it," says the Wife. "And besides, we don't have to mix up with everybody."

"He says they butt right in on you," I told her.

"They'll get a cold reception from me," she says.

But between the curves and the fear o' Palm Beach not bein' so exclusive as it used to be, she couldn't eat no supper, and I had another big meal.

The next mornin' we landed in Jacksonville three hours behind time and narrowly missed connections for St. Augustine by over an hour and a half. They wasn't another train till one-thirty in the afternoon, so we had some time to kill. I went shoppin' and bought a shave and five or six rickeys. The Wife helped herself to a chair in the writin'-room of one o' the hotels and told pretty near everybody in Chicago that she wished they was along with us, accompanied by a pitcher o' the Elks' Home or the Germania Club, or Trout Fishin' at Atlantic Beach.

W'ile I was gettin' my dime's worth in the tonsorial parlors, I happened to look up at a calendar on the wall, and noticed it was the twelfth o' February.

"How does it come that everything's open here to-day?" I says to the barber. "Don't you-all know it's Lincoln's birthday?"

"Is that so?" he says. "How old is he?"

III

We'd wired ahead for rooms at the Alcazar, and when we landed in St. Augustine they was a motor-bus from the hotel to meet us at the station.

"Southern hospitality," I says to the Wife, and we was both pleased till they relieved us o' four bits apiece for the ride.

Well, they hadn't neither one of us slept good the night before, w'ile we was joltin' through Georgia; so when I suggested a nap they wasn't no argument.

"But our clo'es ought to be pressed," says the Missus. "Call up the valet and have it done w'ile we sleep."

So I called up the valet, and sure enough, he come.

"Hello, George!" I says. "You see, we're goin' to lay down and take a nap, and we was wonderin' if you could crease up these two suits and have 'em back here by the time we want 'em."

"Certainly, sir," says he.

"And how much will it cost?" I ast him.

"One dollar a suit," he says.

"Are you on parole or haven't you never been caught?" says I.

"Yes, sir," he says, and smiled like it was a joke.

"Let's talk business, George," I says. "The tailor we go to on Sixty-third walks two blocks to get our clo'es, and two blocks to take 'em to his joint, and two blocks to bring 'em back, and he only soaks us thirty-five cents a suit."

"He gets poor pay and he does poor work," says the burglar. "When I press clo'es I press 'em right."

"Well," I says, "the tailor on Sixty-third satisfies us. Suppose you don't do your best this time, but just give us seventy cents' worth."

But they wasn't no chance for a bargain. He'd been in the business so long he'd become hardened and lost all regard for his fellow men.

The Missus slept, but I didn't. Instead, I done a few problems in arithmetic. Outside o' what she'd gave up for postcards and stamps in Jacksonville, I'd spent two bucks for our lunch, about two more for my shave and my refreshments, one for a rough ride in a bus, one more for gettin' our trunk and grips carried round, two for havin' the clo'es pressed, and about half a buck in tips to people that I wouldn't never see again. Somewheres near nine dollars a day, not countin' no hotel bill, and over two weeks of it yet to come!

Oh, you rummy game at home, at half a cent a point!

When our clo'es come back I woke her up and give her the figures.

"But to-day's an exception," she says. "After this our meals will be

included in the hotel bill and we won't need to get our suits pressed
only once a week and you'll be shavin' yourself and they won't be no
bus fare when we're stayin' in one place. Besides, we can practice economy all spring and all summer."

"I guess we need the practice," I says.

"And if you're goin' to crab all the time about expenses," says she,
"I'll wish we had of stayed home."

"That'll make it unanimous," says I.

Then she begin sobbin' about how I'd spoiled the trip and I had to
promise I wouldn't think no more o' what we were spendin'. I might
just as well of promised to not worry when the White Sox lost or when
I'd forgot to come home to supper.

We went in the dinin'-room about six-thirty and was showed to a
table where they was another couple settin'. They was husband and
wife, I guess, but I don't know which was which. She was wieldin' the
pencil and writin' down their order.

"I guess I'll have clams," he says.

"They disagreed with you last night," says she.

"All right," he says. "I won't try 'em. Give me cream-o'-tomato
soup."

"You don't like tomatoes," she says.

"Well, I won't have no soup," says he. "A little o' the blue-fish."

"The blue-fish wasn't no good at noon," she says. "You better try
the bass."

"All right, make it bass," he says. "And them sweet-breads and a
little roast beef and sweet potatoes and peas and vanilla ice cream and
coffee."

"You wouldn't touch sweet-breads at home," says she, "and you
can't tell what they'll be in a hotel."

"All right, cut out the sweet-breads," he says.

"I should think you'd have the stewed chicken," she says, "and leave
out the roast beef."

"Stewed chicken it is," says he.

"Stewed chicken and mashed potatoes and string beans and buttered
toast and coffee. Will that suit you?"

"Sure!" he says, and she give the slip to the waiter.

George looked at it long enough to of read it three times if he could
of read it once and then went out in the kitchen and got a trayful o'
whatever was handy.

But the poor guy didn't get more'n a taste of anything. She was
watchin' him like a hawk, and no sooner would he delve into one victual

than she'd yank the dish away from him and tell him to remember that health was more important than temporary happiness. I felt so sorry for him that I couldn't enjoy my own repast and I told the Wife that we'd have our breakfast apart from that stricken soul if I had to carry the case to old Al Cazar himself.

In the evenin' we strolled acrost the street to the Ponce—that's supposed to be even sweller yet than where we were stoppin' at. We walked all over the place without recognizin' nobody from our set. I finally warned the Missus that if we didn't duck back to our room I'd probably have a heart attack from excitement; but she'd read in her Florida guide that the decorations and pitchers was worth goin' miles to see, so we had to stand in front o' them for a couple hours and try to keep awake. Four or five o' them was thrillers, at that. Their names was Adventure, Discovery, Contest, and so on, but what they all should of been called was Lady Who Had Mislaid Her Clo'es.

The hotel's named after the fella that built it. He come from Spain and they say he was huntin' for some water that if he'd drunk it he'd feel young. I don't see myself how you could expect to feel young on water. But, anyway, he'd heard that this here kind o' water could be found in St. Augustine, and when he couldn't find it he went into the hotel business and got even with the United States by chargin' five dollars a day and up for a room.

Sunday mornin' we went in to breakfast early and I ast the head waiter if we could set at another table where they wasn't no convalescent and his mate. At the same time I give the said head waiter somethin' that spoke louder than words. We was showed to a place way acrost the room from where we'd been the night before. It was a table for six, but the other four didn't come into our life till that night at supper.

Meanw'ile we went sight-seein'. We visited Fort Marion, that'd be a great protection against the Germans, provided they fought with paper wads. We seen the city gate and the cathedral and the slave market, and then we took the boat over to Anastasia Island, that the ocean's on the other side of it. This trip made me homesick, because the people that was along with us on the boat looked just like the ones we'd often went with to Michigan City on the Fourth o' July. The boat landed on the bay side o' the island and from there we was drug over to the ocean side on a horse car, the horse walkin' to one side o' the car instead of in front, so's he wouldn't get ran over.

We stuck on the beach till dinner-time and then took the chariot back to the pavilion on the bay side, where a whole family served the meal and their pigs put on a cabaret. It was the best meal I had in dear old Dixie—fresh oysters and chicken and mashed potatoes and gravy and fish and pie. And they charged two bits a plate.

"Goodness gracious!" says the Missus, when I told her the price. "This is certainly reasonable. I wonder how it happens."

"Well," I says, "the family was probably washed up here by the tide and don't know they're in Florida."

When we got back to the hotel they was only just time to clean up and go down to supper. We hadn't no sooner got seated when our table companions breezed in. It was a man about forty-five, that looked like he'd made his money in express and general haulin', and he had his wife along and both their mother-in-laws. The shirt he had on was the one he'd started from home with, if he lived in Yokohama. His womenfolks wore mournin' with a touch o' gravy here and there.

"You order for us, Jake," says one o' the ladies.

So Jake grabbed the bill o' fare and his wife took the slip and pencil and waited for the dictation.

"Let's see," he says. "How about oyster cocktail?"

"Yes," says the three Mrs. Black.

"Four oyster cocktails, then," says Jake, "and four orders o' bluepoints."

"The oysters is nice, too," says I.

They all give me a cordial smile and the ice was broke.

"Everything's good here," says Jake.

"I bet you know," I says.

He seemed pleased at the compliment and went on dictatin'.

"Four chicken soups with rice," he says, "and four o' the blue-fish and four veal chops breaded and four roast chicken and four boiled potatoes—"

But it seemed his wife would rather have sweet potatoes.

"All right," says Jake; "four boiled potatoes and four sweets. And chicken salad and some o' that tapioca puddin' and ice cream and tea. Is that satisfactory?"

"Fine!" says one o' the mother-in-laws.

"Are you goin' to stay long?" says Mrs. Jake to my Missus.

The party addressed didn't look very clubby, but she was too polite to pull the cut direct.

"We leave to-morrow night," she says.

Nobody ast her where we was goin'.

"We leave for Palm Beach," she says.

"That's a nice place, I guess," says one o' the old ones. "More people goes there than comes here. It ain't so expensive there, I guess."

"You're some guesser," says the Missus and freezes up.

I ast Jake if he'd been to Florida before.

"No," he says; "this is our first trip, but we're makin' up for lost time. We're seein' all they is to see and havin' everything the best."

"You're havin' everything, all right," I says, "but I don't know if it's the best or not. How long have you been here?"

"A week to-morrow," says he. "And we stay another week and then go to Ormond."

"Are you standin' the trip O. K.?" I ast him.

"Well," he says, "I don't feel quite as good as when we first come."

"Kind o' logy?" I says.

"Yes; kind o' heavy," says Jake.

"I know what you ought to do," says I. "You ought to go to a European plan hotel."

"Not w'ile this war's on," he says, "and besides, my mother's a poor sailor."

"Yes," says his mother; "I'm a very poor sailor."

"Jake's mother can't stand the water," says Mrs. Jake.

So I begun to believe that Jake's wife's mother-in-law was a total failure as a jolly tar.

Social intercourse was put an end to when the waiter staggered in with their order and our'n. The Missus seemed to of lost her appetite and just set there lookin' grouchy and tappin' her fingers on the table-cloth and actin' like she was in a hurry to get away. I didn't eat much, neither. It was more fun watchin'.

"Well," I says, when we was out in the lobby, "we finally got acquainted with some real people."

"Real people!" says the Missus, curlin' her lip. "What did you talk to 'em for?"

"I couldn't resist," I says. "Anybody that'd order four oyster cocktails and four rounds o' blue-points is worth knowin'."

"Well," she says, "if they're there when we go in to-morrow mornin' we'll get our table changed again or you can eat with 'em alone."

But they was absent from the breakfast board.

"They're probably stayin' in bed to-day to get their clo'es washed," says the Missus.

"Or maybe they're sick," I says. "A change of oysters affects some people."

I was for goin' over to the island again and gettin' another o' them quarter banquets, but the program was for us to walk round town all mornin' and take a ride in the afternoon.

First, we went to St. George Street and visited the oldest house in the United States. Then we went to Hospital Street and seen the oldest house in the United States. Then we turned the corner and went down St. Francis Street and inspected the oldest house in the United States. Then we dropped into a soda fountain and I had an egg phosphate, made from the oldest egg in the Western Hemisphere. We passed up lunch and got into a carriage drawn by the oldest horse in Florida, and we rode through the country all afternoon and the driver told us some o' the oldest jokes in the book. He felt it was only fair to give his customers a good time when he was chargin' a dollar an hour, and he had his gags rehearsed so's he could tell the same one a thousand times and never change a word. And the horse knowed where the point come in every one and stopped to laugh.

We done our packin' before supper, and by the time we got to our table Jake and the mourners was through and gone. We didn't have to ask the waiter if they'd been there. He was perspirin' like an evangelist.

After supper we said good-by to the night clerk and twenty-two bucks. Then we bought ourself another ride in the motor-bus and landed at the station ten minutes before train-time; so we only had an hour to wait for the train.

Say, I don't know how many stations they is between New York and San Francisco, but they's twice as many between St. Augustine and Palm Beach. And our train stopped twice and started twice at every one. I give up tryin' to sleep and looked out the window, amusin' myself by readin' the names o' the different stops. The only one that expressed my sentiments was Eau Gallie. We was an hour and a half late pullin' out o' that joint and I figured we'd be two hours to the bad gettin' into our destination. But the guy that made out the time-table must of had the engineer down pat, because when we went acrost the bridge over Lake Worth and landed at the Poinciana depot, we was ten minutes ahead o' time.

They was about two dozen uniformed Ephs on the job to meet us. And when I seen 'em all grab for our baggage with one hand and hold the other out, face up, I knowed why they called it Palm Beach.

IV

The Poinciana station's a couple hundred yards from one end o' the hotel, and that means it's close to five miles from the clerk's desk. By the time we'd registered and been gave our key and marathoned another five miles or so to where our room was located at, I was about ready for the inquest. But the Missus was full o' pep and wild to get down to breakfast and look over our stable mates. She says we would eat without changin' our clo'es; people'd forgive us for not dressin' up on account o' just gettin' there. W'ile she was lookin' out the window at the royal palms and buzzards, I moseyed round the room inspectin' where the different doors led to. Pretty near the first one I opened went into a private bath.

"Here," I says; "they've give us the wrong room."

Then my wife seen it and begin to squeal.

"Goody!" she says. "We've got a bath! We've got a bath!"

"But," says I, "they promised we wouldn't have none. It must be a mistake."

"Never you mind about a mistake," she says. "This is our room and they can't chase us out of it."

"We'll chase ourself out," says I. "Rooms with a bath is fifteen and sixteen dollars and up. Rooms without no bath is bad enough."

"We'll keep this room or I won't stay here," she says.

"All right, you win," I says; but I didn't mean it.

I made her set in the lobby down-stairs w'ile I went to the clerk pretendin' that I had to see about our trunk.

"Say," I says to him, "you've made a bad mistake. You told your man in Chicago that we couldn't have no room with a bath, and now you've give us one."

"You're lucky," he says. "A party who had a bath ordered for these two weeks canceled their reservation and now you've got it."

"Lucky, am I?" I says. "And how much is the luck goin' to cost me?"

"It'll be seventeen dollars per day for that room," he says, and turned away to hide a blush.

I went back to the Wife.

"Do you know what we're payin' for that room?" I says. "We're payin' seventeen dollars."

"Well," she says, "our meals is throwed in."

"Yes," says I, "and the hotel furnishes a key."

"You promised in St. Augustine," she says, "that you wouldn't worry no more about expenses."

Well, rather than make a scene in front o' the bellhops and the few millionaires that was able to be about at that hour o' the mornin', I just says "All right!" and led her into the dinin'-room.

The head waiter met us at the door and turned us over to his assistant. Then some more assistants took hold of us one at a time and we was relayed to a beautiful spot next door to the kitchen and bounded on all sides by posts and pillars. It was all right for me, but a whole lot too private for the Missus; so I had to call the fella that had been our pacemaker on the last lap.

"We don't like this table," I says.

"It's the only one I can give you," he says.

I slipped him half a buck.

"Come to think of it," he says, "I believe they's one I forgot all about."

And he moved us way up near the middle o' the place.

Say, you ought to seen that dinin'-room! From one end of it to the other is a toll call, and if a man that was settin' at the table farthest from the kitchen ordered roast lamb he'd get mutton. At that, they was crowded for fair and it kept the head waiters hustlin' to find trough space for one and all.

It was round nine o'clock when we put in our modest order for orange juice, oatmeal, liver and bacon, and cakes and coffee, and a quarter to ten or so when our waiter returned from the nearest orange grove with Exhibit A. We amused ourself meanw'ile by givin' our neighbors the once over and wonderin' which o' them was goin' to pal with us. As far as I could tell from the glances we received, they wasn't no immediate danger of us bein' annoyed by attentions.

They was only a few womenfolks on deck and they was dressed pretty quiet; so quiet that the Missus was scared she'd shock 'em with the sport shirt she'd bought in Chi. Later on in the day, when the girls come out for their dress parade, the Missus' costume made about as much noise as eatin' marshmallows in a foundry.

After breakfast we went to the room for a change o' raiment. I put on my white trousers and wished to heaven that the sun'd go under a cloud till I got used to tellin' people without words just where my linen began and I left off. The rest o' my outfit was white shoes that hurt, and white sox, and a two-dollar silk shirt that showed up a zebra, and a red tie and a soft collar and a blue coat. The Missus wore a sport suit that I won't try and describe—you'll probably see it on her sometime in the next five years.

We went down-stairs again and out on the porch, where some o' the old birds was takin' a sun bath.

"Where now?" I says.

"The beach, o' course," says the Missus.

"Where is it at?" I ast her.

"I suppose," she says, "that we'll find it somewheres near the ocean."

"I don't believe you can stand this climate," says I.

"The ocean," she says, "must be down at the end o' that avenue, where most everybody seems to be headed."

"Havin' went to our room and back twice, I don't feel like another five-mile hike," I says.

"It ain't no five miles," she says; "but let's ride, anyway."

"Come on," says I, pointin' to a street-car that was standin' in the middle o' the avenue.

"Oh, no," she says. "I've watched and found out that the real people takes them funny-lookin' wheel chairs."

I was wonderin' what she meant when one o' them pretty near run over us. It was part bicycle, part go-cart and part African. In the one we dodged they was room for one passenger, but some o' them carried two.

"I wonder what they'd soak us for the trip," I says.

"Not more'n a dime, I don't believe," says the Missus.

But when we'd hired one and been w'isked down under the palms and past the golf field to the bath-house, we was obliged to part with fifty cents legal and tender.

"I feel much refreshed," I says. "I believe when it comes time to go back I'll be able to walk."

The bath-house is acrost the street from the other hotel, the Breakers, that the man had told us was full for the season. Both buildin's fronts on the ocean; and, boy, it's some ocean! I bet they's fish in there that never seen each other!

"Oh, let's go bathin' right away!" says the Missus.

"Our suits is up to the other beanery," says I, and I was glad of it. They wasn't nothin' temptin' to me about them man-eatin' waves.

But the Wife's a persistent cuss.

"We won't go to-day," she says, "but we'll go in the bath-house and get some rooms for to-morrow."

The bath-house porch was a ringer for the *Follies*. Here and down on the beach was where you seen the costumes at this time o' day. I was so busy rubberin' that I passed the entrance door three times without noticin' it. From the top o' their heads to the bottom o' their feet the girls was a mess o' colors. They wasn't no two dressed alike and if any one o' them had of walked down State Street we'd of had an epidemic o' stiff neck to contend with in Chi. Finally the Missus grabbed me and hauled me into the office.

"Two private rooms," she says to the clerk. "One lady and one gent."

"Five dollars a week apiece," he says. "But we're all filled up."

"You ought to be all locked up!" I says.

"Will you have anything open to-morrow?" ast the Missus.

"I think I can fix you then," he says.

"What do we get for the five?" I ast him.

"Private room and we take care o' your bathin' suit," says he.

"How much if you don't take care o' the suit?" I ast him. "My suit's been gettin' along fine with very little care."

"Five dollars a week apiece," he says, "and if you want the rooms you better take 'em, because they're in big demand."

By the time we'd closed this grand bargain, everybody'd moved offen the porch and down to the water, where a couple dozen o' them went in for a swim and the rest set and watched. They was a long row o' chairs on the beach for spectators and we was just goin' to flop into two o' them when another bandit come up and told us it'd cost a dime apiece per hour.

"We're goin' to be here two weeks," I says. "Will you sell us two chairs?"

He wasn't in no comical mood, so we sunk down on the sand and seen the show from there. We had plenty o' company that preferred these kind o' seats free to the chairs at ten cents a whack.

Besides the people that was in the water gettin' knocked down by the waves and pretendin' like they enjoyed it, about half o' the gang on the sand was wearin' bathin' suits just to be clubby. You could tell by lookin' at the suits that they hadn't never been wet and wasn't intended for no such ridic'lous purpose. I wisht I could describe 'em to you, but it'd take a female to do it right.

One little girl, either fourteen or twenty-four, had white silk slippers and sox that come pretty near up to her ankles, and from there to her knees it was just plain Nature. Northbound from her knees was a pair o' bicycle trousers that disappeared when they come to the bottom of her Mother Hubbard. This here garment was a thing without no neck or sleeves that begin bulgin' at the top and spread out gradual all the way down, like a croquette. To top her off, she had a jockey cap; and —believe me—I'd of played her mount acrost the board. They was plenty o' class in the field with her, but nothin' that approached her speed. Later on I seen her several times round the hotel, wearin' some-thin' near the same outfit, without the jockey cap and with longer croquettes.

We set there in the sand till people begun to get up and leave. Then

we trailed along back o' them to the Breakers' porch, where they was
music to dance and stuff to inhale.

"We'll grab a table," I says to the Missus. "I'm dyin' o' thirst."

But I was allowed to keep on dyin'.

"I can serve you somethin' soft," says the waiter.

"I'll bet you can't!" I says.

"You ain't got no locker here?" he says.

"What do you mean—locker?" I ast him.

"It's the locker liquor law," he says. "We can serve you a drink if
you own your own bottles."

"I'd just as soon own a bottle," I says. "I'll become the proprietor
of a bottle o' beer."

"It'll take three or four hours to get it for you," he says, "and you'd
have to order it through the order desk. If you're stoppin' at one o' the
hotels and want a drink once in a w'ile, you better get busy and put in
an order."

So I had to watch the Missus put away a glass of orange juice that
cost forty cents and was just the same size as they give us for breakfast
free for nothin'. And, not havin' had nothin' to make me forget that
my feet hurt, I was obliged to pay another four bits for an Afromobile
to cart us back to our own boardin' house.

"Well," says the Missus when we got there, "it's time to wash up
and go to lunch."

"Wash up and go to lunch, then," I says; "but I'm goin' to investigate
this here locker liquor or liquor locker law."

So she got her key and beat it, and I limped to the bar.

"I want a highball," I says to the boy.

"What's your number?" says he.

"It varies," I says. "Sometimes I can hold twenty and sometimes four
or five makes me sing."

"I mean, have you got a locker here?" he says.

"No; but I want to get one," says I.

"The gent over there to the desk will fix you," says he.

So over to the desk I went and ast for a locker.

"What do you drink?" ast the gent.

"I'm from Chicago," I says. "I drink bourbon."

"What's your name and room number?" he says, and I told him.

Then he ast me how often did I shave and what did I think o' the
Kaiser and what my name was before I got married, and if I had any
intentions of ever running an elevator. Finally he says I was all right.

"I'll order you some bourbon," he says. "Anything else?"

I was goin' to say no, but I happened to remember that the Wife generally always wants a bronix before dinner. So I had to also put in a bid for a bottle o' gin and bottles o' the Vermouth brothers, Tony and Pierre. It wasn't till later that I appreciated what a grand law this here law was. When I got my drinks I paid ten cents apiece for 'em for service, besides payin' for the bottles o' stuff to drink. And, besides that, about every third highball or bronix I ordered, the waiter'd bring back word that I was just out of ingredients and then they'd be another delay w'ile they sent to the garage for more. If they had that law all over the country they'd soon be an end o' drinkin', because everybody'd get so mad they'd kill each other.

My cross-examination had took quite a long time, but when I got to my room the Wife wasn't back from lunch yet and I had to cover the Marathon route all over again and look her up. We only had the one key to the room, and o' course couldn't expect no more'n that at the price.

The Missus had bought one o' the daily programs they get out and she knowed just what we had to do the rest o' the day.

"For the next couple hours," she says, "we can suit ourself."

"All right," says I. "It suits me to take off my shoes and lay down."

"I'll rest, too," she says; "but at half past four we have to be in the Cocoanut Grove for tea and dancin'. And then we come back to the room and dress for dinner. Then we eat and then we set around till the evenin' dance starts. Then we dance till we're ready for bed."

"Who do we dance all these dances with?" I ast her.

"With whoever we get acquainted with," she says.

"All right," says I; "but let's be careful."

Well, we took our nap and then we followed schedule and had our tea in the Cocoanut Grove. You know how I love tea! My feet was still achin' and the Missus couldn't talk me into no dance.

When we'd set there an hour and was saturated with tea, the Wife says it was time to go up and change into our Tuxedos. I was all in when we reached the room and willin' to even pass up supper and nestle in the hay, but I was informed that the biggest part o' the day's doin's was yet to come. So from six o'clock till after seven I wrestled with studs, and hooks and eyes that didn't act like they'd ever met before and wasn't anxious to get acquainted, and then down we went again to the dinin'-room.

"How about a little bronix before the feed?" I says.

"It would taste good," says the Missus.

So I called Eph and give him the order. In somethin' less than half an hour he come back empty-handed.

"You ain't got no cocktail stuff," he says.

"I certainly have," says I. "I ordered it early this afternoon."

"Where at?" he ast me.

"Over in the bar," I says.

"Oh, the regular bar!" he says. "That don't count. You got to have stuff at the service bar to get it served in here."

"I ain't as thirsty as I thought I was," says I.

"Me, neither," says the Missus.

So we went ahead and ordered our meal, and w'ile we was waitin' for it a young couple come and took the other two chairs at our table. They didn't have to announce through a megaphone that they was honeymooners. It was wrote all over 'em. They was reachin' under the table for each other's hand every other minute, and when they wasn't doin' that they was smilin' at each other or gigglin' at nothin'. You couldn't feel that good and be payin' seventeen dollars a day for room and board unless you was just married or somethin'.

I thought at first their company'd be fun, but after a few meals it got like the southern cookin' and begun to undermine the health.

The conversation between they and us was what you could call limited. It took place the next day at lunch. The young husband thought he was about to take a bite o' the entry, which happened to be roast mutton with sirup; but he couldn't help from lookin' at her at the same time and his empty fork started for his face prongs up.

"Look out for your eye," I says.

He dropped the fork and they both blushed till you could see it right through the sunburn. Then they give me a Mexican look and our acquaintance was at an end.

This first night, when we was through eatin', we wandered out in the lobby and took seats where we could watch the passin' show. The men was all dressed like me, except I was up to date and had on a mushroom shirt, w'ile they was sportin' the old-fashioned concrete bosom. The women's dresses begun at the top with a belt, and some o' them stopped at the mezzanine floor w'ile others went clear down to the basement and helped keep the rugs clean. They was one that must of thought it was the Fourth o' July. From the top of her head to where the top of her bathin' suit had left off, she was a red, red rose. From there to the top of her gown was white, and her gown, what they was of it—was blue.

"My!" says the Missus. "What stunnin' gowns!"

"Yes," I says; "and you could have one just like 'em if you'd take the shade offen the piano lamp at home and cut it down to the right size."

Round ten o'clock we wandered in the Palm Garden, where the dancin' had been renewed. The Wife wanted to plunge right in the mazes o' the foxy trot.

"I'll take some courage first," says I. And then was when I found out that it cost you ten cents extra besides the tip to pay for a drink that you already owned in fee simple.

Well, I guess we must of danced about six dances together and had that many quarrels before she was ready to go to bed. And oh, how grand that old hay-pile felt when I finally bounced into it!

The next day we went to the ocean at the legal hour—half past eleven. I never had so much fun in my life. The surf was runnin' high, I heard 'em say; and I don't know which I'd rather do, go bathin' in the ocean at Palm Beach when the surf is runnin' high, or have a dentist get one o' my molars ready for a big inlay at a big outlay. Once in a w'ile I managed to not get throwed on my head when a wave hit me. As for swimmin', you had just as much chance as if you was at State and Madison at the noon hour. And before I'd been in a minute they was enough salt in my different features to keep the Blackstone hotel runnin' all through the onion season.

The Missus enjoyed it just as much as me. She tried to pretend at first, and when she got floored she'd give a squeal that was supposed to mean heavenly bliss. But after she'd been bruised from head to feet and her hair looked and felt like spinach with French dressin', and she'd drank all she could hold o' the Gulf Stream, she didn't resist none when I drug her in to shore and staggered with her up to our private rooms at five a week per each.

Without consultin' her, I went to the desk at the Casino and told 'em they could have them rooms back.

"All right," says the clerk, and turned our keys over to the next in line.

"How about a refund?" I ast him; but he was waitin' on somebody else.

After that we done our bathin' in the tub. But we was down to the beach every morning at eleven-thirty to watch the rest o' them get batted round.

And at half past twelve every day we'd follow the crowd to the Breakers' porch and dance together, the Missus and I. Then it'd be back to the other hostelry, sometimes limpin' and sometimes in an Afromobile, and a drink or two in the Palm Garden before lunch. And after lunch we'd lay down; or we'd pay some Eph two or three dollars to pedal us through the windin' jungle trail, that was every bit as wild as the Art Institute; or we'd ferry acrost Lake Worth to West Palm Beach and take in a movie, or we'd stand in front o' the portable Fifth Avenue stores w'ile the Missus wished she could have this dress or that hat, or somethin' else that she wouldn't of looked at if she'd been home and in her right mind. But always at half past four we had to live up to the rules and be in the Cocoanut Grove for tea and some more foxy trottin'. And then it was dress for dinner, eat dinner, watch the parade and wind up the glorious day with more dancin'.

I bet you any amount you name that the Castles in their whole life haven't danced together as much as I and the Missus did at Palm Beach. I'd of gave five dollars if even one o' the waiters had took her offen my hands for one dance. But I knowed that if I made the offer public they'd of been a really serious quarrel between us instead o' just the minor brawls occasioned by steppin' on each other's feet.

She made a discovery one night. She found out that they was a place called the Beach Club where most o' the real people disappeared to every evenin' after dinner. She says we would have to go there too.

"But I ain't a member," I says.

"Then find out how you get to be one," she says.

So to the Beach Club I went and made inquiries.

"You'll have to be introduced by a guy that already belongs," says the man at the door.

"Who belongs?" I ast him.

"Hundreds o' people," he says. "Who do you know?"

"Two waiters, two barkeepers and one elevator boy," I says.

He laughed, but his laugh didn't get me no membership card and I had to dance three or four extra times the next day to square myself with the Missus.

She made another discovery and it cost me six bucks. She found out that, though the meals in the regular dinin'-room was included in the triflin' rates per day, the real people had at least two o' their meals in the garden grill and paid extra for 'em. We tried it for one meal and I must say I enjoyed it—all but the check.

"We can't keep up that clip," I says to her.

"We could," says she, "if you wasn't spendin' so much on your locker."

"The locker's a matter o' life and death," I says. "They ain't no man in the world that could dance as much with their own wife as I do and live without liquid stimulus."

When we'd been there four days she got to be on speakin' terms with the ladies' maid that hung round the lobby and helped put the costumes back on when they slipped off. From this here maid the Missus learned who was who, and the information was relayed to me as soon as they was a chance. We'd be settin' on the porch when I'd feel an elbow in my ribs all of a sudden. I'd look up at who was passin' and then try and pretend I was excited.

"Who is it?" I'd whisper.

"That's Mrs. Vandeventer," the Wife'd say. "Her husband's the biggest street-car conductor in Philadelphia."

Or somebody'd set beside us at the beach or in the Palm Garden and my ribs would be all battered up before the Missus was calm enough to tip me off.

"The Vincents," she'd say; "the canned prune people."

It was a little bit thrillin' at first to be rubbin' elbows with all them celeb's; but it got so finally that I could walk out o' the dinin'-room right behind Scotti, the opera singer, without forgettin' that my feet hurt.

The Washington's Birthday Ball brought 'em all together at once, and the Missus pointed out eight and nine at a time and got me so mixed up that I didn't know Pat Vanderbilt from Maggie Rockefeller. The only one you couldn't make no mistake about was a Russian count that you couldn't pronounce. He was buyin' bay mules or somethin' for the Russian government, and he was in ambush.

"They say he can't hardly speak a word of English," says the Missus.

"If I knowed the word for barber shop in Russia," says I, "I'd tell him they was one in this hotel."

V

In our mail box the next mornin' they was a notice that our first week was up and all we owed was one hundred and forty-six dollars and fifty cents. The bill for room and meals was one hundred and nineteen dollars. The rest was for gettin' clo'es pressed and keepin' the locker damp.

I didn't have no appetite for breakfast. I told the Wife I'd wait up in the room and for her to come when she got through. When she blew in I had my speech prepared.

"Look here," I says; "this is our eighth day in Palm Beach society. You're on speakin' terms with a maid and I've got acquainted with half a dozen o' the male hired help. It's cost us about a hundred and sixty-five dollars, includin' them private rooms down to the Casino and our Afromobile trips, and this and that. You know a whole lot o' swell people by sight, but you can't talk to 'em. It'd be just as much satisfaction and hundreds o' dollars cheaper to look up their names in the telephone directory at home; then phone to 'em and, when you got 'em, tell 'em it was the wrong number. That way, you'd get 'em to speak to you at least.

"As for sport," I says, "we don't play golf and we don't play tennis and we don't swim. We go through the same program o' doin' nothin' every day. We dance, but we don't never change partners, For twelve dollars I could buy a phonograph up home and I and you could trot round the livin'-room all evenin' without no danger o' havin' some o' them fancy birds cave our shins in. And we could have twice as much liquid refreshments up there at about a twentieth the cost.

"That Gould I met on the train comin' down," I says, "was a even bigger liar than I give him credit for. He says that when he was here people pestered him to death by comin' up and speakin' to him. We ain't had to dodge nobody or hike behind a cocoanut tree to remain exclusive. He says Palm Beach was too common for him. What he should of said was that it was too lonesome. If they was just one white man here that'd listen to my stuff I wouldn't have no kick. But it ain't no pleasure tellin' stories to the Ephs. They laugh whether it's good or not, and then want a dime for laughin'.

"As for our clo'es," I says, "they would be all right for a couple o' days' stay. But the dames round here, and the men, too, has somethin' different to put on for every mornin', afternoon, and night. You've wore your two evenin' gowns so much that I just have to snap my finger at the hooks and they go and grab the right eyes.

"The meals would be grand," I says, "if the cook didn't keep gettin' mixed up and puttin' puddin' sauce on the meat and gravy on the pie.

"I'm glad we've been to Palm Beach," I says. "I wouldn't of missed it for nothin'. But the ocean won't be no different to-morrow than it was yesterday, and the same for the daily program. It don't even rain here, to give us a little variety.

"Now what do you say," I says, "to us just settlin' this bill, and whatever we owe since then, and beatin' it out o' here just as fast as we can go?"

The Missus didn't say nothin' for a w'ile. She was too busy cryin'. She knowed that what I'd said was the truth, but she wouldn't give up without a struggle.

"Just three more days," she says finally. "If we don't meet somebody worth meetin' in the next three days I'll go wherever you want to take me."

"All right," I says; "three more days it is. What's a little matter o' sixty dollars?"

Well, in them next two days and a half she done some desperate flirtin', but as it was all with women I didn't get jealous. She picked out some o' the E-light o' Chicago and tried every trick she could think up. She told 'em their noses was shiny and offered 'em her powder. She stepped on their white shoes just so's to get a chance to beg their pardon. She told 'em their clo'es was unhooked, and then unhooked 'em so's she could hook 'em up again. She tried to loan 'em her finger-nail tools. When she seen one fannin' herself she'd say: "Excuse me, Mrs. So-and-So; but we got the coolest room in the hotel, and I'd be glad to have you go up there and quit perspirin'." But not a rise did she get.

Not till the afternoon o' the third day o' grace. And I don't know if I ought to tell you this or not—only I'm sure you won't spill it nowheres.

We'd went up in our room after lunch. I was tired out and she was discouraged. We'd set round for over an hour, not sayin' or doin' nothin'.

I wanted to talk about the chance of us gettin' away the next mornin', but I didn't dast bring up the subject.

The Missus complained of it bein' hot and opened the door to leave the breeze go through. She was settin' in a chair near the doorway, pretendin' to read the *Palm Beach News*. All of a sudden she jumped up and kind o' hissed at me.

"What's the matter?" I says, springin' from the lounge.

"Come here!" she says, and went out the door into the hall.

I got there as fast as I could, thinkin' it was a rat or a fire. But the Missus just pointed to a lady walkin' away from us, six or seven doors down.

"It's Mrs. Potter," she says; "*the* Mrs. Potter from Chicago!"

"Oh!" I says, puttin' all the excitement I could into my voice.

And I was just startin' back into the room when I seen Mrs. Potter stop and turn round and come to'rd us. She stopped again maybe twenty feet from where the Missus was standin'.

"Are you on this floor?" she says.

The Missus shook like a leaf.

"Yes," says she, so low you couldn't hardly hear her.

"Please see that they's some towels put in 559," says *the* Mrs. Potter from Chicago.

VI

About five o'clock the Wife quieted down and I thought it was safe to talk to her. "I've been readin' in the guide about a pretty river trip," I says. "We can start from here on the boat to-morrow mornin'. They run to Fort Pierce to-morrow and stay there to-morrow night. The next day they go from Fort Pierce to Rockledge, and the day after that from Rockledge to Daytona. The fare's only five dollars apiece. And we can catch a north-bound train at Daytona."

"All right, I don't care," says the Missus.

So I left her and went down-stairs and acrost the street to ask Mr. Foster. Ask Mr. Foster happened to be a girl. She sold me the boat tickets and promised she would reserve a room with bath for us at Fort Pierce, where we was to spend the followin' night. I bet she knowed all the w'ile that rooms with a bath in Fort Pierce is scarcer than toes on a sturgeon.

I went back to the room and helped with the packin' in an advisory capacity. Neither one of us had the heart to dress for dinner. We ordered somethin' sent up and got soaked an extra dollar for service. But we was past carin' for a little thing like that.

At nine o'clock next mornin' the good ship *Constitution* stopped at the Poinciana dock w'ile we piled aboard. One bellhop was down to see us off and it cost me a quarter to get that much attention. Mrs. Potter must of overslept herself.

The boat was loaded to the guards and I ain't braggin' when I say that we was the best-lookin' people aboard. And as for manners, why, say, old Bill Sykes could of passed off for Henry Chesterfield in that gang! Each one o' them occupied three o' the deck chairs and sprayed orange juice all over their neighbors. We could of talked to plenty o' people here, all right; they were as clubby a gang as I ever seen. But I was afraid if I said somethin' they'd have to answer; and, with their mouths as full o' citrus fruit as they was, the results might of been fatal to my light suit.

We went up the lake to a canal and then through it to Indian River. The boat run aground every few minutes and had to be pried loose. About twelve o'clock a cullud gemman come up on deck and told us lunch was ready. At half past one he served it at a long family table in the cabin. As far as I was concerned, he might as well of left it on the stove. Even if you could of bit into the food, a glimpse of your fellow diners would of strangled your appetite.

After the repast I called the Missus aside.

"Somethin' tells me we're not goin' to live through three days o' this," I says. "What about takin' the train from Fort Pierce and beatin' it for Jacksonville, and then home?"

"But that'd get us to Chicago too quick," says she. "We told people how long we was goin' to be gone and if we got back ahead o' time they'd think they was somethin' queer."

"They's too much queer on this boat," I says. "But you're goin' to have your own way from now on."

We landed in Fort Pierce about six. It was only two or three blocks to the hotel, but when they laid out that part o' town they overlooked some o' the modern conveniences, includin' sidewalks. We staggered through the sand with our grips and sure had worked up a hunger by the time we reached Ye Inn.

"Got reservations for us here?" I ast the clerk.

"Yes," he says, and led us to 'em in person.

The room he showed us didn't have no bath, or even a chair that you could set on w'ile you pulled off your socks.

"Where's the bath?" I ast him.

"This way," he says, and I followed him down the hall, outdoors and up an alley.

Finally we come to a bathroom complete in all details, except that it didn't have no door. I went back to the room, got the Missus and went down to supper. Well, sir, I wish you could of been present at that supper. The choice o' meats was calves' liver and onions or calves' liver and onions. And I bet if them calves had of been still livin' yet they could of gave us some personal reminiscences about Garfield.

The Missus give the banquet one look and then laughed for the first time in several days.

"The guy that named this burg got the capitals mixed," I says. "It should of been Port Fierce."

And she laughed still heartier. Takin' advantage, I says:

"How about the train from here to Jacksonville?"

"You win!" says she. "We can't get home too soon to suit me."

VII

The mornin' we landed in Chicago it was about eight above and a wind was comin' offen the Lake a mile a minute. But it didn't feaze us.

"Lord!" says the Missus. "Ain't it grand to be home!"

"You said somethin'," says I. "But wouldn't it of been grander if we hadn't never left?"

"I don't know about that," she says. "I think we both of us learned a lesson."

"Yes," I says; "and the tuition wasn't only a matter o' close to seven hundred bucks!"

"Oh," says she, "we'll get that back easy!"

"How?" I ast her. "Do you expect some tips on the market from Mrs. Potter and the rest o' your new friends?"

"No," she says. "We'll win it. We'll win it in the rummy game with the Hatches."

CHAMPION

Midge Kelly scored his first knockout when he was seventeen. The knockee was his brother Connie, three years his junior and a cripple. The purse was a half dollar given to the younger Kelly by a lady whose electric had just missed bumping his soul from his frail little body.

Connie did not know Midge was in the house, else he never would have risked laying the prize on the arm of the least comfortable chair in the room, the better to observe its shining beauty. As Midge entered from the kitchen, the crippled boy covered the coin with his hand, but the movement lacked the speed requisite to escape his brother's quick eye.

"Watcha got there?" demanded Midge.

"Nothin'," said Connie.

"You're a one legged liar!" said Midge.

He strode over to his brother's chair and grasped the hand that concealed the coin.

"Let loose!" he ordered.

Connie began to cry.

"Let loose and shut up your noise," said the elder, and jerked his brother's hand from the chair arm.

The coin fell onto the bare floor. Midge pounced on it. His weak mouth widened in a triumphant smile.

"Nothin', huh?" he said. "All right, if it's nothin' you don't want it."

"Give that back," sobbed the younger.

"I'll give you a red nose, you little sneak! Where'd you steal it?"

"I didn't steal it. It's mine. A lady give it to me after she pretty near hit me with a car."

"It's a crime she missed you," said Midge.

Midge started for the front door. The cripple picked up his crutch, rose from his chair with difficulty, and, still sobbing, came toward Midge. The latter heard him and stopped.

"You better stay where you're at," he said.

"I want my money," cried the boy.

"I know what you want," said Midge.

Doubling up the fist that held the half dollar, he landed with all his

190

strength on his brother's mouth. Connie fell to the floor with a thud, the crutch tumbling on top of him. Midge stood beside the prostrate form.

"Is that enough?" he said. "Or do you want this, too?"

And he kicked him in the crippled leg.

"I guess that'll hold you," he said.

There was no response from the boy on the floor. Midge looked at him a moment, then at the coin in his hand, and then went out into the street, whistling.

An hour later, when Mrs. Kelly came home from her day's work at Faulkner's Steam Laundry, she found Connie on the floor, moaning. Dropping on her knees beside him, she called him by name a score of times. Then she got up and, pale as a ghost, dashed from the house. Dr. Ryan left the Kelly abode about dusk and walked toward Halsted Street. Mrs. Dorgan spied him as he passed her gate.

"Who's sick, Doctor?" she called.

"Poor little Connie," he replied. "He had a bad fall."

"How did it happen?"

"I can't say for sure, Margaret, but I'd almost bet he was knocked down."

"Knocked down!" exclaimed Mrs. Dorgan. "Why, who—?"

"Have you seen the other one lately?"

"Michael? No, not since mornin'. You can't be thinkin'—"

"I wouldn't put it past him, Margaret," said the doctor gravely. "The lad's mouth is swollen and cut, and his poor, skinny little leg is bruised. He surely didn't do it to himself and I think Helen suspects the other one."

"Lord save us!" said Mrs. Dorgan. "I'll run over and see if I can help."

"That's a good woman," said Doctor Ryan, and went on down the street.

Near midnight, when Midge came home, his mother was sitting at Connie's bedside. She did not look up.

"Well," said Midge, "what's the matter?"

She remained silent. Midge repeated his question.

"Michael, you know what's the matter," she said at length.

"I don't know nothin'," said Midge.

"Don't lie to me, Michael. What did you do to your brother?"

"Nothin'."

"You hit him."

"Well, then, I hit him. What of it? It ain't the first time."

Her lips pressed tightly together, her face like chalk, Ellen Kelly rose from her chair and made straight for him. Midge backed against the door.

"Lay off'n me, Ma. I don't want to fight no woman."

Still she came on breathing heavily.

"Stop where you're at, Ma," he warned.

There was a brief struggle and Midge's mother lay on the floor before him.

"You ain't hurt, Ma. You're lucky I didn't land good. And I told you to lay off'n me."

"God forgive you, Michael!"

Midge found Hap Collins in the showdown game at the Royal.

"Come on out a minute," he said.

Hap followed him out on the walk.

"I'm leavin' town for a w'ile," said Midge.

"What for?"

"Well, we had a little run-in up to the house. The kid stole a half buck off'n me, and when I went after it he cracked me with his crutch. So I nailed him. And the old lady came at me with a chair and I took it off'n her and she fell down."

"How is Connie hurt?"

"Not bad."

"What are you runnin' away for?"

"Who the hell said I was runnin' away? I'm sick and tired o' gettin' picked on; that's all. So I'm leavin' for a w'ile and I want a piece o' money."

"I ain't only got six bits," said Happy.

"You're in bad shape, ain't you? Well, come through with it."

Happy came through.

"You oughtn't to hit the kid," he said.

"I ain't astin' you who can I hit," snarled Midge. "You try to put somethin' over on me and you'll get the same dose. I'm goin' now."

"Go as far as you like," said Happy, but not until he was sure that Kelly was out of hearing.

Early the following morning, Midge boarded a train for Milwaukee. He had no ticket, but no one knew the difference. The conductor remained in the caboose.

On a night six months later, Midge hurried out of the "stage door" of the Star Boxing Club and made for Duane's saloon, two blocks away. In his pocket were twelve dollars, his reward for having battered up one Demon Dempsey through the six rounds of the first preliminary.

It was Midge's first professional engagement in the manly art. Also it was the first time in weeks that he had earned twelve dollars.

On the way to Duane's he had to pass Niemann's. He pulled his cap over his eyes and increased his pace until he had gone by. Inside Niemann's stood a trusting bartender, who for ten days had staked Midge to drinks and allowed him to ravage the lunch on a promise to come in and settle the moment he was paid for the "prelim."

Midge strode into Duane's and aroused the napping bartender by slapping a silver dollar on the festive board.

"Gimme a shot," said Midge.

The shooting continued until the wind-up at the Star was over and part of the fight crowd joined Midge in front of Duane's bar. A youth in the early twenties, standing next to young Kelly, finally summoned sufficient courage to address him.

"Wasn't you in the first bout?" he ventured.

"Yeh," Midge replied.

"My name's Hersch," said the other.

Midge received the startling information in silence.

"I don't want to butt in," continued Mr. Hersch, "but I'd like to buy you a drink."

"All right," said Midge, "but don't overstrain yourself."

Mr. Hersch laughed uproariously and beckoned to the bartender.

"You certainly gave that wop a trimmin' tonight," said the buyer of the drink, when they had been served. "I thought you'd kill him."

"I would if I hadn't let up," Midge replied. "I'll kill 'em all."

"You got the wallop all right," the other said admiringly.

"Have I got the wallop?" said Midge. "Say, I can kick like a mule. Did you notice them muscles in my shoulders?"

"Notice 'em? I couldn't help from noticin' 'em," said Hersch. "I says to the fella settin' alongside o' me, I says: 'Look at them shoulders! No wonder he can hit,' I says to him."

"Just let me land and it's good-by, baby," said Midge. "I'll kill 'em all."

The oral manslaughter continued until Duane's closed for the night. At parting, Midge and his new friend shook hands and arranged for a meeting the following evening.

For nearly a week the two were together almost constantly. It was Hersch's pleasant role to listen to Midge's modest revelations concerning himself, and to buy every time Midge's glass was empty. But there came an evening when Hersch regretfully announced that he must go home to supper.

"I got a date for eight bells," he confided. "I could stick till then, only I must clean up and put on the Sunday clo'es, 'cause she's the prettiest little thing in Milwaukee."

"Can't you fix it for two?" asked Midge.

"I don't know who to get," Hersch replied. "Wait, though. I got a sister and if she ain't busy, it'll be O. K. She's no bum for looks herself."

So it came about that Midge and Emma Hersch and Emma's brother and the prettiest little thing in Milwaukee foregathered at Wall's and danced half the night away. And Midge and Emma danced every dance together, for though every little onestep seemed to induce a new thirst of its own, Lou Hersch stayed too sober to dance with his own sister.

The next day, penniless at last in spite of his phenomenal ability to make someone else settle, Midge Kelly sought out Doc Hammond, matchmaker for the Star, and asked to be booked for the next show.

"I could put you on with Tracy for the next bout," said Doc.

"What's they in it?" asked Midge.

"Twenty if you cop," Doc told him.

"Have a heart," protested Midge. "Didn't I look good the other night?"

"You looked all right. But you aren't Freddie Welsh yet by a consid'able margin."

"I ain't scared of Freddie Welsh or none of 'em," said Midge.

"Well, we don't pay our boxers by the size of their chests," Doc said. "I'm offerin' you this Tracy bout. Take it or leave it."

"All right; I'm on," said Midge, and he passed a pleasant afternoon at Duane's on the strength of his booking.

Young Tracy's manager came to Midge the night before the show.

"How do you feel about this go?" he asked.

"Me?" said Midge, "I feel all right. What do you mean, how do I feel?"

"I mean," said Tracy's manager, "that we're mighty anxious to win, 'cause the boy's got a chanct in Philly if he cops this one."

"What's your proposition?" asked Midge.

"Fifty bucks," said Tracy's manager.

"What do you think I am, a crook? Me lay down for fifty bucks. Not me!"

"Seventy-five, then," said Tracy's manager.

The market closed on eighty and the details were agreed on in short order. And the next night Midge was stopped in the second round by a terrific slap on the forearm.

This time Midge passed up both Niemann's and Duane's, having a

sizable account at each place, and sought his refreshment at Stein's farther down the street.

When the profits of his deal with Tracy were gone, he learned, by
firsthand information from Doc Hammond and the matchmakers at the
other "clubs," that he was no longer desired for even the cheapest of
preliminaries. There was no danger of his starving or dying of thirst
while Emma and Lou Hersch lived. But he made up his mind, four
months after his defeat by Young Tracy, that Milwaukee was not the
ideal place for him to live.

"I can lick the best of 'em," he reasoned, "but there ain't no more
chanct for me here. I can maybe go east and get on somewheres. And
besides—"

But just after Midge had purchased a ticket to Chicago with the
money he had "borrowed" from Emma Hersch "to buy shoes," a heavy
hand was laid on his shoulders and he turned to face two strangers.

"Where are you goin', Kelly?" inquired the owner of the heavy hand.

"Nowheres," said Midge. "What the hell do you care?"

The other stranger spoke:

"Kelly, I'm employed by Emma Hersch's mother to see that you do
right by her. And we want you to stay here till you've done it."

"You won't get nothin' but the worst of it, monkeying with me,"
said Midge.

Nevertheless, he did not depart for Chicago that night. Two days
later, Emma Hersch became Mrs. Kelly, and the gift of the groom, when
once they were alone, was a crushing blow on the bride's pale cheek.

Next morning, Midge left Milwaukee as he had entered it—by fast
freight.

"They's no use kiddin' ourself any more," said Tommy Haley. "He
might get down to thirty-seven in a pinch, but if he done below that a
mouse could stop him. He's a welter; that's what he is and he knows it
as well as I do. He's growed like a weed in the last six mont's. I told
him, I says, 'If you don't quit growin' they won't be nobody for you to
box, only Willard and them.' He says, 'Well, I wouldn't run away from
Willard if I weighed twenty pounds more.' "

"He must hate himself," said Tommy's brother.

"I never seen a good one that didn't," said Tommy. "And Midge is
a good one; don't make no mistake about that. I wisht we could of got
Welsh before the kid growed so big. But it's too late now. I won't make
no holler, though, if we can match him up with the Dutchman."

"Who do you mean?"

"Young Goetz, the welter champ. We mightn't not get so much dough for the bout itself, but it'd roll in afterward. What a drawin' card we'd be, 'cause the people pays their money to see the fella with the wallop, and that's Midge. And we'd keep the title just as long as Midge could make the weight."

"Can't you land no match with Goetz?"

"Sure, 'cause he needs the money. But I've went careful with the kid so far and look at the results I got! So what's the use of takin' a chanct? The kid's comin' every minute and Goetz is goin' back faster'n big Johnson did. I think we could lick him now; I'd bet my life on it. But six mont's from now they won't be no risk. He'll of licked hisself before that time. Then all as we'll have to do is sign up with him and wait for the referee to stop it. But Midge is so crazy to get at him now that I can't hardly hold him back."

The brothers Haley were lunching in a Boston hotel. Dan had come down from Holyoke to visit with Tommy and to watch the latter's protege go twelve rounds, or less, with Bud Cross. The bout promised little in the way of a contest, for Midge had twice stopped the Baltimore youth and Bud's reputation for gameness was all that had earned him the date. The fans were willing to pay the price to see Midge's hay-making left, but they wanted to see it used on an opponent who would not jump out of the ring the first time he felt its crushing force. Bud Cross was such an opponent, and his willingness to stop boxing-gloves with his eyes, ears, nose, and throat had long enabled him to escape the horrors of honest labor. A game boy was Bud, and he showed it in his battered, swollen, discolored face.

"I should think," said Dan Haley, "that the kid'd do whatever you tell him after all you done for him."

"Well," said Tommy, "he's took my dope pretty straight so far, but he's so sure of hisself that he can't see no reason for waitin'. He'll do what I say, though; he'd be a sucker not to."

"You got a contrac' with him?"

"No, I don't need no contrac'. He knows it was me that drug him out o' the gutter and he ain't goin' to turn me down now, when he's got the dough and bound to get more. Where'd he of been at if I hadn't listened to him when he first come to me? That's pretty near two years ago now, but it seems like last week. I was settin' in the s'loon acrost from the Pleasant Club in Philly, waitin' for McCann to count the dough and come over, when this little bum blowed in and tried to stand the house off for a drink. They told him nothin' doin' and to beat it out o' there, and then he seen me and come over to where I was settin' and ast me wasn't I a boxin' man and I told him who I was. Then he ast me for money to buy a shot and I told him to set down and I'd buy it for him.

"Then we got talkin' things over and he told me his name and told me about fightin' a couple o' prelims out to Milwaukee. So I says, 'Well, boy, I don't know how good or how rotten you are, but you won't never get nowheres trainin' on that stuff.' So he says he'd cut it out if he could get on in a bout and I says I would give him a chanct if he played square with me and didn't touch no more to drink. So we shook hands and I took him up to the hotel with me and give him a bath and the next day I bought him some clo'es. And I staked him to eats and sleeps for over six weeks. He had a hard time breakin' away from the polish, but finally I thought he was fit and I give him his chanct. He went on with Smiley Sayer and stopped him so quick that Smiley thought sure he was poisoned.

"Well, you know what he's did since. The only beatin' in his record was by Tracy in Milwaukee before I got hold of him, and he's licked Tracy three times in the last year.

"I've gave him all the best of it in a money way and he's got seven thousand bucks in cold storage. How's that for a kid that was in the gutter two years ago? And he'd have still more yet if he wasn't so nuts over clo'es and got to stop at the good hotels and so forth."

"Where's his home at?"

"Well, he ain't really got no home. He came from Chicago and his mother canned him out o' the house for bein' no good. She give him a raw deal, I guess, and he says he won't have nothin' to do with her unless she comes to him first. She's got a pile o' money, he says, so he ain't worryin' about her."

The gentleman under discussion entered the café and swaggered to Tommy's table, while the whole room turned to look.

Midge was the picture of health despite a slightly colored eye and an ear that seemed to have no opening. But perhaps it was not his healthiness that drew all eyes. His diamond horse-shoe tie pin, his purple cross-striped shirt, his orange shoes, and his light blue suit fairly screamed for attention.

"Where you been?" he asked Tommy. "I been lookin' all over for you."

"Set down," said his manager.

"No time," said Midge. "I'm goin' down to the w'arf and see 'em unload the fish."

"Shake hands with my brother Dan," said Tommy.

Midge shook with the Holyoke Haley.

"If you're Tommy's brother, you're O. K. with me," said Midge, and the brothers beamed with pleasure.

Dan moistened his lips and murmured an embarrassed reply, but it was lost on the young gladiator.

"Leave me take twenty," Midge was saying. "I prob'ly won't need it, but I don't like to be caught short."

Tommy parted with a twenty dollar bill and recorded the transaction in a small black book the insurance company had given him for Christmas.

"But," he said, "it won't cost you no twenty to look at them fish. Want me to go along?"

"No," said Midge hastily. "You and your brother here prob'ly got a lot to say to each other."

"Well," said Tommy, "don't take no bad money and don't get lost. And you better be back at four o'clock and lay down a w'ile."

"I don't need no rest to beat this guy," said Midge. "He'll do enough layin' down for the both of us."

And laughing even more than the jest called for, he strode out through the fire of admiring and startled glances.

The corner of Boylston and Tremont was the nearest Midge got to the wharf, but the lady awaiting him was doubtless a more dazzling sight than the catch of the luckiest Massachusetts fisherman. She could talk, too—probably better than the fish.

"O you Kid!" she said, flashing a few silver teeth among the gold. "O you fighting man!"

Midge smiled up at her.

"We'll go somewheres and get a drink," he said. "One won't hurt."

In New Orleans, five months after he had rearranged the map of Bud Cross for the third time, Midge finished training for his championship bout with the Dutchman.

Back in his hotel after the final workout, Midge stopped to chat with some of the boys from up north, who had made the long trip to see a champion dethroned, for the result of this bout was so nearly a foregone conclusion that even the experts had guessed it.

Tommy Haley secured the key and the mail and ascended to the Kelly suite. He was bathing when Midge came in, half an hour later.

"Any mail?" asked Midge.

"There on the bed," replied Tommy from the tub.

Midge picked up the stack of letters and postcards and glanced them over. From the pile he sorted out three letters and laid them on the table. The rest he tossed into the waste-basket. Then he picked up the three and sat for a few moments holding them, while his eyes gazed off into space. At length he looked again at the three unopened letters in his hand; then he put one in his pocket and tossed the other two at the basket. They missed their target and fell on the floor.

"Hell!" said Midge, and stooping over picked them up.

He opened one postmarked Milwaukee and read:

Dear Husband:

I have wrote to you so manny times and got no anser and I dont know if you ever got them, so I am writeing again in the hopes you will get this letter and anser. I dont like to bother you with my trubles and I would not only for the baby and I am not asking you should write to me but only send a little money and I am not asking for myself but the baby has not been well a day sence last Aug. and the dr. told me she cant live much longer unless I give her better food and thats impossible the way things are. Lou has not been working for a year and what I make dont hardley pay for the rent. I am not asking for you to give me any money, but only you should send what I loaned when convenient and I think it amts. to about $36.00. Please try and send that amt. and it will help me, but if you cant send the whole amt. try and send me something.

Your wife,

Emma.

Midge tore the letter into a hundred pieces and scattered them over the floor.

"Money, money, money!" he said. "They must think I'm made o' money. I s'pose the old woman's after it too."

He opened his mother's letter:

dear Michael Connie wonted me to rite and say you must beet the dutchman and he is sur you will and wonted me to say we wont you to rite and tell us about it, but I gess you havent no time to rite or we herd from you long beffore this but I wish you would rite jest a line or 2 boy becaus it wuld be better for Connie then a barl of medisin. It wuld help me to keep things going if you send me money now and then when you can spair it but if you cant send no money try and fine time to rite a letter onley a

few lines and it will please Connie. jest think boy he hasent got
out of bed in over 3 yrs. Connie says good luck.

Your Mother,
Ellen F. Kelly.

"I thought so," said Midge. "They're all alike."
The third letter was from New York. It read:

Hon:—This is the last letter you will get from me before your
champ, but I will send you a telegram Saturday, but I can't say
as much in a telegram as in a letter and I am writeing this to let
you know I am thinking of you and praying for good luck.

Lick him good hon and don't wait no longer than you have to
and don't forget to wire me as soon as its over. Give him that
little old left of yours on the nose hon and don't be afraid of
spoiling his good looks because he couldn't be no homlier than
he is. But don't let him spoil my baby's pretty face. You won't
will you hon.

Well hon I would give anything to be there and see it, but I
guess you love Haley better than me or you wouldn't let him keep
me away. But when your champ hon we can do as we please and
tell Haley to go to the devil.

Well hon I will send you a telegram Saturday and I almost
forgot to tell you I will need some more money, a couple hundred
say and you will have to wire it to me as soon as you get this.
You will won't you hon.

I will send you a telegram Saturday and remember hon I am
pulling for you.

Well good-by sweetheart and good luck.

Grace.

"They're all alike," said Midge. "Money, money, money."
Tommy Haley, shining from his ablutions, came in from the adjoining room.

"Thought you'd be layin' down," he said.
"I'm goin' to," said Midge, unbuttoning his orange shoes.
"I'll call you at six and you can eat up here without no bugs to pester
you. I got to go down and give them birds their tickets."
"Did you hear from Goldberg?" asked Midge.
"Didn't I tell you? Sure; fifteen weeks at five hundred, if we win. And

we can get a guarantee o' twelve thousand, with privileges either in New York or Milwaukee."

"Who with?"

"Anybody that'll stand up in front of you. You don't care who it is, do you?"

"Not me. I'll make 'em all look like a monkey."

"Well you better lay down aw'ile."

"Oh, say, wire two hundred to Grace for me, will you? Right away; the New York address."

"Two hundred! You just sent her three hundred last Sunday."

"Well, what the hell do you care?"

"All right, all right. Don't get sore about it. Anything else?"

"That's all," said Midge, and dropped onto the bed.

"And I want the deed done before I come back," said Grace as she rose from the table. "You won't fall down on me, will you, hon?"

"Leave it to me," said Midge. "And don't spend no more than you have to."

Grace smiled a farewell and left the café. Midge continued to sip his coffee and read his paper.

They were in Chicago and they were in the middle of Midge's first week in vaudeville. He had come straight north to reap the rewards of his glorious victory over the broken down Dutchman. A fortnight had been spent in learning his act, which consisted of a gymnastic exhibition and a ten minutes' monologue on the various excellences of Midge Kelly. And now he was twice daily turning 'em away from the Madison Theater.

His breakfast over and his paper read, Midge sauntered into the lobby and asked for his key. He then beckoned to a bell-boy, who had been hoping for that very honor.

"Find Haley, Tommy Haley," said Midge. "Tell him to come up to my room."

"Yes, sir, Mr. Kelly," said the boy, and proceeded to break all his former records for diligence.

Midge was looking out of his seventh-story window when Tommy answered the summons.

"What'll it be?" inquired his manager.

There was a pause before Midge replied.

"Haley," he said, "twenty-five per cent's a whole lot o' money."

"I guess I got it comin', ain't I?" said Tommy.

"I don't see how you figger it. I don't see where you're worth it to me."

"Well," said Tommy, "I didn't expect nothin' like this. I thought you was satisfied with the bargain. I don't want to beat nobody out o' nothin', but I don't see where you could have got anybody else that would of did all I done for you."

"Sure, that's all right," said the champion. "You done a lot for me in Philly. And you got good money for it, didn't you?"

"I ain't makin' no holler. Still and all, the big money's still ahead of us yet. And if it hadn't of been for me, you wouldn't of never got within grabbin' distance."

"Oh, I guess I could of went along all right," said Midge. "Who was it that hung that left on the Dutchman's jaw, me or you?"

"Yes, but you wouldn't been in the ring with the Dutchman if it wasn't for how I handled you."

"Well, this won't get us nowheres. The idear is that you ain't worth no twenty-five per cent now and it don't make no diff'rence what come off a year or two ago."

"Don't it?" said Tommy. "I'd say it made a whole lot of difference."

"Well, I say it don't and I guess that settles it."

"Look here, Midge," Tommy said, "I thought I was fair with you, but if you don't think so, I'm willin' to hear what you think is fair. I don't want nobody callin' me a Sherlock. Let's go down to business and sign up a contrac'. What's your figger?"

"I ain't namin' no figger," Midge replied. "I'm sayin' that twenty-five's too much. Now what are you willin' to take?"

"How about twenty?"

"Twenty's too much," said Kelly.

"What ain't too much?" asked Tommy.

"Well, Haley, I might as well give it to you straight. They ain't nothin' that ain't too much."

"You mean you don't want me at no figger?"

"That's the idear."

There was a minute's silence. Then Tommy Haley walked toward the door.

"Midge," he said, in a choking voice, "you're makin' a big mistake, boy. You can't throw down your best friends and get away with it. That damn woman will ruin you."

Midge sprang from his seat.

"You shut your mouth!" he stormed. "Get out o' here before they have to carry you out. You been spongin' off o' me long enough. Say one more word about the girl or about anything else and you'll get what the Dutchman got. Now get out!"

And Tommy Haley, having a very vivid memory of the Dutchman's face as he fell, got out.

Grace came in later, dropped her numerous bundles on the lounge and perched herself on the arm of Midge's chair.

"Well?" she said.

"Well," said Midge, "I got rid of him."

"Good boy!" said Grace. "And now I think you might give me that twenty-five per cent."

"Besides the seventy-five you're already gettin'?" said Midge.

"Don't be no grouch, hon. You don't look pretty when you're grouchy."

"It ain't my business to look pretty," Midge replied.

"Wait till you see how I look with the stuff I bought this mornin'!"

Midge glanced at the bundles on the lounge.

"There's Haley's twenty-five per cent," he said, "and then some."

The champion did not remain long without a manager. Haley's successor was none other than Jerome Harris, who saw in Midge a better meal ticket than his popular-priced musical show had been.

The contract, giving Mr. Harris twenty-five per cent of Midge's earnings, was signed in Detroit the week after Tommy Haley had heard his dismissal read. It had taken Midge just six days to learn that a popular actor cannot get on without the ministrations of a man who thinks, talks, and means business. At first Grace objected to the new member of the firm, but when Mr. Harris had demanded and secured from the vaudeville people a one-hundred-dollar increase in Midge's weekly stipend, she was convinced that the champion had acted for the best.

"You and my missus will have some great old times," Harris told Grace. "I'd of wired her to join us here, only I seen the Kid's bookin' takes us to Milwaukee next week, and that's where she is."

But when they were introduced in the Milwaukee hotel, Grace admitted to herself that her feeling for Mrs. Harris could hardly be called love at first sight. Midge, on the contrary, gave his new manager's wife the many times over and seemed loath to end the feast of his eyes.

"Some doll," he said to Grace when they were alone.

"Doll is right," the lady replied, "and sawdust where her brains ought to be."

"I'm li'ble to steal that baby," said Midge, and he smiled as he noted the effect of his words on his audience's face.

On Tuesday of the Milwaukee week the champion successfully defended his title in a bout that the newspapers never reported. Midge was alone in his room that morning when a visitor entered without knocking. The visitor was Lou Hersch.

Midge turned white at sight of him.

"What do you want?" he demanded.

"I guess you know," said Lou Hersch. "Your wife's starvin' to death and your baby's starvin' to death and I'm starvin' to death. And you're dirty with money."

"Listen," said Midge, "if it wasn't for you, I wouldn't never saw your sister. And, if you ain't man enough to hold a job, what's that to me? The best thing you can do is keep away from me."

"You give me a piece o' money and I'll go."

Midge's reply to the ultimatum was a straight right to his brother-in-law's narrow chest.

"Take that home to your sister."

And after Lou Hersch had picked himself up and slunk away, Midge thought: "It's lucky I didn't give him my left or I'd of croaked him. And if I'd hit him in the stomach, I'd of broke his spine."

There was a party after each evening performance during the Milwaukee engagement. The wine flowed freely and Midge had more of it than Tommy Haley ever would have permitted him. Mr. Harris offered no objection, which was possibly just as well for his own physical comfort.

In the dancing between drinks, Midge had his new manager's wife for a partner as often as Grace. The latter's face as she floundered round in the arms of the portly Harris, belied her frequent protestations that she was having the time of her life.

Several times that week, Midge thought Grace was on the point of starting the quarrel he hoped to have. But it was not until Friday night that she accommodated. He and Mrs. Harris had disappeared after the matinee and when Grace saw him again at the close of the night show, she came to the point at once.

"What are you tryin' to pull off?" she demanded.

"It's none o' your business, is it?" said Midge.

"You bet it's my business; mine and Harris's. You cut it short or you'll find out."

"Listen," said Midge, "have you got a mortgage on me or somethin'? You talk like we was married."

"We're goin' to be, too. And to-morrow's as good a time as any."

"Just about," Midge said. "You got as much chanct o' marryin' me to-morrow as the next day or next year and that ain't no chanct at all."

"We'll find out," said Grace.

"You're the one that's got somethin' to find out."

"What do you mean?"

"I mean I'm married already."

"You lie!"

"You think so, do you? Well, s'pose you go to this here address and get acquainted with my missus."

Midge scrawled a number on a piece of paper and handed it to her. She stared at it unseeingly.

"Well," said Midge, "I ain't kiddin' you. You go there and ask for Mrs. Michael Kelly, and if you don't find her, I'll marry you to-morrow before breakfast."

Still Grace stared at the scrap of paper. To Midge it seemed an age before she spoke again.

"You lied to me all this w'ile."

"You never ast me was I married. What's more, what the hell diff'rence did it make to you? You got a split, didn't you? Better'n fifty-fifty."

He started away.

"Where you goin'?"

"I'm goin' to meet Harris and his wife."

"I'm goin' with you. You're not goin' to shake me now."

"Yes, I am, too," said Midge quietly. "When I leave town to-morrow night, you're going to stay here. And if I see where you're goin' to make a fuss, I'll put you in a hospital where they'll keep you quiet. You can get your stuff to-morrow mornin' and I'll slip you a hundred bucks. And then I don't want to see no more o' you. And don't try and tag along now or I'll have to add another K. O. to the old record."

When Grace returned to the hotel that night, she discovered that Midge and the Harrises had moved to another. And when Midge left town the following night, he was again without a manager, and Mr. Harris was without a wife.

Three days prior to Midge Kelly's ten-round bout with Young Milton in New York City, the sporting editor of the *News* assigned Joe Morgan to write two or three thousand words about the champion to run with a picture lay-out for Sunday.

Joe Morgan dropped in at Midge's training quarters Friday afternoon. Midge, he learned, was doing road work, but Midge's manager, Wallie Adams, stood ready and willing to supply reams of dope about the greatest fighter of the age.

"Let's hear what you've got," said Joe, "and then I'll try to fix up something."

So Wallie stepped on the accelerator of his imagination and shot away.

"Just a kid; that's all he is; a regular boy. Get what I mean? Don't know the meanin' o' bad habits. Never tasted liquor in his life and would prob'bly get sick if he smelled it. Clean livin' put him up where he's at. Get what I mean? And modest and unassumin' as a school girl. He's so quiet you wouldn't never know he was round. And he'd go to jail before he'd talk about himself.

"No job at all to get him in shape, 'cause he's always that way. The only trouble we have with him is gettin' him to light into these poor bums they match him up with. He's scared he'll hurt somebody. Get what I mean? He's tickled to death over this match with Milton, 'cause everybody says Milton can stand the gaff. Midge'll maybe be able to cut loose a little this time. But the last two bouts he had, the guys hadn't no business in the ring with him, and he was holdin' back all the w'ile for the fear he'd kill somebody. Get what I mean?"

"Is he married?" inquired Joe.

"Say, you'd think he was married to hear him rave about them kiddies he's got. His fam'ly's up in Canada to their summer home and Midge is wild to get up there with 'em. He thinks more o' that wife and them kiddies than all the money in the world. Get what I mean?"

"How many children has he?"

"I don't know, four or five, I guess. All boys and every one of 'em a dead ringer for their dad."

"Is his father living?"

"No, the old man died when he was a kid. But he's got a grand old mother and a kid brother out in Chi. They're the first ones he thinks about after a match, them and his wife and kiddies. And he don't forget to send the old woman a thousand bucks after every bout. He's goin' to buy her a new home as soon as they pay him off for this match."

"How about his brother? Is he going to tackle the game?"

"Sure, and Midge says he'll be a champion before he's twenty years old. They're a fightin' fam'ly and all of 'em honest and straight as a die. Get what I mean? A fella that I can't tell you his name come to Midge in Milwaukee onct and wanted him to throw a fight and Midge give him such a trimmin' in the street that he couldn't go on that night. That's the kind he is. Get what I mean?"

Joe Morgan hung around the camp until Midge and his trainers returned.

"One o' the boys from the *News*," said Wallie by way of introduction. "I been givin' him your fam'ly hist'ry."

"Did he give you good dope?" he inquired.

"He's some historian," said Joe.

"Don't call me no names," said Wallie smiling. "Call us up if they's anything more you want. And keep your eyes on us Monday night. Get what I mean?"

The story in Sunday's *News* was read by thousands of lovers of the manly art. It was well written and full of human interest. Its slight inaccuracies went unchallenged, though three readers, besides Wallie Adams and Midge Kelly, saw and recognized them. The three were Grace, Tommy Haley, and Jerome Harris and the comments they made were not for publication.

Neither the Mrs. Kelly in Chicago nor the Mrs. Kelly in Milwaukee knew that there was such a paper as the New York *News*. And even if they had known of it and that it contained two columns of reading matter about Midge, neither mother nor wife could have bought it. For the *News* on Sunday is a nickel a copy.

Joe Morgan could have written more accurately, no doubt, if instead of Wallie Adams, he had interviewed Ellen Kelly and Connie Kelly and Emma Kelly and Lou Hersch and Grace and Jerome Harris and Tommy Haley and Hap Collins and two or three Milwaukee bartenders.

But a story built on their evidence would never have passed the sporting editor.

"Suppose you can prove it," that gentleman would have said. "It wouldn't get us anything but abuse to print it. The people don't want to see him knocked. He's champion."

THE FACTS

I

The engagement was broken off before it was announced. So only a thousand or so of the intimate friends and relatives of the parties knew anything about it. What they knew was that there had been an engagement and that there was one no longer. The cause of the breach they merely guessed, and most of the guesses were, in most particulars, wrong.

Each intimate and relative had a fragment of the truth. It remained for me to piece the fragments together. It was a difficult job, but I did it. Part of my evidence is hearsay; the major portion is fully corroborated. And not one of my witnesses had anything to gain through perjury.

So I am positive that I have at my tongue's end the facts, and I believe that in justice to everybody concerned I should make them public.

Ellen McDonald had lived on the North Side of Chicago for twenty-one years. Billy Bowen had been a South-Sider for seven years longer. But neither knew of the other's existence until they met in New York, the night before the Army-Navy game.

Billy, sitting with a business acquaintance at a neighboring table in Tonio's, was spotted by a male member of Ellen's party, a Chicagoan, too. He was urged to come on over. He did, and was introduced. The business acquaintance was also urged, came, was introduced and forgotten; forgotten, that is, by every one but the waiter, who observed that he danced not nor told stories, and figured that his function must be to pay. The business acquaintance had been Billy's guest. Now he became host, and without seeking the office.

It was not that Billy and Miss McDonald's male friends were niggards. But unfortunately for the b. a., the checks always happened to arrive when everybody else was dancing or so hysterical over Billy's repartee as to be potentially insolvent.

Billy was somewhere between his fourteenth and twenty-first high-ball; in other words, at his best, from the audience's standpoint. His dialogue was simply screaming and his dancing just heavenly. He was Frank Tinney doubling as Vernon Castle. On the floor he tried and accomplished twinkles that would have spelled catastrophe if attempted under the fourteen mark, or over the twenty-one. And he said the cutest things—one right after the other.

II

You can be charmed by a man's dancing, but you can't fall in love with his funniness. If you're going to fall in love with him at all, you'll do it when you catch him in a serious mood.

Miss McDonald caught Billy Bowen in one at the game next day. Entirely by accident or a decree of fate, her party and his sat in adjoining boxes. Not by accident, Miss McDonald sat in the chair that was nearest Billy's. She sat there first to be amused; she stayed to be conquered.

Here was a different Billy from the Billy of Tonio's. Here was a Billy who trained his gun on your heart and let your risibles alone. Here was a dreamy Billy, a Billy of romance.

How calm he remained through the excitement! How indifferent to the thrills of the game! There was depth to him. He was a man. Her escort and the others round her were children, screaming with delight at the puerile deeds of pseudo heroes. Football was a great sport, but a sport. It wasn't Life. Would the world be better or worse for that nine-yard gain that Elephant or Oliphant, or whatever his name was, had just made? She knew it wouldn't. Billy knew, too, for Billy was deep. He was thinking man's thoughts. She could tell by his silence, by his inattention to the scene before him. She scarcely could believe that here was the same person who, last night, had kept his own, yes, and the neighboring tables, roaring with laughter. What a complex character his!

In sooth, Mr. Bowen was thinking man's thoughts. He was thinking that if this pretty Miss McDowell, or Donnelly, were elsewhere, he could go to sleep. And that if he could remember which team he had bet on and could tell which team was which, he would have a better idea of whether he was likely to win or lose.

When, after the game, they parted, Billy rallied to the extent of asking permission to call. Ellen, it seemed, would be very glad to have him, but she couldn't tell exactly when she would have to be back in Chicago; she still had three more places to visit in the East. Could she possibly let him know when she did get back? Yes, she could and would; if he really wanted her to, she would drop him a note. He certainly wanted her to.

This, thought Billy, was the best possible arrangement. Her note would tell him her name and address, and save him the trouble of 'phoning to all the McConnells, McDowells, and Donnellys on the North Side. He did want to see her again; she was pretty, and, judging from last night, full of pep. And she had fallen for him; he knew it from that look.

He watched her until she was lost in the crowd. Then he hunted round for his pals and the car that had brought them up. At length he gave up the search and wearily climbed the elevated stairs. His hotel was on Broadway, near Forty-fourth. He left the train at Forty-second, the third time it stopped there.

"I guess you've rode far enough," said the guard. "Fifteen cents' worth for a nickel. I guess we ought to have a Pullman on these here trains."

"I guess," said Billy, "I guess——"

But the repartee well was dry. He stumbled down-stairs and hurried toward Broadway to replenish it.

III

Ellen McDonald's three more places to visit in the East must have been deadly dull. Anyway, on the sixth of December, scarcely more than a week after his parting with her in New York, Billy Bowen received the promised note. It informed him merely that her name was Ellen McDonald, that she lived at so-and-so Walton Place, and that she was back in Chicago.

That day, if you'll remember, was Monday. Miss McDonald's parents had tickets for the opera. But Ellen was honestly just worn out, and would they be mad at her if she stayed home and went to bed? They wouldn't. They would take Aunt Mary in her place.

On Tuesday morning, Paul Potter called up and wanted to know if she would go with him that night to "The Follies." She was horribly sorry, but she'd made an engagement. The engagement, evidently, was to study, and the subject was harmony, with Berlin, Kern, and Van Alstyne as instructors. She sat on the piano-bench from half-past seven till quarter after nine, and then went to her room vowing that she would accept any and all invitations for the following evening.

Fortunately, no invitations arrived, for at a quarter of nine Wednesday night, Mr. Bowen did. And in a brand-new mood. He was a bit shy and listened more than he talked. But when he talked, he talked well, though the sparkling wit of the night at Tonio's was lacking. Lacking, too, was the preoccupied air of the day at the football game. There was no problem to keep his mind busy, but even if the Army and Navy had been playing football in this very room, he could have told at a glance which was which. Vision and brain were perfectly clear. And he had been getting his old eight hours, and, like the railroad hen, sometimes nine and sometimes ten, every night since his arrival home from Gotham, N. Y. Mr. Bowen was on the wagon.

They talked of the East, of Tonio's, of the game (this was where Billy did most of his listening), of the war, of theatres, of books, of college, of automobiles, of the market. They talked, too, of their immediate families. Billy's, consisting of one married sister in South Bend, was soon exhausted. He had two cousins here in town whom he saw frequently, two cousins and their wives, but they were people who simply couldn't stay home nights. As for himself, he preferred his rooms and a good book to the so-called gay life. Ellen should think that a man who danced so well would want to be doing it all the time. It was nice of her to say that he danced well, but really he didn't, you know. Oh, yes, he did. She guessed she could tell. Well, anyway, the giddy whirl made no appeal to him, unless, of course, he was in particularly charming company. His avowed love for home and quiet surprised Ellen a little. It surprised Mr. Bowen a great deal. Only last night, he remembered, he had been driven almost desperate by that quiet of which he was now so fond; he had been on the point of busting loose, but had checked himself in time. He had played Canfield till ten, though the book-shelves were groaning with their load.

Ellen's family kept them busy for an hour and a half. It was a dear family and she wished he could meet it. Mother and father were out playing bridge somewhere to-night. Aunt Mary had gone to bed. Aunts Louise and Harriet lived in the next block. Sisters Edith and Wilma would be home from Northampton for the holidays about the twentieth. Brother Bob and his wife had built the cutest house; in Evanston. Her younger brother, Walter, was a case! He was away to-night, had gone out right after dinner. He'd better be in before mother and father came. He had a new love-affair every week, and sixteen years old last August. Mother and father really didn't care how many girls he was interested in, so long as they kept him too busy to run round with those crazy schoolmates of his. The latter were older than he; just at the age when it seems smart to drink beer and play cards for money. Father said if he ever found out that Walter was doing those things, he'd take him out of school and lock him up somewhere.

Aunts Louise and Mary and Harriet did a lot of settlement work. They met all sorts of queer people, people you'd never believe existed. The three aunts were unmarried.

Brother Bob's wife was dear, but absolutely without a sense of humor. Bob was full of fun, but they got along just beautifully together. You never saw a couple so much in love.

Edith was on the basket-ball team at college and terribly popular. Wilma was horribly clever and everybody said she'd make Phi Beta Kappa.

Ellen, so she averred, had been just nothing in school; not bright; not athletic, and, of course, not popular.

"Oh, of course not," said Billy, smiling.

"Honestly," fibbed Ellen.

"You never could make me believe it," said Billy.

Whereat Ellen blushed, and Billy's unbelief strengthened.

At this crisis, the Case burst into the room with his hat on. He removed it at sight of the caller and awkwardly advanced to be introduced.

"I'm going to bed," he announced, after the formality.

"I hoped," said Ellen, "you'd tell us about the latest. Who is it now? Beth?"

"Beth nothing!" scoffed the Case. "We split up the day of the Keewatin game."

"What was the matter?" asked his sister.

"I'm going to bed," said the Case. "It's pretty near midnight."

"By George, it is!" exclaimed Billy. "I didn't dream it was that late!"

"No," said Walter. "That's what I tell dad—the clock goes along some when you're having a good time."

Billy and Ellen looked shyly at each other, and then laughed; laughed harder, it seemed to Walter, than the joke warranted. In fact, he hadn't thought of it as a joke. If it was that good, he'd spring it on Kathryn to-morrow night. It would just about clinch her.

The Case, carrying out his repeated threat, went to bed and dreamed of Kathryn. Fifteen minutes later Ellen retired to dream of Billy. And an hour later than that, Billy was dreaming of Ellen, who had become suddenly popular with him, even if she hadn't been so at Northampton, which he didn't believe.

IV

They saw "The Follies" Friday night. A criticism of the show by either would have been the greatest folly of all. It is doubtful that they could have told what theatre they'd been to ten minutes after they'd left it. From wherever it was, they walked to a dancing place and danced. Ellen was so far gone that she failed to note the change in Billy's trotting. Foxes would have blushed for shame at its awkwardness and lack of variety. If Billy was a splendid dancer, he certainly did not prove it this night. All he knew or cared to know was that he was with the girl he wanted. And she knew only that she was with Billy, and happy.

On the drive home, the usual superfluous words were spoken. They were repeated inside the storm-door at Ellen's father's house, while the taxi driver, waiting, wondered audibly why them suckers of explorers beat it to the Pole to freeze when the North Side was so damn handy.

Ellen's father was out of town. So in the morning she broke the news to mother and Aunt Mary, and then sat down and wrote it to Edith and Wilma. Next she called up Bob's wife in Evanston, and after that she hurried to the next block and sprang it on Aunts Louise and Harriet. It was decided that Walter had better not be told. He didn't know how to keep a secret. Walter, therefore, was in ignorance till he got home from school. The only person he confided in the same evening was Kathryn, who was the only person he saw.

Bob and his wife and Aunts Louise and Harriet came to Sunday dinner, but were chased home early in the afternoon. Mr. McDonald was back and Billy was coming to talk to him. It would embarrass Billy to death to find such a crowd in the house. They'd all meet him soon, never fear, and when they met him, they'd be crazy about him. Bob and Aunt Mary and mother would like him because he was so bright and said such screaming things, and the rest would like him because he was so well-read and sensible, and so horribly good-looking.

Billy, I said, was coming to talk to Mr. McDonald. When he came, he did very little of the talking. He stated the purpose of his visit, told what business he was in and affirmed his ability to support a wife. Then he assumed the rôle of audience while Ellen's father delivered an hour's lecture. The speaker did not express his opinion of Tyrus Cobb or the Kaiser, but they were the only subjects he overlooked. Sobriety and industry were words frequently used.

"I don't care," he prevaricated, in conclusion, "how much money a man is making if he is sober and industrious. You attended college, and I presume you did all the fool things college boys do. Some men recover from their college education, others don't. I hope you're one of the former."

The Sunday-night supper, just cold scraps you might say, was partaken of by the happy but embarrassed pair, the trying-to-look happy but unembarrassed parents, and Aunt Mary. Walter, the Case, was out. He had stayed home the previous evening.

"He'll be here to-morrow night and the rest of the week, or I'll know the reason why," said Mr. McDonald.

"He won't, and I'll tell you the reason why," said Ellen.

"He's a real boy, Sam," put in the real boy's mother. "You can't expect him to stay home every minute."

"I can't expect anything of him," said the father. "You and the girls and Mary here have let him have his own way so long that he's past managing. When I was his age, I was in my bed at nine o'clock."

"Morning or night?" asked Ellen.

Her father scowled. It was evident he could not take a joke, not even a good one.

After the cold scraps had been ruined, Mr. McDonald drew Billy into the smoking-room and offered him a cigar. The prospective son-in-law was about to refuse and express a preference for cigarettes when something told him not to. A moment later he was deeply grateful to the something.

"I smoke three cigars a day," said the oracle, "one after each meal. That amount of smoking will hurt nobody. More than that is too much. I used to smoke to excess, four or five cigars per day, and maybe a pipe or two. I found it was affecting my health, and I cut down. Thank heaven, no one in my family ever got the cigarette habit; disease, rather. How any sane, clean-minded man can start on those things is beyond me."

"Me, too," agreed Billy, taking the proffered cigar with one hand and making sure with the other that his silver pill-case was as deep down in his pocket as it would go.

"Cigarettes, gambling, and drinking go hand in hand," continued the man of the house. "I couldn't trust a cigarette fiend with a nickel."

"There are only two or three kinds he could get for that," said Billy.

"What say?" demanded Mr. McDonald, but before Billy was obliged to wriggle out of it, Aunt Mary came in and reminded her brother-in-law that it was nearly church time.

Mr. McDonald and Aunt Mary went to church. Mrs. McDonald, pleading weariness, stayed home with "the children." She wanted a

chance to get acquainted with this pleasant-faced boy who was going
to rob her of one of her five dearest treasures.

The three were no sooner settled in front of the fireplace than Ellen
adroitly brought up the subject of auction bridge, knowing that it would
relieve Billy of the conversational burden.

"Mother is really quite a shark, aren't you, mother?" she said.

"I don't fancy being called a fish," said the mother.

"She's written two books on it, and she and father have won so many
prizes that they may have to lease a warehouse. If they'd only play for
money, just think how rich we'd all be!"

"The game is fascinating enough without adding to it the excitements
and evils of gambling," said Mrs. McDonald.

"It is a fascinating game," agreed Billy.

"It is," said Mrs. McDonald, and away she went.

Before father and Aunt Mary got home from church, Mr. Bowen
was a strong disciple of conservativeness in bidding and thoroughly
convinced that all the rules that had been taught were dead wrong. He
saw the shark's points so quickly and agreed so whole-heartedly with
her arguments that he impressed her as one of the most intelligent young
men she had ever talked to. It was too bad it was Sunday night, but
some evening soon he must come over for a game.

"I'd like awfully well to read your books," said Billy.

"The first one's usefulness died with the changes in the rules," replied
Mrs. McDonald. "But I think I have one of the new ones in the house,
and I'll be glad to have you take it."

"I don't like to have you give me your only copy."

"Oh, I believe we have two."

She knew perfectly well she had two dozen.

Aunt Mary announced that Walter had been seen in church with
Kathryn. He had made it his business to be seen. He and the lady had
come early and had manœuvred into the third row from the back, on
the aisle leading to the McDonald family pew. He had nudged his aunt
as she passed on the way to her seat, and she had turned and spoken
to him. She could not know that he and Kathryn had "ducked" before
the end of the processional.

After reporting favorably on the Case, Aunt Mary launched into a
description of the service. About seventy had turned out. The music had
been good, but not quite as good as in the morning. Mr. Pratt had sung
"Fear Ye Not, O Israel!" for the offertory. Dr. Gish was still sick and
a lay reader had served. She had heard from Allie French that Dr. Gish

expected to be out by the middle of the week and certainly would be able to preach next Sunday morning. The church had been cold at first, but very comfortable finally.

Ellen rose and said she and Billy would go out in the kitchen and make some fudge.

"I was afraid Aunt Mary would bore you to death," she told Billy, when they had kissed for the first time since five o'clock. "She just lives for the church and can talk on no other subject."

"I wouldn't hold that against her," said Billy charitably.

The fudge was a failure, as it was bound to be. But the Case, who came in just as it was being passed round, was the only one rude enough to say so.

"Is this a new stunt?" he inquired, when he had tested it.

"Is what a new stunt?" asked Ellen.

"Using cheese instead of chocolate."

"That will do, Walter," said his father. "You can go to bed."

Walter got up and started for the hall. At the threshold he stopped.

"I don't suppose there'll be any of that fudge left," he said. "But if there should be, you'd better put it in the mouse trap."

Billy called a taxi and departed soon after Walter's exit. When he got out at his South Side abode, the floor of the tonneau was littered with recent cigarettes.

And that night he dreamed that he was president of the anti-cigarette league; that Dr. Gish was vice-president, and that the motto of the organization was "No trump."

Billy Bowen's business took him out of town the second week in December, and it was not until the twentieth that he returned. He had been East and had ridden home from Buffalo on the same train with Wilma and Edith McDonald. But he didn't know it and neither did they. They could not be expected to recognize him from Ellen's description—that he was horribly good-looking. The dining-car conductor was all of that.

Ellen had further written them that he (not the dining-car conductor) was a man of many moods; that sometimes he was just nice and deep, and sometimes he was screamingly funny, and sometimes so serious and silent that she was almost afraid of him.

They were wild to see him and the journey through Ohio and Indiana would not have been half so long in his company. Edith, the athletic, would have revelled in his wit. Wilma would gleefully have fathomed his depths. They would both have been proud to flaunt his looks before the hundreds of their kind aboard the train. Their loss was greater than

Billy's, for he, smoking cigarettes as fast as he could light them and playing bridge that would have brought tears of compassion to the shark's eyes, enjoyed the trip, every minute of it.

Ellen and her father were at the station to meet the girls. His arrival on this train had not been heralded, and it added greatly to the hysterics of the occasion.

Wilma and Edith upbraided him for not knowing by instinct who they were. He accused them of recognizing him and purposely avoiding him. Much more of it was pulled in the same light vein, pro and con.

He was permitted at length to depart for his office. On the way he congratulated himself on the improbability of his ever being obliged to play basket-ball versus Edith. She must be a whizz in condition. Chances were she'd train down to a hundred and ninety-five before the big games. The other one, Wilma, was a splinter if he ever saw one. You had to keep your eyes peeled or you'd miss her entirely. But suppose you did miss her; what then! If she won her Phi Beta Kappa pin, he thought, it would make her a dandy belt.

These two, he thought, were a misdeal. They should be reshuffled and cut nearer the middle of the deck. Lots of other funny things he thought about these two.

Just before he had left Chicago on this trip, his stenographer had quit him to marry an elevator-starter named Felix Bond. He had 'phoned one of his cousins and asked him to be on the lookout for a live stenographer who wasn't likely to take the eye of an elevator-starter. The cousin had had one in mind.

Here was her card on Billy's desk when he reached the office. It was not a business-card visiting-card, at $3 per hundred. "Miss Violet Moore," the engraved part said. Above was written: "Mr. Bowen—Call me up any night after seven. Calumet 2678."

Billy stowed the card in his pocket and plunged into a pile of uninteresting letters.

On the night of the twenty-second there was a family dinner at McDonald's, and Billy was in on it. At the function he met the rest of them—Bob and his wife, and Aunt Harriet and Aunt Louise.

Bob and his wife, despite the former's alleged sense of humor, spooned every time they were contiguous. That they were in love with each other, as Ellen had said, was easy to see. The wherefore was more of a puzzle.

Bob's hirsute adornment having been disturbed by his spouse's digits during one of the orgies, he went up-stairs ten minutes before dinner time to effect repairs. Mrs. Bob was left alone on the davenport. In performance of his social duties, Billy went over and sat down beside her. She was not, like Miss Muffet, frightened away, but terror or some other fiend rendered her temporarily dumb. The game Mr. Bowen was making his fifth attempt to pry open a conversation when Bob came back.

To the impartial observer the scene on the davenport appeared heartless enough. There was a generous neutral zone between Billy and Flo, that being an abbreviation of Mrs. Bob's given name, which, as a few may suspect, was Florence. Billy was working hard and his face was flushed with the effort. The flush may have aroused Bob's suspicions. At any rate, he strode across the room, scowling almost audibly, shot a glance at Billy that would have made the Kaiser wince, halted magnificently in front of his wife, and commanded her to accompany him to the hall.

Billy's flush became ace high. He was about to get up and break a chair when a look from Ellen stopped him. She was at his side before the pair of Bobs had skidded out of the room.

"Please don't mind," she begged. "He's crazy. I forgot to tell you that he's insanely jealous."

"Did I understand you to say he had a sense of humor?"

"It doesn't work where Flo's concerned. If he sees her talking to a man he goes wild."

"With astonishment, probably," said Billy.

"You're a nice boy," said Ellen irrelevantly.

Dinner was announced and Mr. Bowen was glad to observe that Flo's terrestrial body was still intact. He was glad, too, to note that Bob was no longer frothing. He learned for the first time that the Case and Kathryn were of the party. Mrs. McDonald had wanted to make sure of Walter's presence; hence the presence of his crush.

Kathryn giggled when she was presented to Billy. It made him uncomfortable and he thought for a moment that a couple of studs had fallen out. He soon discovered, however, that the giggle was permanent, just as much a part of Kathryn as her fraction of a nose. He looked forward with new interest to the soup course, but was disappointed to find that she could negotiate it without disturbing the giggle or the linen.

He next centred his attention on Wilma and Edith. Another disappointment was in store. There were as many and as large oysters in Wilma's soup as in any one's. She ate them all, and, so far as appearances went, was the same Wilma. He had expected that Edith would either diet or plunge. But Edith was as prosaic in her consumption of victuals as Ellen, for instance, or Aunt Louise.

He must content himself for the present with Aunt Louise. She was sitting directly opposite and he had an unobstructed view of the widest part he had ever seen in woman's hair.

"Ogden Avenue," he said to himself.

Aunt Louise was telling about her experiences and Aunt Harriet's among the heathen of Peoria Street.

"You never would dream there were such people!" said she.

"I suppose most of them are foreign born," supposed her brother, who was Mr. McDonald.

"Practically all of them," said Aunt Louise.

Billy wanted to ask her whether she had ever missionaried among the Indians. He thought possibly an attempt to scalp her had failed by a narrow margin.

Between courses Edith worked hard to draw out his predicated comicality and Wilma worked as hard to make him sound his low notes. Their labors were in vain. He was not sleepy enough to be deep, and he was fourteen highballs shy of comedy.

In disgust, perhaps, at her failure to be amused, the major portion of the misdeal capsized her cocoa just before the close of the meal and drew a frown from her father, whom she could have thrown in ten minutes, straight falls, any style.

"She'll never miss that ounce," thought Billy.

When they got up from the table and started for the living-room, Mr. Bowen found himself walking beside Aunt Harriet, who had been so silent during dinner that he had all but forgotten her.

"Well, Miss McDonald," he said, "it's certainly a big family, isn't it?"

"Well, young man," said Aunt Harriet, "it ain't no small family, that's sure."

"I should say not," repeated Billy.

Walter and his giggling crush intercepted him.

"What do you think of Aunt Harriet's grammar?" demanded Walter.

"I didn't notice it," lied Billy.

"No, I s'pose not. 'Ain't no small family.' I s'pose you didn't notice it. She isn't a real aunt like Aunt Louise and Aunt Mary. She's just an adopted aunt. She kept house for dad and Aunt Louise after their mother died, and when dad got married, she just kept on living with Aunt Louise."

"Oh," was Billy's fresh comment, and it brought forth a fresh supply of giggles from Kathryn.

Ellen had already been made aware of Billy's disgusting plans. He had to catch a night train for St. Louis, and he would be there all day to-morrow, and he'd be back Friday, but he wouldn't have time to see her, and he'd surely call her up. And Friday afternoon he was going to South Bend to spend Christmas Day with his married sister, because it was probably the last Christmas he'd be able to spend with her.

"But I'll hustle home from South Bend Sunday morning," he said, "and don't you dare make any engagement for the afternoon."

"I do wish you could be with us Christmas Eve. The tree won't be a bit of fun without you."

"You know I wish I could. But you see how it is."

"I think your sister's mean."

Billy didn't deny it.

"Who's going to be here Christmas Eve?"

"Just the people we had to-night, except Kathryn and you. Why?"

"Oh, nothing," said Billy.

"Look here, sir," said his betrothed. "Don't you do anything foolish. You're not supposed to buy presents for the whole family. Just a little, tiny one for me, if you want to, but you mustn't spend much on it. And if you get anything for any one else in this house, I'll be mad."

"I'd like to see you mad," said Billy.

"You'd wish you hadn't," Ellen retorted.

When Billy had gone, Ellen returned to the living-room and faced the assembled company.

"Well," she said, "now that you've all seen him, what's the verdict?"

The verdict seemed to be unanimously in his favor.

"But," said Bob, "I thought you said he was so screamingly funny."

"Yes," said Edith, "you told me that, too."

"Give him a chance," said Ellen. "Wait till he's in a funny mood. You'll simply die laughing!"

V

It is a compound fracture of the rules to have so important a character as Tommy Richards appear in only one chapter. But remember, this isn't a regular story, but a simple statement of what occurred when it occurred. During Chapter Four, Tommy had been on his way home from the Pacific Coast, where business had kept him all fall. His business out there and what he said en route to Chicago are collateral.

Tommy had been Billy's pal at college. Tommy's home was in Minnesota, and Billy was his most intimate, practically his only friend in the so-called metropolis of the Middle West. So Tommy, not knowing that Billy had gone to St. Louis, looked forward to a few pleasant hours with him between the time of the coast train's arrival and the Minnesota train's departure.

The coast train reached Chicago about noon. It was Thursday noon, the twenty-third. Tommy hustled from the station to Billy's office, and there learned of the St. Louis trip. Disappointed, he roamed the streets a while and at length dropped into the downtown ticket office of his favorite Minnesota road. He was told that everything for the night was sold out. Big Christmas business. Tommy pondered.

The coast train reached Chicago about noon. It was Thursday noon, the twenty-third.

"How about to-morrow night?" he inquired.

"I can give you a lower to-morrow night on the six-thirty," replied Leslie Painter, that being the clerk's name.

"I'll take it," said Tommy.

He did so, and the clerk took $10.05.

"I'll see old Bill after all," said Tommy.

Leslie Painter made no reply.

In the afternoon Tommy sat through a vaudeville show, and at night he looped the loop. He retired early, for the next day promised to be a big one.

Billy got in from St. Louis at seven Friday morning and had been in his office an hour when Tommy appeared. I have no details of the meeting.

At half-past eight Tommy suggested that they'd better go out and h'ist one.

"Still on it, eh?" said Billy.

"What do you mean?"

"I mean that I'm off of it."

"Good Lord! For how long?"

"The last day of November."

"Too long! You look sick already."

"I feel great," averred Billy.

"Well, I don't. So come along and bathe in vichy."

On the way "along" Billy told Tommy about Ellen. Tommy's congratulations were physical and jarred Billy from head to heels.

"Good stuff!" cried Tommy so loudly that three pedestrians jumped sideways. "Old Bill hooked! And do you think you're going to celebrate this occasion with water?"

"I think I am," was Billy's firm reply.

"You think you are! What odds?"

"A good lunch against a red hot."

"You're on!" said Tommy. "And I'm going to be mighty hungry at one o'clock."

"You'll be hungry and alone."

"What's the idea? If you've got a lunch date with the future, I'm in on it."

"I haven't," said Billy. "But I'm going to South Bend on the one-forty, and between now and then I have nothing to do but clean up my mail and buy a dozen Christmas presents."

They turned in somewhere.

"Don't you see the girl at all to-day?" asked Tommy.

"Not to-day. All I do is call her up."

"Well, then, if you get outside of a couple, who'll be hurt? Just for old time's sake."

"If you need lunch money, I'll give it to you."

"No, no. That bet's off."

"It's not off. I won't call it off."

"Suit yourself," said Tommy graciously.

At half-past nine, it was officially decided that Billy had lost the bet. At half-past twelve, Billy said it was time to pay it.

"I'm not hungry enough," said Tommy.

"Hungry or no hungry," said Billy, "I buy your lunch now or I don't buy it. See? Hungry or no hungry."

"What's the hurry?" asked Tommy.

"I guess you know what's the hurry. Me for South Bend on the one-forty, and I got to go to the office first. Hurry or no hurry."

"Listen to reason, Bill. How are you going to eat lunch, go to the office, buy a dozen Christmas presents and catch the one-forty?"

"Christmas presents! I forgot 'em! What do you think of that? I forgot 'em. Good night!"

"What are you going to do?"

"Do! What can I do? You got me into this mess. Get me out!"

"Sure, I'll get you out if you'll listen to reason!" said Tommy. "Has this one-forty train got anything on you? Are you under obligations to it? Is the engineer your girl's uncle?"

"I guess you know better than that. I guess you know I'm not engaged to a girl who's got an uncle for an engineer."

"Well, then, what's the next train?"

"That's the boy, Tommy! That fixes it! I'll go on the next train."

"You're sure there is one?" asked Tommy.

"Is one! Say, where do you think South Bend is? In Europe?"

"I wouldn't mind," said Tommy.

"South Bend's only a two-hour run. Where did you think it was? Europe?"

"I don't care where it is. The question is, what's the next train after one-forty?"

"Maybe you think I don't know," said Billy. He called the gentleman with the apron. "What do you know about this, Charley? Here's an old pal of mine who thinks I don't know the time-table to South Bend."

"He's mistaken, isn't he?" said Charley.

"Is he mistaken? Say, Charley, if you knew as much as I do about the time-table to South Bend, you wouldn't be here."

"No, sir," said Charley. "I'd be an announcer over in the station."

"There!" said Billy triumphantly. "How's that, Tommy? Do I know the time-table or don't I?"

"I guess you do," said Tommy. "But I don't think you ought to have secrets from an old friend."

"There's no secrets about it, Charley."

"My name is Tommy," corrected his friend.

"I know that. I know your name as well as my own, better'n my own. I know your name as well as I know the time-table."

"If you'd just tell me the time of that train, we'd all be better off."

"I'll tell you, Tommy. I wouldn't hold out anything on you, old boy. It's five twenty-five."

"You're sure?"

"Sure! Say, I've taken it a hundred times if I've taken it once."

"All right," said Tommy. "That fixes it. We'll go in and have lunch and be through by half-past one. That'll give you four hours to do your shopping, get to your office and make your train."

"Where you going while I shop?"

"Don't bother about me."

"You go along with me."

"Nothing doing."

"Yes, you do."

"No, I don't."

But this argument was won by Mr. Bowen. At ten minutes of three, when they at last called for the check, Mr. Richards looked on the shopping expedition in an entirely different light. Two hours before, it had not appealed to him at all. Now he could think of nothing that would afford more real entertainment. Mr. Richards was at a stage corresponding to Billy's twenty-one. Billy was far past it.

"What we better do," said Tommy, "is write down a list of all the people so we won't forget anybody."

"That's the stuff!" said Billy. "I'll name 'em, you write 'em."

So Tommy produced a pencil and took dictation on the back of a menu-card.

"First, girl's father, Sam'l McDonald."

"Samuel McDonald," repeated Tommy. "Maybe you'd better give me some dope on each one, so if we're shy of time, we can both be buying at once."

"All right," said Billy. "First, Sam'l McDonal'. He's an ol' crab. Raves about cig'rettes."

"Like 'em?"

"No. Hates 'em."

"Sam'l McDonald, cigarettes," wrote Tommy. "Old crab," he added.

When the important preliminary arrangement had at last been completed, the two old college chums went out into the air.

"Where do we shop?" asked Tommy.

"Marsh's," said Billy. " 'S only place I got charge account."

"Maybe we better take a taxi and save time," suggested Tommy.

So they waited five minutes for a taxi and were driven to Marsh's, two blocks away.

"We'll start on the first floor and work up," said Tommy, who had evidently appointed himself captain.

They found themselves among the jewelry and silverware.

"You might get something for the girl here," suggested Tommy.

"Don't worry 'bout her," said Billy. "Leave her till las'."

"What's the limit on the others?"

"I don't care," said Billy. "Dollar, two dollars, three dollars."

"Well, come on," said Tommy. "We got to make it snappy."

But Billy hung back.

"Say, ol' boy," he wheedled. "You're my ol'st frien'. Is that right?"

"That's right," agreed Tommy.

"Well, say, ol' frien', I'm pretty near all in."

"Go home, then, if you want to. I can pull this all right alone."

"Nothin' doin'. But if I could jus' li'l nap, ten, fifteen minutes—you could get couple things here on fir'-floor and then come get me."

"Where?"

"Third floor waitin'-room."

"Go ahead. But wait a minute. Give me some of your cards. And will I have any trouble charging things?"

"Not a bit. Tell 'em you're me."

It was thus that Tommy Richards was left alone in a large store, with Billy Bowen's charge account, Billy Bowen's list, and Billy Bowen's cards.

He glanced at the list.

" 'Samuel McDonald, cigarettes. Old crab,' " he read.

He approached a floor-walker.

"Say, old pal," he said. "I'm doing some shopping and I'm in a big hurry. Where'd I find something for an old cigarette fiend?"

"Cigarette-cases, two aisles down and an aisle to your left," said Old Pal.

Tommy raised the limit on the cigarette-case he picked out for Samuel McDonald. It was $3.75.

"I'll cut down somewhere else," he thought. "The father-in-law ought to be favored a little."

"Charge," he said in response to a query. "William Bowen, Bowen and Company, 18 South La Salle. And here's a card for it. That go out to-night sure?"

He looked again at the list.

"Mrs. Samuel McDonald, bridge bug. Miss Harriet McDonald, reverse English. Miss Louise McDonald, thin hair. Miss Mary Carey, church stuff. Bob and Wife, 'The Man Who Married a Dumb Wife' and gets mysteriously jealous. Walter McDonald, real kid. Edith, fat lady. Wilma, a splinter."

He consulted Old Pal once more. Old Pal's advice was to go to the third floor and look over the books. The advice proved sound. On the third floor Tommy found for Mother "The First Principles of Auction Bridge," and for Aunt Harriet an English grammar. He also bumped into a counter laden with hymnals, chant books, and Books of Common Prayer.

"Aunt Mary!" he exclaimed. And to the clerk: "How much are your medium prayer-books?"

"What denomination?" asked the clerk, whose name was Freda Swanson.

"One or two dollars," said Tommy.

"What church, I mean?" inquired Freda.

"How would I know?" said Tommy. "Are there different books for different churches?"

"Sure. Catholic, Presbyterian, Episcopal, Lutheran——"

"Let's see. McDonald, Carey. How much are the Catholic ones?"

"Here's one at a dollar and a half. In Latin, too."

"That's it. That'll give her something to work on."

Tommy figured on the back of his list.

"Good work, Tommy!" he thought. "Four and a half under the top limit for those three. Walter's next."

He plunged on Walter. A nice poker set, discovered on the fourth floor, came to five even. Tommy wished he could keep it for himself. He also wished constantly that the women shoppers had taken a course in dodging. He was almost as badly battered as the day he played guard against the Indians.

"Three left besides the queen herself," he observed. "Lord, no. I forgot Bob and his missus."

He moved down-stairs again to the books.

"Have you got 'The Man Who Married a Dumb Wife'?" he queried.

Anna Henderson looked, but could not find it.

"Never mind!" said Tommy. "Here's one that'll do."

And he ordered "The Green-Eyed Monster" for the cooing doves in Evanston.

"Now," he figured, "there's just Wilma and Edith and Aunt Louise." Once more he started away from the books, but a title caught his eye: "Eat and Grow Thin."

"Great!" exclaimed Tommy. "It'll do for Edith. By George! It'll do for both of them. 'Eat' for Wilma, and the 'Grow Thin' for Edith. I guess that's doubling up some! And now for Aunt Louise."

The nearest floor-walker told him, in response to his query, that switches would be found on the second floor.

"I ought to have a switch-engine to take me round," said Tommy, who never had felt better in his life. But the floor-walker did not laugh, possibly because he was tired.

"Have you anything to match it with?" asked the lady in the switch-yard.

"No, I haven't."

"Can you give me an idea of the color?"

"What colors have you got?" demanded Tommy.

"Everything there is. I'll show them all to you, if you've got the time."

"Never mind," said Tommy. "What's your favorite color in hair?"

The girl laughed.

"Golden," she said.

"You're satisfied, aren't you?" said Tommy, for the girl had chosen the shade of her own shaggy mane. "All right, make it golden. And a merry Christmas to you."

He forgot to ask the price of switches. He added up the rest and found that the total was $16.25.

"About seventy-five cents for the hair," he guessed. "That will make it seventeen even. I'm some shopper. And all done in an hour and thirteen minutes."

He discovered Billy asleep in the waiting-room and it took him three precious minutes to bring him to.

"Everybody's fixed but the girl herself," he boasted. "I got books for most of 'em."

"Where you been?" asked Billy. "What time is it?"

"You've got about thirty-three minutes to get a present for your lady love and grab your train. You'll have to pass up the office."

"What time is it? Where you been?"

"Don't bother about that. Come on."

On the ride down, Billy begged every one in the elevator to tell him the time, but no one seemed to know. Tommy hurried him out of the store and into a taxi.

"There's a flock of stores round the station," said Tommy. "You can find something there for the dame."

But the progress of the cab through the packed down-town streets was painfully slow and the station clock, when at last they got in sight of it, registered 5.17.

"You can't wait!" said Tommy. "Give me some money and tell me what to get."

Billy fumbled clumsily in seven pockets before he located his pocketbook. In it were two fives and a ten.

"I gotta have a feevee," he said.

"All right. I'll get something for fifteen. What'll it be?"

"Make it a wrist-watch."

"Sure she has none?"

"She's got one. That's for other wris'."

"I used your last card. Have you got another?"

"Pocketbook," said Billy.

Tommy hastily searched and found a card. He pushed Billy toward the station entrance.

"Good-by and merry Christmas," said Tommy.

"Goo'-by and God bless you!" said Billy, but he was talking to a large policeman.

"Where are you trying to go?" asked the latter.

"Souse Ben'," said Billy.

"Hurry up, then. You've only got a minute."

The minute and six more were spent in the purchase of a ticket. And when Billy reached the gate, the 5.25 had gone and the 5.30 was about to chase it.

"Where to?" inquired the gateman.

"Souse Ben'," said Billy.

"Run then," said the gateman.

Billy ran. He ran to the first open vestibule of the Rock Island train, bound for St. Joe, Missouri.

"Where to?" asked a porter.

"Souse," said Billy.

"Ah can see that," said the porter. "But where you goin'?"

The train began to move and Billy, one foot dragging on the station platform, moved with it. The porter dexterously pulled him aboard. And he was allowed to ride to Englewood.

Walking down Van Buren Street, it suddenly occurred to the genial Mr. Richards that he would have to go some himself to get his baggage and catch the 6.30 for the northwest. He thought of it in front of a Van Buren jewelry shop. He stopped and went in.

Three-quarters of an hour later, a messenger-boy delivered a particularly ugly and frankly inexpensive wrist-watch at the McDonald home. The parcel was addressed to Miss McDonald and the accompanying card read:

"Mr. Bowen: Call me up any night after seven. Calumet 2678. Miss Violet Moore."

There was no good-will toward men in the McDonald home this Christmas. Ellen spent the day in bed and the orders were that she must not be disturbed.

Down-stairs, one person smiled. It was Walter. He smiled in spite of the fact that his father had tossed his brand-new five-dollar poker set into the open fireplace. He smiled in spite of the fact that he was not allowed to leave the house, not even to take Kathryn to church.

"Gee!" he thought, between smiles, "Billy sure had nerve!"

Bob walked round among his relatives seeking to dispel the gloom with a remark that he thought apt and nifty:

"Be grateful," was the remark, "that he had one of his screamingly funny moods before it was too late."

But no one but Bob seemed to think much of the remark, and no one seemed grateful.

Those are the facts, and it was quite a job to dig them up. But I did it.

HARMONY

Even a baseball writer must sometimes work. Regretfully I yielded my seat in the P. G., walked past the section where Art Graham, Bill Cole, Lefty Parks and young Waldron were giving expert tonsorial treatment to "Sweet Adeline," and flopped down beside Ryan, the manager.

"Well, Cap," I said, "we're due in Springfield in a little over an hour and I haven't written a line."

"Don't let me stop you," said Ryan.

"I want you to start me," I said.

"Lord!" said Ryan. "You oughtn't to have any trouble grinding out stuff these days, with the club in first place and young Waldron gone crazy. He's worth a story any day."

"That's the trouble," said I. "He's been worked so much that there's nothing more to say about him. Everybody in the country knows that he's hitting .420, that he's made nine home runs, twelve triples and twenty-some doubles, that he's stolen twenty-five bases, and that he can play the piano and sing like Carus'. They've run his picture oftener than Billy Sunday and Mary Pickford put together. Of course, you might come through with how you got him."

"Oh, that's the mystery," said Ryan.

"So I've heard you say," I retorted. "But it wouldn't be a mystery if you'd let me print it."

"Well," said Ryan, "if you're really hard up I suppose I might as well come through. Only there's really no mystery at all about it; it's just what I consider the most remarkable piece of scouting ever done. I've been making a mystery of it just to have a little fun with Dick Hodges. You know he's got the Jackson club and he's still so sore about my stealing Waldron he'll hardly speak to me.

"I'll give you the dope if you want it, though it's a boost for Art Graham, not me. There's lots of people think the reason I've kept the thing a secret is because I'm modest.

"They give me credit for having found Waldron myself. But Graham is the bird that deserves the credit and I'll admit that he almost had to get down on his knees to make me take his tip. Yes, sir, Art Graham was the scout, and now he's sitting on the bench and the boy he recommended has got his place."

"That sounds pretty good," I said. "And how did Graham get wise?"

"I'm going to tell you. You're in a hurry; so I'll make it snappy.

"You weren't with us last fall, were you? Well, we had a day off in Detroit, along late in the season. Graham's got relatives in Jackson; so he asked me if he could spend the day there. I told him he could and asked him to keep his eyes peeled for good young pitchers, if he happened to go to the ball game. So he went to Jackson and the next morning he came back all excited. I asked him if he'd found me a pitcher and he said he hadn't, but he'd seen the best natural hitter he'd ever looked at—a kid named Waldron.

" 'Well,' I said, 'you're the last one that ought to be recommending outfielders. If there's one good enough to hold a regular job, it might be your job he'd get.'

"But Art said that didn't make any difference to him—he was looking out for the good of the club. Well, I didn't see my way clear to asking the old man to dig up good money for an outfielder nobody'd ever heard of, when we were pretty well stocked with them, so I tried to stall Art; but he kept after me and kept after me till I agreed to stick in a draft for the kid just to keep Art quiet. So the draft went in and we got him. Then, as you know, Hodges tried to get him back, and that made me suspicious enough to hold on to him. Hodges finally came over to see me and wanted to know who'd tipped me to Waldron. That's where the mystery stuff started, because I saw that Hodges was all heated up and wanted to kid him along. So I told him we had some mighty good scouts working for us, and he said he knew our regular scouts and they couldn't tell a ballplayer from a torn ligament. Then he offered me fifty bucks if I'd tell him the truth and I just laughed at him. I said: 'A fella happened to be in Jackson one day and saw him work. But I won't tell you who the fella was, because you're too anxious to know.' Then he insisted on knowing what day the scout had been in Jackson. I said I'd tell him that if he'd tell me why he was so blame curious. So he gave me his end of it.

"It seems his brother, up in Ludington, had seen this kid play ball on the lots and had signed him right up for Hodges and taken him to Jackson, and of course, Hodges knew he had a world beater the minute he saw him. But he also knew he wasn't going to be able to keep him in Jackson, and, naturally he began to figure how he could get the most money for him. It was already August when the boy landed in Jackson; so there wasn't much chance of getting a big price last season. He decided to teach the kid what he didn't know about baseball and to keep him under cover till this year. Then everybody would be touting him and there'd be plenty of competition. Hodges could sell to the highest bidder.

"He had Waldron out practising every day, but wouldn't let him play in a game, and every player on the Jackson club had promised to keep the secret till this year. So Hodges wanted to find out from me which one of his players had broken the promise.

"Then I asked him if he was perfectly sure that Waldron hadn't played in a game, and he said he had gone in to hit for somebody just once. I asked him what date that was and he told me. It was the day Art had been in Jackson. So I said:

" 'There's your mystery solved. That's the day my scout saw him, and you'll have to give the scout a little credit for picking a star after seeing him make one base hit.'

"Then Hodges said:

" 'That makes it all the more a mystery. Because, in the first place, he batted under a fake name. And, in the second place, he didn't make a base hit. He popped out.'

"That's about all there is to it. You can ask Art how he picked the kid out for a star from seeing him pop out once. I've asked him myself, and he's told me that he liked the way Waldron swung. Personally, I believe one of those Jackson boys got too gabby. But Art swears not."

"That *is* a story," I said gratefully. "An old outfielder who must know he's slipping recommends a busher after seeing him pop out once. And the busher jumps right in and gets his job."

I looked down the aisle toward the song birds. Art Graham, now a bench warmer, and young Waldron, whom he had touted and who was the cause of his being sent to the bench, were harmonizing at the tops of their strong and not too pleasant voices.

"And probably the strangest part of the story," I added, "is that Art doesn't seem to regret it. He and the kid appear to be the best of friends."

"Anybody who can sing is Art's friend," said Ryan.

I left him and went back to my seat to tear off my seven hundred words before we reached Springfield. I considered for a moment the advisability of asking Graham for an explanation of his wonderful bit of scouting, but decided to save that part of it for another day. I was in a hurry and, besides, Waldron was just teaching them a new "wallop," and it would have been folly for me to interrupt.

"It's on the word 'you,' " Waldron was saying. "I come down a tone;

Lefty goes up a half tone, and Bill comes up two tones. Art just sings it like always. Now try her again," I heard him direct the song birds. They tried her again, making a worse noise than ever:

"I only know I love you;
 Love me, and the world (the world) is mine (the world is mine)."

"No," said Waldron. "Lefty missed it. If you fellas knew music, I could teach it to you with the piano when we get to Boston. On the word 'love,' in the next to the last line, we hit a regular F chord. Bill's singing the low F in the bass and Lefty's hitting middle C in the baritone, and Art's on high F and I'm up to A. Then, on the word 'you,' I come down to G, and Art hits E, and Lefty goes up half a tone to C sharp, and Cole comes up from F to A in the bass. That makes a good wallop. It's a change from the F chord to the A chord. Now let's try her again," Waldron urged.

They tried her again:

"I only know I love you——"

"No, no!" said young Waldron. "Art and I were all right; but Bill came up too far, and Lefty never moved off that C. Half a tone up, Lefty. Now try her again."

We were an hour late into Springfield, and it was past six o'clock when we pulled out. I had filed my stuff, and when I came back in the car the concert was over for the time, and Art Graham was sitting alone.

"Where are your pals?" I asked.

"Gone to the diner," he replied.

"Aren't you going to eat?"

"No," he said, "I'm savin' up for the steamed clams." I took the seat beside him.

"I sent in a story about you," I said.

"Am I fired?" he asked.

"No, nothing like that."

"Well," he said, "you must be hard up when you can't find nothin' better to write about than a old has-been."

"Cap just told me who it was that found Waldron," said I.

"Oh, that," said Art. "I don't see no story in that."

"I thought it was quite a stunt," I said. "It isn't everybody that can pick out a second Cobb by just seeing him hit a fly ball."

Graham smiled.

"No," he replied, "they's few as smart as that."

"If you ever get through playing ball," I went on, "you oughtn't to have any trouble landing a job. Good scouts don't grow on trees."

"It looks like I'm pretty near through now," said Art, still smiling. "But you won't never catch me scoutin' for nobody. It's too lonesome a job."

I had passed up lunch to retain my seat in the card game; so I was hungry. Moreover, it was evident that Graham was not going to wax garrulous on the subject of his scouting ability. I left him and sought the diner. I found a vacant chair opposite Bill Cole.

"Try the minced ham," he advised, "but lay off'n the sparrow-grass. It's tougher'n a double-header in St. Louis."

"We're over an hour late," I said.

"You'll have to do a hurry-up on your story, won't you?" asked Bill. "Or did you write it already?"

"All written and on the way."

"Well, what did you tell 'em?" he inquired. "Did you tell 'em we had a pleasant trip, and Lenke lost his shirt in the poker game, and I'm goin' to pitch to-morrow, and the Boston club's heard about it and hope it'll rain?"

"No," I said. "I gave them a regular story to-night—about how Graham picked Waldron."

"Who give it to you?"

"Ryan," I told him.

"Then you didn't get the real story," said Cole, "Ryan himself don't know the best part of it, and he ain't goin' to know it for a w'ile. He'll maybe find it out after Art's got the can, but not before. And I hope nothin' like that'll happen for twenty years. When it does happen, I want to be sent along with Art, 'cause I and him's been roomies now since 1911, and I wouldn't hardly know how to act with him off'n the club. He's a nut all right on the singin' stuff, and if he was gone I might get a chanct to give my voice a rest. But he's a pretty good guy, even if he is crazy."

"I'd like to hear the real story," I said.

"Sure you would," he answered, "and I'd like to tell it to you. I will tell it to you if you'll give me your promise not to spill it till Art's gone. Art told it to I and Lefty in the club-house at Cleveland pretty near a month ago, and the three of us and Waldron is the only ones that knows it. I figure I've did pretty well to keep it to myself this long, but it seems like I got to tell somebody."

"You can depend on me," I assured him, "not to say a word about it till Art's in Minneapolis, or wherever they're going to send him."

"I guess I can trust you," said Cole. "But if you cross me, I'll shoot my fast one up there in the press coop some day and knock your teeth loose."

"Shoot," said I.

"Well," said Cole, "I s'pose Ryan told you that Art fell for the kid after just seein' him pop out."

"Yes, and Ryan said he considered it a remarkable piece of scouting."

"It was all o' that. It'd of been remarkable enough if Art'd saw the bird pop out and then recommended him. But he didn't even see him pop out."

"What are you giving me?"

"The fac's," said Bill Cole. "Art not only didn't see him pop out, but he didn't even see him with a ball suit on. He wasn't never inside the Jackson ball park in his life."

"Waldron?"

"No. Art I'm talkin' about."

"Then somebody tipped him off," I said, quickly.

"No, sir. Nobody tipped him off, neither. He went to Jackson and spent the ev'nin' at his uncle's house, and Waldron was there. Him and Art was together the whole ev'nin'. But Art didn't even ask him if he could slide feet first. And then he come back to Detroit and got Ryan to draft him. But to give you the whole story, I'll have to go back a ways. We ain't nowheres near Worcester yet, so they's no hurry, except that Art'll prob'ly be sendin' for me pretty quick to come in and learn Waldron's lost chord.

"You wasn't with this club when we had Mike McCann. But you must of heard of him; outside his pitchin', I mean. He was on the stage a couple o' winters, and he had the swellest tenor voice I ever heard. I never seen no grand opera, but I'll bet this here C'ruso or McCormack or Gadski or none o' them had nothin' on him for a pure tenor. Every note as clear as a bell. You couldn't hardly keep your eyes dry when he'd tear off 'Silver Threads' or 'The River Shannon.'

"Well, when Art was still with the Washin'ton club yet, I and Lefty and Mike used to pal round together and onct or twict we'd hit up some harmony. I couldn't support a fam'ly o' Mormons with my voice, but it was better in them days than it is now. I used to carry the lead, and Lefty'd hit the baritone and Mike the tenor. We didn't have no bass. But most o' the time we let Mike do the singin' alone, 'cause he

had us outclassed, and the other boys kept tellin' us to shut up and give
'em a treat. First it'd be 'Silver Threads' and then 'Jerusalem' and then
'My Wild Irish Rose' and this and that, whatever the boys ast him for.
Jake Martin used to say he couldn't help a short pair if Mike wasn't
singin'.

"Finally Ryan pulled off the trade with Griffith, and Graham come
on our club. Then they wasn't no more solo work. They made a bass
out o' me, and Art sung the lead, and Mike and Lefty took care o' the
tenor and baritone. Art didn't care what the other boys wanted to hear.
They could holler their heads off for Mike to sing a solo, but no
sooner'd Mike start singin' than Art'd chime in with him and pretty
soon we'd all four be goin' it. Art's a nut on singin', but he don't care
nothin' about list'nin', not even to a canary. He'd rather harmonize than
hit one past the outfielders with two on.

"At first we done all our serenadin' on the train. Art'd get us out o'
bed early so's we could be through breakfast and back in the car in
time to tear off a few before we got to wherever we was goin'.

"It got so's Art wouldn't leave us alone in the different towns we played
at. We couldn't go to no show or nothin'. We had to stick in the hotel
and sing, up in our room or Mike's. And then he went so nuts over it
that he got Mike to come and room in the same house with him at
home, and I and Lefty was supposed to help keep the neighbors awake
every night. O' course we had mornin' practice w'ile we was home, and
Art used to have us come to the park early and get in a little harmony
before we went on the field. But Ryan finally nailed that. He says that
when he ordered mornin' practice he meant baseball and not no minstrel
show.

"Then Lefty, who wasn't married, goes and gets himself a girl. I met
her a couple o' times, and she looked all right. Lefty might of married
her if Art'd of left him alone. But nothin' doin'. We was home all
through June onct, and instead o' comin' round nights to sing with us,
Lefty'd take this here doll to one o' the parks or somewheres. Well, sir,
Art was pretty near wild. He scouted round till he'd found out why
Lefty'd quit us and then he tried pretty near everybody else on the club
to see if they wasn't some one who could hit the baritone. They wasn't
nobody. So the next time we went on the road, Art give Lefty a earful
about what a sucker a man was to get married, and looks wasn't everything and the girl was prob'ly after Lefty's money and he wasn't
bein' a good fella to break up the quartette and spoil our good times,

and so on, and kept pesterin' and teasin' Lefty till he give the girl up.
I'd of saw Art in the Texas League before I'd of shook a girl to please
him, but you know these left-handers.

"Art had it all framed that we was goin' on the stage, the four of us,
and he seen a vaudeville man in New York and got us booked for eight
hundred a week—I don't know if it was one week or two. But he sprung
it on me in September and says we could get solid bookin' from October
to March; so I ast him what he thought my Missus would say when I
told her I couldn't get enough o' bein' away from home from March to
October, so I was figurin' on travelin' the vaudeville circuit the other
four or five months and makin' it unanimous? Art says I was tied to a
woman's apron and all that stuff, but I give him the cold stare and he
had to pass up that dandy little scheme.

"At that, I guess we could of got by on the stage all right. Mike was
better than this here Waldron and I hadn't wore my voice out yet on
the coachin' line, tellin' the boys to touch all the bases.

"They was about five or six songs that we could kill. 'Adeline' was
our star piece. Remember where it comes in, 'Your fair face beams'?
Mike used to go away up on 'fair.' Then they was 'The Old Millstream'
and 'Put on Your Old Gray Bonnet.' I done some fancy work in that
one. Then they was 'Down in Jungle Town' that we had pretty good.
And then they was one that maybe you never heard. I don't know the
name of it. It run somethin' like this."

Bill sottoed his voice so that I alone could hear the beautiful refrain:

> " 'Years, years, I've waited years
>   Only to see you, just to call you "dear."
>   Come, come, I love but thee,
>   Come to your sweetheart's arms; come back to me.'

"That one had a lot o' wallops in it, and we didn't overlook none
o' them. The boys used to make us sing it six or seven times a night.
But 'Down in the Cornfield' was Art's favor-ight. They was a part in
that where I sung the lead down low and the other three done a banjo
stunt. Then they was 'Castle on the Nile' and 'Come Back to Erin' and
a whole lot more.

"Well, the four of us wasn't hardly ever separated for three years.
We was practisin' all the w'ile like as if we was goin' to play the big
time, and we never made a nickel off'n it. The only audience we had
was the ball players or the people travelin' on the same trains or stoppin'

at the same hotels, and they got it all for nothin'. But we had a good time, 'specially Art.

"You know what a pitcher Mike was. He could go in there stone cold and stick ten out o' twelve over that old plate with somethin' on 'em. And he was the willin'est guy in the world. He pitched his own game every third or fourth day, and between them games he was warmin' up all the time to go in for somebody else. In 1911, when we was up in the race for aw'ile, he pitched eight games out o' twenty, along in September, and win seven o' them, and besides that, he finished up five o' the twelve he didn't start. We didn't win the pennant, and I've always figured that them three weeks killed Mike.

"Anyway, he wasn't worth nothin' to the club the next year; but they carried him along, hopin' he'd come back and show somethin'. But he was pretty near through, and he knowed it. I knowed it, too, and so did everybody else on the club, only Graham. Art never got wise till the trainin' trip two years ago this last spring. Then he come to me one day.

" 'Bill,' he says, 'I don't believe Mike's comin' back.'

" 'Well,' I says, 'you're gettin's so's they can't nobody hide nothin' from you. Next thing you'll be findin' out that Sam Crawford can hit.'

" 'Never mind the comical stuff,' he says. 'They ain't no joke about this!'

" 'No,' I says, 'and I never said they was. They'll look a long w'ile before they find another pitcher like Mike.'

" 'Pitcher my foot!' says Art. 'I don't care if they have to pitch the bat boy. But when Mike goes, where'll our quartette be?'

" 'Well,' I says, 'do you get paid every first and fifteenth for singin' or for crownin' that old pill?'

" 'If you couldn't talk about money, you'd be deaf and dumb,' says Art.

" 'But you ain't playin' ball because it's fun, are you?'

" 'No,' he says, 'they ain't no fun for me in playin' ball. They's no fun doin' nothin' but harmonizin', and if Mike goes, I won't even have that.'

" 'I and you and Lefty can harmonize,' I says.

" 'It'd be swell stuff harmonizin' without no tenor,' says Art. 'It'd be like swingin' without no bat.'

"Well, he ast me did I think the club'd carry Mike through another season, and I told him they'd already carried him a year without him bein' no good to them, and I figured if he didn't show somethin' his first time out, they'd ask for waivers. Art kept broodin' and broodin' about it till they wasn't hardly no livin' with him. If he ast me onct he ast me a thousand times if I didn't think they might maybe hold onto Mike another season on account of all he'd did for 'em. I kept tellin' him I didn't think so; but that didn't satisfy him and he finally went to Ryan and ast him point blank.

" 'Are you goin' to keep McCann?' Art ast him.

" 'If he's goin' to do us any good, I am,' says Ryan. 'If he ain't, he'll have to look for another job.'

"After that, all through the trainin' trip, he was right on Mike's heels.

" 'How does the old souper feel?' he'd ask him.

" 'Great!' Mike'd say.

"Then Art'd watch him warm up, to see if he had anything on the ball.

" 'He's comin' fine,' he'd tell me. 'His curve broke to-day just as good as I ever seen it.'

"But that didn't fool me, or it didn't fool Mike neither. He could throw about four hooks and then he was through. And he could of hit you in the head with his fast one and you'd of thought you had a rash.

"One night, just before the season opened up, we was singin' on the train, and when we got through, Mike says:

" 'Well, boys, you better be lookin' for another C'ruso.'

" 'What are you talkin' about?' says Art.

" 'I'm talkin' about myself,' says Mike. 'I'll be up there in Minneapolis this summer, pitchin' onct a week and swappin' stories about the Civil War with Joe Cantillon.'

" 'You're crazy,' says Art. 'Your arm's as good as I ever seen it.'

" 'Then,' says Mike, 'you must of been playin' blindfolded all these years. This is just between us, 'cause Ryan'll find it out for himself; my arm's rotten, and I can't do nothin' to help it.'

"Then Art got sore as a boil.

" 'You're a yellow, quittin' dog,' he says. 'Just because you come round a little slow, you talk about Minneapolis. Why don't you resign off'n the club?'

" 'I might just as well,' Mike says, and left us.

"You'd of thought that Art would of gave up then, 'cause when a ball player admits he's slippin', you can bet your last nickel that he's through. Most o' them stalls along and tries to kid themself and everybody else long after they know they're gone. But Art kept talkin' like they was still some hope o' Mike comin' round, and when Ryan told us one night in St. Louis that he was goin' to give Mike his chanct, the next day, Art was as nervous as a bride goin' to get married. I wasn't nervous. I just felt sorry, 'cause I knowed the old boy was hopeless.

"Ryan had told him he was goin' to work if the weather suited him. Well, the day was perfect. So Mike went out to the park along about noon and took Jake with him to warm up. Jake told me afterwards that Mike was throwin', just easy like, from half-past twelve till the rest of us got there. He was tryin' to heat up the old souper and he couldn't of ast for a better break in the weather, but they wasn't enough sunshine in the world to make that old whip crack.

"Well, sir, you'd of thought to see Art that Mike was his son or his brother or somebody and just breakin' into the league. Art wasn't in the outfield practisin' more than two minutes. He come in and stood behind Mike w'ile he was warmin' up and kept tellin' how good he looked, but the only guy he was kiddin' was himself.

"Then the game starts and our club goes in and gets three runs.

" 'Pretty soft for you now, Mike,' says Art, on the bench. 'They can't score three off'n you in three years.'

"Say, it's lucky he ever got the side out in the first innin'. Everybody that come up hit one on the pick, but our infield pulled two o' the greatest plays I ever seen and they didn't score. In the second, we got three more, and I thought maybe the old bird was goin' to be lucky enough to scrape through.

"For four or five innin's, he got the grandest support that was ever gave a pitcher; but I'll swear that what he throwed up there didn't have no more on it than September Morning. Every time Art come to the bench, he says to Mike, 'Keep it up, old boy. You got more than you ever had.'

"Well, in the seventh, Mike still had 'em shut out, and we was six runs to the good. Then a couple o' the St. Louis boys hit 'em where they couldn't nobody reach 'em and they was two on and two out. Then somebody got a hold o' one and sent it on a line to the left o' second base. I forgot who it was now; but whoever it was, he was supposed to be a right field hitter, and Art was layin' over the other way for him. Art started with the crack o' the bat, and I never seen a man make a better try for a ball. He had it judged perfect; but Cobb or Speaker or none o' them couldn't of catched it. Art just managed to touch it by stretchin' to the limit. It went on to the fence and everybody come in. They didn't score no more in that innin'.

"Then Art come in from the field and what do you think he tried to pull?

" 'I don't know what was the matter with me on that fly ball,' he says. 'I ought to caught it in my pants pocket. But I didn't get started till it was right on top o' me.'

" 'You misjudged it, didn't you?' says Ryan.

" 'I certainly did,' says Art without crackin'.

" 'Well,' says Ryan, 'I wisht you'd misjudge all o' them that way. I never seen a better play on a ball.'

"So then Art knowed they wasn't no more use trying to alibi the old boy.

"Mike had a turn at bat and when he come back, Ryan ast him how he felt.

" 'I guess I can get six more o' them out,' he says.

"Well, they didn't score in the eighth, and when the ninth come Ryan sent I and Lefty out to warm up. We throwed a few w'ile our club was battin'; but when it come St. Louis' last chanct, we was too much interested in the ball game to know if we was throwin' or bakin' biscuits.

"The first guy hits a line drive, and somebody jumps a mile in the air and stabs it. The next fella fouled out, and they was only one more to get. And then what do you think come off? Whoever it was hittin' lifted a fly ball to centre field. Art didn't have to move out of his tracks. I've saw him catch a hundred just like it behind his back. But you know what he was thinkin'. He was sayin' to himself, 'If I nail this one, we're li'ble to keep our tenor singer a w'ile longer.' And he dropped it.

"Then they was five base hits that sounded like the fourth o' July, and they come so fast that Ryan didn't have time to send for I or Lefty. Anyway, I guess he thought he might as well leave Mike in there and take it.

"They wasn't no singin' in the clubhouse after that game. I and Lefty always let the others start it. Mike, o' course, didn't feel like no jubilee, and Art was so busy tryin' not to let nobody see him cry that he kept his head clear down in his socks. Finally he beat it for town all alone, and we didn't see nothin' of him till after supper. Then he got us together and we all went up to Mike's room.

" 'I want to try this here "Old Girl o' Mine," ' he says.

" 'Better sing our old stuff,' says Mike. 'This looks like the last time.'

"Then Art choked up and it was ten minutes before he could get goin'. We sung everything we knowed, and it was two o'clock in the mornin' before Art had enough. Ryan come in after midnight and set a w'ile listenin', but he didn't chase us to bed. He knowed better'n any of us that it was a farewell. When I and Art was startin' for our room, Art turned to Mike and says:

" 'Old boy, I'd of gave every nickel I ever owned to of caught that fly ball.'

" 'I know you would,' Mike says, 'and I know what made you drop it. But don't worry about it, 'cause it was just a question o' time, and if I'd of got away with that game, they'd of murdered some o' the infielders next time I started.'

"Mike was sent home the next day, and we didn't see him again. He was shipped to Minneapolis before we got back. And the rest o' the season I might as well of lived in a cemetery w'ile we was on the road. Art was so bad that I thought onct or twict I'd have to change roomies. Onct in a w'ile he'd start hummin' and then he'd break off short and growl at me. He tried out two or three o' the other boys on the club to see if he couldn't find a new tenor singer, but nothin' doin'. One night he made Lefty try the tenor. Well, Lefty's voice is bad enough down low. When he gets up about so high, you think you're in the stockyards.

"And Art had a rotten year in baseball, too. The old boy's still pretty near as good on a fly ball as anybody in the league; but you ought to saw him before his legs begin to give out. He could cover as much ground as Speaker and he was just as sure. But the year Mike left us, he missed pretty near half as many as he got. He told me one night, he says:

" 'Do you know, Bill, I stand out there and pray that nobody'll hit one to me. Every time I see one comin' I think o' that one I dropped for Mike in St. Louis, and then I'm just as li'ble to have it come down on my bean as in my glove.'

" 'You're crazy,' I says, 'to let a thing like that make a bum out o' you.'

"But he kept on droppin' fly balls till Ryan was talkin' about settin' him on the bench where it wouldn't hurt nothin' if his nerve give out. But Ryan didn't have nobody else to play out there, so Art held on.

"He come back the next spring—that's a year ago—feelin' more cheerful and like himself than I'd saw him for a long w'ile. And they was a kid named Burton tryin' out for second base that could sing pretty near as good as Mike. It didn't take Art more'n a day to find this out, and every mornin' and night for a few days the four of us would be together, hittin' her up. But the kid didn't have no more idea o' how to play the bag than Charley Chaplin. Art seen in a minute that he couldn't never beat Cragin out of his job, so what does he do but take him out and try and learn him to play the outfield. He wasn't no worse there than at second base; he couldn't of been. But before he'd practised out there three days they was bruises all over his head and shoulders where fly balls had hit him. Well, the kid wasn't with us long enough to see the first exhibition game, and after he'd went, Art was Old Man Grump again.

" 'What's the matter with you?' I says to him. 'You was all smiles the day we reported and now you could easy pass for a undertaker.'

" 'Well,' he says, 'I had a great winter, singin' all the w'ile. We got a good quartette down home and I never enjoyed myself as much in my life. And I kind o' had a hunch that I was goin' to be lucky and find somebody amongst the bushers that could hit up the old tenor.'

" 'Your hunch was right,' I says. 'That Burton kid was as good a tenor as you'd want.'

" 'Yes,' he says, 'and my hunch could of played ball just as good as him.'

"Well, sir, if you didn't never room with a corpse, you don't know what a whale of a time I had all last season. About the middle of August he was at his worst.

" 'Bill,' he says, 'I'm goin' to leave this old baseball flat on its back if somethin' don't happen. I can't stand these here lonesome nights. I ain't like the rest o' the boys that can go and set all ev'nin' at a pitcher show or hang round them Dutch gardens. I got to be singin' or I am mis'rable.'

" 'Go ahead and sing,' says I. 'I'll try and keep the cops back.'

" 'No,' he says, 'I don't want to sing alone. I want to harmonize and we can't do that 'cause we ain't got no tenor.'

"I don't know if you'll believe me or not, but sure as we're settin' here he went to Ryan one day in Philly and tried to get him to make a trade for Harper.

" 'What do I want him for?' says Ryan.

" 'I hear he ain't satisfied,' says Art.

" 'I ain't runnin' no ball players' benefit association,' says Ryan, and Art had to give it up. But he didn't want Harper on the club for no other reason than because he's a tenor singer!

"And then come that Dee-troit trip, and Art got permission to go to Jackson. He says he intended to drop in at the ball park, but his uncle wanted to borry some money off'n him on a farm, so Art had to drive out and see the farm. Then, that night, this here Waldron was up to call on Art's cousin—a swell doll, Art tells me. And Waldron set down to the py-ana and begin to sing and play. Then it was all off; they wasn't

no spoonin' in the parlor that night. Art wouldn't leave the kid get off'n
the py-ana stool long enough to even find out if the girl was a blonde
or a brunette.

"O' course Art knowed the boy was with the Jackson club as soon
as they was interduced, 'cause Art's uncle says somethin' about the both
o' them bein' ball players, and so on. But Art swears he never thought
o' recommendin' him till the kid got up to go home. Then he ast him
what position did he play and found out all about him, only o' course
Waldron didn't tell him how good he was 'cause he didn't know himself.

"So Art ast him would he like a trial in the big show, and the kid
says he would. Then Art says maybe the kid would hear from him, and
then Waldron left and Art went to bed, and he says he stayed awake
all night plannin' the thing out and wonderin' would he have the nerve
to pull it off. You see he thought that if Ryan fell for it, Waldron'd join
us as soon as his season was over and then Ryan'd see he wasn't no
good; but he'd prob'ly keep him till we was through for the year, and
Art could alibi himself some way, say he'd got the wrong name or
somethin'. All he wanted, he says, was to have the kid along the last
month or six weeks, so's we could harmonize. A nut? I guess not.

"Well, as you know, Waldron got sick and didn't report, and when
Art seen him on the train this spring he couldn't hardly believe his eyes.
He thought surely the kid would of been canned durin' the winter with-
out no trial.

"Here's another hot one. When we went out the first day for practice,
Art takes the kid off in a corner and tries to learn him enough baseball
so's he won't show himself up and get sent away somewheres before
we had a little benefit from his singin'. Can you imagine that? Tryin'
to learn this kid baseball, when he was born with a slidin' pad on.

"You know the rest of it. They wasn't never no question about Waldron makin' good. It's just like everybody says—he's the best natural ball
player that's broke in since Cobb. They ain't nothin' he can't do. But
it *is* a funny thing that Art's job should be the one he'd get. I spoke
about that to Art when he give me the story.

" 'Well,' he says, 'I can't expect everything to break right. I figure
I'm lucky to of picked a guy that's good enough to hang on. I'm in
stronger with Ryan right now, and with the old man, too, than when I
was out there playin' every day. Besides, the bench is a pretty good
place to watch the game from. And this club won't be shy a tenor singer
for nine years.'

" 'No,' I says, 'but they'll be shy a lead and a baritone and a bass
before I and you and Lefty is much older.'

" 'What of it?' he says. 'We'll look up old Mike and all go some-wheres and live together.' "

We were nearing Worcester. Bill Cole and I arose from our table and started back toward our car. In the first vestibule we encountered Buck, the trainer.

"Mr. Graham's been lookin' all over for you, Mr. Cole," he said.

"I've been rehearsin' my part," said Bill.

We found Art Graham, Lefty, and young Waldron in Art's seat. The kid was talking.

"Lefty missed it again. If you fellas knew music, I could teach it to you on the piano when we get to Boston. Lefty, on the word 'love,' in the next to the last line, you're on middle C. Then, on the word 'you,' you slide up half a tone. That'd ought to be a snap, but you don't get it. I'm on high A and come down to G and Bill's on low F and comes up to A. Art just sings the regular two notes, F and E. It's a change from the F chord to the A chord. It makes a dandy wallop and it ought to be a——"

"Here's Bill now," interrupted Lefty, as he caught sight of Cole.

Art Graham treated his roommate to a cold stare.

"Where the h—l have you been?" he said angrily.

"Lookin' for the lost chord," said Bill.

"Set down here and learn this," growled Art. "We won't never get it if we don't work."

"Yes, let's tackle her again," said Waldron. "Bill comes up two full tones, from F to A. Lefty goes up half a tone, Art sings just like always, and I come down a tone. Now try her again."

Two years ago it was that Bill Cole told me that story. Two weeks ago Art Graham boarded the evening train on one of the many roads that lead to Minneapolis.

The day Art was let out, I cornered Ryan in the club-house after the others had dressed and gone home.

"Did you ever know," I asked, "that Art recommended Waldron without having seen him in a ball suit?"

"I told you long ago how Art picked Waldron," he said.

"Yes," said I, "but you didn't have the right story."

So I gave it to him.

"You newspaper fellas," he said when I had done, "are the biggest suckers in the world. Now I've never given you a bad steer in my life. But you don't believe what I tell you and you go and fall for one of Bill

Cole's hop dreams. Don't you know that he was the biggest liar in baseball? He'd tell you that Walter Johnson was Jack's father if he thought he could get away with it. And that bunk he gave you about Waldron. Does it sound reasonable?"

"Just as reasonable," I replied, "as the stuff about Art's grabbing him after seeing him pop out."

"I don't claim he did," said Ryan. "That's what Art told me. One of those Jackson ball players could give you the real truth, only of course he wouldn't, because if Hodges ever found it out he'd shoot him full of holes. Art Graham's no fool. He isn't touting ball players because they can sing tenor or alto or anything else."

Nevertheless, I believe Bill Cole; else I wouldn't print the story. And Ryan would believe, too, if he weren't in such a mood these days that he disagrees with everybody. For in spite of Waldron's wonderful work, and he is at his best right now, the club hasn't done nearly as well as when Art and Bill and Lefty were still with us.

There seems to be a lack of harmony.

MY ROOMY

I

No—I ain't signed for next year; but there won't be no trouble about that. The dough part of it is all fixed up. John and me talked it over and I'll sign as soon as they send me a contract. All I told him was that he'd have to let me pick my own roommate after this and not sic no wild man on to me.

You know I didn't hit much the last two months o' the season. Some o' the boys, I notice, wrote some stuff about me gettin' old and losin' my battin' eye. That's all bunk! The reason I didn't hit was because I wasn't gettin' enough sleep. And the reason for that was Mr. Elliott.

He wasn't with us after the last part o' May, but I roomed with him long enough to get the insomny. I was the only guy in the club game enough to stand for him; but I was sorry afterward that I done it, because it sure did put a crimp in my little old average.

And do you know where he is now? I got a letter today and I'll read it to you. No—I guess I better tell you somethin' about him first. You fellers never got acquainted with him and you ought to hear the dope to understand the letter. I'll make it as short as I can.

He didn't play in no league last year. He was with some semi-pros over in Michigan and somebody writes John about him. So John sends Needham over to look at him. Tom stayed there Saturday and Sunday, and seen him work twice. He was playin' the outfield, but as luck would have it they wasn't a fly ball hit in his direction in both games. A base hit was made out his way and he booted it, and that's the only report Tom could get on his fieldin'. But he wallops two over the wall in one day and they catch two line drives off him. The next day he gets four blows and two o' them is triples.

So Tom comes back and tells John the guy is a whale of a hitter and fast as Cobb, but he don't know nothin' about his fieldin'. Then John signs him to a contract—twelve hundred or somethin' like that. We'd been in Tampa a week before he showed up. Then he comes to the hotel and just sits round all day, without tellin' nobody who he was. Finally the bellhops was going to chase him out and he says he's one o' the ballplayers. Then the clerk gets John to go over and talk to him. He tells John his name and says he hasn't had nothin' to eat for three days, because he was broke. John told me afterward that he'd drew about three hundred in advance—last winter sometime. Well, they took him in the dinin' room and they tell me he inhaled about four meals at once. That night they roomed him with Heine.

Next mornin' Heine and me walks out to the grounds together and Heine tells me about him. He says:

"Don't never call me a bug again. They got me roomin' with the champion o' the world."

"Who is he?" I says.

"I don't know and I don't want to know," says Heine; "but if they stick him in there with me again I'll jump to the Federals. To start with, he ain't got no baggage. I ast him where his trunk was and he says he didn't have none. Then I ast him if he didn't have no suitcase, and he says: 'No. What do you care?' I was goin' to lend him some pajamas, but he put on the shirt o' the uniform John give him last night and slept in that. He was asleep when I got up this mornin'. I seen his collar layin' on the dresser and it looked like he had wore it in Pittsburgh every day for a year. So I throwed it out the window and he comes down to breakfast with no collar. I ast him what size collar he wore and he says he didn't want none, because he wasn't goin' out nowheres. After breakfast he beat it up to the room again and put on his uniform. When I got up there he was lookin' in the glass at himself, and he done it all the time I was dressin'."

When we got out to the park I got my first look at him. Pretty good-lookin' guy, too, in his unie—big shoulders and well put together; built somethin' like Heine himself. He was talkin' to John when I come up.

"What position do you play?" John was askin' him.

"I play anywheres," says Elliott.

"You're the kind I'm lookin' for," says John. Then he says: "You was an outfielder up there in Michigan, wasn't you?"

"I don't care where I play," says Elliott.

John sends him to the outfield and forgets all about him for a while. Pretty soon Miller comes in and says:

"I ain't goin' to shag for no bush outfielder!"

John ast him what was the matter, and Miller tells him that Elliott ain't doin' nothin' but just standin' out there; that he ain't makin' no attemp' to catch the fungoes, and that he won't even chase 'em. Then John starts watchin' him, and it was just like Miller said. Larry hit one pretty near in his lap and he stepped out o' the way. John calls him in and ast him:

"Why don't you go after them fly balls?"

"Because I don't want 'em," says Elliott.

John gets sarcastic and says:

"What do you want? Of course we'll see that you get anythin' you want!"

"Give me a ticket back home," says Elliott.

"Don't you want to stick with the club?" says John, and the busher tells him, no, he certainly did not. Then John tells him he'll have to pay his own fare home and Elliott don't get sore at all. He just says:

"Well, I'll have to stick, then—because I'm broke."

We was havin' battin' practice and John tells him to go up and hit a few. And you ought to of seen him bust 'em!

Lavender was in there workin' and he'd been pitchin' a little all winter, so he was in pretty good shape. He lobbed one up to Elliott, and he hit it 'way up in some trees outside the fence—about a mile, I guess. Then John tells Jimmy to put somethin' on the ball. Jim comes through with one of his fast ones and the kid slams it agin the right-fieldwall on a line.

"Give him your spitter!" yells John, and Jim handed him one. He pulled it over first base so fast that Bert, who was standin' down there, couldn't hardly duck in time. If it'd hit him it'd killed him.

Well, he kep' on hittin' everythin' Jim give him—and Jim had somethin' too. Finally John gets Pierce warmed up and sends him out to pitch, tellin' him to hand Elliott a flock o' curve balls. He wanted to see if lefthanders was goin' to bother him. But he slammed 'em right along, and I don't b'lieve he hit more'n two the whole mornin' that wouldn't of been base hits in a game.

They sent him out to the outfield again in the afternoon, and after a lot o' coaxin' Leach got him to go after fly balls; but that's all he did do—just go after 'em. One hit him on the bean and another on the shoulder. He run back after the short ones and 'way in after the ones that went over his head. He catched just one—a line drive that he couldn't get out o' the way of; and then he acted like it hurt his hands.

I come back to the hotel with John. He ast me what I thought of Elliott.

"Well," I says, "he'd be the greatest ballplayer in the world if he could just play ball. He sure can bust 'em."

John says he was afraid he couldn't never make an outfielder out o' him. He says:

"I'll try him on the infield to-morrow. They must be some place he can play. I never seen a lefthand hitter that looked so good agin lefthand pitchin'—and he's got a great arm; but he acts like he'd never saw a fly ball."

Well, he was just as bad on the infield. They put him at short and he was like a sieve. You could of drove a hearse between him and second base without him gettin' near it. He'd stoop over for a ground ball about the time it was bouncin' up agin the fence; and when he'd try to cover the bag on a peg he'd trip over it.

They tried him at first base and sometimes he'd run 'way over in the coachers' box and sometimes out in right field lookin' for the bag. Once Heine shot one acrost at him on a line and he never touched it with his hands. It went bam! right in the pit of his stomach—and the lunch he'd ate didn't do him no good.

Finally John just give up and says he'd have to keep him on the bench and let him earn his pay by bustin' 'em a couple o' times a week or so. We all agreed with John that this bird would be a whale of a pinch hitter—and we was right too. He was hittin' 'way over five hundred when the blowoff come, along about the last o' May.

II

Before the trainin' trip was over, Elliott had roomed with pretty near everybody in the club. Heine raised an awful holler after the second night down there and John put the bug in with Needham. Tom stood him for three nights. Then he doubled up with Archer, and Schulte, and Miller, and Leach, and Saier— and the whole bunch in turn, averagin' about two nights with each one before they put up a kick. Then John tried him with some o' the youngsters, but they wouldn't stand for him no more'n the others. They all said he was crazy and they was afraid he'd get violent some night and stick a knife in 'em.

He always insisted on havin' the water run in the bathtub all night, because he said it reminded him of the sound of the dam near his home. The fellers might get up four or five times a night and shut off the faucet, but he'd get right up after 'em and turn it on again. Carter, a big bush pitcher from Georgia, started a fight with him about it one night, and Elliott pretty near killed him. So the rest o' the bunch, when they'd saw Carter's map next mornin', didn't have the nerve to do nothin' when it come their turn.

Another o' his habits was the thing that scared 'em, though. He'd brought a razor with him—in his pocket, I guess—and he used to do his shavin' in the middle o' the night. Instead o' doin' it in the bathroom he'd lather his face and then come out and stand in front o' the lookin'-

glass on the dresser. Of course he'd have all the lights turned on, and
that was bad enough when a feller wanted to sleep; but the worst of it
was that he'd stop shavin' every little while and turn round and stare
at the guy who was makin' a failure o' tryin' to sleep. Then he'd wave
his razor round in the air and laugh, and begin shavin' agin. You can
imagine how comf'table his roomies felt!

John had bought him a suitcase and some clothes and things, and
charged 'em up to him. He'd drew so much dough in advance that he
didn't have nothin' comin' till about June. He never thanked John and
he'd wear one shirt and one collar till some one throwed 'em away.

Well, we finally gets to Indianapolis, and we was goin' from there to
Cincy to open. The last day in Indianapolis John come and ast me how
I'd like to change roomies. I says I was perfectly satisfied with Larry.
Then John says:

"I wisht you'd try Elliott. The other boys all kicks on him, but he
seems to hang round you a lot and I b'lieve you could get along all
right."

"Why don't you room him alone?" I ast.

"The boss or the hotels won't stand for us roomin' alone," says John.
"You go ahead and try it, and see how you make out. If he's too much
for you let me know; but he likes you and I think he'll be diff'rent with
a guy who can talk to him like you can."

So I says I'd tackle it, because I didn't want to throw John down.
When we got to Cincy they stuck Elliott and me in one room, and we
was together till he quit us.

III

I went to the room early that night, because we was goin' to open next
day and I wanted to feel like somethin'. First thing I done when I got
undressed was turn on both faucets in the bathtub. They was makin'
an awful racket when Elliott finally come in about midnight. I was layin'
awake and I opened right up on him. I says:

"Don't shut off that water, because I like to hear it run."

Then I turned over and pretended to be asleep. The bug got his
clothes off, and then what did he do but go in the bathroom and shut
off the water! Then he come back in the room and says:

"I guess no one's goin' to tell me what to do in here."

But I kep' right on pretendin' to sleep and didn't pay no attention.
When he'd got into his bed I jumped out o' mine and turned on all the
lights and begun stroppin' my razor. He says:

"What's comin' off?"

"Some o' my whiskers," I says. "I always shave along about this time."

"No, you don't!" he says. "I was in your room one mornin' down in Louisville and I seen you shavin' then."

"Well," I says, "the boys tell me you shave in the middle o' the night; and I thought if I done all the things you do mebbe I'd get so's I could hit like you."

"You must be superstitious!" he says. And I told him I was. "I'm a good hitter," he says, "and I'd be a good hitter if I never shaved at all. That don't make no diff'rence."

"Yes, it does," I says. "You prob'ly hit good because you shave at night; but you'd be a better fielder if you shaved in the mornin'."

You see, I was tryin' to be just as crazy as him—though that wasn't hardly possible.

"If that's right," says he, "I'll do my shavin' in the mornin'—because I seen in the papers where the boys says that if I could play the outfield like I can hit I'd be as good as Cobb. They tell me Cobb gets twenty thousand a year."

"No," I says; "he don't get that much—but he gets about ten times as much as you do."

"Well," he says, "I'm goin' to be as good as him, because I need the money."

"What do you want with money?" I says.

He just laughed and didn't say nothin'; but from that time on the water didn't run in the bathtub nights and he done his shavin' after breakfast. I didn't notice, though, that he looked any better in fieldin' practice.

IV

It rained one day in Cincy and they trimmed us two out o' the other three; but it wasn't Elliott's fault.

They had Larry beat four to one in the ninth innin' o' the first game. Archer gets on with two out, and John sends my roomy up to hit— though Benton, a lefthander, is workin' for them. The first thing Benton serves up there Elliott cracks it a mile over Hobby's head. It would of been good for three easy—only Archer—playin' safe, o' course—pulls up at third base. Tommy couldn't do nothin' and we was licked.

The next day he hits one out o' the park off the Indian; but we was 'way behind and they was nobody on at the time. We copped the last one without usin' no pinch hitters.

I didn't have no trouble with him nights durin' the whole series. He come to bed pretty late while we was there and I told him he'd better not let John catch him at it.

"What would he do?" he says.

"Fine you fifty," I says.

"He can't fine me a dime," he says, "because I ain't got it."

Then I told him he'd be fined all he had comin' if he didn't get in the hotel before midnight; but he just laughed and says he didn't think John had a kick comin' so long as he kep' bustin' the ball.

"Some day you'll go up there and you won't bust it," I says.

"That'll be an accident," he says.

That stopped me and I didn't say nothin'. What could you say to a guy who hated himself like that?

The "accident" happened in St. Louis the first day. We needed two runs in the eighth and Saier and Brid was on, with two out. John tells Elliott to go up in Pierce's place. The bug goes up and Griner gives him two bad balls—'way outside. I thought they was goin' to walk him— and it looked like good judgment, because they'd heard what he done in Cincy. But no! Griner comes back with a fast one right over and Elliott pulls it down the right foul line, about two foot foul. He hit it so hard you'd of thought they'd sure walk him then; but Griner gives him another fast one. He slammed it again just as hard, but foul. Then Griner gives him one 'way outside and it's two and three. John says, on the bench:

"If they don't walk him now he'll bust that fence down."

I thought the same and I was sure Griner wouldn't give him nothin' to hit; but he come with a curve and Rigler calls Elliott out. From where we sat the last one looked low, and I thought Elliott'd make a kick. He come back to the bench smilin'.

John starts for his position, but stopped and ast the bug what was the matter with that one. Any busher I ever knowed would of said, "It was too low," or "It was outside," or "It was inside." Elliott says:

"Nothin' at all. It was right over the middle."

"Why didn't you bust it, then?" says John.

"I was afraid I'd kill somebody," says Elliott, and laughed like a big boob.

John was pretty near chokin'.

"What are you laughin' at?" he says.

"I was thinkin' of a nickel show I seen in Cincinnati," says the bug.

"Well," says John, so mad he couldn't hardly see, "that show and that laugh'll cost you fifty."

We got beat, and I wouldn't of blamed John if he'd fined him his whole season's pay.

Up'n the room that night I told him he'd better cut out that laughin' stuff when we was gettin' trimmed or he never would have no pay day. Then he got confidential.

"Pay day wouldn't do me no good," he says. "When I'm all squared up with the club and begin to have a pay day I'll only get a hundred bucks at a time, and I'll owe that to some o' you fellers. I wisht we could win the pennant and get in on that World's Series dough. Then I'd get a bunch at once."

"What would you do with a bunch o' dough?" I ast him.

"Don't tell nobody, sport," he says; "but if I ever get five hundred at once I'm goin' to get married."

"Oh!" I says. "And who's the lucky girl?"

"She's a girl up in Muskegon," says Elliott; "and you're right when you call her lucky."

"You don't like yourself much, do you?" I says.

"I got reason to like myself," says he. "You'd like yourself, too, if you could hit 'em like me."

"Well," I says, "you didn't show me no hittin' to-day."

"I couldn't hit because I was laughin' too hard," says Elliott.

"What was it you was laughin' at?" I says.

"I was laughin' at that pitcher," he says. "He thought he had somethin' and he didn't have nothin'."

"He had enough to whiff you with," I says.

"He didn't have nothin'!" says he again. "I was afraid if I busted one off him they'd can him, and then I couldn't never hit agin him no more."

Naturally I didn't have no comeback to that. I just sort o' gasped and got ready to go to sleep; but he wasn't through.

"I wisht you could see this bird!" he says.

"What bird?" I says.

"This dame that's nuts about me," he says.

"Good-looker?" I ast.

"No," he says; "she ain't no bear for looks. They ain't nothin' about her for a guy to rave over till you hear her sing. She sure can holler some."

"What kind o' voice has she got?" I ast.

"A bear," says he.

"No," I says; "I mean is she a barytone or an air?"

"I don't know," he says; "but she's got the loudest voice I ever hear on a woman. She's pretty near got me beat."

"Can you sing?" I says; and I was sorry right afterward that I ast him that question.

I guess it must of been bad enough to have the water runnin' night after night and to have him wavin' that razor round; but that couldn't of been nothin' to his singin'. Just as soon as I'd pulled that boner he says, "Listen to me?" and starts in on 'Silver Threads Among the Gold.' Mind you, it was after midnight and they was guests all round us tryin' to sleep!

They used to be noise enough in our club when we had Hofman and Sheckard and Richie harmonizin'; but this bug's voice was louder'n all o' theirn combined. We once had a pitcher named Martin Walsh— brother o' Big Ed's—and I thought he could drownd out the Subway; but this guy made a boiler factory sound like Dummy Taylor. If the whole hotel wasn't awake when he'd howled the first line it's a pipe they was when he cut loose, which he done when he come to "Always young and fair to me." Them words could of been heard easy in East St. Louis.

He didn't get no encore from me, but he goes right through it again—or starts to. I knowed somethin' was goin' to happen before he finished—and somethin' did. The night clerk and the house detective come bangin' at the door. I let 'em in and they had plenty to say. If we made another sound the whole club'd be canned out o' the hotel. I tried to salve 'em, and I says:

"He won't sing no more."

But Elliott swelled up like a poisoned pup.

"Won't I?" he says. "I'll sing all I want to."

"You won't sing in here," says the clerk.

"They ain't room for my voice in here anyways," he says. "I'll go outdoors and sing."

And he puts his clothes on and ducks out. I didn't make no attemp' to stop him. I heard him bellowin' 'Silver Threads' down the corridor and down the stairs, with the clerk and the dick chasin' him all the way and tellin' him to shut up.

Well, the guests make a holler the next mornin'; and the hotel people tells Charlie Williams that he'll either have to let Elliott stay somewheres else or the whole club'll have to move. Charlie tells John, and John was thinkin' o' settlin' the question by releasin' Elliott.

I guess he'd about made up his mind to do it; but that afternoon they had us three to one in the ninth, and we got the bases full, with two down and Larry's turn to hit. Elliott had been sittin' on the bench sayin' nothin'.

"Do you think you can hit one today?" says John.

"I can hit one any day," says Elliott.

"Go up and hit that lefthander, then," says John, "and remember there's nothin' to laugh at."

Sallee was workin'—and workin' good; but that didn't bother the bug. He cut into one, and it went between Oakes and Whitted like a shot. He come into third standin' up and we was a run to the good. Sallee was so sore he kind o' forgot himself and took pretty near his full wind-up pitchin' to Tommy. And what did Elliott do but steal home and get away with it clean!

Well, you couldn't can him after that, could you? Charlie gets him a room somewheres and I was relieved of his company that night. The next evenin' we beat it for Chi to play about two weeks at home. He didn't tell nobody where he roomed there and I didn't see nothin' of him, 'cep' out to the park. I ast him what he did with himself nights and he says:

"Same as I do on the road—borrow some dough some place and go to the nickel shows."

"You must be stuck on 'em," I says.

"Yes," he says; "I like the ones where they kill people—because I want to learn how to do it. I may have that job some day."

"Don't pick on me," I says.

"Oh," says the bug, "you never can tell who I'll pick on."

It seemed as if he just couldn't learn nothin' about fieldin', and finally John told him to keep out o' the practice.

"A ball might hit him in the temple and croak him," says John.

But he busted up a couple o' games for us at home, beatin' Pittsburgh once and Cincy once.

V

They give me a great big room at the hotel in Pittsburgh; so the fellers picked it out for the poker game. We was playin' along about ten o'clock one night when in come Elliott—the earliest he'd showed up since we'd been roomin' together. They was only five of us playin' and Tom ast him to sit in.

"I'm busted," he says.

"Can you play poker?" I ast him.

"They's nothin' I can't do!" he says. "Slip me a couple o' bucks and I'll show you."

So I slipped him a couple o' bucks and honestly hoped he'd win, because I knowed he never had no dough. Well, Tom dealt him a hand and he picks it up and says:

"I only got five cards."

"How many do you want?" I says.

"Oh," he says, "if that's all I get I'll try to make 'em do."

The pot was cracked and raised, and he stood the raise. I says to myself: "There goes my two bucks!" But no—he comes out with three queens and won the dough. It was only about seven bucks; but you'd of thought it was a million to see him grab it. He laughed like a kid.

"Guess I can't play this game!" he says; and he had me fooled for a minute—I thought he must of been kiddin' when he complained of only havin' five cards.

He copped another pot right afterward and was sittin' there with about eleven bucks in front of him when Jim opens a roodle pot for a buck. I stays and so does Elliott. Him and Jim both drawed one card and I took three. I had kings or queens—I forget which. I didn't help 'em none; so when Jim bets a buck I throws my hand away.

"How much can I bet?" says the bug.

"You can raise Jim a buck if you want to," I says.

So he bets two dollars. Jim comes back at him. He comes right back at Jim. Jim raises him again and he tilts Jim right back. Well, when he'd boosted Jim with the last buck he had, Jim says:

"I'm ready to call. I guess you got me beat. What have you got?"

"I know what I've got, all right," says Elliott. "I've got a straight." And he throws his hand down. Sure enough, it was a straight, eight high. Jim pretty near fainted and so did I.

The bug had started pullin' in the dough when Jim stops him.

"Here! Wait a minute!" says Jim. "I thought you had somethin'. I filled up." Then Jim lays down his nine full.

"You beat me, I guess," says Elliott, and he looked like he'd lost his last friend.

"Beat you?" says Jim. "Of course I beat you! What did you think I had?"

"Well," says the bug, "I thought you might have a small flush or somethin'."

When I regained consciousness he was beggin' for two more bucks.

"What for?" I says. "To play poker with? You're barred from the game for life!"

"Well," he says, "if I can't play no more I want to go to sleep, and you fellers will have to get out o' this room."

Did you ever hear o' nerve like that? This was the first night he'd came in before twelve and he orders the bunch out so's he can sleep! We politely suggested to him to go to Brooklyn.

Without sayin' a word he starts in on his 'Silver Threads'; and it wasn't two minutes till the game was busted up and the bunch—all but me—was out o' there. I'd of beat it too, only he stopped yellin' as soon as they'd went.

"You're some buster!" I says. "You bust up ball games in the afternoon and poker games at night."

"Yes," he says; "that's my business—bustin' things."

And before I knowed what he was about he picked up the pitcher of ice-water that was on the floor and throwed it out the window—through the glass and all.

Right then I give him a plain talkin' to. I tells him how near he come to gettin' canned down in St. Louis because he raised so much Cain singin' in the hotel.

"But I had to keep my voice in shape," he says. "If I ever get dough enough to get married the girl and me'll go out singin' together."

"Out where?" I ast.

"Out on the vaudeville circuit," says Elliott.

"Well," I says, "if her voice is like yours you'll be wastin' money if you travel round. Just stay up in Muskegon and we'll hear you, all right!"

I told him he wouldn't never get no dough if he didn't behave himself. That, even if we got in the World's Series, he wouldn't be with us— unless he cut out the foolishness.

"We ain't goin' to get in no World's Series," he says, "and I won't never get a bunch o' money at once; so it looks like I couldn't get married this fall."

Then I told him we played a city series every fall. He'd never thought o' that and it tickled him to death. I told him the losers always got about five hundred apiece and that we were about due to win it and get about eight hundred. "But," I says, "we still got a good chance for the old pennant; and if I was you I wouldn't give up hope o' that yet—not where John can hear you, anyway."

"No," he says, "we won't win no pennant, because he won't let me play reg'lar; but I don't care so long as we're sure o' that city-series dough."

"You ain't sure of it if you don't behave," I says.

"Well," says he, very serious, "I guess I'll behave." And he did—till we made our first Eastern trip.

VI

We went to Boston first, and that crazy bunch goes out and piles up a three-run lead on us in seven innin's the first day. It was the pitcher's turn to lead off in the eighth, so up goes Elliott to bat for him. He kisses the first thing they hands him for three bases; and we says, on the bench: "Now we'll get 'em!"—because, you know, a three-run lead wasn't nothin' in Boston.

"Stay right on that bag!" John hollers to Elliott.

Mebbe if John hadn't said nothin' to him everythin' would of been all right; but when Perdue starts to pitch the first ball to Tommy, Elliott starts to steal home. He's out as far as from here to Seattle.

If I'd been carryin' a gun I'd of shot him right through the heart. As it was, I thought John'd kill him with a bat, because he was standin' there with a couple of 'em, waitin' for his turn; but I guess John was too stunned to move. He didn't even seem to see Elliott when he went to the bench. After I'd cooled off a little I says:

"Beat it and get into your clothes before John comes in. Then go to the hotel and keep out o' sight."

When I got up in the room afterward, there was Elliott, lookin' as innocent and happy as though he'd won fifty bucks with a pair o' treys.

"I thought you might of killed yourself," I says.

"What for?" he says.

"For that swell play you made," says I.

"What was the matter with the play?" ast Elliott, surprised. "It was all right when I done it in St. Louis."

"Yes," I says; "but they was two out in St. Louis and we wasn't no three runs behind."

"Well," he says, "if it was all right in St. Louis I don't see why it was wrong here."

"It's a diff'rent climate here," I says, too disgusted to argue with him.

"I wonder if they'd let me sing in this climate?" says Elliott.

"No," I says. "Don't sing in this hotel, because we don't want to get fired out o' here—the eats is too good."

"All right," he says. "I won't sing." But when I starts down to supper he says: "I'm li'ble to do somethin' worse'n sing."

He didn't show up in the dinin' room and John went to the boxin' show after supper; so it looked like him and Elliott wouldn't run into each other till the murder had left John's heart. I was glad o' that—because a Mass'chusetts jury might not consider it justifiable hommer-cide if one guy croaked another for givin' the Boston club a game.

I went down to the corner and had a couple o' beers; and then I come straight back, intendin' to hit the hay. The elevator boy had went for a drink or somethin', and they was two old ladies already waitin' in the car when I stepped in. Right along after me comes Elliott.

"Where's the boy that's supposed to run this car?" he says. I told him the boy'd be right back; but he says: "I can't wait. I'm much too sleepy."

And before I could stop him he'd slammed the door and him and I and the poor old ladies was shootin' up.

"Let us off at the third floor, please!" says one o' the ladies, her voice kind o' shakin'.

"Sorry, madam," says the bug; "but this is a express and we don't stop at no third floor."

I grabbed his arm and tried to get him away from the machinery; but he was as strong as a ox and he throwed me agin the side o' the car like I was a baby. We went to the top faster'n I ever rode in an elevator before. And then we shot down to the bottom, hittin' the bumper down there so hard I thought we'd be smashed to splinters.

The ladies was too scared to make a sound durin' the first trip; but while we was goin' up and down the second time—even faster'n the first—they begun to scream. I was hollerin' my head off at him to quit and he was makin' more noise than the three of us—pretendin' he was the locomotive and the whole crew o' the train.

Don't never ask me how many times we went up and down! The women fainted on the third trip and I guess I was about as near it as I'll ever get. The elevator boy and the bellhops and the waiters and the night clerk and everybody was jumpin' round the lobby screamin'; but no one seemed to know how to stop us.

Finally—on about the tenth trip, I guess—he slowed down and stopped at the fifth floor, where we was roomin'. He opened the door and beat it for the room, while I, though I was tremblin' like a leaf, run the car down to the bottom.

The night clerk knowed me pretty well and knowed I wouldn't do nothin' like that; so him and I didn't argue, but just got to work together to bring the old women to. While we was doin' that Elliott must of run down the stairs and slipped out o' the hotel, because when they sent the officers up to the room after him he'd blowed.

They was goin' to fire the club out; but Charlie had a good standin' with Amos, the proprietor, and he fixed it up to let us stay—providin' Elliott kep' away. The bug didn't show up at the ball park next day and we didn't see no more of him till we got on the rattler for New York. Charlie and John both bawled him, but they give him a berth— an upper—and we pulled into the Grand Central Station without him havin' made no effort to wreck the train.

VII

I'd studied the thing pretty careful, but hadn't come to no conclusion. I was sure he wasn't no stew, because none o' the boys had ever saw him even take a glass o' beer, and I couldn't never detect the odor o' booze on him. And if he'd been a dope I'd of knew about it—roomin' with him.

There wouldn't of been no mystery about it if he'd been a left-hand pitcher—but he wasn't. He wasn't nothin' but a whale of a hitter and he throwed with his right arm. He hit lefthanded, a' course; but so did Saier and Brid and Schulte and me, and John himself; and none of us was violent. I guessed he must of been just a plain nut and li'ble to break out any time.

They was a letter waitin' for him at New York, and I took it, in- tendin' to give it to him at the park, because I didn't think they'd let him room at the hotel; but after breakfast he come up to the room, with his suitcase. It seems he'd promised John and Charlie to be good, and made it so strong they b'lieved him.

I give him his letter, which was addressed in a girl's writin' and come from Muskegon.

"From the girl?" I says.

"Yes," he says; and, without openin' it, he tore it up and throwed it out the window.

"Had a quarrel?" I ast.

"No, no," he says; "but she can't tell me nothin' I don't know al- ready. Girls always writes the same junk. I got one from her in Pitts- burgh, but I didn't read it."

"I guess you ain't so stuck on her," I says.

He swells up and says:

"Of course I'm stuck on her! If I wasn't, do you think I'd be goin' round with this bunch and gettin' insulted all the time? I'm stickin' here because o' that series dough, so's I can get hooked."

"Do you think you'd settle down if you was married?" I ast him.

"Settle down?" he says. "Sure, I'd settle down. I'd be so happy that I wouldn't have to look for no excitement."

Nothin' special happened that night 'cep' that he come in the room about one o'clock and woke me up by pickin' up the foot o' the bed and droppin' it on the floor, sudden-like.

"Give me a key to the room," he says.

"You must of had a key," I says, "or you couldn't of got in."

"That's right!" he says, and beat it to bed.

One o' the reporters must of told Elliott that John had ast for waivers on him and New York had refused to waive, because next mornin' he come to me with that dope.

"New York's goin' to win this pennant!" he says.

"Well," I says, "they will if some one else don't. But what of it?"

"I'm goin' to play with New York," he says, "so's I can get the World's Series dough."

"How you goin' to get away from this club?" I ast.

"Just watch me!" he says. "I'll be with New York before this series is over."

Well, the way he goes after the job was original, anyway. Rube'd had one of his good days the day before and we'd got a trimmin'; but this second day the score was tied up at two runs apiece in the tenth, and Big Jeff'd been wabblin' for two or three innin's.

Well, he walks Saier and me, with one out, and Mac sends for Matty, who was warmed up and ready. John sticks Elliott in in Brid's place and the bug pulls one into the right-field stand.

It's a cinch McGraw thinks well of him then, and might of went after him if he hadn't went crazy the next afternoon. We're tied up in the ninth and Matty's workin'. John sends Elliott up with the bases choked; but he doesn't go right up to the plate. He walks over to their bench and calls McGraw out. Mac tells us about it afterward.

"I can bust up this game right here!" says Elliott.

"Go ahead," says Mac; "but be careful he don't whiff you."

Then the bug pulls it.

"If I whiff," he says, "will you get me on your club?"

"Sure!" says Mac, just as anybody would.

By this time Bill Koem was hollerin' about the delay; so up goes Elliott and gives the worst burlesque on tryin' to hit that you ever see. Matty throws one a mile outside and high, and the bug swings like it was right over the heart. Then Matty throws one at him and he ducks out o' the way—but swings just the same. Matty must of been wise by this time, for he pitches one so far outside that the Chief almost has to go to the coachers' box after it. Elliott takes his third healthy and runs through the field down to the clubhouse.

We got beat in the eleventh; and when we went in to dress he has his street clothes on. Soon as he seen John comin' he says: "I got to see McGraw!" And he beat it.

John was goin' to the fights that night; but before he leaves the hotel he had waivers on Elliott from everybody and had sold him to Atlanta.

"And," says John, "I don't care if they pay for him or not."

My roomy blows in about nine and got the letter from John out of his box. He was goin' to tear it up, but I told him they was news in it. He opens it and reads where he's sold. I was still sore at him; so I says:

"Thought you was goin' to get on the New York club?"

"No," he says. "I got turned down cold. McGraw says he wouldn't have me in his club. He says he'd had Charlie Faust—and that was enough for him."

He had a kind o' crazy look in his eyes; so when he starts up to the room I follows him.

"What are you goin' to do now?" I says.

"I'm goin' to sell this ticket to Atlanta," he says, "and go back to Muskegon, where I belong."

"I'll help you pack," I says.

"No," says the bug. "I come into this league with this suit o'clothes and a collar. They can have the rest of it." Then he sits down on the bed and begins to cry like a baby. "No series dough for me," he blubbers, "and no weddin' bells! My girl'll die when she hears about it!"

Of course that made me feel kind o' rotten, and I says:

"Brace up, boy! The best thing you can do is go to Atlanta and try hard. You'll be up here again next year."

"You can't tell me where to go!" he says, and he wasn't cryin' no more. "I'll go where I please—and I'm li'ble to take you with me."

I didn't want no argument, so I kep' still. Pretty soon he goes up to the lookin'-glass and stares at himself for five minutes. Then, all of a sudden, he hauls off and takes a wallop at his reflection in the glass. Naturally he smashed the glass all to pieces and he cut his hand somethin' awful.

Without lookin' at it he come over to me and says: "Well, good-by, sport!"—and holds out his other hand to shake. When I starts to shake with him he smears his bloody hand all over my map. Then he laughed like a wild man and run out o' the room and out o' the hotel.

VIII

Well, boys, my sleep was broke up for the rest o' the season. It might of been because I was used to sleepin' in all kinds o' racket and excitement, and couldn't stand for the quiet after he'd went—or it might of been because I kep' thinkin' about him and feelin' sorry for him.

I of'en wondered if he'd settle down and be somethin' if he could get married; and finally I got to b'lievin' he would. So when we was dividin' the city series dough I was thinkin' of him and the girl. Our share o' the money—the losers', as usual—was twelve thousand seven hundred sixty bucks or somethin' like that. They was twenty-one of us and that meant six hundred seven bucks apiece. We was just goin' to cut it up that way when I says:

"Why not give a divvy to poor old Elliott?"

About fifteen of 'em at once told me that I was crazy. You see, when he got canned he owed everybody in the club. I guess he'd stuck me for the most—about seventy bucks—but I didn't care nothin' about that. I knowed he hadn't never reported to Atlanta, and I thought he was prob'ly busted and a bunch o' money might make things all right for him and the other songbird.

I made quite a speech to the fellers, tellin' 'em how he'd cried when he left us and how his heart'd been set on gettin' married on the series dough. I made it so strong that they finally fell for it. Our shares was cut to five hundred eighty apiece, and John sent him a check for a full share.

For a while I was kind o' worried about what I'd did. I didn't know if I was doin' right by the girl to give him the chance to marry her.

He'd told me she was stuck on him, and that's the only excuse I had for tryin' to fix it up between 'em; but, b'lieve me, if she was my sister or a friend o' mine I'd just as soon of had her manage the Cincinnati Club as marry that bird. I thought to myself:

"If she's all right she'll take acid in a month—and it'll be my fault; but if she's really stuck on him they must be somethin' wrong with her too, so what's the diff'rence?"

Then along comes this letter that I told you about. It's from some friend of hisn up there—and they's a note from him. I'll read 'em to you and then I got to beat it for the station:

DEAR SIR: They have got poor Elliott locked up and they are goin' to take him to the asylum at Kalamazoo. He thanks you for

the check, and we will use the money to see that he is made
comf'table.

When the poor boy come back here he found that his girl was
married to Joe Bishop, who runs a soda fountain. She had wrote
to him about it, but he did not read her letters. The news drove
him crazy—poor boy—and he went to the place where they was
livin' with a baseball bat and very near killed 'em both. Then he
marched down the street singin' 'Silver Threads Among the Gold'
at the top of his voice. They was goin' to send him to prison for
assault with intent to kill, but the jury decided he was crazy.

He wants to thank you again for the money.

Yours truly,   JIM——

I can't make out his last name—but it don't make no diff'rence. Now
I'll read you his note:

OLD ROOMY: I was at bat twice and made two hits; but I guess
I did not meet 'em square. They tell me they are both alive yet,
which I did not mean 'em to be. I hope they got good curve-ball
pitchers where I am goin'. I sure can bust them curves—can't I,
sport?

Yours,   B. ELLIOTT.

P.S.—The B stands for Buster.

That's all of it, fellers; and you can see I had some excuse for not
hittin'. You can also see why I ain't never goin' to room with no bug
again—not for John or nobody else!

THE YOUNG IMMIGRUNTS

Preface

The person whose name is signed to this novel was born on the nine-teenth day of August, 1915, and was therefore four years and three months old when the manuscript was found, late in November, 1919. The narrative is substantially true, with the following exceptions:

1. "My Father," the leading character in the work, is depicted as a man of short temper, whereas the person from whom the character was drawn is in reality as pleasant a fellow as one would care to meet and seldom has a cross word for any one, let alone women and children.

2. The witty speeches accredited to "My Father" have, possibly ow-ing to the limitations of a child's memory, been so garbled and twisted that they do not look half so good in print as they sounded in the open air.

3. More stops for gas were made than are mentioned in the story.

As the original manuscript was written on a typewriter with a rather frayed ribbon, and as certain words were marked out and others hand-written in, I have taken the liberty of copying the entire work with a fresh ribbon and the inclusion of the changes which the author indicated in pencil in the first draft. Otherwise the story is presented to the reader exactly as it was first set down.

THE FATHER.

Chapter I

MY PARENTS

My parents are both married and ½ of them are very good looking. The balance is tall and skiny and has a swarty complexion with moles but you hardily ever notice them on account of your gaze being rapped up in his feet which would be funny if brevvity wasnt the soul of wit. Everybody says I have his eyes and I am glad it didnt half to be some-thing else tho Rollie Zeider the ball player calls him owl eyes for a nick name but if I was Rollie Zeider and his nose I wouldnt pick on some-bodys else features.

He wears pretty shirts which he bought off of another old ball player Artie Hofman to attrack tension off of his feet and must of payed a big price for them I heard my ant tell my uncle when they thorght I was a sleep down to the lake tho I guess he pays even more for his shoes if they sell them by the frunt foot.

I was born in a hospittle in Chicago 4 years ago and liked it very much and had no idear we were going to move till 1 day last summer I heard my mother arsk our nurse did she think she could get along O. K. with myself and 3 brothers John Jimmie and David for 10 days wilst she and my old man went east to look for a costly home.

Well yes said our nurse barshfully.

I may as well exclaim to the reader that John is 7 and Jimmie is 5 and I am 4 and David is almost nothing as yet you might say and tho I was named for my father they call me Bill thank God.

The conversation amungst my mother and our nurse took place right after my father came back from Toledo where Jack Dempsey knocked Jessie Willard for a gool tho my father liked the big fellow and bet on him.

David was in his bath at the time and my mother and our nurse and myself and 2 elder brothers was standing around admireing him tho I notice that when the rest of the family takes their bath they dont make open house of the occassion.

Well my parents went east and dureing their absents myself and brothers razed hell with David on the night shift but when they come back my mother said to the nurse were they good boys.

Fine replid our nurse lamely and where are you going to live.

Connecticut said my mother.

Our nurse forced a tired smile.

Here we will leave my parents to unpack and end this chapter.

Chapter 2

STARTING GAILY

We spent the rest of the summer on my granmother in Indiana and my father finley went to the worst series to write it up as he has followed sports of all sorts for years and is a expert so he bet on the wite sox and when he come home he acted rarther cross.

Well said my mother simperingly I suppose we can start east now.

We will start east when we get good and ready said my father with a lordly sneeze.

The next thing was how was we going to make the trip as my father had boughten a new car that the cheepest way to get it there was drive it besides carrying a grate deal of our costly bagage but if all of us went in it they would be no room left for our costly bagage and besides 2 of my brothers always acts like devils incarnite when they get in a car so my mother said to our nurse.

If you think you can manage the 2 older boys and David on the train myself and husband will take Bill in the car said my mother to our nurse.

Fine replid our nurse with a gastly look witch my mother did not see.

Myself and parents left Goshen Indiana on a fine Monday morning leaveing our nurse and brothers to come latter in the weak on the railway. Our plans was to reach Detroit that night and stop with my uncle and ant and the next evening take the boat to Buffalo and thence to Connecticut by motor so the first town we past through was Middlebury.

Elmer Flick the old ball player use to live here said my father modestly.

My mother forced a smile and soon we were acrost the Michigan line and my mother made the remark that she was thirsty.

We will stop at Coldwater for lunch said my father with a strate face as he pulls most of his lines without changeing expressions.

Sure enough we puled up to 1 side of the road just after leaveing Coldwater and had our costly viands of frid chicken and doughnuts and milk fernished by my grate ant and of witch I partook freely.

We will stop at Ypsilanti for supper said my father in calm tones that is where they have the state normal school.

I was glad to hear this and hoped we would get there before dark as I had always wanted to come in contack with normal peaple and see what they are like and just at dusk we entered a large size town and drove past a large size football field.

Heavens said my mother this must be a abnormal school to have such a large football field.

My father wore a qeer look.

This is not Ypsilanti this is Ann Arbor he crid.

But I thorght you said we would go south of Ann Arbor and direct to Ypsilanti said my mother with a smirk.

I did say that but I thorght I would surprise you by comeing into Ann Arbor replid my father with a corse jesture.

Personly I think the surprise was unanimous.

Well now we are here said my mother we might as well look up Bill.

Bill is my uncle Bill so we stoped at the Alfa Delt house and got him and took him down to the hotel for supper and my old man called up Mr. Yost the football coach of the Michigan football team and he come down and visited with us.

What kind of a team have you got coach said my father lamely.

I have got a determined team replid Mr. Yost they are determined to not play football.

At this junction my unlucky mother changed the subjeck to the league of nations and it was 10 o'clock before Mr. Yost come to a semi colon so we could resume our journey and by the time we past through Ypsilanti the peaple was not only subnormal but unconsius. It was nerly midnight when we puled up in frunt of my ants and uncles house in Detroit that had been seting up since 7 expecting us.

Were sorry to be so late said my mother bruskly.

Were awfully glad you could come at all replid my ant with a ill consealed yawn.

We will now leave my relitives to get some sleep and end this chapter.

Chapter 3

ERIE LAKE

The boat leaves Detroit every afternoon at 5 oclock and reachs Buffalo the next morning at 9 tho I would better exclaim to my readers that when it is 9 oclock in Buffalo it is only 8 oclock in Goshen for instants as Buffalo peaple are qeer.

Well said my father the next morning at brekfus I wander what time we half to get the car on the board of the boat.

I will find out down town and call up and let you know replid my uncle who is a engineer and digs soors or something.

Sure enough he called up dureing the fornoon and said the car must be on the board of the boat at 3 oclock so my father left the house at 2 oclock and drove down to the worf tho he had never drove a car in Detroit before but has nerves of steal. Latter my uncle come out to his home and took myself and mother and ant down to the worf where my old man was waiting for us haveing put the car on the board.

What have you been doing ever since 3 oclock arsked my mother as it was now nerly 5.

Haveing a high ball my father replid.

I thorght Detroit was dry said my mother shyly.

Did you said my father with a rye smile and as it was now nerly time for the boat to leave we said good by to my uncle and ant and went on the boat. A messenger took our costly bagage and put it away wilst myself and parents went out on the porch and set looking at the peaple on the worf. Suddenly they was a grate hub bub on the worf and a young man and lady started up the gangs plank wilst a big crowd throwed rice and old shoes at them and made a up roar.

Bride and glum going to Niagara Falls said my father who is well travelled and seams to know everything.

Instantly the boat give a blarst on the wistle and I started with suprise.

Did that scare you Bill said my father and seamed to enjoy it and I supose he would of laughed out right had I fell overboard and been drowned in the narsty river water.

Soon we were steeming up the river on the city of Detroit 3.

That is Canada over there is it not said my mother.

What did you think it was the Austrian Tyrol replid my father explodeing a cough. Dureing our progress up the river I noticed sevral funny things flotting in the water with lanterns hanging on them and was wandering what they could be when my mother said they seam to have plenty of boys.

They have got nothing on us replid my father quick as a flarsh.

A little latter who should come out on the porch and set themselfs ner us but the bride and glum.

Oh I said to myself I hope they will talk so as I can hear them as I have always wandered what newlyweds talk about on their way to Niagara Falls and soon my wishs was realized.

Some night said the young glum are you warm enough.

I am perfectly comfertible replid the fare bride tho her looks belid her words what time do we arive in Buffalo.

9 oclock said the lordly glum are you warm enough.

I am perfectly comfertible replid the fare bride what time do we arive in Buffalo.

9 oclock said the lordly glum I am afrade it is too cold for you out here.

Well maybe it is replid the fare bride and without farther adieu they went in the spacius parlers.

I wander will he be arsking her 8 years from now is she warm enough said my mother with a faint grimace.

The weather may change before then replid my father.

Are you warm enough said my father after a slite pause.

No was my mothers catchy reply.

Well said my father we arive in Buffalo at 9 oclock and with that we all went inside as it was now pitch dark and had our supper and retired and when we rose the next morning and drest and had brekfus we puled up to the worf in Buffalo and it was 9 oclock so I will leave the city of Detroit 3 tide to the worf and end this chapter.

Chapter 4

BUFFALO TO ROCHESTER 76.4

As we was leaveing the boat who should I see right along side of us but the fare bride and the lordly glum.

We are right on the dot said the glum looking at his costly watch it is just 9 oclock and so they past out of my life.

We had to wait qite a wile wilst the old man dug up his bill of loading and got the costly moter.

We will half to get some gas he said I wonder where they is a garage.

No sooner had the words fell from his lips when a man with a flagrant Adams apple handed him a card with the name of a garage on it.

Go up Genesee st 5 blks and turn to the left or something said the man with the apple.

Soon we reached the garage and had the gas tank filled with gas it was 27 cents in Buffalo and soon we was on our way to Rochester.

Well these are certainly grate roads said my father barshfully.

They have lots better roads in the east than out west replid my mother with a knowing wink.

The roads all through the east are better than out west remarked my father at lenth.

These are wonderfull replid my mother smuggleing me vs her arm.

The time past quickly with my parents in so jocular a mood and all most before I knew it we was on the outer skirts of Batavia.

What town is this quired my mother in a tolerant voice.

Batavia husked my father sloughing down to 15 miles per hour.

Well maybe we would better stop and have lunch here said my mother coyly.

We will have lunch in Rochester replid my father with a loud cough.

My mother forced a smile and it was about ½ past 12 when we arived in Rochester and soon we was on Genesee st and finley stoped in front of a elegant hotel and shared a costly lunch.

Chapter 5

MY FATHER'S IDEAR

Wilst participateing in the lordly viands my father halled out his map and give it the up and down.

Look at here he said at lenth they seams to be a choice of 2 main roads between here and Syracuse but 1 of them gos way up north to Oswego wilst the other gos way south to Geneva where as Syracuse is strate east from here you might say so it looks to me like we would save both millage and time if we was to drive strate east through Lyons the way the railway gos.

Well I dont want to ride on the ties said my mother with a loud cough.

Well you dont half to because they seams to be a little road that gos strate through replid my father removeing a flys cadaver from the costly farina.

Well you would better stick to the main roads said my mother tacklessly.

Well you would better stick to your own business replid my father with a pungent glance.

Soon my father had payed the check and gave the waiter a lordly bribe and once more we sprang into the machine and was on our way. The lease said about the results of my fathers grate idear the soonest mended in a word it turned out to be a holycost of the first water as after we had covered miles and miles of ribald roads we suddenly come to a abrupt conclusion vs the side of a stagnant freight train that was stone deef to honks. My father set there for nerly ½ a hour reciteing the 4 Horses of the Apoplex in a under tone but finely my mother mustard up her curage and said affectedly why dont we turn around and go back somewheres. I cant spell what my father replid.

At lenth my old man decided that Lyons wouldnt never come to Mahomet if we set it out on the same lines all winter so we backed up and turned around and retraced 4 miles of shell holes and finely reached our objective by way of Detour.

Puling up in front of a garage my father beckoned to a dirty mechanic.

How do we get to Syracuse from her arsked my father blushing furiously.

Go strate south to Geneva and then east to Syracuse replid the dirty mechanic with a loud cough.

Isnt there no short cut arsked my father.

Go strate south to Geneva and then east to Syracuse replid the dirty mechanic.

You see daddy we go to Geneva after all I said brokenly but luckly for my piece of mind my father dont beleive in corporeal punishment a specially in front of Lyons peaple.

Soon we was on a fine road and nothing more hapened till we puled into Syracuse at 7 that evening and as for the conversation that changed hands in the car between Lyons and Syracuse you could stick it in a day message and send it for 30 cents.

Chapter 6

SYRACUSE TO HUDSON 183.2

Soon we was on Genesee st in Syracuse but soon turned off a blk or 2 and puled up in front of a hotel that I cant ether spell or pronounce besides witch they must of been a convention of cheese sculpters or something stoping there and any way it took the old man a hour to weedle a parler bed room and bath out of the clerk and put up a cot for me.

Wilst we was enjoying a late and futile supper in the hotel dinning room a man named Duffy reckonized my father and came to our table and arsked him to go to some boxing matchs in Syracuse that night.

Thanks very much said my father with a slite sneeze but you see what I have got on my hands besides witch I have been driveing all day and half to start out again erly in the morning so I guess not.

Between you and I dear reader my old man has been oposed to pugilisms since the 4 of July holycost.

Who is that man arsked my mother when that man had gone away.

Mr. Duffy replid my father shove the ketchup over this way.

Yes I know he is Mr. Duffy but where did you meet him insisted my mother quaintly.

In Boston my father replid where would a person meet a man named Duffy.

When we got up the next morning it was 6 o'clock and purring rain but we eat a costly brekfus and my father said we would save time if we would all walk down to the garage where he had horded the car witch he stated was only 2 short blks away from the hotel. Well if it was only 2 short blks why peaple that lives next door to each other in

Syracuse are by no means neighbors and when we got there the entire party was soping wet and rarther rabid.

We will all catch our death of cold chuckled my mother.

What of it explained my old man with a dirty look at the sky.

Maybe we would better put up the curtains sugested my mother smirking.

Maybe we wouldnt too said my father cordialy.

Well maybe it will clear up said my mother convulsively.

Maybe it wont too replid my father as he capered into the drivers seat.

My father is charming company wilst driveing on strange roads through a purring rain and even when we past through Oneida and he pronounced it like it was a biscuit neither myself or my mother ventured to correct him but finely we reached Utica when we got to witch we puled up along side the kerb and got out and rang ourselfs out to a small extent when suddenly a closed car sored past us on the left.

Why that was Mrs. Heywood in that car explained my mother with a fierce jesture. By this time it was not raining and we got back into the car and presently over took the closed car witch stoped when they reckonized us.

And witch boy is this quired Mrs. Heywood when the usual compliments had been changed.

This is the third he is named for his father replid my mother forcing a smile.

He has his eyes was the comment.

Bill dont you remember Mrs. Heywood said my mother turning on me she use to live in Riverside and Dr. Heywood tended to you that time you had that slite atack of obesity.

Well yes I replid with a slite accent but did not add how rotten the medicine tasted that time and soon we was on Genesee st on our way out of Utica.

I wander why they dont name some of their sts Genesee in these eastren towns said my father for the sun was now shining but no sooner had we reached Herkimer when the clouds bersed with renude vigger and I think my old man was about to say we will stop here and have lunch when my mother sugested it herself.

No replid my father with a corse jesture we will go on to Little Falls.

It was raining cats and dogs when we arived at Little Falls and my father droped a quaint remark.

If Falls is a verb he said the man that baptized this town was a practicle joker.

We will half to change our close replid my mother steping into a mud peddle in front of the hotel with a informal look.

When we had done so we partook of a meger lunch and as it was now only drooling resumed our jurney.

They soked me 5 for that room said my father but what is a extra sokeing or 2 on a day like this.

I didnt mean for you to get a room said my mother violently.

Where did you want us to change our close on the register said my old man turning pail.

Wasnt it funny that we should happen to see Mrs. Heywood in Utica said my mother at lenth.

They live there dont they my father replid.

Why yes my mother replid.

Well then my father replid the real joke would of been if we had of happened to see her in Auburn.

A little wile latter we past a grate many signs reading dine at the Big Nose Mountain Inn.

Rollie Zeider never told me they had named a mountain after him crid my father and soon we past through Fonda.

Soon we past through Amsterdam and I guess I must of dosed off at lease I cant remember anything between there and Schenectady and I must apologize to my readers for my laps as I am unable to ether describe the scenery or report anything that may of been said between these 2 points but I recall that as we entered Albany a remark was adrest to me for the first time since lunch.

Bill said my mother with a ½ smirk this is Albany the capital of New York state.

So this is Albany I thorght to myself.

Who is governor of New York now arsked my mother to my father.

Smith replid my father who seams to know everything.

Queer name said my mother sulkily.

Soon we puled up along side a policeman who my father arsked how de we get acrost the river to the New York road and if Albany pays their policemans by the word I'll say we were in the presents of a rich man and by the time he got through it was dark and still drooling and my old man didnt know the road and under those conditions I will not repete the conversation that transpired between Albany and Hudson but will end my chapter at the city limits of the last named settlemunt.

Chapter 7

HUDSON

We were turing gaily down the main st of Hudson when a man of 12 years capered out from the side walk and hoped on the runing board.

Do you want a good garage he arsked with a dirty look.

Why yes my good man replid my father tenderly but first where is the best hotel.

I will take you there said the man.

I must be a grate favorite in Hudson my father wispered at my mother.

Soon folling the mans directions we puled up in front of a hotel but when my father went at the register the clerk said I am full tonight.

Where do you get it around here arsked my father tenderly.

We have no rooms replid the senile clerk paying no tension to my old mans remark but there is a woman acrost the st that takes loggers.

Not to excess I hope replid my father but soon we went acrost the st and the woman agrede to hord us for the night so myself and mother went to our apartmunts wilst my father and the 12 year old besought the garage. When we finley got reunited and went back to the hotel for supper it was past 8 oclock as a person could of told from the viands. Latter in front of our loggings we again met the young man who had welcomed us to Hudson and called my father to 1 side.

There is a sailer going to spend the night here he said in a horse wisper witch has walked all the way from his home Schenectady and he has got to report on his ship in New York tomorrow afternoon and has got no money so if he dont get a free ride he will be up vs it.

He can ride with us replid my father with a hiccup if tomorrow is anything like today a sailer will not feel out of place in my costly moter.

I will tell him replid the man with a corse jesture.

Will you call us at ½ past 5 my mother reqested to our lanlady as we entered our Hudson barracks.

I will if I am awake she replid useing her handkerchief to some extent.

Latter we wandered how anybody could help from being awake in that hot bed of mones and grones and cat calls and caterwauls and gulish screaks of all kinds and tho we had rose erly at Syracuse and had a day of retchedness we was all more than ready to get up when she wraped on our door long ere day brake.

Where is that sailer that stoped here last night quired my father as we was about to make a lordly outburst.

He wouldnt pay his bill and razed hell so I kicked him out replid the lanlady in her bear feet.

Without farther adieu my father payed his bill and we walked into the dismul st so I will end this chapter by leaveing the fare lanlady flaping in the door way in her sredded night gown.

Chapter 8

HUDSON TO YONKERS 106.5

It was raining a little so my father bad my mother and I stand in the st wilst he went to the garage and retained the costly moter. He returned ½ a hour latter with the story that the garage had been locked and he had to go to the props house and roust him out.

How did you know where he lived quired my mother barshfully.

I used the brains god gave me was my fathers posthumous reply.

Soon we rumpled into Rhinebeck and as it was now day light and the rain had siezed we puled up in front of the Beekman arms for brekfus.

It says this is the oldest hotel in America said my mother reading the programme.

The eggs tastes all right replid my father with a corse jesture.

What is the next town quired my mother when we again set sale.

Pokippsie was my father's reply.

Thats where Vassar is said my mother as my old man stiffled a yawn I wonder if there is a store there that would have a koop for David.

I doubt it they ever heard of him said my father dryly how much do they cost.

Well I dont know.

We entered Pokipsie at lenth and turned to the left up the main st and puled up in front of a big store where myself and mother went in and purchased a koop for my little brother and a kap for me witch only took a ½ hour dureing witch my father lost his temper and when we finley immerged he was barking like a dog and giveing the Vassar yell. 2 men come out of the store with us and tost the koop with the rest of the junk in the back seat and away we went.

Doesnt this look cute on him said my mother in regards to my new kap.

What of it replid my father with a grimace and with that we puled into Garrison.

Isnt this right acrost the river from West Point said my mother with a gastly look.

What of it replid my father tenderly and soon we found ourselfs in Peekskill.

This is where that young girl cousin of mine gos to school said my father from Philadelphia.

What of it said my mother with a loud cough and presently we stoped and bought 15 gals of gas.

I have got a fund of usefull information about every town we come to said my father admireingly for instants this is Harmon where they take off the steem engines and put on the electric bull-gines.

My mother looked at him with ill consealed admiration.

And what do you know about this town she arsked as we frisked into Ossining.

Why this is Ossining where they take off the hair and put on the stripes replid my father qick as a flarsh and the next place is Tarrytown where John D. Rockefeller has a estate.

What is the name of the estate quired my mother breathlessly.

Socony I supose was the sires reply.

With that we honked into Yonkers and up the funny looking main st.

What a funny looking st said my mother and I always thorght it was the home of well to do peaple.

Well yes replid my father it is the home of the ruling class at lease Bill Klem the umpire and Bill Langford the referee lives here.

I will end my chapter on that one.

Chapter 9

THE BUREAU OF MANHATTAN

Isn't it about time said my mother as we past Spuyten Duyvil and entered the Bureau of Manhattan that we made our plans.

What plans said my father all my plans is all ready made.

Well then you might make me your confident sugested my mother with a quaint smirk.

Well then heres the dope uttered my father in a vage tone I am going to drop you at the 125 st station where you will only half to wait 2 hours and a ½ for the rest of the family as the train from the west is do at 350 at 125 st in the meen wile I will drive out to Grenitch with

Bill and see if the house is ready and etc and if the other peaples train is on time you can catch the 4 4 and I an Bill will meet you at the Grenitch station.

If you have time get a qt of milk for David said my mother with a pail look.

What kind of milk arsked my dad.

Oh sour milk my mother screened.

As she was now in a pretty bad temper we will leave her to cool off for 2 hours and a ½ in the 125 st station and end this chapter.

Chapter 10

N.Y. TO GRENITCH 500.0

The lease said about my and my fathers trip from the Bureau of Manhattan to our new home the soonest mended. In some way ether I or he got balled up on the grand concorpse and next thing you know we was thretning to swoop down on Pittsfield.

Are you lost daddy I arsked tenderly.

Shut up he explained.

At lenth we doubled on our tracks and done much better as we finley hit New Rochelle and puled up along side a policeman with falling archs.

What road do I take for Grenitch Conn quired my father with poping eyes.

Take the Boston post replid the policeman.

I have all ready subscribed to one out of town paper said my father and steped on the gas so we will leave the flat foot gaping after us like a prune fed calf and end this chapter.

Chapter 11

HOW IT ENDED

True to our promise we were at the station in Grenitch when the costly train puled in from 125 st. Myself and father hoped out of the lordly moter and helped the bulk of the famly off of the train and I aloud our nurse and my 3 brothers to kiss me tho David left me rarther moist.

Did you have a hard trip my father arsked to our nurse shyly.

Why no she replid with a slite stager.

She did too said my mother they all acted like little devils.

Did you get Davids milk she said turning on my father.

Why no does he like milk my father replid with a gastly smirk.

We got lost mudder I said brokenly.

We did not screened my father and accidently cracked me in the shins with a stray foot.

To change the subjeck I turned my tensions on my brother Jimmie who is nerest my age.

I've seen our house Jimmie I said brokenly I got here first.

Yes but I slept all night on a train and you didnt replid Jimmie with a dirty look.

Nether did you said my brother John to Jimmie you was awake all night.

Were awake said my mother.

Me and David was awake all night and crid said my brother John.

But I only crid once the whole time said my brother Jimmie.

But I didnt cry at all did I I arsked to my mother.

So she replid with a loud cough Bill was a very very good boy.

So now we will say fare well to the characters in this book.

THE BIG TOWN

QUICK RETURNS

This is just a clipping from one of the New York papers; a little kidding piece that they had in about me two years ago. It says:

HOOSIER CLEANS UP IN WALL STREET. Employees of the brokerage firm of H. L. Krause & Co. are authority for the statement that a wealthy Indiana speculator made one of the biggest killings of the year in the Street yesterday afternoon. No very definite information was obtainable, as the Westerner's name was known to only one of the firm's employees, Francis Griffin, and he was unable to recall it last night.

You'd think I was a millionaire and that I'd made a sucker out of Morgan or something, but it's only a kid, see? If they'd of printed the true story they wouldn't of had no room left for that day's selections at Pimlico, and God knows that would of been fatal.

But if you want to hear about it, I'll tell you.

Well, the War wound up in the fall of 1918. The only member of my family that was killed in it was my wife's stepfather. He died of grief when it ended with him two hundred thousand dollars ahead. I immediately had a black bandage sewed round my left funny bone, but when they read us the will I felt all right again and tore it off. Our share was seventy-five thousand dollars. This was after we had paid for the inheritance tax and the amusement stamps on a horseless funeral.

My young sister-in-law, Katie, dragged down another seventy-five thousand dollars and the rest went to the old bird that had been foreman in Papa's factory. This old geezer had been starving to death for twenty years on the wages my step father-in-law give him, and the rest of us didn't make no holler when his name was read off for a small chunk, especially as he didn't have no teeth to enjoy it with.

I could of had this old foreman's share, maybe, if I'd of took advantage of the offer "Father" made me just before his daughter and I was married. I was over in Niles, Michigan, where they lived, and he insisted on me seeing his factory, which meant smelling it too. At that time I was knocking out about eighteen hundred dollars per annum selling cigars out of South Bend, and the old man said he would start me in

280

with him at only about a fifty per cent cut, but we would also have the privilege of living with him and my wife's kid sister.

"They's a lot to be learnt about this business," he says, "but if you would put your mind on it you might work up to manager. Who knows?"

"My nose knows," I said, and that ended it.

The old man had lost some jack and went into debt a good many years ago, and for a long wile before the war begin about all as he was able to do was support himself and the two gals and pay off a part of what he owed. When the war broke loose and leather went up to hell and gone I and my wife thought he would get prosperous, but before this country went in his business went on about the same as usual.

"I don't know how they do it," he would say. "Other leather men is getting rich on contracts with the Allies, but I can't land a one."

I guess he was trying to sell razor strops to Russia.

Even after we got into it and he begin to clean up, with the factory running day and night, all as we knew was that he had contracts with the U.S. Government, but he never confided in us what special stuff he was turning out. For all as we knew, it may of been medals for the ground navy.

Anyway, he must of been hitting a fast clip when the armistice come and ended the war for everybody but Congress! It's a cinch he wasn't amongst those arrested for celebrating too loud on the night of November 11. On the contrary they tell me that when the big news hit Niles the old bird had a stroke that he didn't never recover from, and though my wife and Katie hung round the bedside day after day in the hopes he would tell how much he was going to leave he was keeping his fiscal secrets for Oliver Lodge or somebody, and it wasn't till we seen the will that we knew we wouldn't have to work no more, which is pretty fair consolation even for the loss of a step father-in-law that ran a perfume mill.

"Just think," said my wife, "after all his financial troubles, Papa died a rich man!"

"Yes," I said to myself, "and a patriot. His only regret was that he just had one year to sell leather to his country."

If the old codger had of only been half as fast a salesman as his two daughters this clipping would of been right when it called me a wealthy Hoosier. It wasn't two weeks after we seen the will when the gals had disposed of the odor factory and the old home in Niles, Michigan. Katie, it seemed, had to come over to South Bend and live with us. That was agreeable to me, as I figured that if two could live on eighteen hundred dollars a year three could struggle along some way on the income off one hundred and fifty thousand dollars.

Only for me, though, Ella and Sister Kate would of shot the whole wad into a checking account so as the bank could enjoy it wile it lasted. I argued and fought and finally persuaded them to keep five thousand apiece for pin money and stick the rest into bonds.

The next thing they done was run over to Chi and buy all the party dresses that was vacant. Then they come back to South Bend and wished somebody would give a party. But between you and I the people we'd always ran round with was birds that was ready for bed as soon as they got home from the first show, and even though it had been printed in the *News-Times* that we had fell heir to a lot of jack we didn't have to hire no extra clerical help to tend to invitations received from the demi-Monday.

Finally Ella said we would start something ourselves. So she got a lot of invitations printed and sent them to all our friends that could read and hired a cater and a three-piece orchestra and everything, and made me buy a dress suit.

Well, the big night arrived and everybody come that had somebody to leave their baby with. The hosts wore evening clothes and the rest of the merrymakers prepared for the occasion with a shine or a clean collar. At first the cat had everybody's tongue, but when we sat down to eat some of the men folks begun to get comical. For instance, they would say to my wife or Katie, "Ain't you afraid you'll catch cold?" And they'd say to me, "I didn't know you was a waiter at the Oliver." Before the fish course everybody was in a fair way to get the giggles.

After supper the musicians come and hid behind a geranium and played a jazz. The entire party set out the first dance. The second was a solo between Katie and I, and I had the third with my wife. Then Kate and the Mrs. had one together, wile I tried holds with a lady named Mrs. Eckhart, who seemed to think that somebody had ast her to stand for a time exposure. The men folks had all drifted over behind the plant to watch the drummer, but after the stalemate between Mrs. Eckhart and I, I grabbed her husband and took him out in the kitchen and showed him a bottle of bourbon that I'd been saving for myself, in the hopes it would loosen him up. I told him it was my last bottle, but he must of thought I said it was the last bottle in the world. Anyway, when he got through they was international prohibition.

We went back in the ballroom and sure enough he ast Katie to dance. But he hadn't no sooner than win one fall when his wife challenged him to take her home and that started the epidemic that emptied the house of everybody but the orchestra and us. The orchestra had been hired to stay till midnight, which was still two hours and a half distance, so I invited both of the gals to dance with me at once, but it seems like they was surfeited with that sport and wanted to cry a little. Well, the musicians had ran out of blues, so I chased them home.

"Some party!" I said, and the two girls give me a dirty look like it was my fault or something. So we all went to bed and the ladies beat me to it on account of being so near ready.

Well, they wasn't no return engagements even hinted at and the only other times all winter when the gals had a chance to dress up was when some secondhand company would come to town with a show and I'd have to buy a box. We couldn't ask nobody to go with us on account of not having no friends that you could depend on to not come in their stocking feet.

Finally it was summer and the Mrs. said she wanted to get out of town.

"We've got to be fair to Kate," she said.

"We don't know no young unmarried people in South Bend and it's no fun for a girl to run round with her sister and brother-in-law. Maybe if we'd go to some resort somewheres we might get acquainted with people that could show her a good time."

So I hired us rooms in a hotel down to Wawasee Lake and we stayed there from the last of June till the middle of September. During that time I caught a couple of bass and Kate caught a couple of carp from Fort Wayne. She was getting pretty friendly with one of them when along come a wife that he hadn't thought was worth mentioning. The other bird was making a fight against the gambling fever, but one night it got the best of him and he dropped forty-five cents in the nickel machine and had to go home and make a new start.

About a week before we was due to leave I made the remark that it would seem good to be back in South Bend and get some home cooking.

"Listen!" says my wife. "I been wanting for a long wile to have a serious talk with you and now's as good a time as any. Here are I and Sis and you with an income of over eight thousand dollars a year and having pretty near as good a time as a bird with habitual boils. What's more, we can't never have a good time in South Bend, but have got to move somewheres where we are unknown."

"South Bend is certainly all of that," I said.

"No, it isn't," said the Mrs. "We're acquainted there with the kind of people that makes it impossible for us to get acquainted with the other kind. Kate could live there twenty years and never meet a decent man. She's a mighty attractive girl, and if she had a chance they's nobody she couldn't marry. But she won't never have a chance in South Bend. And they's no use of you saying 'Let her move,' because I'm going to keep her under my eye till she's married and settled down. So in other words, I want us to pack up and leave South Bend for good and all and move somewheres where we'll get something for our money."

"For instance, where?" I ast her.

"They's only one place," she said; "New York City."

"I've heard of it," said I, "but I never heard that people who couldn't enjoy themselves on eight thousand a year in South Bend could go to New York and tear it wide open."

"I'm not planning to make no big splurge," she says. "I just want to be where they's Life and fun; where we can meet real live people. And as for not living there on eight thousand, think of the families that's already living there on half of that and less!"

"And think of the Life and fun they're having!" I says.

"But when you talk about eight thousand a year," said the Mrs., "why do we have to hold ourselves to that? We can sell some of those bonds and spend a little of our principal. It will just be taking money out of one investment and putting it in another."

"What other?" I ast her.

"Kate," said the wife. "You let me take her to New York and manage her and I'll get her a husband that'll think our eight thousand a year fell out of his vest."

"Do you mean," I said, "that you'd let a sister of yours marry for money?"

"Well," she says, "I know a sister of hers that wouldn't mind if she had."

So I argued and tried to compromise on somewheres in America, but it was New York or nothing with her. You see, she hadn't never been here, and all as she knew about it she'd read in books and magazines, and for some reason another when authors starts in on that subject it ain't very long till they've got a weeping jag. Besides, what chance did I have when she kept reminding me that it was her stepfather, not mine, that had croaked and made us all rich?

When I had give up she called Kate in and told her, and Kate squealed and kissed us both, though God knows I didn't deserve no remuneration or ask for none.

Ella had things all planned out. We was to sell our furniture and take a furnished apartment here, but we would stay in some hotel till we found a furnished apartment that was within reason.

"Our stay in some hotel will be life-long," I said.

The furniture, when we come to sell it, wasn't worth nothing, and that's what we got. We didn't have nothing to ship, as Ella found room for our books in my collar box. I got two lowers and an upper in spite of the Government, and with two taxi drivers and the baggage-man thronging the station platform we pulled out of South Bend and set forth to see Life.

The first four miles of the journey was marked by considerable sniveling on the part of the heiresses.

"If it's so painful to leave the Bend let's go back," I said.

"It isn't leaving the Bend," said the Mrs., "but it makes a person sad to leave any place."

"Then we're going to have a muggy trip," said I. "This train stops pretty near everywheres to either discharge passengers or employees."

They were still sobbing when we left Mishawaka and I had to pull some of my comical stuff to get their minds off. My wife's mighty easy to look at when she hasn't got those watery blues, but I never did see a gal that knocked you for a goal when her nose was in full bloom.

Katie had brought a flock of magazines and started in on one of them at Elkhart, but it's pretty tough trying to read with the Northern Indiana mountains to look out at, to say nothing about the birds of prey that kept prowling up and down the aisle in search of a little encouragement or a game of rhum.

I noticed a couple of them that would of give a lady an answer if she'd approached them in a nice way, but I've done some traveling myself and I know what kind of men it is that allows themselves to be drawed into a flirtation on trains. Most of them has made the mistake of getting married some time, but they don't tell you that. They tell you that you and a gal they use to be stuck on is as much alike as a pair of corsets, and if you ever come to Toledo to give them a ring, and they hand you a telephone number that's even harder to get than the ones there are; and they ask you your name and address and write it down, and the next time they're up at the Elks they show it to a couple of the brothers and tell what they'd of done if they'd only been going all the way through.

"Say, I hate to talk about myself! But say!"

Well, I didn't see no sense in letting Katie waste her time on those kind of guys, so every time one of them looked our way I give him the

fish eye and the non-stop signal. But this was my first long trip since
the Government started to play train, and I didn't know the new rules
in regards to getting fed; otherwise I wouldn't of never cleaned up in
Wall Street.

In the old days we use to wait till the boy come through and announced that dinner was now being served in the dining car forward;
then we'd saunter into the washroom and wash our hands if necessary,
and ramble into the diner and set right down and enjoy as big a meal
as we could afford. But the Government wants to be economical, so
they've cut down the number of trains, to say nothing about the victuals;
and they's two or three times as many people traveling, because they
can't throw their money away fast enough at home. So the result is that
the wise guys keeps an eye on their watch and when it's about twenty
minutes to dinner time they race to the diner and park against the door
and get quick action; and after they've eat the first time they go out and
stand in the vestibule and wait till it's their turn again, as one Federal
meal don't do nothing to your appetite only whet it, you might say.

Well, anyway, I was playing the old rules and by the time I and the
two gals started for the diner we run up against the outskirts of a crowd
pretty near as big as the ones that waits outside restaurant windows to
watch a pancake turn turtle. About eight o'clock we got to where we
could see the wealthy dining car conductor in the distance, but it was
only about once every quarter of an hour that he raised a hand, and
then he seemed to of had all but one of his fingers shot off.

I have often heard it said that the way to a man's heart is through
his stomach, but every time I ever seen men and women keep waiting
for their eats it was always the frail sex that give the first yelp, and
personally I've often wondered what would of happened in the trenches
Over There if ladies had of been occupying them when the rations failed
to show up. I guess the bombs bursting round would of sounded like
Sweet and Low sang by a quextette of deef mutes.

Anyway, my two charges was like wild animals, and when the con
finally held up two fingers I didn't have no more chance or desire to
stop them than as if they was the Center College Football Club right
after opening prayer.

The pair of them was ushered to a table for four where they already
was a couple of guys making the best of it, and it wasn't more than ten
minutes later when one of these birds dipped his bill in the finger bowl
and staggered out, but by the time I took his place the other gent and
my two gals was talking like barbers.

The guy was Francis Griffin that's in the clipping. But when Ella

introduced us all as she said was, "This is my husband," without mentioning his name, which she didn't know at that time, or mine, which
had probably slipped her memory.

Griffin looked at me like I was a side dish that he hadn't ordered.
Well, I don't mind snubs except when I get them, so I ast him if he
wasn't from Sioux City—you could tell he was from New York by his
blue collar.

"From Sioux City!" he says. "I should hope not!"

"I beg your pardon," I said. "You look just like a photographer I
used to know out there."

"I'm a New Yorker," he said, "and I can't get home too soon."

"Not on this train, you can't," I said.

"I missed the Century," he says.

"Well," I says with a polite smile, "the Century's loss is our gain."

"Your wife's been telling me," he says, "that you're moving to the
Big Town. Have you ever been there?"

"Only for a few hours," I says.

"Well," he said, "when you've been there a few weeks you'll wonder
why you ever lived anywhere else. When I'm away from old Broadway
I always feel like I'm only camping out."

Both the gals smiled their appreciation, so I says: "That certainly
expresses it. You'd ought to remember that line and give it to Georgie
Cohan."

"Old Georgie!" he says. "I'd give him anything I got and welcome.
But listen! Your wife mentioned something about a good hotel to stop
at wile you're looking for a home. Take my advice and pick out one
that's near the center of things; you'll more than make up the difference
in taxi bills. I lived up in the Hundreds one winter and it averaged me
ten dollars a day in cab fares."

"You must of had a pleasant home life," I says.

"Me!" he said. "I'm an old bachelor."

"Old!" says Kate, and her and the Mrs. both giggled.

"But seriously," he says, "if I was you I would go right to the Baldwin, where you can get a room for twelve dollars a day for the three
of you; and you're walking distance from the theaters or shops or cafés
or anywheres you want to go."

"That sounds grand!" said Ella.

"As far as I'm concerned," I said, "I'd just as lief be overseas from
any of the places you've mentioned. What I'm looking for is a home
with a couple of beds and a cookstove in the kitchen, and maybe a
bath."

"But we want to see New York first," said Katie, "and we can do that better without no household cares."

"That's the idear!" says Griffin. "Eat, drink and be merry; to-morrow we may die."

"I guess we won't drink ourselves to death," I said, "not if the Big Town's like where we been living."

"Oh, say!" says our new friend. "Do you think little old New York is going to stand for prohibition? Why, listen! I can take you to thirty places to-morrow night where you can get all you want in any one of them."

"Let's pass up the other twenty-nine," I says.

"But that isn't the idear," he said. "What makes we New Yorkers sore is to think they should try and wish a law like that on Us. Isn't this supposed to be a government of the people, for the people and by the people?"

"People!" I said. "Who and the hell voted for prohibition if it wasn't the people?"

"The people of where?" he says. "A lot of small-time hicks that couldn't buy a drink if they wanted it."

"Including the hicks," I says, "that's in the New York State legislature."

"But not the people of New York City," he said. "And you can't tell me it's fair to spring a thing like this without warning on men that's got their fortunes tied up in liquor that they can't never get rid of now, only at a sacrifice."

"You're right," I said. "They ought to give them some warning. Instead of that they was never even a hint of what was coming off till Maine went dry seventy years ago."

"Maine?" he said. "What the hell is Maine?"

"I don't know," I said. "Only they was a ship or a boat or something named after it once, and the Spaniards sunk it and we sued them for libel or something."

"You're a smart Aleck," he said. "But speaking about war, where was you?"

"In the shipyards at South Bend painting a duck boat," I says. "And where was you?"

"I'd of been in there in a few more weeks," he says. "They wasn't no slackers in the Big Town."

"No," said I, "and America will never forget New York for coming in on our side."

By this time the gals was both giving me dirty looks, and we'd eat all we could get, so we paid our checks and went back in our car and I felt kind of apologetic, so I dug down in the old grip and got out a bottle of bourbon that a South Bend pal of mine, George Hull, had give me the day before; and Griffin and I went in the washroom with it and before the evening was over we was pretty near ready to forget national boundaries and kiss.

The old bourb' helped me save money the next morning, as I didn't care for no breakfast. Ella and Kate went in with Griffin and you could of knocked me over with a coupling pin when the Mrs. come back and reported that he'd insisted on paying the check. "He told us all about himself," she said. "His name is Francis Griffin and he's in Wall Street. Last year he cleared twenty thousand dollars in commissions and everything."

"He's a piker," I says. "Most of them never even think under six figures."

"There you go!" said the Mrs. "You never believe nothing. Why shouldn't he be telling the truth? Didn't he buy our breakfast?"

"I been buying your breakfast for five years," I said, "but that don't prove that I'm knocking out twenty thousand per annum in Wall Street."

Francis and Katie was setting together four or five seats ahead of us.

"You ought to of seen the way he looked at her in the diner," said the Mrs. "He looked like he wanted to eat her up."

"Everybody gets desperate in a diner these days," I said. "Did you and Kate go fifty-fifty with him? Did you tell him how much money we got?"

"I should say not!" says Ella. "But I guess we did say that you wasn't doing nothing just now and that we was going to New York to see Life, after being cooped up in a small town all these years. And Sis told him you'd made us put pretty near everything in bonds, so all we can spend is eight thousand a year. He said that wouldn't go very far in the Big Town."

"I doubt if it ever gets as far as the Big Town," I said. "It won't if he makes up his mind to take it away from us."

"Oh, shut up!" said the Mrs. "He's all right and I'm for him, and I hope Sis is too. They'd make a stunning couple. I wished I knew what they're talking about."

"Well," I said, "they're both so reserved that I suppose they're telling each other how they're affected by cucumbers."

When they come back and joined us Ella said: "We was just remarking how well you two young things seemed to be getting along.

We was wondering what you found to say to one another all this time."

"Well," said Francis, "just now I think we were discussing you. Your sister said you'd been married five years and I pretty near felt like calling her a fibber. I told her you looked like you was just out of high school."

"I've heard about you New Yorkers before," said the Mrs. "You're always trying to flatter somebody."

"Not me," said Francis. "I never say nothing without meaning it."

"But sometimes," says I, "you'd ought to go on and explain the meaning."

Along about Schenectady my appetite begin to come back. I'd made it a point this time to find out when the diner was going to open, and then when it did our party fell in with the door.

"The wife tells me you're on the stock exchange," I says to Francis when we'd give our order.

"Just in a small way," he said. "But they been pretty good to me down there. I knocked out twenty thousand last year."

"That's what he told us this morning," said Ella.

"Well," said I, "they's no reason for a man to forget that kind of money between Rochester and Albany, even if this is a slow train."

"Twenty thousand isn't a whole lot in the Big Town," said Francis, "but still and all, I manage to get along and enjoy myself a little on the side."

"I suppose it's enough to keep one person," I said.

"Well," says Francis, "they say two can live as cheap as one."

Then him and Kate and Ella all giggled, and the waiter brought in a part of what he thought we'd ordered and we eat what we could and ast for the check. Francis said he wanted it and I was going to give in to him after a long hard struggle, but the gals reminded him that he'd paid for breakfast, so he said all right, but we'd all have to take dinner with him some night.

I and Francis set a wile in the washroom and smoked, and then he went to entertain the gals, but I figured the wife would go right to sleep like she always does when they's any scenery to look out at, so I stuck where I was and listened to what a couple of toothpick salesmen from Omsk would of done with the League of Nations if Wilson had of had sense enough to leave it to them.

Pulling into the Grand Central Station, Francis apologized for not being able to steer us over to the Baldwin and see us settled, but said he had to rush right downtown and report on his Chicago trip before the office closed. To see him when he parted with the gals you'd of thought he was going clear to Siberia to compete in the Olympic Games, or whatever it is we're in over there.

Well, I took the heiresses to the Baldwin and got a regular Big Town welcome. Ella and Kate set against a pillar wile I tried different tricks to make an oil-haired clerk look at me. New York hotel clerks always seem to of just dropped something and can't take their eyes off the floor. Finally I started to pick up the register and the guy give me the fish eye and ast what he could do for me.

"Well," I said, "when I come to a hotel I don't usually want to buy a straw hat."

He ast me if I had a reservation and I told him no.

"Can't do nothing for you then," he says. "Not till to-morrow morning anyway."

So I went back to the ladies.

"We'll have to go somewheres else," I said. "This joint's a joint. They won't give us nothing till to-morrow."

"But we can't go nowheres else," said the Mrs. "What would Mr. Griffin think, after recommending us to come here?"

"Well," I said, "if you think I'm going to park myself in a four-post chair all night just because we got a tip on a hotel from Wall Street you're Queen of the Cuckoos."

"Are you sure they haven't anything at all?" she says.

"Go ask them yourself!" I told her.

Well, she did, and in about ten minutes she come back and said everything was fixed.

"They'll give us a single room with bath and a double room with bath for fifteen dollars a day," she said.

" 'Give us' is good!" said I.

"I told him we'd wired for reservations and it wasn't our fault if the wire didn't get here," she said. "He was awfully nice."

Our rooms was right close to each other on the twenty-first floor. On the way up we decided by two votes to one that we'd dress for dinner. I was still monkeying with my tie when Katie come in for Ella to look her over. She had on the riskiest dress she'd bought in Chi.

"It's a pretty dress," she said, "but I'm afraid maybe it's too daring for just a hotel dining room."

Say, we hadn't no sooner than set down in the hotel dining room when two other gals come in that made my team look like they was dressed for a sleigh ride with Doc Cook.

"I guess you don't feel so daring now," I said. "Compared to that baby in black you're wearing Jess Willard's ulster."

"Do you know what that black gown cost?" said Ella. "Not a cent under seven hundred dollars."

"That would make the material twenty-one hundred dollars a yard," I says.

"I'd like to know where she got it," said Katie.

"Maybe she cut up an old stocking," said I.

"I wished now," said the Mrs., "that we'd waited till we got here before we bought our clothes."

"You can bet one thing," says Katie. "Before we're ast out anywheres on a real party we'll have something to wear that isn't a year old."

"First thing to-morrow morning," says the Mrs., "we'll go over on Fifth Avenue and see what we can see."

"They'll only be two on that excursion," I says.

"Oh, we don't want you along," said Ella. "But I do wished you'd go to some first-class men's store and get some ties and shirts and things that don't look like an embalmer."

Well, after a wile one of the waiters got it in his head that maybe we hadn't came in to take a bath, so he fetched over a couple of programs.

"Never mind them," I says. "What's ready? We're in a hurry."

"The Long Island Duckling's very nice," he said. "And how about some nice au gratin potatoes and some nice lettuce and tomato salad with Thousand Island dressing, and maybe some nice French pastry?"

"Everything seems to be nice here," I said. "But wait a minute. How about something to drink?"

He give me a mysterious smile.

"Well," he said, "they're watching us pretty close here, but we serve something we call a cup. It comes from the bar and we're not supposed to know what the bartender puts in it."

"We'll try and find out," I said. "And rush this order through, as we're starved."

So he frisked out and was back again in less than an hour with another guy to help carry the stuff, though Lord knows he could of parked the three ducklings on one eyelid and the whole meal on the back of his hand. As for the cup, when you tasted it they wasn't no big mystery about what the bartender had put in it—a bottle of seltzer and a prune and a cherry and an orange peel, and maybe his finger. The check come to eighteen dollars and Ella made me tip him the rest of a twenty.

Before dinner the gals had been all for staying up a wile and looking the crowd over, but when we was through they both owned up that they hadn't slept much on the train and was ready for bed.

Ella and Kate was up early in the morning. They had their breakfast without me and went over to stun Fifth Avenue. About ten o'clock Francis phoned to say he'd call round for us that evening and take us to dinner. The gals didn't get back till late in the afternoon, but from one o'clock on I was too busy signing for packages to get lonesome. Ella finally staggered in with some more and I told her about our invitation.

"Yes, I know," she said.

"How do you know?" I ast her.

"He told us," she said. "We had to call him up to get a check cashed."

"You got plenty nerve!" I said. "How does he know your checks is good?"

"Well, he likes us," she said. "You'll like us too when you see us in some of the gowns we bought."

"Some!" I said.

"Why, yes," said the Mrs. "You don't think a girl can go round in New York with one evening dress!"

"How much money did you spend to-day?" I ast her.

"Well," she said, "things are terribly high—that is, nice things. And then, of course, there's suits and hats and things besides the gowns. But remember, it's our money. And as I told you, it's an investment. When young Mister Wall Street sees Kate to-night it'll be all off."

"I didn't call on you for no speech," I says. "I ast you how much you spent."

"Not quite sixteen hundred dollars."

I was still out on my feet when the phone rung. Ella answered it and then told me it was all right about the tickets.

"What tickets?" I said.

"Why, you see," she says, "after young Griffin fixing us up with that check and inviting us to dinner and everything we thought it would be nice to take him to a show to-night. Kate wanted to see *Ups and Downs*, but the girl said she couldn't get us seats for it. So I ast that nice clerk that took care of us yesterday and he's fixed it."

"All right," I said, "but when young Griffin starts a party, why and the hell not let him finish it?"

"I suppose he would of took us somewheres after dinner," says the Mrs., "but I couldn't be sure. And between you and I, I'm positive that if he and Kate is throwed together a whole evening, and her look-ing like she'll look to-night, we'll get mighty quick returns on our investment."

Well, to make a short story out of it, the gals finally got what they called dressed, and I wished Niles, Michigan, or South Bend could of seen them. If boxers wore bathing skirts I'd of thought I was in the ring with a couple of bantams.

"Listen!" I said. "What did them two girdles cost?"

"Mine was three hundred and Kate's three hundred and fifty," said the Mrs.

"Well," I says, "don't you know that you could of went to any cut-rate drugstore and wrapped yourself up just as warm in thirty-two cents' worth of adhesive tape? Listen!" I said. "What's the use of me paying a burglar for tickets to a show like *Ups and Downs* when I could set round here and look at you for nothing?"

Then Griffin rung up to say that he was waiting and we went down-stairs. Francis took us in the same dining room we'd been in the night before, but this time the waiters all fought each other to get to us first.

I don't know what we eat, as Francis had something on the hip that kind of dazed me for a wile, but afterwards I know we got a taxi and went to the theater. The tickets was there in my name and only cost me thirteen dollars and twenty cents.

Maybe you seen this show wile it was here. Some show! I didn't read the program to see who wrote it, but I guess the words was by Noah and the music took the highest awards at the St. Louis Fair. They had a good system on the gags. They didn't spring none but what you'd heard all your life and knew what was coming, so instead of just laugh-ing at the point you laughed all the way through it.

I said to Ella, I said, "I bet the birds that run this don't want pro-hibition. If people paid $3.30 apiece and come in here sober they'd come back the next night with a machine gun."

"I think it's dandy," she says, "and you'll notice every seat is full. But listen! Will you do something for me? When this is over suggest that we go up to the Castle Roof for a wile."

"What for?" I said. "I'm sleepy."

"Just this once," she says. "You know what I told you about quick returns!"

Well, I give in and made the suggestion, and I never seen people so easy coaxed. I managed to get a ringside table for twenty-two bucks. Then I ast the boy how about getting a drink and he ast me if I knew any of the head waiters.

"I do," says Francis. "Tell Hector it's for Frank Griffin's party."

So we ordered four Scotch highballs and some chicken à la King, and then the dinge orchestra tore loose some jazz and I was expecting a dance with Ella, but before she could ask me Francis had ast her, and I had one with Kate.

"Your Wall Street friend's a fox," I says, "asking an old married lady to dance so's to stand in with the family."

"Old married lady!" said Kate. "Sis don't look a day over sixteen to-night."

"How are you and Francis coming?" I ast her.

"I don't know," she says. "He acts kind of shy. He hasn't hardly said a word to me all evening."

Well, they was another jazz and I danced it with Ella; then her and Francis had another one and I danced again with Kate. By this time our food and refreshments was served and the show was getting ready to start.

I could write a book on what I don't remember about that show. The first sip of their idear of a Scotch highball put me down for the count of eight and I was practic'lly unconscious till the waiter woke me up with a check for forty bucks.

Francis seen us home and said he would call up again soon, and when Ella and I was alone I made the remark that I didn't think he'd ever strain his larnix talking to Kate.

"He acts gun-shy when he's round her," I says. "You seem to be the one that draws him out."

"It's a good sign," she says. "A man's always embarrassed when he's with a girl he's stuck on. I'll bet you anything you want to bet that within a week something'll happen."

Well, she win. She'd of win if she'd of said three days instead of a week. It was a Wednesday night when we had that party, and on the Friday Francis called up and said he had tickets for the Palace. I'd been laid up mean wile with the Scotch influenza, so I told the gals to cut me out. I was still awake yet when Ella come in a little after midnight.

"Well," I said, "are we going to have a brother-in-law?"

"Mighty soon," she says.

So I ast her what had come off.

"Nothing—to-night," she says, "except this: He wrote me a note. He wants me to go with him to-morrow afternoon and look at a little furnished apartment. And he ast me if I could come without Sis, as he wants to pull a surprise on her. So I wondered if you couldn't think of some way to fix it so's I can sneak off for a couple of hours."

"Sure!" I said. "Just tell her you didn't sleep all night and you're wore out and you want to take a nap."

So she pulled this gag at lunch Saturday and Katie said she was tired too. She went up to her room and Ella snuck out to keep her date with Francis. In less than an hour she romped into our room again and throwed herself on the bed.

"Well," I says, "it must of been a little apartment if it didn't only take you this long to see it."

"Oh, shut up!" she said. "I didn't see no apartment. And don't say a word to me or I'll scream."

Well, I finally got her calmed down and she give me the details. It seems that she'd met Francis, and he'd got a taxi and they'd got in the taxi and they hadn't no sooner than got in the taxi when Francis give her a kiss.

"Quick returns," I says.

"I'll kill you if you say another word!" she says.

So I managed to keep still.

Well, I didn't know Francis' home address, and Wall Street don't run Sundays, so I spent the Sabbath training on a quart of rye that a bell hop picked up at a bargain sale somewheres for fifteen dollars. Mean wile Katie had been let in on the secret and staid in our room all day, moaning like a prune-fed calf.

"I'm afraid to leave her alone," says Ella. "I'm afraid she'll jump out the window."

"You're easily worried," I said. "What I'm afraid of is that she won't."

Monday morning finally come, as it generally always does, and I told the gals I was going to some first-class men's store and buy myself some ties and shirts that didn't look like a South Bend embalmer.

So the only store I knew about was H. L. Krause & Co. in Wall Street, but it turned out to be an office. I ast for Mr. Griffin and they ast me my name and I made one up, Sam Hall or something, and out he come.

If I told you the rest of it you'd think I was bragging. But I did bust a few records. Charley Brickley and Walter Eckersall both kicked five goals from field in one football game, and they was a bird named Robertson or something out at Purdue that kicked seven. Then they was one of the old-time ball players, Bobby Lowe or Ed Delehanty, that hit four or five home runs in one afternoon. And out to Toledo that time Dempsey made big Jess set down seven times in one round.

Well, listen! In a little less than three minutes I floored this bird nine times and I kicked him for eight goals from the field and I hit him over the fence for ten home runs. Don't talk records to me!

So that's what they meant in the clipping about a Hoosier cleaning up in Wall Street. But it's only a kid, see?

RITCHEY

Well, I was just getting used to the Baldwin and making a few friends round there when Ella suddenly happened to remember that it was Griffin who had recommended it. So one day, wile Kate was down to the chiropodist's, Ella says it was time for us to move and she had made up her mind to find an apartment somewheres.

"We could get along with six rooms," she said. "All as I ask is for it to be a new building and on some good street, some street where the real people lives."

"You mean Fifth Avenue," said I.

"Oh, no," she says. "That's way over our head. But we'd ought to be able to find something, say, on Riverside Drive." "A six room apartment," I says, "in a new building on Riverside Drive? What was you expecting to pay?"

"Well," she said, "you remember that time I and Kate visited the Kitchells in Chi? They had a dandy apartment on Sheridan Road, six rooms and brand new. It cost them seventy-five dollars a month. And Sheridan Road is Chicago's Riverside Drive."

"Oh, no," I says. "Chicago's Riverside Drive is Canal Street. But listen: Didn't the Kitchells have their own furniture?"

"Sure they did," said Ella.

"And are you intending to furnish us all over complete?" I asked her.

"Of course not," she says. "I expect to get a furnished apartment. But that don't only make about twenty-five dollars a month difference."

"Listen," I said: "It was six years ago that you visited the Kitchells; beside which, that was Chi and this is the Big Town. If you find a six room furnished apartment for a hundred dollars in New York City to-day, we'll be on Pell Street in Chinatown, and maybe Katie can marry into a laundry or a joss house."

"Well," said the wife, "even if we have to go to $150 a month for a place on the Drive, remember half of it's my money and half of it's Kate's, and none of it's yours."

"You're certainly letter perfect in that speech," I says.

"And further and more," said Ella, "you remember what I told you the other day. Wile one reason we moved to New York was to see Life, the main idear was to give Kate a chance to meet real men. So every nickel we spend making ourself look good is just an investment."

"I'd rather feel good than look good," I says, "and I hate to see us spending so much money on a place to live that they won't be nothing left to live on. For three or four hundred a month you might get a joint on the Drive with a bed and two chairs, but I can't drink furniture."

"This trip wasn't planned as no spree for you," says Ella. "On the other hand, I believe Sis would stand a whole lot better show of landing the right kind of a man if the rumor was to get out that her brother-in-law stayed sober once in a wile."

"Well," I said, "I don't think my liberal attitude on the drink question affected the results of our deal in Wall Street. That investment would of turned out just as good whether I was a teetotaler or a lush."

"Listen," she says: "The next time you mention ancient history like that, I'll make a little investment in a lawyer. But what's the use of arguing? I and Kate has made up our mind to do things our own way with our own money, and to-day we're going up on the Drive with a real estate man. We won't pay no more than we can afford. All as we want is a place that's good enough and big enough for Sis to entertain her gentleman callers in it, and she certainly can't do that in this hotel."

"Well," I says, "all her gentleman callers that's been around here in the last month, she could entertain them in one bunch in a telephone booth."

"The reason she's been let alone so far," says the Mrs., "is because I won't allow her to meet the kind of men that stays at hotels. You never know who they are."

"Why not?" I said. "They've all got to register their name when they come in, which is more than you can say for people that lives in $100 apartments on Riverside Drive."

Well, my arguments went so good that for the next three days the two gals was on a home-seekers' excursion and I had to spend my time learning the eastern inter-collegiate kelly pool rules up to Doyle's. I win about seventy-five dollars.

When the ladies come home the first two nights they was all wore out and singing the landlord blues, but on the third afternoon they busted in all smiles.

"We've found one," says Ella. "Six rooms, too."

"Where at?" I asked her.

"Just where we wanted it," she says. "On the Drive. And it fronts right on the Hudson."

"No!" I said. "I thought they built them all facing the other way."

"It almost seems," said Katie, "like you could reach out and touch New Jersey."

"It's what you might call a near beer apartment," I says.

"And it's almost across the street from Grant's Tomb," says Ella.

"How many rooms has he got?" I says.

"We was pretty lucky," said Ella. "The people that had it was forced to go south for the man's health. He's a kind of a cripple. And they decided to sublet it furnished. So we got a bargain."

"Come on," I says. "What price?"

"Well," she says, "they don't talk prices by the month in New York. They give you the price by the year. So it sounds a lot more than it really is. We got it for $4,000."

"Sweet patootie!" I said. "That's only half your income."

"Well, what of it?" says Ella. "It won't only be for about a year and it's in the nicest kind of a neighborhood and we can't meet nothing only the best kind of people. You know what I told you."

And she give me a sly wink.

Well, it seems like they had signed up a year's lease and paid a month's rent in advance, so what was they left for me to say? All I done was make the remark that I didn't see how we was going to come even close to a trial balance.

"Why not?" said Katie. "With our rent paid we can get along easy on $4,000 a year if we economize."

"Yes," I said. "You'll economize just like the rest of the Riverside Drivers, with a couple of servants and a car and four or five new evening dresses a month. By the end of six months the bank'll be figuring our account in marks."

"What do you mean 'our' account?" says Ella.

"But speaking about a car," said Katie, "do you suppose we could get a good one cheap?"

"Certainly," I said. "They're giving away the good ones for four double coupons."

"But I mean an inexpensive one," says Kate.

"You can't live on the River and ride in a flivver," I said. "Besides, the buses limp right by the door."

"Oh, I love the buses!" said Ella.

"Wait till you see the place," says Katie to me. "You'll go simply wild! They's a colored boy in uniform to open the door and they's two elevators."

"How high do we go?" I said.

"We're on the sixth floor," says Katie.

"I should think we could get that far in one elevator," I says.

"What was it the real estate man told us?" said Ella. "Oh, yes, he said the sixth floor was the floor everybody tried to get on."

"It's a wonder he didn't knock it," I said.

Well, we was to have immediate possession, so the next morning we checked out of this joint and swooped up on the Drive. The colored boy, who I nicknamed George, helped us up with the wardrobe. Ella had the key and inside of fifteen minutes she'd found it.

We hadn't no sooner than made our entree into our new home when I knew what ailed the previous tenant. He'd crippled himself stumbling over the furniture. The living room was big enough to stage the high hurdles, and that's what was in it, only they'd planted them every two feet apart. If a stew with the blind staggers had of walked in there in the dark, the folks on the floor below would of thought he'd knocked the head pin for a goal.

"Come across the room," said Ella, "and look at the view."

"I guess I can get there in four downs," I said, "but you better have a substitute warming up."

"Well," she says, when I'd finally fell acrost the last white chalk mark, "what do you think of it?"

"It's a damn pretty view," I says, "but I've often seen the same view from the top of a bus for a thin dime."

Well, they showed me over the whole joint and it did look O. K., but not $4,000 worth. The best thing in the place was a half full bottle of rye in the kitchen that the cripple hadn't gone south with. I did.

We got there at eleven o'clock in the morning, but at three p.m. the gals was still hanging up their Follies costumes, so I beat it out and over to Broadway and got myself a plate of pea soup. When I come back, Ella and Katie was laying down exhausted. Finally I told Ella that I was going to move back to the hotel unless they served meals in this dump, so her and Kate got up and went marketing. Well, when you move from Indiana to the Big Town, of course you can't be expected to do your own cooking, so what we had that night was from the delicatessen, and for the next four days we lived on dill pickles with dill pickles.

"Listen," I finally says: "The only reason I consented to leave the hotel was in the hopes I could get a real home cook meal once in a wile and if I don't get a real home cook meal once in a wile, I leave this dive."

"Have a little bit of patience," says Ella. "I advertised in the paper for a cook the day before we come here, the day we rented this apartment. And I offered eight dollars a week."

"How many replies did you get?" I asked her.

"Well," she said, "I haven't got none so far, but it's probably too soon to expect any."

"What did you advertise in, the world almanac?" I says.

"No, sir," she says. "I advertised in the two biggest New York papers, the ones the real estate man recommended."

"Listen," I said: "Where do you think you're at, in Niles, Michigan? If you get a cook here for eight dollars a week, it'll be a one-armed leper that hasn't yet reached her teens."

"What would you do, then?" she asked me.

"I'd write to an employment agency," I says, "and I'd tell them we'll pay good wages."

So she done that and in three days the phone rung and the agency said they had one prospect on hand and did we want her to come out and see us. So Ella said we did and out come a colleen for an interview. She asked how much we was willing to pay.

"Well," said Ella, "I'd go as high as twelve dollars. Or I'd make it fifteen if you done the washing."

Kathleen Mavourneen turned her native color.

"Well," I said, "how much do you want?"

"I'll work for ninety dollars a month," she said, only I can't get the brogue. "That's for the cookin' only. No washin'. And I would have to have a room with a bath and all day Thursdays and Sunday evenin's off."

"Nothing doing," said Ella, and the colleen started for the door.

"Wait a minute," I says. "Listen: Is that what you gals is getting in New York?"

"We're a spalpeen if we ain't," says the colleen bawn.

Well, I was desperate, so I called the wife to one side and says: "For heaven's sakes, take her on a month's trial. I'll pay the most of it with a little piece of money I picked up last week down to Doyle's. I'd rather do that than get dill pickled for a goal."

"Could you come right away?" Ella asked her.

"Not for a couple days," says Kathleen.

"It's off, then," I said. "You cook our supper to-night or go back to Greece."

"Well," she says, "I guess I could make it if I hurried."

So she went away and come back with her suitcase, and she cooked our supper that night. And Oh darlint!

Well, Beautiful Katie still had the automobile bug and it wasn't none of my business to steer her off of it and pretty near every day she would go down to the "row" and look them over. But every night she'd come home whistling a dirge.

"I guess I've seen them all," she'd say, "but they're too expensive or else they look like they wasn't."

But one time we was all coming home in a taxi from a show and come up Broadway and all of a sudden she yelled for the driver to stop.

"That's a new one in that window," she says, "and one I never see before."

Well, the dive was closed at the time and we couldn't get in, but she insisted on going down there the first thing in the morning and I and Ella must go along. The car was a brand new model Bam Eight.

"How much?" I asked him.

"Four thousand," he says.

"When could I get one?" says Katie.

"I don't know," said the salesman.

"What do you mean?" I asked him. "Haven't they made none of them?"

"I don't know," says the salesman. "This is the only one we got."

"Has anybody ever rode in one?" I says.

"I don't know," said the guy.

So I asked him what made it worth four thousand.

"Well," he says, "what made this lady want one?"

"I don't know," I said.

"Could I have this one that's on the floor?" says Katie.

"I don't know," said the salesman.

"Well, when do you think I could get one?" says Katie.

"We can't promise no deliveries," says the salesman.

Well, that kind of fretted me, so I asked him if they wasn't a salesman we could talk to.

"You're talking to one," he said.

"Yes, I know," said I. "But I used to be a kind of a salesman myself, and when I was trying to sell things, I didn't try and not sell them."

"Yes," he says, "but you wasn't selling automobiles in New York in 1920. Listen," he says: "I'll be frank with you. We got the New York agency for this car and was glad to get it because it sells for four thousand and anything that sells that high, why the people will eat up, even if it's a pearl-handle ketchup bottle. If we ever do happen to get a consignment of these cars, they'll sell like oil stock. The last word we got from the factory was that they'd send us three cars next September. So that means we'll get two cars a year from next October and if we can spare either of them, you can have one."

So then he begin to yawn and I said, "Come on, girls," and we got a taxi and beat it home. And I wouldn't of said nothing about it, only if Katie had of been able to buy her Bam, what come off might of never came off.

It wasn't only two nights later when Ella come in from shopping all excited. "Well," she said, "talk about experiences! I just had a ride home and it wasn't in a street car and it wasn't in a taxi and it wasn't on the subway and it wasn't on a bus."

"Let's play charades," said I.

"Tell us, Sis," says Katie.

"Well," said the wife, "I was down on Fifth Avenue, waiting for a bus, and all of a sudden a big limousine drew up to the curb with a livery chauffeur, and a man got out of the back seat and took off his hat and asked if he couldn't see me home. And of course I didn't pay no attention to him."

"Of course not," I said.

"But," says Ella, "he says, 'Don't take no offense. I think we're next door neighbors. Don't you live acrost the hall on the sixth floor of the Lucius?' So of course I had to tell him I did."

"Of course," I said.

"And then he said," says Ella, " 'Is that your sister living with you?' 'Yes,' I said, 'she lives with my husband and I.' 'Well,' he says, 'if you'll get in and let me take you home, I'll tell you what a beautiful girl I think she is.' So I seen then that he was all right, so I got in and come home with him. And honestly, Sis, he's just wild about you!"

"What is he like?" says Katie.

"He's stunning," says the wife. "Tall and wears dandy clothes and got a cute mustache that turns up."

"How old?" says Kate, and the Mrs. kind of stalled.

"Well," she said, "he's the kind of a man that you can't tell how old they are, but he's not old. I'd say he was, well, maybe he's not even that old."

"What's his name?" asked Kate.

"Trumbull," said the Mrs. "He said he was keeping bachelor quarters, but I don't know if he's really a bachelor or a widower. Anyway, he's a dandy fella and must have lots of money. Just imagine living alone in one of these apartments!"

"Imagine living in one of them whether you're a bachelor or a Mormon," I says.

"Who said he lived alone?" asked Katie.

"He did," says the Mrs. "He told me that him and his servants had the whole apartment to themselves. And that's what makes it so nice, because he's asked the three of us over there to dinner to-morrow night."

"What makes it so nice?" I asked her.

"Because it does," said Ella, and you can't ever beat an argument like that.

So the next night the two girls donned their undress uniforms and made me put on the oysters and horse radish and we went acrost the hall to meet our hero. The door was opened by a rug peddler and he showed us into a twin brother to our own living room, only you could get around it without being Houdini.

"Mr. Trumbull will be right out," said Omar.

The ladies was shaking like an aspirin leaf, but in a few minutes, in come mine host. However old Ella had thought he wasn't, she was wrong. He'd seen baseball when the second bounce was out. If he'd of started his career as a barber in Washington, he'd of tried to wish a face massage on Zachary Taylor. The only thing young about him was his teeth and his clothes. His dinner suit made me feel like I was walking along the station platform at Toledo, looking for hot boxes.

"Ah, here you are!" he says. "It's mighty nice of you to be neighborly. And so this is the young sister. Well," he says to me, "you had your choice, and as far as I can see, it was heads you win and tails you win. You're lucky."

So when he'd spread all the salve, he rung the bell and in come Allah with cocktails. I don't know what was in them, but when Ella and Katie had had two apiece, they both begin to trill.

Finally we was called in to dinner and every other course was hootch. After the solid and liquid diet, he turned on the steam piano and we all danced. I had one with Beautiful Katie and the rest of them was with my wife, or, as I have nicknamed them, quarrels. Well, the steam run out of three of us at the same time, the piano inclusive, and Ella sat down in a chair that was made for Eddie Foy's family and said how comfortable it was.

"Yes," says Methuselah, "that's my favorite chair. And I bet you wouldn't believe me if I told you how much it cost."

"Oh, I'd like to know," says Ella.

"Two hundred dollars," says mine host.

"Do you still feel comfortable?" I asked her.

"Speaking about furniture," said the old bird, "I've got a few bits that I'm proud of. Would you like to take a look at them?"

So the gals said they would and we had to go through the entire apartment, looking at bits. The best bits I seen was tastefully wrapped up in kegs and cases. It seemed like every time he opened a drawer, a cork popped up. He was a hundred per cent proofer than the governor of New Jersey. But he was giving us a lecture on the furniture itself, not the polish.

"I picked up this dining room suit for eighteen hundred," he says.

"Do you mean the one you've got on?" I asked him, and the gals give me a dirty look.

"And this rug," he says, stomping on an old rag carpet. "How much do you suppose that cost?"

It was my first guess, so I said fifty dollars.

"That's a laugh," he said. "I paid two thousand for that rug."

"The guy that sold it had the laugh," I says.

Finally he steered us into his bedroom.

"Do you see that bed?" he says. "That's Marie Antoinette's bed. Just a cool thousand."

"What time does she usually get in?" I asked him.

"Here's my hobby," he said, opening up a closet, "dressing gowns and bathrobes."

Well, they was at least a dozen of them hanging on hangers. They was all colors of the rainbow including the Scandinavian. He dragged one down that was redder than Ella's and Katie's cheeks.

"This is my favorite bathrobe," he said. "It's Rose D. Barry."

So I asked him if he had all his household goods and garments named after some dame.

"This bathrobe cost me an even two hundred," he says.

"I always take baths bare," I said. "It's a whole lot cheaper."

"Let's go back in the living room," says Katie.

"Come on," said Ella, tugging me by the sleeve.

"Wait a minute," I says to her. "I don't know how much he paid for his toothbrush."

Well, when we got back in the living room, the two gals acted kind of drowsy and snuggled up together on the davenport and I and the old bird was left to ourself.

"Here's another thing I didn't show you," he says, and pulls a pair of African golf balls out of a drawer in his desk. "These dice is real ivory and they cost me twelve and a half berries."

"You mean up to now," I said.

"All right," he said. "We'll make it a twenty-five dollar limit."

Well, I didn't have no business in a game with him, but you know how a guy gets sometimes. So he took them first and rolled a four.

"Listen," I says: "Do you know how many times Willard set down in the first round?"

And sure enough he sevened.

"Now solid ivory dice," I said, "how many days in the week?"

So out come a natural. And as sure as I'm setting here, I made four straight passes with the whole roll riding each time and with all that wad parked on the two thousand dollar rug, I shot a five and a three. "Ivory," I said, "we was invited here to-night, so don't make me pay for the entertainment. Show me eighter from Decatur."

And the lady from Decatur showed.

Just then they was a stir on the davenport, and Ella woke up long enough to make the remark that we ought to go home. It was the first time she ever said it in the right place.

"Oh," I says, "I've got to give Mr. Trumbull a chance to get even." But I wasn't in earnest.

"Don't bother about that," said Old Noah. "You can accommodate me some other time."

"You're certainly a sport," I says.

"And thanks for a wonderful time," said Ella. "I hope we'll see you again soon."

"Soon is to-morrow night," said mine host. "I'm going to take you all up the river to a place I know."

"Well," I says to Katie, when we was acrost the hall and the door shut, "how do you like him?"

"Oh, shut up!" says Katie.

So the next night he come over and rung our bell and said Ritchey was waiting with the car and would we come down when we was ready. Well, the gals had only had all day to prepare for the trip, so in another half hour they had their wraps on and we went downstairs. They wasn't nothing in front but a Rools-Royce with a livery chauffeur that looked like he'd been put there by a rubber stamp.

"What a stunning driver!" said Katie when we'd parked ourself in the back seat.

"Ritchey?" says mine host. "He is a nice looking boy, but better than that, he's a boy I can trust."

Well, anyway, the boy he could trust took us out to a joint called the Indian Inn where you wouldn't of never knew they was an eighteenth amendment only that the proprietor was asking twenty berries a quart for stuff that used to cost four. But that didn't seem to bother Methuselah and he ordered two of them. Not only that but he got us a table so close to the orchestra that the cornet player thought we was his mute.

"Now, what'll we eat?" he says.

So I looked at the program and the first item I seen was "Guinea Hen, $4.50."

"That's what Katie'll want," I says to myself, and sure enough that's what she got.

Well, we eat and then we danced and we danced and we danced, and finally along about eleven I and Ella was out on the floor pretending like we was enjoying ourself, and we happened to look over to the table and there was Katie and Trumbull setting one out and to look at either you could tell that something was wrong.

"Dance the next one with her," says Ella, "and find out what's the matter."

So I danced the next one with Katie and asked her.

"He squeezed my hand," she says. "I don't like him."

"Well," said I, "if you'd of ordered guinea hen on me I wouldn't of stopped at your hand. I'd of went at your throat."

"I've got a headache," she says. "Take me out to the car."

So they was nothing to it but I had to take her out to the car and come back and tell Ella and Trumbull that she wasn't feeling any too good and wanted to go home.

"She don't like me," says the old guy. "That's the whole trouble."

"Give her time," says Ella. "Remember she's just a kid."

"Yes, but what a kid!" he says.

So then he paid the check without no competition and we went out and clumb in the big limmie. Katie was pretending like she was asleep and neither Ella or Trumbull acted like they wanted to talk, so the conversation on the way home was mostly one-sided, with me in the title role. Katie went in the apartment without even thanking mine host for the guinea hen, but he kept Ella and I outside long enough to say that Ritchey and the car was at our service any time we wanted them.

So Ella told her that the next noon at breakfast. "And you'd ought to be ashamed of yourself," says Ella, "for treating a man like that like that."

"He's too fresh," says Katie.

"Well," said Ella, "if he was a little younger, you wouldn't mind him being fresh."

"No," said Katie, "if he was fresh, I wouldn't care if he was fresh. But what's the number of the garage?"

And she didn't lose no time taking advantage of the old bird. That same afternoon it seemed she had to go shopping and the bus wasn't good enough no more. She was out in Trumbull's limmie from two o'clock till pretty near seven. The old guy himself come to our place long about five and wanted to know if we knew where she was at. "I haven't no idear," said Ella. "I expected her home long ago. Did you want to use the car?"

"What's the difference," I said, "if he wanted to use the car or not? He's only the owner."

"Well," says Trumbull, "when I make an offer I mean it, and that little girl is welcome to use my machine whenever she feels like it."

So Ella asked him to stay to dinner and he said he would if we'd allow him to bring in some of his hootch, and of course I kicked on that proposition, but he insisted. And when Katie finally did get home, we was all feeling good and so was she and you'd never of thought they'd been any bad feelings the night before.

Trumbull asked her what she'd been buying.

"Nothing," she says. "I was looking at dresses, but they want too much money."

"You don't need no dresses," he says.

"No, of course not," said Katie. "But lots of girls is wearing them."

"Where did you go?" said Ella.

"I forget," says Katie. "What do you say if we play cards?"

So we played rummy till we was all blear-eyed and the old guy left, saying we'd all go somewheres next day. After he'd gone Ella begin to talk serious.

"Sis," she says, "here's the chance of a lifetime. Mr. Trumbull's head over heels in love with you and all as you have to do is encourage him a little. Can't you try and like him?"

"They's nobody I have more respect for," said Katie, "unless it's George Washington."

And then she give a funny laugh and run off to bed.

"I can't understand Sis no more," said Ella, when we was alone.

"Why not?" I asked her.

"Why, look at this opportunity staring her in the face," says the Mrs.

"Listen," I said: "The first time I stared you in the face, was you thinking about opportunity?"

Well, to make a short story out of it, I was the only one up in the house the next morning when Kathleen said we had a caller. It was the old boy.

"I'm sorry to be so early," he says, "but I just got a telegram and it means I got to run down to Washington for a few days. And I wanted to tell you that wile I'm gone Ritchey and the car is at your service."

So I thanked him and he said good-by and give his regards to the Mrs. and especially Katie, so when they got up I told them about it and I never seen a piece of bad news received so calm as Katie took it.

"But now he's gone," I said at the breakfast table, "why not the three of us run out to Bridgeport and call on the Wilmots?"

They're cousins of mine.

"Oh, fine!" said Ella.

"Wait a minute," says Katie. "I made a kind of an engagement with a dressmaker for to-day."

Well, as I say, to make a short story out of it, it seems like she'd made engagements with the dressmaker every day, but they wasn't no dresses ever come home.

In about a week Trumbull come back from Washington and the first thing he done was look us up and we had him in to dinner and I don't remember how the conversation started, but all of a sudden we was on the subject of his driver, Ritchey.

"A great boy," says Trumbull, "and a boy you can trust. If I didn't like him for nothing else, I'd like him for how he treats his family."

"What family?" says Kate.

"Why," says Trumbull, "his own family: his wife and two kids."

"My heavens!" says Katie, and kind of fell in a swoon.

So it seems like we didn't want to live there no more and we moved back to the Baldwin, having sublet the place on the Drive for three thousand a year.

So from then on, we was paying a thousand per annum for an apartment we didn't live in two weeks. But as I told the gals, we was getting pretty near as much for our money as the people that rented New York apartments and lived in them, too.

LADY PERKINS

Along the first week in May they was a couple hot days, and Katie can't stand the heat. Or the cold, or the medium. Anyway, when it's hot she always says: "I'm simply stifling." And when it's cold: "I'm simply frozen." And when it ain't neither one: "I wished the weather would do one thing another." I don't s'pose she knows what she's saying when she says any one of them things, but she's one of these here gals that can't bear to see a conversation die out and thinks it's her place to come through with a wise crack whenever they's a vacuum.

So during this hot spell we was having dinner with a bird named Gene Buck that knowed New York like a book, only he hadn't never read a book, and Katie made the remark that she was simply stifling.

"If you think this is hot," says our friend, "just wait till the summer comes. The Old Town certainly steams up in the Old Summer Time."

So Kate asked him how people could stand it.

"They don't," he says. "All the ones that's got a piece of change ducks out somewheres where they can get the air."

"Where do they go?" Katie asked him.

"Well," he says, "the most of my pals goes to Newport or Maine or up in the Adirondacks. But of course them places is out of most people's reach. If I was you folks I'd go over on Long Island somewheres and either take a cottage or live in one of them good hotels."

"Where, for instance?" says my Mrs.

"Well," he said, "some people takes cottages, but the rents is something fierce, and besides, the desirable ones is probably all eat up by this time. But they's plenty good hotels where you get good service and swell meals and meet good people; they won't take in no riffraff. And they give you a pretty fair rate if they know you're going to make a stay."

So Ella asked him if they was any special one he could recommend.

"Let's think a minute," he says.

"Let's not strain ourself," I said.

"Don't get cute!" said the Mrs. "We want to get some real information and Mr. Buck can give it to us."

"How much would you be willing to pay?" said Buck.

It was Ella's turn to make a wise crack.

"Not no more than we have to," she says.

"I and my sister has got about eight thousand dollars per annum between us," said Katie, "though a thousand of it has got to go this year to a man that cheated us up on Riverside Drive.

"It was about a lease. But Papa left us pretty well off; over a hundred and fifty thousand dollars."

"Don't be so secret with Mr. Buck," I says. "We've knew him pretty near a week now. Tell him about them four-dollar stockings you bought over on Fifth Avenue and the first time you put them on they got as many runs as George Sisler."

"Well," said Buck, "I don't think you'd have no trouble getting comfortable rooms in a good hotel on seven thousand dollars. If I was you I'd try the Hotel Decker. It's owned by a man named Decker."

"Why don't he call it the Griffith?" I says.

"It's located at Tracy Estates," says Buck. "That's one of the garden spots of Long Island. It's a great big place, right up to the minute, and they give you everything the best. And they's three good golf courses within a mile of the hotel."

The gals told him they didn't play no golf.

"You don't know what you've missed," he says.

"Well," I said, "I played a game once myself and missed a whole lot."

"Do they have dances?" asked Kate.

"Plenty of them," says Buck, "and the guests is the nicest people you'd want to meet. Besides all that, the meals is included in the rates, and they certainly set a nasty table."

"I think it sounds grand," said the Mrs. "How do you get there?"

"Go over to the Pennsylvania Station," says Buck, "and take the Long Island Railroad to Jamaica. Then you change to the Haverton branch. It don't only take a half hour altogether."

"Let's go over to-morrow morning and see can we get rooms," said Katie.

So Ella asked how that suited me.

"Go just as early as you want to," I says. "I got a date to run down to the Aquarium and see the rest of the fish."

"You won't make no mistake stopping at the Decker," says Buck.

So the gals thanked him and I paid the check so as he would have more to spend when he joined his pals up to Newport.

Well, when Ella and Kate come back the next afternoon, I could see without them telling me that it was all settled. They was both grinning like they always do when they've pulled something nutty.

"It's a good thing we met Mr. Buck," said the Mrs., "or we mightn't never of heard of this place. It's simply wonderful. A double room with a bath for you and I and a room with a bath for Katie. The meals is throwed in, and we can have it all summer."

"How much?" I asked her.

"Two hundred a week," she said. "But you must remember that's for all three of us and we get our meals free."

"And I s'pose they also furnish knobs for the bedroom doors," says I.

"We was awful lucky," said the wife. "These was the last two rooms they had, and they wouldn't of had those only the lady that had engaged them canceled her reservation."

"I wished I'd met her when I was single," I says.

"So do I," says Ella.

"But listen," I said. "Do you know what two hundred a week

amounts to? It amounts to over ten thousand a year, and our income is seven thousand."

"Yes," says Katie, "but we aren't only going to be there twenty weeks, and that's only four thousand."

"Yes," I said, "and that leaves us three thousand for the other thirty-two weeks, to pay for board and room and clothes and show tickets and a permanent wave every other day."

"You forget," said Kate, "that we still got our principal, which we can spend some of it and not miss it."

"And you also forget," said the Mrs., "that the money belongs to Sis and I, not you."

"I've got a sweet chance of forgetting that," I said. "It's hammered into me three times a day. I hear about it pretty near as often as I hear that one of you's lost their new silk bag."

"Well, anyway," says Ella, "it's all fixed up and we move out there early tomorrow morning, so you'll have to do your packing to-night."

I'm not liable to celebrate the anniversary of the next day's trip. Besides the trunks, the gals had a suitcase and a grip apiece and I had a suitcase. So that give me five pieces of baggage to wrestle, because of course the gals had to carry their parasol in one hand and their wrist watch in the other. A redcap helped load us on over to the station, but oh you change at Jamaica! And when we got to Tracy Estates we seen that the hotel wasn't only a couple of blocks away, so the ladies said we might as well walk and save taxi fare.

I don't know how I covered them two blocks, but I do know that when I reeled into the Decker my hands and arms was paralyzed and Ella had to do the registering.

Was you ever out there? Well, I s'pose it's what you might call a family hotel, and a good many of the guests belongs to the cay-nine family. A few of the couples that can't afford dogs has got children, and you're always tripping over one or the other. They's a dining room for the grown-ups and another for the kids, wile the dogs and their nurses eats in the grill-room à la carte. One part of the joint is bachelor quarters. It's located right next to the dogs' dormitories, and they's a good deal of rivalry between the dogs and the souses to see who can make the most noise nights. They's also a ballroom and a couple card rooms and a kind of a summer parlor where the folks sets round in the evening and listen to a three-piece orchestra that don't know they's been any music wrote since Poets and Peasants. The men get up about eight o'clock and go down to New York to Business. They don't never go to work. About nine the women begins limping downstairs and either goes to call on their dogs or take them for a walk in the front yard. This is a great big yard with a whole lot of benches strewed round it, but you can't set on them in the daytime because the women or the nurses uses them for a place to read to the dogs or kids, and in the evenings you would have to share them with the waitresses, which you have already had enough of them during the day.

When the women has prepared themselves for the long day's grind with a four-course breakfast, they set round on the front porch and discuss the big questions of the hour, like for instance the last trunk murder or whether an Airedale is more loving than a Golden Bantam. Once in a wile one of them cracks that it looks like they was bound to be a panic pretty soon and a big drop in prices, and so forth. This shows they're broad-minded and are giving a good deal of thought to up-to-date topics. Every so often one of them'll say: "The present situation can't keep up." The hell it can't!

By one o'clock their appetites is whetted so keen from brain exercise that they make a bum out of a plate of soup and an order of Long Island duckling, which they figure is caught fresh every day, and they wind up with salad and apple pie à la mode and a stein of coffee. Then they totter up to their rooms to sleep it off before Dear gets home from Business.

Saturday nights everybody puts on their evening clothes like something was going to happen. But it don't. Sunday mornings the husbands and bachelors gets up earlier than usual to go to their real business, which is golf. The womenfolks are in full possession of the hotel till Sunday night supper and wives and husbands don't see one another all day long, but it don't seem as long as if they did. Most of them's approaching their golden-wedding jubilee and haven't nothing more to say to each other than you could call a novelty. The husband may make the remark, Sunday night, that he would of broke one hundred and twenty in the afternoon round if the caddy hadn't of handed him a spoon when he asked for a nut pick, and the wife'll probably reply that she's got to go in Town some day soon and see a chiropodist. The rest of the Sabbath evening is spent in bridge or listening to the latest song hit from *The Bohemian Girl*.

The hotel's got all the modern conveniences like artificial light and a stopper in the bathtubs. They even got a barber and a valet, but you can't get a shave wile he's pressing your clothes, so it's pretty near impossible for a man to look their best at the same time.

Well, the second day we was there I bought me a deck of cards and got so good at solitary that pretty soon I could play fifty games between

breakfast and lunch and a hundred from then till suppertime. During
the first week Ella and Kate got on friendly terms with over a half dozen
people—the head waiter, our waitress, some of the clerks and the manager and the two telephone gals. It wasn't from lack of trying that they
didn't meet even more people. Every day one or the other of them would
try and swap a little small talk with one of the other squatters, but it
generally always wound up as a short monologue.

Ella said to me one day, she says: "I don't know if we can stick it
out here or not. Every hotel I was ever at before, it was easy enough to
make a lot of friends, but you could stick a bottle of cream alongside
one of these people and it'd stay sweet a week. Unless they looked at
it. I'm sick of talking to you and Sis and the hired help, and Kate's so
lonesome that she cries herself to sleep nights."

Well, if I'd of only had sense enough to insist on staying we'd of
probably packed up and took the next train to Town. But instead of
that I said: "What's to prevent us from going back to New York?"

"Don't be silly!" says the Mrs. "We come out here to spend the
summer and here is where we're going to spend the summer."

"All right," I says, "and by September I'll be all set to write a book
on one-handed card games."

"You'd think," says Ella, "that some of these women was titled roy-
alties the way they snap at you when you try and be friends with them.
But they's only one in the bunch that's got any handle to her name;
that's Lady Perkins."

I asked her which one was that.

"You know," says Ella. "I pointed her out to you in the dining room.
She's a nice-looking woman, about thirty-five, that sets near our table
and walks with a cane."

"If she eats like some of the rest of them," I says, "she's lucky they
don't have to w'eel her."

"She's English," says Ella. "They just come over and her husband's
in Texas on some business and left her here. She's the one that's got
that dog."

"That dog!" I said. "You might just as well tell me she's the one that
don't play the mouth organ. They've all got a dog."

"She's got two," said the wife. "But the one I meant is that big
German police dog that I'm scared to death of him. Haven't you saw
her out walking with him and the little chow?"

"Yes," I said, "if that's what it is. I always wondered what the boys
in the Army was talking about when they said they eat chow."

"They probably meant chowchow," says the Mrs. "They wouldn't of had these kind of chows, because in the first place, who would eat a dog, and besides these kind costs too much."

"Well," I says, "I'm not interested in the price of chows, but if you want to get acquainted with Lady Perkins, why I can probably fix it for you."

"Yes, you'll fix it!" said Ella. "I'm beginning to think that if we'd of put you in storage for the summer the folks round here wouldn't shy away from us like we was leopards that had broke out of a pest-house. I wished you would try and dress up once in a wile and not always look like you was just going to do the chores. Then maybe I and Sis might get somewheres."

Well, of course when I told her I could probably fix it up with Lady Perkins, I didn't mean nothing. But it wasn't only the next morning when I started making good. I was up and dressed and downstairs about half past eight, and as the gals wasn't ready for their breakfast yet I went out on the porch and set down. They wasn't nobody else there, but pretty soon I seen Lady Perkins come up the path with her two whelps. When she got to the porch steps their nurse popped out of the servants' quarters and took them round to the grillroom for their breakfast. I s'pose the big one ordered sauerkraut and kalter Aufschnitt, wile the chow had tea and eggs fo yung. Anyway, the Perkins dame come up on the porch and flopped into the chair next to mine.

In a few minutes Ed Wurz, the manager of the hotel, showed, with a bag of golf instruments and a trick suit. He spotted me and asked me if I didn't want to go along with him and play.

"No," I said. "I only played once in my life."

"That don't make no difference," he says. "I'm a bum myself. I just play shinny, you might say."

"Well," I says, "I can't anyway, on account of my dogs. They been giving me a lot of trouble."

Of course I was referring to my feet, but he hadn't no sooner than went on his way when Lady Perkins swung round on me and says: "I didn't know you had dogs. Where do you keep them?"

At first I was going to tell her "In my shoes," but I thought I might as well enjoy myself, so I said: "They're in the dog hospital over to Haverton."

"What ails them?" she asked me.

Well, I didn't know nothing about cay-nine diseases outside of hydrophobia, which don't come till August, so I had to make one up.

"They got blanny," I told her.

"Blanny!" she says. "I never heard of it before."

"No," I said. "It hasn't only been discovered in this country just this year. It got carried up here from Peru some way another."

"Oh, it's contagious, then!" says Lady Perkins.

"Worse than measles or lockjaw," says I. "You take a dog that's been in the same house with a dog that's got blanny, and it's a miracle if they don't all get it."

She asked me if I'd had my dogs in the hotel.

"Only one day," I says, "the first day we come, about a week ago. As soon as I seen what was the matter with them, I took them over to Haverton in a sanitary truck."

"Was they mingling with the other dogs here?" she says.

"Just that one day," I said.

"Heavens!" said Lady Perkins. "And what's the symptoms?"

"Well," I said, "first you'll notice that they keep their tongue stuck out a lot and they're hungry a good deal of the time, and finally they show up with a rash."

"Then what happens?" she says.

"Well," said I, "unless they get the best of treatment, they kind of dismember."

Then she asked me how long it took for the symptoms to show after a dog had been exposed. I told her any time between a week and four months.

"My dogs has been awful hungry lately," she says, "and they most always keeps their tongue stuck out. But they haven't no rash."

"You're all right, then," I says. "If you give them treatments before the rash shows up, they's no danger."

"What's the treatment?" she asked me.

"You rub the back of their neck with some kind of dope," I told her. "I forget what it is, but if you say the word, I can get you a bottle of it when I go over to the hospital this afternoon."

"I'd be ever so much obliged," she says, "and I hope you'll find your dear ones a whole lot better."

"Dear ones is right," I said. "They cost a pile of jack, and the bird I bought them off of told me I should ought to get them insured, but I didn't. So if anything happens to them now, I'm just that much out."

Next she asked me what kind of dogs they was.

"Well," I said, "you might maybe never of heard of them, as they don't breed them nowheres only way down in Dakota. They call them yaphounds—I don't know why; maybe on account of the noise they make. But they're certainly a grand-looking dog and they bring a big price."

She set there a wile longer and then got up and went inside, probably to the nursery to look for signs of rash.

Of course I didn't tell the Mrs. and Kate nothing about this incidence. They wouldn't of believed it if I had of, and besides, it would be a knock-out if things broke right and Lady Perkins come up and spoke to me wile they was present, which is just what happened.

During the afternoon I strolled over to the drugstore and got me an empty pint bottle. I took it up in the room and filled it with water and shaving soap. Then I laid low till evening, so as Perk would think I had went to Haverton.

I and Ella and Kate breezed in the dining room kind of late and we hadn't no more than ordered when I seen the Lady get up and start out. She had to pass right past us, and when I looked at her and smiled she stopped.

"Well," she said, "how's your dogs?"

I got up from the table.

"A whole lot better, thank you," says I, and then I done the honors. "Lady Perkins," I said, "meet the wife and sister-in-law."

The two gals staggered from their chairs, both pop-eyed. Lady Perkins bowed to them and told them to set down. If she hadn't the floor would of bounced up and hit them in the chin.

"I got a bottle for you," I said. "I left it upstairs and I'll fetch it down after supper."

"I'll be in the red card room," says Perk, and away she went.

I wished you could of see the two gals. They couldn't talk for a minute, for the first time in their life. They just set there with their mouth open like a baby blackbird. Then they both broke out with a rash of questions that come so fast I couldn't understand none of them, but the general idear was, What the hell!

"They's no mystery about it," I said. "Lady Perkins was setting out on the porch this morning and you two was late getting down to breakfast, so I took a walk, and when I come back she noticed that I kind of limped and asked me what ailed my feet. I told her they always swoll up in warm weather and she said she was troubled the same way and did I know any medicine that shrank them. So I told her I had a preparation and would bring her a bottle of it."

"But," says Kate, "I can't understand a woman like she speaking to a man she don't know."

"She's been eying me all week," I said. "I guess she didn't have the nerve to break the ice up to this morning; then she got desperate."

"She must of," said Ella.

"I wished," said Kate, "that when you introduce me to people you'd give them my name."

"I'm sorry," I said, "but I couldn't recall it for a minute, though your face is familiar."

"But listen," says the wife. "What ails your dogs is a corn. You haven't got no swelled feet and you haven't got no medicine for them."

"Well," I says, "what I give her won't hurt her. It's just a bottle of soap and water that I mixed up, and pretty near everybody uses that once in a wile without no bad after effects."

Now, the whole three of us had been eating pretty good ever since we'd came to the Decker. After living à la carte at Big Town prices for six months, the American plan was sweet patootie. But this night the gals not only skrimped themselves but they was in such a hurry for me to get through that my molars didn't hardly have time to identify what all was scampering past them. Ella finally got so nervous that I had to take off the feed bag without dipping my bill into the stewed rhubarb.

"Lady Perkins will get tired waiting for you," she says. "And besides, she won't want us horning in there and interrupting them after their game's started."

"Us!" said I. "How many do you think it's going to take to carry this bottle?"

"You don't mean to say we can't go with you!" said Kate.

"You certainly can't," I says. "I and the nobility won't have our little romance knocked for a gool by a couple of country gals that can't get on speaking terms with nobody but the chambermaid."

"But they'll be other people there," says Kate. "She can't play cards alone."

"Who told you she was going to play cards?" I says. "She picked the red card room because we ain't liable to be interrupted there. As for playing cards alone, what else have I done all week? But when I get there she won't have to play solitary. It'll be two-handed hearts; where if you was to crowd in, it couldn't be nothing but rummy."

Well, they finally dragged me from the table, and the gals took a seat in the lobby wile I went upstairs after the medicine. But I hadn't no sooner than got a hold of the bottle when Ella come in the room.

"Listen," she says. "They's a catch in this somewheres. You needn't to try and tell me that a woman like Lady Perkins is trying to start a flirtation with a yahoo. Let's hear what really come off."

"I already told you," I said. "The woman's nuts over me and you should ought to be the last one to find fault with her judgment."

Ella didn't speak for a wile. Then she says: "Well, if you're going to forget your marriage vows and flirt with an old hag like she, I guess two can play at that little game. They's several men round this hotel that I like their looks and all as they need is a little encouragement."

"More than a little, I guess," says I, "or else they'd of already been satisfied with what you and Kate has give them. They can't neither one of you pretend that you been fighting on the defense all week, and the reason you haven't copped nobody is because this place is a hotel, not a home for the blind."

I wrapped a piece of newspaper round the bottle and started for the door. But all of a sudden I heard snuffles and stopped.

"Look here," I said. "I been kidding you. They's no need for you to get sore and turn on the tear ducks. I'll tell you how this thing happened if you think you can see a joke."

So I give her the truth, and afterwards I says: "They'll be plenty of time for you and Kate to get acquainted with the dame, but I don't want you tagging in there with me to-night. She'd think we was too cordial. To-morrow morning, if you can manage to get up, we'll all three of us go out on the porch and lay for her when she brings the whelps back from their hike. She's sure to stop and inquire about my kennel. And don't forget, wile she's talking, that we got a couple of yaphounds that's suffering from blanny, and if she asks any questions let me do the answering, as I can think a lot quicker. You better tell Kate the secret, too, before she messes everything up, according to custom."

Then I and the Mrs. come downstairs and her and Katie went out to listen to the music wile I beat it to the red card room. I give Perkie the bottle of rash poison and she thanked me and said she would have the dogs' governess slap some of it onto them in the morning. She was playing bridge w'ist with another gal and two dudes. To look at their faces they wasn't playing for just pins. I had sense enough to not talk, but I stood there watching them a few minutes. Between hands Perk introduced me to the rest of the party. She had to ask my name first. The other skirt at the table was a Mrs. Snell and one of the dudes was a Doctor Platt. I didn't get the name of Lady Perkins' partner.

"Mr. Finch," says Perk, "is also a dog fancier. But his dogs is sick with a disease called blanny and he's got them over to the dog hospital at Haverton."

"What kind of dogs?" asked Platt.

"I never heard of the breed before," says Perk. "They're yaphounds."

"They raise them in South Dakota," I says.

Platt gives me a funny look and said: "I been in South Dakota several times and I never heard of a yaphound neither; or I never heard of a disease named blanny."

"I s'pose not," says I. "You ain't the only old-fashioned doctor that left themself go to seed when they got out of school. I bet you won't admit they's such a thing as appendicitis."

Well, this got a laugh from Lady Perkins and the other dude, but it didn't go very big with Doc or Mrs. Snell. Wile Doc was trying to figure out a come-back I said I must go and look after my womenfolks. So I told the party I was glad to of met them and walked out.

I found Ella and Katie in the summer parlor, and they wasn't alone. A nice-looking young fella named Codd was setting alongside of them, and after we was introduced Ella leaned over and w'ispered to me that he was Bob Codd, the famous aviator. It come out that he had invented some new kind of an aeroplane and had came to demonstrate it to the Williams Company. The company—Palmer Williams and his brother, you know—they've got their flying field a couple miles from the hotel. Well, a guy with nerve enough to go up in one of them things certainly ain't going to hesitate about speaking to a strange gal when he likes their looks. So this Codd baby had give himself an introduction to my Mrs. and Kate, and I guess they hadn't sprained an ankle running away from him.

Of course Ella wanted to know how I'd came out with Lady Perkins. I told her that we hadn't had much chance to talk because she was in a bridge game with three other people, but I'd met them and they'd all seemed to fall for me strong. Ella wanted to know who they was and I told her their names, all but the one I didn't get. She squealed when I mentioned Mrs. Snell.

"Did you hear that, Sis?" she says to Kate. "Tom's met Mrs. Snell. That's the woman, you know, that wears them funny clothes and has the two dogs."

"You're describing every woman in the hotel," I said.

"But this is *the* Mrs. Snell," said the wife. "Her husband's the sugar man and she's the daughter of George Henkel, the banker. They say she's a wonderful bridge player and don't never play only for great big stakes. I'm wild to meet her."

"Yes," I said, "if they's one person you should ought to meet, it's a wonderful bridge player that plays for great big stakes, especially when our expenses is making a bum out of our income and you don't know a grand slam from no dice."

"I don't expect to gamble with her," says Ella. "But she's just the kind of people we want to know."

Well, the four of us set there and talked about this and that, and Codd said he hadn't had time to get his machine put together yet, but when he had her fixed and tested her a few times he would take me up for a ride.

"You got the wrong number," I says. "I don't feel flighty."

"Oh, I'd just love it!" said Kate.

"Well," says Codd, "you ain't barred. But I don't want to have no passengers along till I'm sure she's working O. K."

When I and Ella was upstairs she said that Codd had told them he expected to sell his invention to the Williamses for a cold million. And he had took a big fancy to Kate.

"Well," I said, "they say that the reckless aviators makes the best ones, so if him and Kate gets married he'll be better than ever. He won't give a damn after that."

"You're always saying something nasty about Sis," said the Mrs.; "but I know you just talk to hear yourself talk. If I thought you meant it I'd walk out on you."

"I'd hate to lose you," I says, "but if you took her along I wouldn't write it down as a total loss."

The following morning I and the two gals was down on the porch bright and early and in a few minutes, sure enough, along came Lady Perkins, bringing the menagerie back from the parade. She turned them over to the nurse and joined us. She said that Martha, the nurse, had used the rash poison and it had made a kind of a lather on the dogs' necks and she didn't know whether to wash it off or not, but it had dried up in the sun. She asked me how many times a day the dope should ought to be put on, and I told her before every meal and at bedtime.

"But," I says, "it's best to not take the dogs right out in the sun where the lather'll dry. The blanny germ can't live in that kind of lather, so the longer it stays moist, why, so much the better."

Then she asked me was I going to Haverton to see my pets that day and I said yes, and she said she hoped I'd find them much improved. Then Ella cut in and said she understood that Lady Perkins was very fond of bridge.

"Yes, I am," says Perk. "Do you people play?"

"No, we don't," says Ella, "but we'd like to learn."

"It takes a long wile to learn to play good," said Perk. "But I do wished they was another real player in the hotel so as we wouldn't have to take Doctor Platt in. He knows the game, but he don't know enough to keep still. I don't mind people talking wile the cards is being dealt, but once the hands is picked up they ought to be absolute silence. Last night I lost about three hundred and seventy dollars just because he talked at the wrong time."

"Three hundred and seventy dollars!" said Kate. "My, you must play for big stakes!"

"Yes, we do," says Lady Perkins; "and when a person is playing for sums like that it ain't no time to trifle, especially when you're playing against an expert like Mrs. Snell."

"The game must be awfully exciting," said Ella. "I wished we could watch it sometime."

"I guess it wouldn't hurt nothing," says Perkie; "not if you kept still. Maybe you'd bring me luck."

"Was you going to play to-night?" asked Kate.

"No," says the Lady. "They's going to be a little dance here to-night and Mr. Snell's dance mad, so he insists on borrowing his wife for the occasion. Doctor Platt likes to dance too."

"We're all wild about it," says Kate. "Is this an invitation affair?"

"Oh, no," says Perk. "It's for the guests of the hotel."

Then she said good-by to us and went in the dining room. The rest of our conversation all day was about the dance and what should we wear, and how nice and democratic Lady Perkins was, and to hear her talk you wouldn't never know she had a title. I s'pose the gals thought she ought to stop every three or four steps and declare herself.

I made the announcement about noon that I wasn't going to partake in the grand ball. My corn was the alibi. But they wasn't no way to escape from dressing up and escorting the two gals into the grand ball-room and then setting there with them.

The dance was a knock-out. Outside of Ella and Kate and the aviator and myself, they was three couple. The Snells was there and so was Doctor Platt. He had a gal with him that looked like she might be his mother with his kid sister's clothes on. Then they was a pair of young shimmy shakers that ought to of been give their bottle and tucked in the hay at six p.m. A corn wouldn't of bothered them the way they danced; their feet wasn't involved in the transaction.

I and the Mrs. and Kate was the only ones there in evening clothes. The others had attended these functions before and knew that they wouldn't be enough suckers on hand to make any difference whether you wore a monkey suit or rompers. Besides, it wasn't Saturday night.

The music was furnished by the three-piece orchestra that usually done their murder in the summer parlor.

Ella was expecting me to introduce her and Kate to the Snell gal, but her and her husband was so keen for dancing that they called it off in the middle of the second innings and beat it upstairs. Then Ella said she wouldn't mind meeting Platt, but when he come past us and I spoke to him he give me a look like you would expect from a flounder that's been wronged.

So poor Codd danced one with Kate and one with Ella, and so on, and so on, till finally it got pretty late, a quarter to ten, and our party was the only merry-makers left in the joint. The orchestra looked over at us to see if we could stand some more punishment. The Mrs. told me to go and ask them to play a couple more dances before they quit. They done what I asked them, but maybe I got my orders mixed up.

The next morning I asked Wurz, the manager, how often the hotel give them dances.

"Oh," he says, "once or twice a month."

I told him I didn't see how they could afford it.

Kate went out after supper this next evening to take an automobile ride with Codd. So when I and Ella had set in the summer parlor a little wile, she proposed that we should go in and watch the bridge game. Well, I wasn't keen for it, but when you tell wife you don't want to do something she always says, "Why not?" and even if you've got a reason she'll make a monkey out of it. So we rapped at the door of the red card room and Lady Perkins said, "Come in," and in we went.

The two dudes and Mrs. Snell was playing with her again, but Perk was the only one that spoke.

"Set down," she said, "and let's see if you can bring me some luck."

So we drawed up a couple of chairs and set a little ways behind her. Her and the anonymous dude was partners against Doc and Mrs. Snell, and they didn't change all evening. I haven't played only a few games of bridge, but I know a little about it, and I never see such hands as Perkie held. It was a misdeal when she didn't have the ace, king and four or five others of one suit and a few picture cards and aces on the side. When she couldn't get the bid herself she doubled the other pair and made a sucker out of them. I don't know what they was playing a point, but when they broke up Lady Perkins and her dude was something like seven hundred berries to the good.

I and Ella went to bed wile they was settling up, but we seen her on the porch in the morning. She smiled at us and says: "You two are certainly grand mascots! I hope you can come in and set behind me again to-night. I ain't even yet, but one more run of luck like last night's and I'll be a winner. Then," she says, "I s'pose I'll have to give my mascots some kind of a treat."

Ella was tickled to death and couldn't hardly wait to slip Sis the good news. Kate had been out late and overslept herself and we was half through breakfast when she showed up. The Mrs. told her about the big game and how it looked like we was in strong with the nobility, and Kate said she had some good news of her own; that Codd had as good as told her he was stuck on her.

"And he's going to sell his invention for a million," says Ella. "So I guess we wasn't as crazy coming out to this place as some people thought we was."

"Wait till the machine's made good," I said.

"It has already," says Kate. "He was up in it yesterday and everything worked perfect and he says the Williamses was wild over it. And what do you think's going to come off to-morrow morning? He's going to take me up with him."

"Oh, no, Sis!" said Ella. "S'pose something should happen!"

"No hope," says I.

"But even if something should happen," said Katie, "what would I care as long as it happened to Bob and I together!"

I told the waitress to bring me another order of fried mush.

"To-night," said Kate, "Bob's going in Town to a theater party with some boys he went to college with. So I can help you bring Lady Perkins good luck."

Something told me to crab this proposition and I tried, but it was passed over my veto. So the best I could do was to remind Sis, just before we went in the gambling den, to keep her mouth shut wile the play was going on.

Perk give us a smile of welcome and her partner smiled too.

For an hour the game went along about even. Kate acted like she was bored, and she didn't have nothing to say after she'd told them, wile somebody was dealing, that she was going to have an aeroplane ride in the morning. Finally our side begin to lose, and lose by big scores. They was one time when they was about sixteen hundred points to the bad. Lady Perkins didn't seem to be enjoying herself and when Ella addressed a couple of remarks to her the cat had her tongue.

But the luck switched round again and Lady Perk had all but caught up when the blow-off come.

It was the rubber game, with the score nothing and nothing. The Doc dealt the cards. I was setting where I could see his hand and Perk's both. Platt had the king, jack and ten and five other hearts. Lady Perkins held the ace and queen of hearts, the other three aces and everything else in the deck.

The Doc bid two hearts. The other dude and Mrs. Snell passed.

"Two without," says Lady Perkins.

"Three hearts," says Platt.

The other two passed again and Perk says: "Three without."

Katie had came strolling up and was pretty near behind Perk's chair.

"Well," says Platt, "it looks like——"

But we didn't find out what it looked like, as just then Katie says: "Heavens! Four aces! Don't you wished you was playing penny ante?"

It didn't take Lady Perkins no time at all to forget her title.

"You fool!" she screams, w'eeling round on Kate. "Get out of here, and get out of here quick, and don't never come near me again! I hope your aeroplane falls a million feet. You little fool!"

I don't know how the hand come out. We wasn't there to see it played.

Lady Perkins got part of her hope. The aeroplane fell all right, but only a couple of miles instead of a million feet. They say that they was a defect or something in poor Codd's engine. Anyway, he done an involuntary nose dive. Him and his invention was spilled all over Long Island. But Katie had been awake all night with the hysterics and Ella hadn't managed to get her to sleep till nine a.m. So when Codd had called for her Ella'd told him that Sis would go some other day. Can you beat it?

Wile I and Ella was getting ready for supper I made the remark that I s'posed we'd live in a vale of tears for the next few days.

"No," said Ella. "Sis is taking it pretty calm. She's sensible. She says if that could of happened, why the invention couldn't of been no good after all. And the Williamses probably wouldn't of give him a plugged dime for it."

Lady Perkins didn't only speak to me once afterwards. I seen her setting on the porch one day, reading a book. I went up to her and said: "Hello." They wasn't no answer, so I thought I'd appeal to her sympathies.

"Maybe you're still interested in my dogs," I said. "They was too far gone and the veter'nary had to order them shot."

"That's good," said Perk, and went on reading.

ONLY ONE

About a week after this, the Mrs. made the remark that the Decker wasn't big enough to hold both she and Perkins.

"She treats us like garbage," says the Mrs., "and if I stay here much longer I'll forget myself and do her nose in a braid."

But Perk left first and saved us the trouble. Her husband was down in Texas looking after some oil gag and he wired her a telegram one day to come and join him as it looked like he would have to stay there all summer. If I'd of been him I'd of figured that Texas was a sweet enough summer resort without adding your wife to it.

We was out on the porch when her ladyship and two dogs shoved off.

"Three of a kind," said the Mrs.

And she stuck her tongue out at Perk and felt like that made it all even. A woman won't stop at nothing to revenge insults. I've saw them stagger home in a new pair of 3 double A shoes because some fresh clerk told them the 7 Ds they tried on was too small. So anyway we decided to stay on at the Decker and the two gals prettied themselves up every night for dinner in the hopes that somebody besides the head waiter would look at them twice, but we attracted about as much attention as a dirty finger nail in the third grade.

That is, up till Herbert Daley come on the scene.

Him and Katie spotted each other at the same time. It was the night he come to the Decker. We was pretty near through dinner when the head waiter showed him to a table a little ways from us. The majority of the guests out there belongs to the silly sex and a new man is always a riot, even with the married ones. But Daley would of knocked them dead anywheres. He looked like he was born and raised in Shubert's chorus and the minute he danced in all the womenfolks forgot the feed bag and feasted their eyes on him. As for Daley, after he'd glanced at the bill of fare, he let his peepers roll over towards our table and then they quit rolling. A cold stare from Kate might have scared him off, but if they was ever a gal with "Welcome" embroidered on her pan, she's it.

It was all I could do to tear Ella and Sis from the dining room, though they was usually in a hurry to romp out to the summer parlor and enjoy a few snubs. I'd just as soon of set one place as another, only for the waitress, who couldn't quit till we did and she generally always had a date with the big ski jumper the hotel hires to destroy trunks.

Well, we went out and listened a wile to the orchestra, which had brought a lot of new jazz from the Prince of Pilsen, and we waited for the new dude to show up, but he didn't, and finally I went in to the desk to buy a couple of cigars and there he was, talking to Wurz, the manager. Wurz introduced us and after we'd shook hands Daley excused himself and said he was going upstairs to write a letter. Then Wurz told me he was Daley the horseman.

"He's just came up from the South," says Wurz. "He's going to be with us till the meetings is over at Jamaica and Belmont. He's got a whale of a stable and he expects to clean up round New York with Only One, which he claims can beat any horse in the world outside of Man o' War. They's some other good ones in the bunch, too, and he says he'll tell me when he's going to bet on them. I don't only bet once in a long wile and then never more than $25 at a crack, but I'll take this baby's tips as often as he comes through with them. I guess a man won't make no mistake following a bird that bets five and ten thousand at a clip, though of course it don't mean much to him if he win or lose. He's dirty with it."

I asked Wurz if Daley was married and he said no.

"And listen," he says: "It looks like your little sister-in-law had hit him for a couple of bases. He described where she was setting in the dining room and asked who she was."

"Yes," I said, "I noticed he was admiring somebody at our table, but I thought maybe it was me."

"He didn't mention you," says Wurz, "only to make sure you wasn't Miss Kate's husband."

"If he was smart he'd know that without asking," I said. "If she was my wife I'd be wearing weeds."

I went back to the gals and told them I'd met the guy. They was all steamed up.

"Who is he?" says Kate.

"His name is Herbert Daley," I told her. "He's got a stable over to Jamaica."

"A stable!" says Ella, dropping her jaw. "A man couldn't dress like he and run a livery."

So I had to explain that he didn't run no livery, but owned a string of race horses.

"How thrilling!" says Katie. "I love races! I went to the Grand Circuit once, the time I was in Columbus."

"These is different," I says. "These is thurlbreds."

"So was they thurlbreds!" she says. "You always think a thing can't be no good if you wasn't there."

I let her win that one.

"We must find out when the race is and go," said the Mrs.

"They's six of them every day," I said, "but it costs about five smackers apiece to get in, to say nothing about what you lose betting."

"Betting!" says Katie. "I just love to bet and I never lose. Don't you remember the bet I made with Sammy Pass on the baseball that time? I took him for a five-pound box of candy. I just felt that Cincinnati was going to win."

"So did the White Sox," I says. "But if you bet with the boys over to Jamaica, the only candy they'll take you for is an all-day sucker."

"What did Mr. Daley have to say?" asked Ella.

"He had to say he was pleased to meet me," I told her. "He proved it by chasing upstairs to write a letter."

"Probably to his wife," said Kate.

"No," I said. "Wurz tells me he ain't got no wife. But he's got plenty of jack, so Wurz says."

"Well, Sis," says the Mrs., "that's no objection to him, is it?"

"Don't be silly!" said Katie. "He wouldn't look at me."

"I guess not!" I says. "He was so busy doing it in the dining room, that half his soup never got past his chin. And listen: I don't like to get you excited, but Wurz told me he asked who you was."

"O Sis!" said the Mrs. "It looks like a Romance."

"Wurz didn't say nothing about a Romance," said I. "He may be interested like the rubes who stare with their mouth open at Ringling's 'Strange People.' "

"Oh, you can't tease Sis like that," said Ella. "She's as pretty as a picture to-night and nobody could blame a man from admiring her."

"Especially when we don't know nothing about him," I says. "He may be a snow-eater or his upstairs rooms is unfurnished or something."

"Well," says Ella, "if he shows up again to-night, don't you forget to introduce us."

"Better not be in no hurry," I said.

"Why not?" said Ella. "If him and Sis likes each other's looks, why, the sooner they get acquainted, it won't hurt nothing."

"I don't know," I says. "I've noticed that most of the birds you chose for a brother-in-law only stayed in the family as long as they was strangers."

"Nobody said nothing about Mr. Daley as a brother-in-law," says Ella.

"Oh!" I said. "Then I suppose you want Katie to meet him so as she can land a hostler's job."

Well, in about a half hour, the gals got their wish and Daley showed up. I didn't have to pull no strategy to land him. He headed right to where we was setting like him and I was old pals. I made the introductions and he drawed up a chair and parked. The rest of the guests stared at us goggle-eyed.

"Some hotel!" says Daley.

"We like it," says the Mrs. "They's so many nice people lives here."

"We know by hearsay," I said, but she stepped on my foot.

"It's handy for me," said Daley. "I have a few horses over to the Jamaica race track and it's a whole lot easier to come here than go in Town every night."

"Do you attend the races every day?" says Katie.

"Sure," he says. "It's my business. And they's very few afternoons when one of my nags ain't entered."

"My! You must have a lot of them!" said Kate.

"Not many," says Daley. "About a hundred. And I only shipped thirty."

"Imagine!" said Kate.

"The army's got that many," I said.

"The army ain't got none like mine," says Daley. "I guess they wished they had of had. I'd of been glad to of helped them out, too, if they'd asked me."

"That's why I didn't enlist," I said. "Pershing never even suggested it."

"Oh, I done my bit all right," says Daley. "Two hundred thousand in Liberty Bonds is all."

"Just like throwing it away!" I says.

"Two hundred thousand!" says Ella. "And you've still got money left?"

She said this in a joking way, but she kept the receiver to her ear.

"I ain't broke yet," says Daley, "and I don't expect to be."

"You don't half know this hotel," I says.

"The Decker does charge good prices," said Daley, "but still and all, a person is willing to pay big for the opportunity of meeting young ladies like the present company."

"O Mr. Daley!" said Kate. "I'm afraid you're a flatter."

"I bet he makes them pretty speeches to every woman he meets," says Ella.

"I haven't met none before who I felt like making them," says Daley.

Wile they was still talking along these lines, the orchestra begin to drool a Perfect Day, so I ducked out on the porch for air. The gals worked fast wile I was gone and when I come back it was arranged that Daley was to take us to the track next afternoon in his small car.

His small car was a toy that only had enough room for the people that finds fault with Wilson. I suppose he had to leave his big car in New York on account of the Fifty-ninth Street bridge being so frail.

Before we started I asked our host if they was a chance to get anything to drink over to the track and he says no, but pretty near everybody brought something along on the hip, so I said for them to wait a minute wile I went up to the room and filled a flask. When we was all in the car, the Mrs. wanted to know if it wasn't risky, me taking the hootch along.

"It's against the prohibition law," she says.

"So am I," I said.

"They's no danger," says Daley. "They ain't began to force prohibition yet. I only wished they had. It would save me a little worry about my boy."

"Your boy!" said Katie, dropping her jaw a foot.

"Well, I call him my boy," says Daley. "I mean little Sid Mercer, that rides for me. He's the duke of them all when he lays off the liquor. He's gave me his word that he won't touch nothing as long as he's under contract to me, and he's kept straight so far, but I can't help from worr'ing about him. He ought to be good, though, when I pay him $20,000 for first call, and leave him make all he can on the side. But he ain't got much stren'th of character, you might say, and if something upsets him, he's liable to bust things wide open.

"I remember once he was stuck on a gal down in Louisville and he was supposed to ride Great Scott for Bradley in the Derby. He was the only one that could handle Scott right, and with him up Scott would of win as far as from here to Dallas. But him and the gal had a brawl the day before the race and that night the kid got stiff. When it come time for the race he couldn't of kept a seat on a saw horse. Bradley had to hustle round and dig up another boy and Carney was the only one left that could ride at all and him and Great Scott was strangers. So Bradley lose the race and canned Mercer."

"Whisky's a terrible thing," says Ella. A woman'll sometimes pretend for a long wile like she's stupid and all of a sudden pull a wise crack that proves she's a thinker.

"Well," says Daley, "when Bradley give him the air, I took him, and he's been all right. I guess maybe I know how to handle men."

"Men only?" says Katie, smiling.

"Men and horses," said Daley. "I ain't never tried to handle the fair sex and I don't know if I could or not. But I've just met one that I think could handle me." And he give her a look that you could pour on a waffle.

Daley had a table saved for him in the clubhouse and we eat our lunch. The gals had clubhouse sandwiches, probably figuring they was caught fresh there. They was just one of Daley's horses entered that day and he told us he wasn't going to bet on it, as it hadn't never showed nothing and this was just a try-out. He said, though, that they was other horses on the card that looked good and maybe he would play them after he'd been round and talked to the boys.

"Yes," says Kate, "but the men you'll talk to knows all about the different horses and they'll tell you what horses to bet on and how can I win?"

"Why," says Daley, "if I decide to make a little bet on So-and-So I'll tell you about it and you can bet on the same horse."

"But if I'm betting with you," says Kate, "how can we bet on the same horse?"

"You're betting with me, but you ain't betting against me," said Daley. "This ain't a bet like you was betting with your sister on a football game or something. We place our bets with the bookmakers, that makes their living taking bets. Whatever horse we want to bet on, they take the bet."

"They must be crazy!" says Katie. "Your friends tell you what horse is going to win and you bet on them and the bookbinders is stung."

"My friends makes mistakes," says Daley, "and besides, I ain't the only guy out here that bets. Pretty near everybody at the track bets and the most of them don't know a race horse from a corn plaster. A book-maker that don't finish ahead on the season's a cuckoo. Now," he says, "if you'll excuse me for a few minutes, I'll go down to the paddock and see what's new."

So wile he was gone we had a chance to look round and they was plenty to see. It was a Saturday and a big crowd out. Lots of them was gals that you'd have to have a pick to break through to their regular face. Since they had their last divorce, about the only excitement they could enjoy was playing a long shot. Which reminds me that they's an old saying that nobody loves a fat man, but you go out to a race track or down to Atlantic City or any place where the former wifes hangs out and if you'll notice the birds with them, the gents that broke up their home, you'll find out that the most of them is guys with chins that runs into five and six figures and once round their waist is a sleeper jump.

Besides the Janes and the fat rascals with them, you seen a flock of ham actors that looked like they'd spent the night in a Chinese snowstorm, and maybe a half a dozen losers'-end boxers that'd used the bridge of their nose to block with and always got up in the morning just after the clock had struck ten, thinking they'd been counted out.

Pretty near everybody wore a pair of field glasses on a strap and when the race was going on they'd look through them and tell the world that the horse they'd bet on was three len'ths in front and just as good as in, but I never heard of a bookie paying off on that dope, and personally when someone would insist on lending me a pair to look through I couldn't tell if the things out there racing was horses or gnats.

Daley was back with us in a few minutes and says to Kate: "I guess you'll have to bet on yourself in the first race."

So she asked him what did he mean and he said: "I had a tip on a filly named Sweet and Pretty."

"O Mr. Daley!" says Kate.

"They don't expect her to win," says Daley, "but she's six, two and even, and I'm going to play her place and show."

Then he explained what that was and he said he was going to bet a thousand each way and finally the gals decided to go in for $10 apiece to show. It tickled them to death to find out that they didn't have to put up nothing. We found seats down in front wile Daley went to place the bets. Pretty soon the horses come out and Kate and Ella both screamed when they seen how cute the jockeys was dressed. Sweet and Pretty was No. 10 and had a combination of colors that would knock your eye out. Daley come back and explained that every owner had their own colors and of course the gals wanted to know what his was and he told them Navy blue and orange sleeves with black whoops on them and a blue cap.

"How beautiful!" says Ella. "I can't hardly wait to see them!"

"You must have wonderful taste in colors!" says Kate.

"Not only in colors," he says.

"O Mr. Daley!" she says again.

Well, the race was ran and No. 10 was a Sweet and Pretty last.

"Now," I says, "you O Mr. Daley."

The gals had yelped themself hoarse and didn't have nothing to say, but I could tell from their face that it would take something more than a few pretty speeches to make up for that twenty men.

"Never mind that!" said Daley. "She got a rotten ride. We'll get that back on the next one."

His hunch in the next one was Sena Day and he was betting a thousand on her to place at 4 to 1. He made the gals go in for $20 apiece, though they didn't do it with no pep. I went along with him to place the bets and he introduced me to a bookie so as I could bet a few smackers of my own when I felt like it. You know they's a law against betting unless it's a little bet between friends and in order to be a bookie's friend he's got to know your name. A quick friendship sprung up between I and a guy named Joe Meyer, and he not only give me his card but a whole deck of them. You see the law also says that when you make one of these bets with your pals he can't give you no writing to show for it, but he's generally always a man that makes a lot of friends and it seems like they all want to make friendly bets with him, and he can't remember where all his buddies lives, so he makes them write their name and address on the cards and how much the friendly wager is for and who on, and so forth, and the next day he mails them the bad news and they mail him back a check for same. Once in a wile, of course, you get the bad news and forget to mail him the check and he feels blue over it as they's nothing as sad as breaking up an old friendship.

I laid off Sena Day and she win. Daley smiled at the gals.

"There!" he says. "I'm sorry we didn't play her on the nose, but I was advised to play safe."

"Fine advice!" said Kate. "It's cost Sis and I $60 so far."

"What do you mean?" says Daley.

"We lose $20 on the first race," she says, "and you tell us we'll get it back on the next one and we bet the horse'll come second and it don't."

So we had to explain that if a horse win, why it placed, too, and her and Ella had grabbed $160 on that race and was $140 ahead. He was $2,000 winners himself.

"We'll have a drink on Sena," he says. "I don't believe they was six people out here that bet a nickel on her."

So Katie told him he was wonderful and him and the gals had a sarsaparilla or something and I poured my own. He'd been touting Cleopatra in the third race, but her and everybody else was scratched out of it except Captain Alcock and On Watch. On Watch was 9 to 10 and Alcock even money and Daley wouldn't let us bet.

"On Watch is best," he says, "but he's giving away twenty pounds and you can't tell. Anyway, it ain't worth it at that price."

"Only two horses in the race?" asked Ella.

"That's all," he says.

"Well, then, listen," she says, all excited: "Why not bet on one of them for place?"

Daley laughed and said it was a grand idear only he didn't think the bookbinders would stand for it.

"But maybe they don't know," she says.

"I guess they do," said Daley. "It's almost impossible to keep a secret like that round a race track."

"Besides," I said, "the bookworms owes you and Kate $70 apiece and if you put something like that over on them and they find it out, they'll probably get even by making you a check on the West Bank of the Hudson River."

So we decided to play fair and lay off the race entirely. On Watch come through and the gals felt pretty bad about it till we showed them that they'd of only grabbed off nine smackers apiece if they'd of plunged on him for $20 straight.

Along toward time for the next race, Daley steered us down by the paddock and we seen some of the nags close up. Daley and the gals raved over this one and that one, and wasn't this one a beauty, and so forth. Personally they was all just a horse to me and I never seen one yet that wasn't homelier than the City Hall. If they left it up to me to name the world's champion eyesore, I'd award the elegant barb' wire wash rag to a horse rode by a woman in a derby hat. People goes to the Horse Show to see the Count de Fault; they don't know a case of withers from an off hind hock. And if the Sport of Kings was patronized by just birds that admires equine charms, you could park the Derby Day crowd in a phone booth.

A filly named Tamarisk was the favorite in the fourth race and Daley played her for eight hundred smackers at 4 to 5. The gals trailed along with $8 apiece and she win from here to Worcester. The fifth was the one that Daley had an entry in—a dog named Fly-by-Night. It was different in the daytime. Mercer had the mount and done the best he could, which was finish before supper. Nobody bet, so nobody was hurt.

"He's just a green colt," Daley told us. "I wanted to see how he'd behave."

"Well," I said, "I thought he behaved like a born caboose."

Daley liked the Waterbury entry in the last and him and the gals played it and win. All told, Daley was $4,000 ahead on the day and Ella and Kate had picked up $160 between them. They wanted to kiss everybody on the way out. Daley sent us to the car to wait for him. He wanted to see Mercer a minute. After a wile he come out and brought

Mercer along and introduced him. He's a good-looking kid only for a couple of blotches on his pan and got an under lip and chin that kind of lags behind. He was about Kate's height, and take away his Adams apple and you could mail him to Duluth for six cents. Him and Kate got personal right away and she told him how different he looked now than in his riding make-up. He said he had a new outfit that he'd of wore if he'd knew she was looking on. So I said I hoped he didn't expect to ride Fly-by-Night round the track and keep a suit new, and he laughed, and Daley didn't seem to enjoy the conversation and said we'd have to be going, but when we started off, Kate and Mercer give each other a smile with a future in it. She's one of these gals that can't help from looking open house, even if the guy takes after a pelican.

Daley moved to our table that night and after that we eat breakfast and supper with him pretty near every day. After breakfast the gals would go down to New York to spend what they had win the day before, and I'll admit that Daley give us many a winner. I begin betting a little of my own jack, but I stuck the proceeds in the old sock. I ain't superstitious about living off a woman's money as long as you're legally married, but at the clip the two gals was going, it looked like their old man's war profits was on the way to join their maker, and the more jack I laid by, the less sooner I would have to go to work.

We'd meet every afternoon at the track and after the races Daley'd bring us back to the hotel. After supper we'd set round and chin or play rummy or once in a wile we'd go in Town to a show or visit one of the road houses near the Decker. The mail service on Long Island's kind of rotten and they's a bunch of road houses that hasn't heard of prohibition.

During the time we'd lived in Town Katie had got acquainted with three or four birds that liked her well enough to take her places where they wasn't no cover charge, but since we'd moved to the Decker we hadn't heard from none of them. That is, till a few days after we'd met Daley, when she told us that one of the New York boys, a guy named Goldberg, had called up and wanted her to come in and see a show with him. He's a golf champion or something. Well, Daley offered to drive her in, but she said no, she'd rather go on the train and Goldberg was going to meet her. So she went, and Daley tried to play cards with Ella and I, but he was too restless and finally snuck up to his room.

They wasn't no question about his feelings toward Kate. He was always trying to fix it to be alone with her, but I guess it was the first time in her life when she didn't have to do most of the leading and she kept him at arm's len'th. Her and Ella had many a battle. Ella told her that the first thing she knowed he'd get discouraged and walk out on her; that she'd ought to quit monking and give him to understand that she was ready to yes him when he spoke up. But Katie said she guessed she could run her own love affairs as she'd had a few more of them than Ella.

So Ella says: "Maybe you have, but which one of us has got the husband?"

"You, thank the Lord!" says Katie.

"Thank him twice," I said.

Kate didn't come home from her New York party till two o'clock and she overslept herself till it was too late to go down again and shop. So we all drove over to the track with Daley and most of the way over he acted like a child. Katie kept talking about what a good show she seen and had a grand time, and so forth, and he pretended he wasn't listening. Finally she cut it out and give him the old oil and by the time we got to the clubhouse he'd tossed in the sponge.

That was the last day at Jamaica and a couple of his horses was in. We was all down on them and they both copped, though Mercer had to give one of them a dude ride to pull us through. Daley got maudlin about what a grand rider the kid was and a grand little fella besides, and he had half a notion to bring him along with us back to the hotel and show him a good time. But Kate said what was the use of an extra man, as it would kind of spoil things and she was satisfied with just Daley. So of course that tickled him and everybody was feeling good and after supper him and Kate snuck out alone for the first time. Ella made me set up till they come back, so as she could get the news. Well, Daley had asked her all right, but she told him she wanted a little wile to think.

"Think!" says Ella. "What does she want to think for?"

"The novelty, I suppose," said I.

Only One was in the big stake race the next day, when we shifted over to Belmont. They was five or six others in with him, all of them pretty good, and the price on him was 3 to 1. He hadn't started yet since Daley'd brought him here, but they'd been nursing him along and Mercer and the trainer said he was right.

I suppose of course you've been out to Belmont. At that time they run the wrong way of the track, like you deal cards. Daley's table was in a corner of the clubhouse porch and when you looked up the track, the horses was coming right at you. Even the boys with the trick glasses didn't dast pretend they could tell who's ahead.

The Belmont national hymn is Whispering. The joint's so big and scattered round that a German could sing without disturbing the party at the next table. But they seems to be a rule that when they's anything to be said, you got to murmur it with the lips stuck to the opponent's earlobe. They shush you if you ask out loud for a toothpick. Everywheres you'll see two or three guys with their heads together in a whispering scene. One of them has generally always just been down to the horses' dining room and had lunch with Man o' War or somebody and they told him to play Sea Mint in the next race as Cleopatra had walked the stall all night with her foal. A little ways off they'll be another pair of shushers and one of them's had a phone call from Cleopatra's old dam to put a bet on Cleo as Captain Alcock had got a hold of some wild oats and they couldn't make him do nothing but shimmy.

If they's ten horses in a race you can walk from one end of the clubhouse to the other and get a whisper on all ten of them. I remember the second time Man o' War run there. They was only one horse that wanted to watch him from the track and the War horse was 1 to 100. So just before the race, if you want to call it that, I seen a wise cracker that I'd got acquainted with, that had always been out last night with Madden or Waterbury, so just kidding I walked up to him and asked him who he liked. So he motioned me to come over against the wall where they wasn't nobody near us and whispered, "Man o' War's unbeatable." You see if that remark had of been overheard and the news allowed to spread round, it might of forced the price to, say, 1 to a lump of coal, and spoiled the killing.

Well, wile the Jamaica meeting was on, the gals had spent some of their spare time figuring out how much they'd of been ahead if Daley had of let them bet more than ten to twenty smackers a race. So this day at Belmont, they said that if he liked Only One so much, he should ought to leave them raise the ante just once and play fifty apiece.

But he says: "No, not this time. I'm pretty sure he'll win, but he's in against a sweet field and he ain't raced for a month. I'll bet forty on the nose for the two of you, and if he looks good you can gamble some real money the next time he runs."

So Ella and Kate had to be satisfied with $20 apiece. Daley himself bet $2,000 and I piked along with $200 that I didn't tell the gals nothing about. We all got 3 to 1. A horse named Streak of Lightning was favorite at 6 to 5. It was a battle. Only One caught the Streak in the last step and win by a flea's jaw. Everybody was in hysterics and the gals got all messed up clawing each other.

"Nobody but Mercer could of did it!" says Daley, as soon as he could talk.

"He's some jockey!" yelled Kate. "O you Sid!"

Pretty soon the time was give out and Only One had broke the track record for the distance, whatever it was.

"He's a race horse!" said Daley. "But it's too bad he had to extend himself. We won't get no price the next time out."

Well, altogether the race meant $14,000 to Daley, and he said we'd all go to Town that night and celebrate. But when we got back to the Decker, they was a telegram for him and he had to pack up and beat it for Kentucky.

Daley being away didn't stop us from going to the track. He'd left orders with Ernest, his driver, to take us wherever we wanted to go and the gals had it so bad now that they couldn't hardly wait till afternoon. They kept on trimming the books, too. Kate got a phone call every morning that she said was from this Goldberg and he was giving her tips. Her and Ella played them and I wished I had. I would of if I'd knew who they was from. They was from Mercer, Daley's boy. That's who they was from.

I and Ella didn't wise up till about the third night after Daley'd went. That night, Kate took the train to Town right after supper, saying she had a date with Goldberg. It was a swell night and along about eight, I and Ella decided we might as well have a ride. So we got a hold of Ernest and it wound up by us going to New York too. We seen a picture and batted round till midnight and then Ella says why not go down to the Pennsylvania Station and pick Kate up when she come to take the train, and bring her home. So we done it. But when Katie showed up for the train, it was Mercer that was with her, not Goldberg.

Well, Mercer was pretty near out to the car with us when he happened to think that Daley's driver mustn't see him. So he said good night and left us. But he didn't do it quick enough. Daley's driver had saw him and I seen that he'd saw him and I knowed that he wasn't liable to be stuck on another of Daley's employs that was getting ten times as much money as him and all the cheers, and never had to dirty himself up changing a tire. And I bet it was all Ernest could do was wait till Daley come back so as he could explode the boom.

Kate and Ella didn't know Ernest was hep and I didn't tell them for fear of spoiling the show, so the women done their brawling on the way home in a regular race track whisper. The Mrs. told Kate she was a hick to be monking round with a jockey when Daley was ready and willing to give her a modern home with a platinum stopper in the washbowl. Kate told Ella that she wasn't going to marry nobody for their money, and besides, Mercer was making more than enough to support a wife, and how that boy can dance!

"But listen," she says: "I ain't married to neither one of them yet and don't know if I want to be."

"Well," says Ella, "you won't have no chance to marry Daley if he finds out about you and Mercer."

"He won't find out unless you tell him," said Kate.

"Well, I'll tell him," says Ella, "unless you cut this monkey business out."

"I'll cut it out when I get good and ready," says Kate. "You can tell Daley anything you please."

She knew they wasn't no chance of Ella making good.

"Daley'll be back in a couple of days," says the Mrs. "When he comes he'll want his answer and what are you going to say?"

"Yes or no, according to which way I make up my mind," said Kate. "I don't know yet which one I like best."

"That's ridic'lous!" Ella says. "When a girl says she can't make up her mind, it shows they's nothing to make up. Did you ever see me when I couldn't make up my mind?"

"No," said Katie, "but you never had even one whole man to choose between."

The last half of the ride neither of them were talking. That's a world's record in itself. They kind of made up the next morning after I'd told Ella that the surest way to knock Daley's chances for a gool was to paste Mercer.

"Just lay off of it," I told her. "The best man'll win in fair competition, which it won't be if you keep plugging for Daley."

We had two more pretty fair days at the track on Kate's tips that Mercer give her. We also went on a party with him down Town, but we used the train, not Daley's car.

Daley showed up on a Wednesday morning and had Ernest take him right over to the track. I suppose it was on this trip that Ernest squealed. Daley didn't act no different when we joined him on the clubhouse porch, but that night him and Kate took a ride alone and come back engaged.

They'd been pointing Only One for the Merrick Handicap, the fourth race on Saturday. It was worth about $7,000 to the winner. The distance was seven furlongs and Only One had top weight, 126 pounds. But Thursday he done a trial over the distance in 1.22, carrying 130 pounds, so it looked like a set-up.

Thursday morning I and Ella happened to be in Katie's room when the telephone rung. It was Mercer on the other end. He asked her something and she says: "I told you why in my note."

So he said something else and she says: "Not with no jailbird."

And she hung up.

Well, Ella wanted to know what all the pleasantries was about, but Kate told her to mind her own business.

"You got your wish and I'm engaged to Daley," she says, "and that's all you need to know."

For a gal that was going to marry a dude that was supposed to have all the money in the world, she didn't act just right, but she wouldn't been Kate if she had of, so I didn't think much about it.

Friday morning I got a wire from one of the South Bend boys, Goat Anderson, sent from Buffalo, saying he'd be in New York that night and would I meet him at the Belmont at seven o'clock. So I went in Town from the track and waited round till pretty near nine, but he didn't show up. I started to walk across to the Pennsylvania Station and on the way I dropped in at a place where they was still taking a chance. I had one up at the bar and was throwing it into me when a guy in the back part yelled "Hey! Come here!" It was Mercer yelling and it was me he wanted.

He was setting at a table all alone with a highball. It didn't take no Craig Kennedy to figure out that it wasn't his first one.

"Set down before I bat you down!" he says.

"Listen," I says: "I wished you was champion of the world. You'd hold onto the title just long enough for me to reach over and sock you where most guys has a chin."

"Set down!" he says. "It's your wife I'm going to beat up, not you."

"You ain't going to beat up nobody's wife or nobody's husband," I says, "and if you don't cut out that line of gab you'll soon be asking the nurse how you got there."

"Set down and come clean with me," he says. "Was your wife the one that told Daley about your sister-in-law and I?"

"If she did, what of it?" I says.

"I'm asking you, did she?" he says.

"No, she didn't," I said. "If somebody told him his driver told him. He seen you the other night."

"Ernest!" he says. "Frank and Ernest! I'll Ernest him right in the jaw!"

"You're a fine matchmaker!" I says. "He could knock you for a row of flat tires. Why don't you try and get mad at Dempsey?"

"Set down and have a drink," says Mercer.

"I didn't mean that about your wife. You and her has treated me all right. And your sister-in-law, too, even if she did give me the air. And called me a jailbird. But that's all right. It's Daley I'm after and it's Daley I'm going to get."

"Sweet chance!" I says. "What could you do to him?"

"Wait and see!" said Mercer, and smiled kind of silly.

"Listen," I says. "Have you forgot that you're supposed to ride Only One to-morrow?"

"Supposed to ride is right," he says, and smiled again.

"Ain't you going to ride him?" I said.

"You bet I am!" he says.

"Well, then," I said, "you better call it a day and go home."

"I'm over twenty-one," he says, "and I'm going to set here and enjoy myself. But remember, I ain't keeping you up."

Well, they wasn't nothing I could do only set there and wait for him to get stiff and then see him to his hotel. We had a drink and we had another and a couple more. Finally he opened up. I wished you could of heard him. It took him two hours to tell his story, and everything he said, he said it over and over and repeated it four and five times. And part of the time he talked so thick that I couldn't hardly get him.

"Listen," he says. "Can you keep a secret? Listen," he says. "I'm going to take a chance with you on account of your sister-in-law. I loved that little gal. She's give me the air, but that don't make no difference; I loved that little gal and I don't want her to lose no money. So I'm going to tell you a secret and if you don't keep your clam shut I'll roll you for a natural. In the first place," he says, "how do you and Daley stack up?"

"That ain't no secret," I said. "I think he's all right. He's been a good friend of mine."

"Oh," says Mercer, "so he's been a good friend of yours, has he? All right, then. I'm going to tell you a secret. Do you remember the day I met you and the gals in the car? Well, a couple of days later, Daley was feeling pretty good about something and he asked me how I liked his gal? So I told him she looked good. So he says, 'I'm going to marry that gal,' he says. He says, 'She likes me and her sister and brother-in-law is encouraging it along,' he says. 'They know I've got a little money and they're making a play for me. They're a couple of rats and I'm the cheese. They're going to make a meal off of me. They think they are,' he says. 'But the brother-in-law's a smart Aleck that thinks he's a wise cracker. He'd be a clown in a circus, only that's work. And his wife's fishing for a sucker with her sister for bait. Well, the gal's a pip and I'm going to marry her,' he says, 'but as soon as we're married, it's good-by, family-in-law! Me and them is going to be perfect strangers. They think they'll have free board and lodging at my house,' he says, 'but they won't get no meal unless they come to the back door for it, and when they feel sleepy they can make up a lower for themself on my cement porch.' That's the kind of a friend of yours this baby is," says Mercer.

I didn't say nothing and he went on.

"He's your friend as long as he can use you," he says. "He's been my friend since I signed to ride for him, that is, up till he found out I was stealing his gal. Then he shot my chances for a bull's-eye by telling her about a little trouble I had, five or six years ago. I and a girl went to a party down in Louisville and I seen another guy wink at her and I asked him what he meant by it and he said he had St. Vitus' dance. So I pulled the iron and knocked off a couple of his toes, to cure him. I was in eleven months and that's what Daley told Kate about. And of course he made her promise to not tell, but she wrote me a good-by note and spilled it. That's the kind of a pal he is.

"After I got out I worked for Bradley, and when Bradley turned me loose, he give me a $10,000 contract."

"He told us twenty," I said.

"Sure he did," says Mercer. "He always talks double. When he gets up after a tough night, both his heads aches. And if he ever has a baby he'll invite you over to see the twins. But anyway, what he pays me ain't enough and after to-morrow I'm through riding. What's ten or fifteen thousand a year when you can't drink nothing and you starve to death for the fear you'll pick up an ounce! Listen," he says. "I got a brother down in Oklahoma that's in the oil lease game. He cleaned up $25,000 last year and he wants me to go in with him. And with what I've saved up and what I'm going to win to-morrow, I should worry if we don't make nothing in the next two years."

"How are you going to win to-morrow?" I said. "The price'll be a joke."

"The price on who?" says Mercer.

"Only One," I said.

He give a silly laugh and didn't say nothing for a minute. Then he asked if Daley done the betting for I and the two gals. I told him he had did it at first, but now I was doing it.

"Well," he says, "you do it to-morrow, see? That little lady called me a jailbird, but I don't want her to lose her money."

So I asked him what he meant and he asked me for the tenth or eleventh time if I could keep a secret. He made me hold up my hand and swear I wouldn't crack what he was going to tell me.

"Now," he says, "what's the name of the horse I'm riding to-morrow?"

"Only One," I said.

"That ain't all of it," said Mercer. "His name to-morrow is Only One Left. See? Only One Left."

"Do you mean he's going to get left at the post?" I says.

"You're a Ouija board!" says Mercer. "Your name is Ouija and the horse's name is Only One Left. And listen," he says. "Everything but three horses is going to be scratched out of this race and we'll open at about 1 to 3 and back up to 1 to 5. And Daley's going to bet his right eye. But they's a horse in the race named Sap and that's the horse my two thousand smackers is going down on. And you're a sap, too, if you don't string along with me."

"Suppose you can't hold Only One?"

"Get the name right," said Mercer. "Only One Left. And don't worry about me not handling him. He thinks I'm Billy Sunday and everything I say he believes. Do you remember the other day when I beat Streak of Lightning? Well, the way I done that was whispering in One's ear, coming down the stretch. I says to him, 'One,' I says, 'this Lightning hoss has been spilling it round that your father's grandmother was a zebra. Make a bum out of him!' That's what I whispered to him and he got sore and went past Lightning like he was standing still. And to-morrow, just before we're supposed to go, I'll say to him, 'One, we're back at Jamaica. You're facing the wrong way.' And when Sap and the other dog starts, we'll be headed towards Rhode Island and in no hurry to get there."

"Mercer," I said, "I don't suppose they's any use talking to you, but after all, you're under contract to give Daley the best you've got and it don't look to me just like you was treating him square."

"Listen!" he says. "Him and square don't rhyme. And besides, I won't be under contract to nobody by this time to-morrow. So you save your sermon for your own parish."

I don't know if you'll think I done right or not. Or I don't care. But what was the sense of me tipping off a guy that had said them sweet things about I and Ella? And even if I don't want a sister-in-law of mine running round with a guy that's got a jail record, still Daley squealing on him was rotten dope. And besides, I don't never like to break a promise, especially to a guy that shoots a man's toes off just for having St. Vitus' dance.

Well, anyway, the third race was over and the Merrick Handicap was next, and just like Mercer had said, they all quit but our horse and Sap and a ten-ton truck named Honor Bright. He was 20 to 1 and Sap was 6. Only One was 1 to 3 and Daley hopped on him with fifteen thousand men. Before post time the price was 1 to 5 and 1 to 6.

Daley was off his nut all afternoon and didn't object when I said I'd place the gals' money and save him the trouble. Kate and Ella had figured out what they had win up to date. It was about $1,200 and Daley told them to bet it all.

"You'll only make $400 between you," he says, "but it's a cinch."

"And four hundred's pretty good interest on $1,200," says Kate. "About ten per cent, ain't it?"

I left them and went downstairs. I wrote out a card for a hundred smackers on Sap. Then my feet caught cold and I didn't turn it in. I walked down towards the paddock and got there just as the boys was getting ready to parade. I seen Mercer and you wouldn't of never knew he'd fell off the wagon.

Daley was down there, too, and I heard him say: "Well, Sid, how about you?"

"Never better," says Mercer. "If I don't win this one I'll quit riding."

Then he seen me and smiled.

I chased back to the clubhouse, making up my mind on the way. I decided to not bet a nickel for the gals on anything. If Mercer was crossing me, I'd give Ella and Kate their $400 like they had win it, and say nothing. Personally, I was going to turn in the card I'd wrote on Sap. That was my idear when I got to Joe Meyer. But all of a sudden I had the hunch that Mercer was going through; they wasn't a chance in the world for him to weaken. I left Meyer's stand and went to a bookie named Haynes, who I'd bet with before.

Sap had went up to 8 to 1, and instead of a hundred smackers I bet a thousand.

He finished ahead by three len'ths, probably the most surprised horse in history. Honor Bright got the place, but only by a hair. Only One, after being detained for some reason another, come faster at the end than any horse ever run before. And Mercer give him an unmerciful walloping, pretending to himself, probably, that the hoss was its master.

We come back to our table. The gals sunk down in their chairs. Ella was blubbering and Kate was as white as a ghost. Daley finally joined us, looking like he'd had a stroke. He asked for a drink and I give him my flask.

"I can't understand it!" he says. "I don't know what happened!"

"You don't!" hollered Kate. "I'll tell you what happened. You stole our money! Twelve hundred dollars! You cheat!"

"Oh, shut your fool mouth!" says Daley.

And another Romance was knocked for a row of sour apple trees.

Kate brought the mail in the dining room Monday morning. They was a letter for her and one for me. She read hers and they was a couple of tears in her eyes.

"Mercer's quit riding," she says. "This is a farewell note. He's going to Oklahoma."

Ella picked up my envelope.

"Who's this from?" she says.

"Give it here," I said, and took it away from her. "It's just the statement from Haynes, the bookie."

"Well, open it up," she said.

"What for?" said I. "You know how much you lose, don't you?"

"He might of made a mistake, mightn't he?" she says.

So I opened up the envelope and there was the check for $8,000.

"Gosh!" I said. "It looks like it was me that made the mistake!" And I laid the check down where her and Kate could see it. They screamed and I caught Ella just as she was falling off the chair.

"What does this mean?" says Kate.

"Well," I said, "I guess I was kind of rattled Saturday, and when I come to make my bet I got balled up and wrote down Sap. And I must of went crazy and played him for a thousand men."

"But where's our statement, mine and Sis'?" says Ella.

"That's my mistake again," I said. "I wrote out your ticket, but I must of forgot to turn it in."

They jumped up and come at me, and before I could duck I was kissed from both sides at once.

"O Sis!" yelps the Mrs. "Just think! We didn't lose our twelve hundred! We didn't lose nothing at all. We win eight thousand dollars!"

"Try and get it!" I says.

KATIE WINS A HOME

Oh yes, we been back here quite a wile. And we're liable to be here quite a wile. This town's good enough for me and it suits the Mrs. too, though they didn't neither one of us appreciate it till we'd give New York a try. If I was running the South Bend Boosters' club, I'd make everybody spend a year on the Gay White Way. They'd be so tickled when they got to South Bend that you'd never hear them razz the old burg again. Just yesterday we had a letter from Katie, asking us would we come and pay her a visit. She's a regular New Yorker now. Well, I didn't have to put up no fight with my Mrs. Before I could open my pan she says, "I'll write and tell her we can't come; that you're looking for a job and don't want to go nowheres just now."

Well, they's some truth in that. I don't want to go nowheres and I'll take a job if it's the right kind. We could get along on the interest from Ella's money, but I'm tired of laying round. I didn't do a tap of work all the time I was east and I'm out of the habit, but the days certainly do drag when a man ain't got nothing to do and if I can find something where I don't have to travel, I'll try it out.

But the Mrs. has still got most of what the old man left her and all and all, I'm glad we made the trip. I more than broke even by winning pretty close to $10,000 on the ponies down there. And we got Katie off our hands, which was one of the objects of us going in the first place—that and because the two gals wanted to see Life. So I don't grudge the time we spent, and we had some funny experiences when you look back at them. Anybody does that goes on a tour like that with a cuckoo like Katie. You hear a lot of songs and gags about mother-in-laws. But I could write a book of them about sister-in-laws that's twenty years old and pretty and full of peace and good will towards Men.

Well, after the blow-off with Daley, Long Island got too slow, besides costing us more than we could afford. So the gals suggested moving back in Town, to a hotel called the Graham on Sixty-seventh Street that somebody had told them was reasonable.

They called it a family hotel, but as far as I could see, Ella and I was the only ones there that had ever forced two dollars on the clergy. Outside of the transients, they was two song writers and a couple of gals that had their hair pruned and wrote for the papers, and the rest of the lodgers was boys that had got penned into a sixteen-foot ring with Benny Leonard by mistake. They looked like they'd spent many an evening hanging onto the ropes during the rush hour.

When we'd staid there two days, Ella and Katie was ready to pack up again.

"This is just a joint," said Ella. "The gals may be all right, but they're never in, only to sleep. And the men's impossible; a bunch of low prize-fighters."

I was for sticking, on account of the place being cheap, so I said: "Second prize ain't so low. And you're overlooking the two handsome tune thiefs. Besides, what's the difference who else lives here as long as the rooms is clean and they got a good restaurant? What did our dude cell-mates out on Long Island get us? Just trouble!"

But I'd of lose the argument as usual only for Kate oversleeping herself. It was our third morning at the Graham and her and Ella had it planned to go and look for a better place. But Katie didn't get up till pretty near noon and Ella went without her. So it broke so's Sis had just came downstairs and turned in her key when the two bellhops reeled in the front door bulging with baggage and escorting Mr. Jimmy Ralston. Yes, Jimmy Ralston the comedian. Or comic, as he calls it.

Well, he ain't F. X. Bushman, as you know. But no one that seen him could make the mistake of thinking he wasn't somebody. And he looked good enough to Kate so as she waited till the clerk had him fixed up, and then ast who he was. The clerk told her and she told us when the Mrs. come back from her hunt. Ella begin to name a few joints where we might move, but it seemed like Sis had changed her mind.

"Oh," she says, "let's stay here a wile longer, a week anyway."

"What's came over you!" ast Ella. "You just said last night that you was bored to death here."

"Maybe we won't be so bored now," said Kate, smiling. "The Graham's looking up. We're entertaining a celebrity—Jimmy Ralston of the Follies."

Well, they hadn't none of us ever seen him on the stage, but of course we'd heard of him. He'd only just started with the Follies, but he'd made a name for himself at the Winter Garden, where he broke in two or three years ago. And Kate said that a chorus gal she'd met—Jane Abbott—had told her about Ralston and what a scream he was on a party.

"He's terribly funny when he gets just the right number of drinks," says Kate.

"Well, let's stay then," says Ella. "It'll be exciting to know a real actor."

"I would like to know him," says Katie, "not just because he's on the stage, but I think it'd be fun to set and listen to him talk. He must say the screamingest things! If we had him round we wouldn't have to play cards or nothing for entertainment. Only they say it makes people fat to laugh."

"If I was you, I'd want to get fat," I said. "Looking like an E string hasn't started no landslide your way."

"Is he attractive?" ast the Mrs.

"Well," said Kate, "he isn't handsome, but he's striking looking. You wouldn't never think he was a comedian. But then, ain't it generally always true that the driest people have sad faces?"

"That's a joke!" I said. "Did you ever see Bryan when he didn't look like somebody was tickling his feet?"

"We'll have to think up some scheme to get introduced to him," says Ella.

"It'll be tough," I says. "I don't suppose they's anybody in the world harder to meet than a member of the Follies, unless it's an Elk in a Pullman washroom."

"But listen," says Kate: "We don't want to meet him till we've saw the show. It'd be awfully embarrassing to have him ask us how we liked the Follies and we'd have to say we hadn't been to it."

"Yes," said the Mrs., "but still if we tell him we haven't been to it, he may give us free passes."

"Easy!" I said. "And it'd take a big load off his mind. They say it worries the Follies people half sick wondering what to do with all their free passes."

"Suppose we go to-night!" says Kate. "We can drop in a hotel somewheres and get seats. The longer we don't go, the longer we won't meet him."

"And the longer we don't meet him," I says, "the longer till he gives you the air."

"I'm not thinking of Mr. Ralston as a possible suitor," says Katie, swelling up. "But I do want to get acquainted with a man that don't bore a person to death."

"Well," I says, "if this baby's anything like the rest of your gentleman friends, he won't hardly be round long enough for that."

I didn't make no kick about going to the show. We hadn't spent no money since we'd moved back to Town and I was as tired as the gals of setting up in the room, playing rummy. They said we'd have to dress, and I kicked just from habit, but I'd got past minding that end of it. They was one advantage in dolling up every time you went anywheres. It meant an hour when they was no chance to do something even sillier.

We couldn't stop to put on the nose bag at the Graham because the women was scared we'd be too late to get tickets. Besides, when you're dressed for dinner, you at least want the waiter to be the same. So we took a taxi down to the Spencer, bought Follies seats in the ninth row, and went in to eat. It's been in all the papers that the price of food has came down, but the hotel man can't read. They fined us eleven smackers for a two-course banquet that if the Woman's Guild, here, would dast soak you four bits a plate for it, somebody'd write a nasty letter to the *News-Times*.

We got in the theater a half hour before the show begin. I put in the time finding out what the men will wear, and the gals looked up what scenes Ralston'd be in. He was only on once in each act. They don't waste much time on a comedian in the Follies. It don't take long to spring the two gags they can think up for him in a year, and besides, he just interferes with the big gal numbers, where Bunny Granville or somebody dreams of the different flappers he danced with at the prom, and the souvenirs they give him; and one by one the different gals writhes in, dressed like the stage director thinks they dress at the female colleges—a Wesley gal in pink tights, a Vassar dame in hula-hula, and a Smith gal with a sombrero and a sailor suit. He does a couple of steps with them and they each hand him a flower or a vegetable to remember them by. The song winds up:

> But my most exclusive token
> Is a little hangnail broken
> Off the gal from Gussie's School for Manicures.

And his real sweet patootie comes on made up as a scissors.

You've saw Ralston? He's a good comedian; no getting away from that. The way he fixes up his face, you laugh just to look at him. I yelled when I first seen him. He was supposed to be an office boy and he got back late from lunch and the boss ast him what made him late and he said he stopped to buy the extra. So the boss ast him what extra and he says the extra about the New York society couple getting married. So the boss said, "Why, they wouldn't print an extra about that. They's a New York society couple married most every day." So Ralston said, "Yes, but this couple is both doing it for the first time."

I don't remember what other gags he had, and they're old anyway by now. But he was a hit, especially with Ella and Kate. They screamed so loud I thought we'd get the air. If he didn't say a word, he'd be funny with that fool make-up and that voice.

I guess if it wasn't for me the gals would of insisted on going back to the stage door after the show and waiting for him to come out. I've saw Katie bad a lot of times, but never as cuckoo as this. It wasn't no case of love at first or second sight. You couldn't be stuck on this guy from seeing him. But she'd always been kind of stage-struck and was crazy over the idear of getting acquainted with a celebrity, maybe going round to places with him, and having people see her with Jimmy Ralston, the comedian. And then, of course, most anybody wants to meet a person that can make you laugh.

I managed to persuade them that the best dope would be to go back to the Graham and wait for him to come home; maybe we could fix it up with the night clerk to introduce us. I told them that irregardless of what you read in books, they's some members of the theatrical profession that occasionally visits the place where they sleep. So we went to the hotel and set in the lobby for an hour and a half, me trying to keep awake wile the gals played Ralston's part of the show over again a couple thousand times. They's nothing goes so big with me as listening to people repeat gags out of a show that I just seen.

The clerk had been tipped off and when Ralston finally come in and went to get his key, I strolled up to the desk like I was after mine. The clerk introduced us.

"I want you to meet my wife and sister-in-law," I said.

"Some other time," says Ralston. "They's a matinee to-morrow and I got to run off to bed."

So off he went and I got bawled out for Ziegfeld having matinees. But I squared myself two days afterwards when we went in the restaurant for lunch. He was just having breakfast and the three of us stopped by his table. I don't think he remembered ever seeing me before, but anyway he got up and shook hands with the women. Well, you couldn't never accuse Ella of having a faint heart, and she says:

"Can't we set down with you, Mr. Ralston? We want to tell you how much we enjoyed the Follies."

So he says, sure, set down, but I guess we would of anyway.

"We thought it was a dandy show," says Katie.

"It ain't a bad troupe," says Ralston.

"If you'll pardon me getting personal," said Ella, "we thought you was the best thing in it."

He looked like he'd strain a point and forgive her.

"We all just yelled!" says Katie. "I was afraid they'd put us out, you made us laugh so hard."

"Well," says Ralston, "I guess if they begin putting people out for that, I'd have to leave the troupe."

"It wouldn't be much of a show without you," says Ella.

"Well, all that keeps me in it is friendship for Ziggy," says Ralston. "I said to him last night, I says, 'Ziggy, I'm going to quit the troupe. I'm tired and I want to rest a wile.' So he says, 'Jim, don't quit or I'll have to close the troupe. I'll give you fifteen hundred a week to stay.'

I'm getting a thousand now. But I says to him, I said, 'Ziggy, it ain't a question of money. What I want is a troupe of my own, where I get a chance to do serious work. I'm sick of making a monkey of myself in front of a bunch of saps from Nyack that don't appreciate no art but what's wrapped up in a stocking.' So he's promised that if I'll stick it out this year, he'll star me next season in a serious piece."

"Is he giving you the five hundred raise?" I ast him.

"I wouldn't take it," said Ralston. "I don't need money."

"At that, a person can live pretty cheap at this hotel," I says.

"I didn't move here because it was cheap," he said. "I moved here to get away from the pests—women that wants my autograph or my picture. And all they could say was how much they enjoyed my work and how did I think up all them gags, and so forth. No real artist likes to talk about himself, especially to people that don't understand. So that's the reason why I left the Ritz, so's I'd be left alone, not to save money. And I don't save no money, neither. I've got the best suite in the house—bedroom, bath, and study."

"What do you study?" ast Kate.

"The parts I want to play," he says; "Hamlet and Macbeth and Richard."

"But you're a comedian," says Kate.

"It's just a stepping stone," said Ralston.

He'd finished his breakfast and got up.

"I must go to my study and work," he says. "We'll meet again."

"Yes, indeed," says Ella. "Do you always come right back here nights after the show?"

"When I can get away from the pests," he says.

"Well," says Ella, "suppose you come up to our rooms to-night and we'll have a bite to eat. And I think the husband can give you a little liquid refreshments if you ever indulge."

"Very little," he says. "What is your room number?"

So the Mrs. told him and he said he'd see us after the show that night, and walked out.

"Well," said Ella, "how do you like him?"

"I think he's wonderful!" says Katie. "I didn't have no idear he was so deep, wanting to play Hamlet."

"Pretty near all comedians has got that bug," I says.

"Maybe he's different when you know him better," said Ella.

"I don't want him to be different," says Kate.

"But he was so serious," said the Mrs. "He didn't say nothing funny."

"Sure he did," I says. "Didn't he say artists hate to talk about themselfs?"

Pretty soon the waiter come in with our lunch. He ast us if the other gentleman was coming back.

"No," said Ella. "He's through."

"He forgot his check," says the dish smasher.

"Oh, never mind!" says Ella. "We'll take care of that."

"Well," I says, "I guess the bird was telling the truth when he said he didn't need no money."

I and the gals spent the evening at a picture show and stopped at a delicatessen on the way home to stock up for the banquet. I had a quart and a pint of yearling rye, and a couple of bottles of McAllister that they'd fined me fifteen smackers apiece for and I wanted to save them, so I told Kate that I hoped her friend would get comical enough on the rye.

"He said he drunk very little," she reminded me.

"Remember, don't make him talk about himself," said the Mrs. "What we want is to have him feel at home, like he was with old friends, and then maybe he'll warm up. I hope we don't wake the whole hotel, laughing."

Well, Ralston showed up about midnight. He'd remembered his date and apologized for not getting there before.

"I like to walk home from the theater," he says. "I get some of my funniest idears wile I walk."

I come to the conclusion later that he spent practically his whole life riding.

Ella's and my room wasn't no gymnasium for size and after the third drink, Ralston tried to get to the dresser to look at himself in the glass, and knocked a $30 vase for a corpse. This didn't go very big with the Mrs., but she forced a smile and would of accepted his apology if he'd made any. All he done was mumble something about cramped quarters. They was even more cramped when we set the table for the big feed, and it was my tough luck to have our guest park himself in the chair nearest the clothes closet, where my two bottles of Scotch had been put to bed. The fourth snifter finished the pint of rye and I said I'd get the other quart, but before I could stop her, Ella says:

"Let Mr. Ralston get it. It's right there by him."

So the next thing you know, James has found the good stuff and he comes out with both bottles of it.

"McAllister!" he says. "That's my favorite. If I'd knew you had that, I wouldn't of drank up all your rye."

"You haven't drank it all up," I says. "They's another bottle of it in there."

"It can stay there as long as we got this," he says, and helped himself to the corkscrew.

Well, amongst the knickknacks the gals had picked up at the delicatessen was a roast chicken and a bottle of olives, and at the time I thought Ralston was swallowing bones, stones, and all. It wasn't till the next day that we found all these keepsakes on the floor, along with a couple dozen assorted cigarette butts.

Katie's chorus gal friend had told her how funny the guy was when he'd had just the right number of shots, but I'd counted eight and begin to get discouraged before he started talking.

"My mother could certainly cook a chicken," he says.

"Is your mother living?" Kate ast him.

"No," he says. "She was killed in a railroad wreck. I'll never forget when I had to go and identify her. You wouldn't believe a person could get that mangled! No," he says, "my family's all gone. I never seen my father. He was in the pesthouse with smallpox when I was born and he died there. And my only sister died of jaundice. I can still——"

But Kate was scared we'd wake up the hotel, laughing, so she says: "Do you ever give imitations?"

"You mustn't make Mr. Ralston talk about himself," says Ella.

"Imitations of who?" said Ralston.

"Oh, other actors," said Katie.

"No," he says. "I leave it to the other actors to give imitations of me."

"I never seen none of them do it," says Kate.

"They all do it, but they don't advertise it," he says. "Every comic in New York is using my stuff."

"Oh!" said Ella. "You mean they steal your idears."

"Can't you go after them for it?" ast Katie.

"You could charge them with petit larceny," I said.

"I wouldn't be mean," said Ralston. "But they ain't a comic on the stage to-day that I didn't give him every laugh he's got."

"You ain't only been on the stage three or four years," I says. "How did Hitchcock and Ed Wynn and them fellas get by before they seen you?"

"They wasn't getting by," he says. "I'm the baby that put them on their feet. Take Hitchy. Hitchy come to me last spring and says, 'Jim, I've ran out of stuff. Have you got any notions I could use?' So I says, 'Hitchy, you're welcome to anything I got.' So I give him a couple of

idears and they're the only laughs in his troupe. And you take Wynn.
He opened up with a troupe that looked like a flop and one day I seen
him on Broadway, wearing a long pan, and I says, 'What's the matter,
Eddie?' And he brightened up and says, 'Hello, there, Jim! You're just
the boy I want to see.' So I says, 'Well, Eddie, I'm only too glad to do
anything I can.' So he says, 'I got a flop on my hands unlest I can get
a couple of idears, and you're the baby that can give them to me.' So I
said, 'All right, Eddie.' And I give him a couple of notions to work on
and they made his show. And look at Stone! And Errol! And Jolson and
Tinney! Every one of them come to me at one time another, hollering
for help. 'Jim, give me a couple of notions!' 'Jim, give me a couple of
gags!' And not a one of them went away empty-handed."

"Did they pay you?" ast Ella.

Ralston smiled.

"I wouldn't take no actor's money," he says. "They're all brothers
to me. They can have anything I got, and I can have anything they got,
only they haven't got nothing."

Well, I can't tell you all he said, as I was asleep part of the time.
But I do remember that he was the one that had give Bert Williams the
notion of playing coon parts, and learnt Sarah Bernhardt to talk
French.

Along about four o'clock, when they was less than a pint left in the
second McAllister bottle, he defied all the theater managers in New
York.

"I ain't going to monkey with them much longer!" he says. "I'll let
you folks in on something that'll cause a sensation on Broadway. I'm
going to quit the Follies!"

We was all speechless.

"That's the big secret!" he says. "I'm coming out as a star under my
own management and in a troupe wrote and produced by myself!"

"When?" ast Kate.

"Just as soon as I decide who I'm going to let in as part owner,"
said Ralston. "I've worked for other guys long enough! Why should I
be satisfied with $800 a week when Ziegfeld's getting rich off me!"

"When did he cut you $200?" I says. "You was getting $1,000 last
time I seen you."

He didn't pay no attention.

"And why should I let some manager produce my play," he says,
"and pay me maybe $1,200 a week when I ought to be making six or
seven thousand!"

"Are you working on your play now?" Kate ast him.

"It's done," he says. "I'm just trying to make up my mind who's the right party to let in on it. Whoever it is, I'll make him rich."

"I've got some money to invest," says Katie. "Suppose you tell us about the play."

"I'll give you the notion, if you'll keep it to yourself," says Ralston. "It's a serious play with a novelty idear that'll be a sensation. Suppose I go down to my suite and get the script and read it to you."

"Oh, if you would!" says Kate.

"It'll knock you dead!" he says.

And just the thought of it was fatal to the author. He got up from his chair, done a nose dive acrost the table and laid there with his head in the chili sauce.

I called up the clerk and had him send up the night bellhop with our guest's key. I and the boy acted as pall bearers and got him to his "suite," where we performed the last sad rites. Before I come away I noticed that the "suite" was a ringer for Ella's and mine—a dinky little room with a bath. The "study" was prettily furnished with coat hangers.

When I got back to my room Katie'd ducked and the Mrs. was asleep, so I didn't get a chance to talk to them till we was in the restaurant at noon. Then I ast Kate if she'd figured out just what number drink it was that had started him being comical.

"Now listen," she says: "I don't think that Abbott girl ever met him in her life. Anyway, she had him all wrong. We expected he'd do stunts, like she said, but he ain't that kind that shows off or acts smart. He's too much of a man for that. He's a bigger man than I thought."

"I and the bellhop remarked that same thing," I says.

"And you needn't make fun of him for getting faint," says Katie. "I called him up a wile ago to find out how he was and he apologized and said they must of been something in that second bottle of Scotch."

So I says:

"You tell him they was, but they ain't."

Well, it couldn't of been the Scotch or no other brew that ruined me. Or if it was, it worked mighty slow. I didn't even look at a drink for three days after the party in our room. But the third day I felt rotten, and that night I come down with a fever. Ella got scared and called a doctor and he said it was flu, and if I didn't watch my step it'd be something worse. He advised taking me to a hospital and I didn't have pep enough to say no.

So they took me and I was pretty sick for a couple of weeks—too sick for the Mrs. to give me the news. And it's a wonder I didn't have a relapse when she finally did.

"You'll probably yelp when you hear this," she says. "I ain't crazy about it myself, but it didn't do me no good to argue at first and it's too late for argument now. Well, to begin with, Sis is in love with Ralston."

"What of it!" I said. "She's going through the city directory and she's just got to the R's."

"No, it's the real thing this time," said the Mrs. "Wait till you hear the rest of it. She's going on the stage!"

"I've got nothing against that," I says. "She's pretty enough to get by in the Follies chorus, and if she can earn money that way, I'm for it."

"She ain't going into no chorus," said Ella. "Ralston's quit the Follies and she's going in his show."

"The one he wrote?" I ast.

"Yes," said the Mrs.

"And who's going to put it on?" I ast her.

"That's it," she says. "They're going to put it on themself, Ralston and Sis. With Sis's money. She sold her bonds, fifty thousand dollars' worth."

"But listen," I says. "Fifty thousand dollars! What's the name of the play, Ringling's Circus?"

"It won't cost all that," said Ella. "They figure it'll take less than ten thousand to get started. But she insisted on having the whole thing in a checking account, where she can get at it. If the show's a big success in New York they're going to have a company in Chicago and another on the road. And Ralston says her half of the profits in New York ought to run round $5,000 a week. But anyway, she's sure of $200 a week salary for acting in it."

"Where did she get the idear she can act?" I says.

"She's always had it," said the Mrs., "and I think she made him promise to put her in the show before she agreed to back it. Though she says it's a wonderful investment! She won't be the leading woman, of course. But they's only two woman's parts and she's got one of them."

"Well," I said, "if she's going to play a sap and just acts normal, she'll be a sensation."

"I don't know what she'll be," says Ella. "All I know is that she's mad over Ralston and believes everything he says. And even if you hadn't of been sick we couldn't of stopped her."

So I ast what the play was like, but Ella couldn't tell me.

Ralston had read it out loud to she and Kate, but she couldn't judge from just hearing it that way. But Kate was tickled to death with it. And they'd already been rehearsing a week, but Sis hadn't let Ella see the rehearsals. She said it made her nervous.

"Ralston thinks the main trouble will be finding a theater," said the Mrs. "He says they's a shortage of them and the men that owns them won't want to let him have one on account of jealousy."

"Has the Follies flopped?" I ast her.

"No," she says, "but they've left town."

"They always do, this time of year," I said.

"That's what I thought," says the Mrs., "but Ralston says they'd intended to stay here all the year round, but when the news come out that he'd left, they didn't dast. He's certainly got faith in himself. He must have, to give up a $600 a week salary. That's what he says he was really getting."

"You say Katie's in love," I says. "How about him?"

"I don't know and she don't know," says Ella. "He calls her dearie and everything and holds her hands, but when they're alone together, he won't talk nothing but business. Still, as I say, he calls her dearie."

"Actors calls every gal that," I says. "It's because they can't remember names."

Well, to make a short story out of it, they had another couple weeks' rehearsals that we wasn't allowed to see, and they finally got a theater—the Olney. They had to guarantee a $10,000 business to get it. They didn't go to Atlantic City or nowheres for a tryout. They opened cold. And Ralston didn't tell nobody what kind of a show it was.

Of course he done what they generally always do on a first night. He sent out free passes to everybody that's got a dress suit, and they's enough of them in New York to pretty near fill up a theater. These invited guests is supposed to be for the performance wile it's going on. After it's through, they can go out and ride it all over the island.

Well, the rules wasn't exactly lived up to at "Bridget Sees a Ghost." On account of Ralston writing the play and starring in it, the gang thought it would be comical and they come prepared to laugh. It was comical all right, and they laughed. They didn't only laugh; they yelled. But they yelled in the wrong place.

The programme said it was "a Daring Drama in Three Acts." The three acts was what made it daring. It took nerve to even have one. In the first place, this was two years after the armistice and the play was about the war, and I don't know which the public was most interested in by this time—the war or Judge Parker.

Act 1 was in July, 1917. Ralston played the part of Francis Shaw, a captain in the American army. He's been married a year, and when the curtain goes up, his wife's in their New York home, waiting for him to come in from camp on his weekly leave. She sets reading the war news in the evening paper, and she reads it out loud, like people always do when they're alone, waiting for somebody. Pretty soon in comes Bridget, the Irish maid—our own dear Katie. And I wished you could of heard her brogue. And seen her gestures. What she reminded me most like was a gal in a home talent minstrels giving an imitation of Lew Fields playing the part of the block system on the New York Central. Her first line was, "Ain't der Captain home yed?" But I won't try and give you her dialect.

"No," says Mrs. Shaw. "He's late." So Katie says better late than never, and the wife says, yes, but she's got a feeling that some day it'll be never; something tells her that if he ever goes to France, he won't come back. So Bridget says, "You been reading the war news again and it always makes you sad." "I hate wars!" says Mrs. Shaw, and that line got one of the biggest laughs.

After this they was a couple of minutes when neither of them could think of nothing to add, and then the phone rung and Bridget answered it. It was Capt. Shaw, saying he'd be there pretty soon; so Bridget goes right back to the kitchen to finish getting dinner, but she ain't no sooner than left the stage when Capt. Shaw struts in. He must of called up from the public booth on his front porch.

The audience had a tough time recognizing him without his comic make-up, but when they did they give him a good hand. Mrs. Shaw got up to greet him, but he brushed by her and come down to the footlights to bow. Then he turned and went back to his Mrs., saying "Maizie!" like this was the last place he expected to run acrost her. They kissed and then he ast her "Where is Bobbie, our dear little one?"—for fear she wouldn't know whose little one he meant. So she rung the bell and back come Bridget, and he says "Well, Bridget!" and Bridget says, "Well, it's the master!" This line was another riot. "Bring the little one, Bridget," says Mrs. Shaw, and the audience hollered again.

Wile Bridget was after the little one, the Captain celebrated the re-union by walking round the room, looking at the pictures. Bridget brings the baby in and the Captain uncovers its face and says, "Well, Bobbie!" Then he turns to his wife and says, "Let's see, Maizie. How old is he?" "Two weeks," says Maizie. "Two weeks!" says Captain Shaw, surprised. "Well," he says, "I hope by the time he's old enough to fight for the Stars and Stripes, they won't be no such a thing as war." So Mrs. Shaw says, "And I hope his father won't be called on to make the supreme sacrifice for him and we others that must stay home and wait. I sometimes think that in wartime, it's the women and children that suffers most. Take him back to his cozy cradle, Bridget. We mothers must be careful of our little ones. Who knows when the kiddies will be our only comfort!" So Bridget beat it out with the little one and I bet he hated to leave all the gaiety.

"Well," says Shaw to his wife, "and what's the little woman been doing?"

"Just reading," she says, "reading the news of this horrible war. I don't never pick up the paper but what I think that some day I'll see your name amongst the dead."

"Well," says the Captain bravely, "they's no danger wile I stay on U. S. soil. But only for you and the little one, I would welcome the call to go Over There and take my place in the battle line. The call will come soon, I believe, for they say France needs men." This rumor pretty near caused a riot in the audience and Ralston turned and give us all a dirty look.

Then Bridget come in again and said dinner was ready, and Shaw says, "It'll seem funny to set down wile I eat." Which was the first time I ever knew that army captains took their meals off the mantelpiece.

Wile the Shaws was out eating, their maid stayed in the living room, where she'd be out of their way. It seems that Ralston had wrote a swell speech for her to make in this spot, about what a tough thing war is, to come along and separate a happy young couple like the Shaws that hadn't only been married a year. But the speech started "This is terrible!" and when Bridget got that much of it out, some egg in the gallery hollered "You said a mouthful, kid!" and stopped the show.

The house finally quieted down, but Katie was dumb for the first time in her life. She couldn't say the line that was the cue for the phone to ring, and she had to go over and answer a silent call. It was for the Captain, and him and his wife both come back on the stage.

"Maizie," he says, after he'd hung up, "it's came! That was my general! We sail for France in half an hour!"

"O husband!" says Maizie. "This is the end!"

"Nonsense!" says Shaw with a brave smile. "This war means death for only a small per cent of our men."

"And almost no captains," yells the guy in the gallery.

Shaw gets ready to go, but she tells him to wait till she puts on her wraps; she'll go down to the dock and see him off.

"No, darling," he says. "Our orders is secret. I can't give you the name of our ship or where we're sailing from."

So he goes and she flops on the couch w'ining because he wouldn't tell her whether his ship left from Times Square or Grand Central.

They rung the curtain down here to make you think six days has passed. When it goes up again, Maizie's setting on the couch, holding the little one. Pretty soon Bridget comes in with the evening paper.

"They's a big headline, mum," she says. "A troopship has been torpedoed."

Well, when she handed her the paper, I could see the big headline. It said, "Phillies Hit Grimes Hard." But Maizie may of had a bet on Brooklyn. Anyway, she begin trembling and finally fell over stiff. So Bridget picked up the paper and read it out loud:

"Amongst the men lost was Capt. F. Shaw of New York."

Down went the curtain again and the first act was over, and some jokesmith in the audience yelled "Author! Author!"

"He's sunk!" said the egg in the gallery.

Well, Maizie was the only one in the whole theater that thought Shaw was dead. The rest of us just wished it. Still you couldn't blame her much for getting a wrong idear, as it was Nov. 11, 1918—over a year later—when the second act begins, and she hadn't heard from him in all that time. It wasn't never brought out why. Maybe he'd forgot her name or maybe it was Burleson's fault, like everything else.

The scene was the same old living room and Maizie was setting on the same old couch, but she was all dressed up like Elsie Ferguson. It comes out that she's expecting a gentleman friend, a Mr. Thornton, to dinner. She asks Bridget if she thinks it would be wrong of her to accept the guy the next time he proposed. He's ast her every evening for the last six months and she can't stall him much longer. So Bridget says it's all right if she loves him, but Maizie don't know if she loves him or not, but he looks so much like her late relic that she can't hardly tell the difference and besides, she has got to either marry or go to work, or her and the little one will starve. They's a knock at the door and Thornton comes in. Him and the absent Captain looks as much alike as two brothers, yours and mine. Bridget ducks and Thornton proposes. Maizie says, "Before I answer, I must tell you a secret. Captain Shaw didn't leave me all alone. I have a little one, a boy." "Oh, I love kiddies," says Thornton. "Can I see him?" So she says it's seven o'clock and the little one's supposed to of been put to bed, but she has Bridget go get him.

The little one's entrance was the sensation of this act. In Act 1 he was just three or four towels, but now Bridget can't even carry him acrost the stage, and when she put him on his feet, he comes up pretty near to her shoulder. And when Thornton ast him would he like to have a new papa, he says, "Yes, because my other papa's never coming back."

Well, they say a woman can't keep a secret, but if Thornton had been nosing round for six months and didn't know till now that they was a spanker like Bobbie in the family circle, I wouldn't hardly call Maizie the town gossip.

After the baby'd went back to read himself to sleep and Mrs. Shaw had yessed her new admirer, Bridget dashed in yelling that the armistice was signed and held up the evening paper for Maizie and Thornton to see. The great news was announced in code. It said: "Phillies Hit Grimes Hard." And it seemed kind of silly to not come right out and say "Armistice Signed!" Because as I recall, even we saps out here in South Bend had knew it since three o'clock that morning.

The last act was in the same place, on Christmas Eve, 1918.

Maizie and her second husband had just finished doing up presents for the little one. We couldn't see the presents, but I suppose they was giving him a cocktail shaker and a shaving set. Though when he come on the stage you could see he hadn't aged much since Act 2. He hadn't even begin to get bald.

Thornton and the Mrs. went off somewheres and left the kid alone, but all of a sudden the front door opened and in come old Cap Shaw, on crutches. He seen the kid and called to him. "Who are you?" says the little one. "I'm Santa Claus," says the Cap, "and I've broughten you a papa for Christmas." "I don't want no papa," says Bobbie. "I've just got a new one." Then Bridget popped in and seen "the master" and hollered, "A ghost!" So he got her calmed down and she tells him what's came off. "It was in the paper that Capt. F. Shaw of New York was lost," she says. "It must of been another Capt. F. Shaw!" he says.

"It's an odd name," hollered the guy in the gallery.

The Captain thinks it all over and decides it's his move. He makes Bridget promise to never tell that she seen him and he says good-by to she and the kid and goes out into the night.

Maizie comes in, saying she heard a noise and what was it? Was somebody here? "Just the boy with the evening paper," says Bridget. And the cat's got Bobbie's tongue. And Maizie don't even ask for the paper. She probably figured to herself it was the old story; that Grimes was still getting his bumps.

Well, I wished you could of read what the papers wrote up about the show. One of them said that Bridget seen a ghost at the Olney theater last night and if anybody else wanted to see it, they better go quick because it wouldn't be walking after this week. Not even on crutches. The mildest thing they said about Ralston was that he was even funnier than when he was in the Follies and tried to be. And they said the part of Bridget was played by a young actress that they hoped would make a name for herself, because Ralston had probably called her all he could think of.

We waited at the stage door that night and when Kate come out, she was crying. Ralston had canned her from the show.

"That's nothing to cry about," I says. "Yo're lucky! It's just like as if a conductor had put you off a train a couple of minutes before a big smash-up."

The programme had been to all go somewheres for supper and celebrate the play's success. But all Katie wanted now was to get in a taxi and go home and hide.

On the way, I ast her how much she was in so far.

"Just ten thousand," she says.

"Ten thousand!" I said. "Why, they was only one piece of scenery and that looked like they'd bought it secondhand from the choir boys' minstrels. They couldn't of spent one thousand, let alone ten."

"We had to pay the theater a week's rent in advance," she says. "And Jimmy give five thousand to a man for the idear."

"The idear for what?" I ast.

"The idear for the play," she said.

"That stops me!" I says. "This baby furnishes idears for all the good actors in the world, but when he wants one for himself, he goes out and pays $5,000 for it. And if he got a bargain, you're Mrs. Fiske."

"Who sold him the idear?" ast Ella.

"He wouldn't tell me," says Kate.

"Ponzi," I said.

Ralston called Kate up the next noon and made a date with her at the theater. He said that he was sorry he'd been rough. Before she went I ast her to give me a check for the forty thousand she had left so's I could buy back some of her bonds.

"I haven't got only $25,000," she says. "I advanced Jimmy fifteen thousand for his own account, so's he wouldn't have to bother me every time they was bills to meet."

So I said: "Listen: I'll go see him with you and if he don't come clean with that money, I'll knock him deader'n his play."

"Thank you!" she says. "I'll tend to my own affairs alone."

She come back late in the afternoon, all smiles.

"Everything's all right," she said. "I give him his choice of letting me be in the play or giving me my money."

"And which did he choose?" I ast her.

"Neither one," she says. "We're going to get married."

"Bridget" went into the ashcan Saturday night and the wedding come off Monday. Monday night they left for Boston, where the Follies was playing. Kate told us they'd took Ralston back at the same salary he was getting before.

"How much is that?" I ast her.

"Four hundred a week," she says.

Well, two or three days after they'd left, I got up my nerve and says to the Mrs.:

"Do you remember what we moved to the Big Town for? We done it to see Life and get Katie a husband. Well, we got her a kind of a husband and I'll tell the world we seen Life. How about moseying back to South Bend?"

"But we haven't no home there now."

"Nor we ain't had none since we left there," I says. "I'm going down and see what's the first day we can get a couple of lowers."

"Get uppers if it's quicker," says the Mrs.

So here we are, really enjoying ourselfs for the first time in pretty near two years. And Katie's in New York, enjoying herself, too, I suppose. She ought to be, married to a comedian. It must be such fun to just set and listen to him talk.

SOME LIKE THEM COLD

N. Y., Aug. 3.

DEAR MISS GILLESPIE: How about our bet now as you bet me I would forget all about you the minute I hit the big town and would never write you a letter. Well girlie it looks like you lose so pay me. Seriously we will call all bets off as I am not the kind that bet on a sure thing and it sure was a sure thing that I would not forget a girlie like you and all that is worrying me is whether it may not be the other way round and you are wondering who this fresh guy is that is writing you this letter. I bet you are so will try and refreshen your memory.

Well girlie I am the handsome young man that was wondering round the Lasalle st. station Monday and "happened" to sit down beside of a mighty pretty girlie who was waiting to meet her sister from Toledo and the train was late and I am glad of it because if it had not of been that little girlie and I would never of met. So for once I was a lucky guy but still I guess it was time I had some luck as it was certainly tough luck for you and I to both be liveing in Chi all that time and never get together till a half hour before I was leaveing town for good.

Still "better late than never" you know and maybe we can make up for lost time though it looks like we would have to do our makeing up at long distants unless you make good on your threat and come to N. Y. I wish you would do that little thing girlie as it looks like that was the only way we would get a chance to play round together as it looks like they was little or no chance of me comeing back to Chi as my whole future is in the big town. N. Y. is the only spot and specially for a man that expects to make my liveing in the song writeing game as here is the Mecca for that line of work and no matter how good a man may be they don't get no recognition unless they live in N. Y.

Well girlie you asked me to tell you all about my trip. Well I remember you saying that you would give anything to be makeing it yourself but as far as the trip itself was conserned you ought to be thankfull you did not have to make it as you would of sweat your head off. I know I did specially wile going through Ind. Monday P.M. but Monday night was the worst of all trying to sleep and finely I give it up and just layed there with the prespiration rolling off of me though I was laying on top of the covers and nothing on but my underwear.

Yesterday was not so bad as it rained most of the A.M. comeing through N. Y. state and in the P. M. we road along side of the Hudson all P. M. Some river girlie and just looking at it makes a man forget all about the heat and everything else except a certain girlie who I seen for the first time Monday and then only for a half hour but she is the kind of a girlie that a man don't need to see her only once and they would be no danger of forgetting her. There I guess I better lay off that subject or you will think I am a "fresh guy."

Well that is about all to tell you about the trip only they was one amuseing incidence that come off yesterday which I will tell you. Well they was a dame got on the train at Toledo Monday and had the birth opp. mine but I did not see nothing of her that night as I was out smokeing till late and she hit the hay early but yesterday A. M. she come in the dinner and sit at the same table with me and tried to make me and it was so raw that the dinge waiter seen it and give me the wink and of course I paid no tension and I waited till she got through so as they would be no danger of her folling me out but she stopped on the way out to get a tooth pick and when I come out she was out on the platform with it so I tried to brush right by but she spoke up and asked me what time it was and I told her and she said she geussed her watch was slow so I said maybe it just seemed slow on acct. of the company it was in.

I don't know if she got what I was driveing at or not but any way she give up trying to make me and got off at Albany. She was a good looker but I have no time for gals that tries to make strangers on a train.

Well if I don't quit you will think I am writeing a book but will expect a long letter in answer to this letter and we will see if you can keep your promise like I have kept mine. Don't dissapoint me girlie as I am all alone in a large city and hearing from you will keep me from getting home sick for old Chi though I never thought so much of the old town till I found out you lived there. Don't think that is kidding girlie as I mean it.

You can address me at this hotel as it looks like I will be here right along as it is on 47th st. right off of old Broadway and handy to everything and am only paying $21 per wk. for my rm. and could of got one for $16 but without bath but am glad to pay the differents as am lost without my bath in the A. M. and sometimes at night too.

Tomorrow I expect to commence fighting the "battle of Broadway" and will let you know how I come out that is if you answer this letter. In the mean wile girlie au reservoir and don't do nothing I would not do.   Your new friend (?)   CHAS. F. LEWIS.

                                                    Chicago, Ill., Aug. 6
MY DEAR MR. LEWIS: Well, that certainly was a "surprise party" getting your letter and you are certainly a "wonder man" to keep your word as I am afraid most men of your sex are gay deceivers but maybe you are "different." Any way it sure was a surprise and will gladly pay the bet if you will just tell me what it was we bet. Hope it was not money as I am a "working girl" but if it was not more than a dollar or two will try to dig it up even if I have to "beg, borrow or steal."

Suppose you will think me a "case" to make a bet and then forget what it was, but you must remember, Mr. Man, that I had just met you and was "dazzled." Joking aside I was rather "fussed" and will tell you why. Well, Mr. Lewis, I suppose you see lots of girls like the one you told me about that you saw on the train who tried to "get acquainted" but I want to assure you that I am not one of those kind and sincerely hope you will believe me when I tell you that you was the first man I ever spoke to meeting them like that and my friends and the people who know me would simply faint if they knew I ever spoke to a man without a "proper introduction."

Believe me, Mr. Lewis, I am not that kind and I don't know now why I did it only that you was so "different" looking if you know what I mean and not at all like the kind of men that usually try to force their attentions on every pretty girl they see. Lots of times I act on impulse and let my feelings run away from me and sometimes I do things on the impulse of the moment which I regret them later on, and that is what I did this time, but hope you won't give me cause to regret it and I know you won't as I know you are not that kind of a man a specially after what you told me about the girl on the train. But any way as I say, I was in a "daze" so can't remember what it was we bet, but will try and pay it if it does not "break" me.

Sis's train got in about ten minutes after yours had gone and when she saw me what do you think was the first thing she said? Well, Mr. Lewis, she said: "Why Mibs (That is a pet name some of my friends have given me) what has happened to you? I never seen you have as much color." So I passed it off with some remark about the heat and changed the subject as I certainly was not going to tell her that I had just been talking to a man who I had never met or she would of dropped dead from the shock. Either that or she would not of believed me as it would be hard for a person who knows me well to imagine me doing a thing like that as I have quite a reputation for "squelching" men who try to act fresh. I don't mean anything personal by that, Mr. Lewis, as am a good judge of character and could tell without you telling me that you are not that kind.

Well, Sis and I have been on the "go" ever since she arrived as I took yesterday and today off so I could show her the "sights" though she says she would be perfectly satisfied to just sit in the apartment and listen to me "rattle on." Am afraid I am a great talker, Mr. Lewis, but Sis says it is as good as a show to hear me talk as I tell things in such a different way as I cannot help from seeing the humorous side of everything and she says she never gets tired of listening to me, but of course she is my sister and thinks the world of me, but she really does laugh like she enjoyed my craziness.

Maybe I told you that I have a tiny little apartment which a girl friend of mine and I have together and it is hardly big enough to turn round in, but still it is "home" and I am a great home girl and hardly ever care to go out evenings except occasionally to the theatre or dance. But even if our "nest" is small we are proud of it and Sis complimented us on how cozy it is and how "homey" it looks and she said she did not see how we could afford to have everything so nice and Edith (my girl friend) said: "Mibs deserves all the credit for that. I never knew a girl who could make a little money go a long ways like she can." Well, of course she is my best friend and always saying nice things about me, but I do try and I hope I get results. Have always said that good taste and being careful is a whole lot more important than lots of money though it is nice to have it.

You must write and tell me how you are getting along in the "battle of Broadway" (I laughed when I read that) and whether the publishers like your songs though I know they will. Am crazy to hear them and hear you play the piano as I love good jazz music even better than classical, though I suppose it is terrible to say such a thing. But I usually say just what I think though sometimes I wish afterwards I had not of. But still I believe it is better for a girl to be her own self and natural instead of always acting. But am afraid I will never have a chance to hear you play unless you come back to Chi and pay us a visit as my "threat" to come to New York was just a "threat" and I don't see any hope of ever getting there unless some rich New Yorker should fall in love with me and take me there to live. Fine chance for poor little me, eh Mr. Lewis?

Well, I guess I have "rattled on" long enough and you will think I
am writing a book unless I quit and besides, Sis has asked me as a special
favor to make her a pie for dinner. Maybe you don't know it, Mr. Man,
but I am quite famous for my pie and pastry, but I don't suppose a
"genius" is interested in common things like that.

Well, be sure and write soon and tell me what N.Y. is like and all
about it and don't forget the little girlie who was "bad" and spoke to
a strange man in the station and have been blushing over it ever since.

Your friend (?)   MABELLE GILLESPIE.

N. Y., Aug. 10

DEAR GIRLIE: I bet you will think I am a fresh guy commenceing that
way but Miss Gillespie is too cold and a man can not do nothing cold
in this kind of weather specially in this man's town which is the hottest
place I ever been in and I guess maybe the reason why New Yorkers is
so bad is because they think they are all ready in H—— and can not
go no worse place no matter how they behave themselves. Honest girlie
I certainly envy you being where there is a breeze off the old Lake and
Chi may be dirty but I never heard of nobody dying because they was
dirty but four people died here yesterday on acct. of the heat and I seen
two different women flop right on Broadway and had to be taken away
in the ambulance and it could not of been because they was dressed too
warm because it would be impossible for the women here to leave off
any more cloths.

Well have not had much luck yet in the battle of Broadway as all
the heads of the big music publishers is out of town on their vacation
and the big boys is the only ones I will do business with as it would be
silly for a man with the stuff I have got to waste my time on somebody
that is just on the staff and have not got the final say. But I did play a
couple of my numbers for the people up to Levy's and Goebel's and
they went crazy over them in both places. So it looks like all I have to
do is wait for the big boys to get back and then play my numbers for
them and I will be all set. What I want is to get taken on the staff of
one of the big firms as that gives a man the inside and they will plug
your numbers more if you are on the staff. In the mean wile have not
got nothing to worry me but am just seeing the sights of the big town
as have saved up enough money to play round for a wile and any way
a man that can play piano like I can don't never have to worry about
starveing. Can certainly make the old music box talk girlie and am
always good for a $75 or $100 job.

Well have been here a week now and on the go every minute and I thought I would be lonesome down here but no chance of that as I have been treated fine by the people I have met and have sure met a bunch of them. One of the boys liveing in the hotel is a vaudeville actor and he is a member of the Friars club and took me over there to dinner the other night and some way another the bunch got wise that I could play piano so of course I had to sit down and give them some of my numbers and everybody went crazy over them. One of the boys I met there was Paul Sears the song writer but he just writes the lyrics and has wrote a bunch of hits and when he heard some of my melodies he called me over to one side and said he would like to work with me on some numbers. How is that girlie as he is one of the biggest hit writers in N. Y.

N. Y. has got some mighty pretty girlies and I guess it would not be hard to get acquainted with them and in fact several of them has tried to make me since I been here but I always figure that a girl must be something wrong with her if she tries to make a man that she don't know nothing about so I pass them all up. But I did meet a couple of pips that a man here in the hotel went up on Riverside Drive to see them and insisted on me going along and they got on some way that I could make a piano talk so they was nothing but I must play for them so I sit down and played some of my own stuff and they went crazy over it.

One of the girls wanted I should come up and see her again, and I said I might but I think I better keep away as she acted like she wanted to vamp me and I am not the kind that likes to play round with a gal just for their company and dance with them etc. but when I see the right gal that will be a different thing and she won't have to beg me to come and see her as I will camp right on her trail till she says yes. And it won't be none of these N. Y. fly by nights neither. They are all right to look at but a man would be a sucker to get serious with them as they might take you up and next thing you know you would have a wife on your hands that don't know a dish rag from a waffle iron.

Well girlie will quit and call it a day as it is too hot to write any more and I guess I will turn on the cold water and lay in the tub a wile and then turn in. Don't forget to write to

Your friend,   CHAS. F. LEWIS.

DEAR MR. MAN: Hope you won't think me a "silly Billy" for starting my letter that way but "Mr. Lewis" is so formal and "Charles" is too much the other way and any way I would not dare call a man by their first name after only knowing them only two weeks. Though I may as well confess that Charles is my favorite name for a man and have always been crazy about it as it was my father's name. Poor old dad, he died of cancer three years ago, but left enough insurance so that mother and we girls were well provided for and do not have to do anything to support ourselves though I have been earning my own living for two years to make things easier for mother and also because I simply can't bear to be doing nothing as I feel like a "drone." So I flew away from the "home nest" though mother felt bad about it as I was her favorite and she always said I was such a comfort to her as when I was in the house she never had to worry about how things would go.

But there I go gossiping about my domestic affairs just like you would be interested in them though I don't see how you could be though personaly I always like to know all about my friends, but I know men are different so will try and not bore you any longer. Poor Man, I certainly feel sorry for you if New York is as hot as all that. I guess it has been very hot in Chi, too, at least everybody has been complaining about how terrible it is. Suppose you will wonder why I say "I guess" and you will think I ought to know if it is hot. Well, sir, the reason I say "I guess" is because I don't feel the heat like others do or at least I don't let myself feel it. That sounds crazy I know, but don't you think there is a good deal in mental suggestion and not letting yourself feel things? I believe that if a person simply won't allow themselves to be affected by disagreeable things, why such things won't bother them near as much. I know it works with me and that is the reason why I am never cross when things go wrong and "keep smiling" no matter what happens and as far as the heat is concerned, why I just don't let myself feel it and my friends say I don't even look hot no matter if the weather is boiling and Edith, my girl friend, often says that I am like a breeze and it cools her off just to have me come in the room. Poor Edie suffers terribly during the hot weather and says it almost makes her mad at me to see how cool and unruffled I look when everybody else is perspiring and have red faces etc.

I laughed when I read what you said about New York being so hot that people thought it was the "other place." I can appreciate a joke, Mr. Man, and that one did not go "over my head." Am still laughing at some of the things you said in the station though they probably struck me funnier than they would most girls as I always see the funny side and sometimes something is said and I laugh and the others wonder what I am laughing at as they cannot see anything in it themselves, but it is just the way I look at things so of course I cannot explain to them why I laughed and they think I am crazy. But I had rather part with almost anything rather than my sense of humour as it helps me over a great many rough spots.

Sis has gone back home though I would of liked to of kept her here much longer, but she had to go though she said she would of liked nothing better than to stay with me and just listen to me "rattle on." She always says it is just like a show to hear me talk as I always put things in such a funny way and for weeks after she has been visiting me she thinks of some of the things I said and laughs over them. Since she left Edith and I have been pretty quiet though poor Edie wants to be on the "go" all the time and tries to make me go out with her every evening to the pictures and scolds me when I say I had rather stay home and read and calls me a "book worm." Well, it is true that I had rather stay home with a good book than go to some crazy old picture and the last two nights I have been reading myself to sleep with Robert W. Service's poems. Don't you love Service or don't you care for "highbrow" writings?

Personly there is nothing I love more than to just sit and read a good book or sit and listen to somebody play the piano, I mean if they can really play and I really believe I like popular music better than the classical though I suppose that is a terrible thing to confess, but I love all kinds of music but a specially the piano when it is played by somebody who can really play.

Am glad you have not "fallen" for the "ladies" who have tried to make your acquaintance in New York. You are right in thinking there must be something wrong with girls who try to "pick up" strange men as no girl with self respect would do such a thing and when I say that, Mr. Man, I know you will think it is a funny thing for me to say on account of the way our friendship started, but I mean it and I assure you that was the first time I ever done such a thing in my life and would never of thought of doing it had I not known you were the right kind of a man as I flatter myself that I am a good judge of character and can tell pretty well what a person is like by just looking at them and I assure you I had made up my mind what kind of a man you were before I allowed myself to answer your opening remark. Otherwise I am the last girl in the world that would allow myself to speak to a person without being introduced to them.

When you write again you must tell me all about the girl on Riverside Drive and what she looks like and if you went to see her again and all about her. Suppose you will think I am a little old "curiosity shop" for asking all those questions and will wonder why I want to know. Well, sir, I won't tell you why, so there, but I insist on you answering all questions and will scold you if you don't. Maybe you will think that the reason why I am so curious is because I am "jealous" of the lady in question. Well, sir, I won't tell you whether I am or not, but will keep you "guessing." Now, don't you wish you knew?

Must close or you will think I am going to "rattle on" forever or maybe you have all ready become disgusted and torn my letter up. If so all I can say is poor little me—she was a nice little girl and meant well, but the man did not appreciate her.

There! Will stop or you will think I am crazy if you do not all ready.

Yours (?)   MABELLE.

N. Y., Aug. 20

DEAR GIRLIE: Well girlie I suppose you thought I was never going to answer your letter but have been busier than a one armed paper hanger the last week as have been working on a number with Paul Sears who is one of the best lyric writers in N. Y. and has turned out as many hits as Berlin or Davis or any of them. And believe me girlie he has turned out another hit this time that is he and I have done it together. It is all done now and we are just waiting for the best chance to place it but will not place it nowheres unless we get the right kind of a deal but maybe will publish it ourselves.

The song is bound to go over big as Sears has wrote a great lyric and I have give it a great tune or at least every body that has heard it goes crazy over it and it looks like it would go over bigger than any song since Mammy and would not be surprised to see it come out the hit of the year. If it is handled right we will make a bbl. of money and Sears says it is a cinch we will clean up as much as $25000 apiece which is pretty fair for one song but this one is not like the most of them but has got a great lyric and I have wrote a melody that will knock them out of their seats. I only wish you could hear it girlie and hear it the way I play it. I had to play it over and over about 50 times at the Friars last night.

I will copy down the lyric of the chorus so you can see what it is like and get the idea of the song though of course you can't tell much about it unless you hear it played and sang. The title of the song is When They're Like You and here is the chorus:

> "Some like them hot, some like them cold.
> Some like them when they're not too darn old.
> Some like them fat, some like them lean.
> Some like them only at sweet sixteen.

Some like them dark, some like them light.
Some like them in the park, late at night.
Some like them fickle, some like them true,
But the time I like them is when they're like you."

How is that for a lyric and I only wish I could play my melody for you as you would go nuts over it but will send you a copy as soon as the song is published and you can get some of your friends to play it over for you and I know you will like it though it is a different melody when I play it or when somebody else plays it.

Well girlie you will see how busy I have been and am libel to keep right on being busy as we are not going to let the grass grow under our feet but as soon as we have got this number placed we will get busy on another one as a couple like that will put me on Easy st. even if they don't go as big as we expect but even 25 grand is a big bunch of money and if a man could only turn out one hit a year and make that much out of it I would be on Easy st. and no more hammering on the old music box in some cabaret.

Who ever we take the song to we will make them come across with one grand for advance royaltys and that will keep me going till I can turn out another one. So the future looks bright and rosey to yours truly and I am certainly glad I come to the big town though sorry I did not do it a whole lot quicker.

This is a great old town girlie and when you have lived here a wile you wonder how you ever stood for a burg like Chi which is just a hick town along side of this besides being dirty etc. and a man is a sucker to stay there all their life specially a man in my line of work as N. Y. is the Mecca for man that has got the musical gift. I figure that all the time I spent in Chi I was just wasteing my time and never really started to live till I come down here and I have to laugh when I think of the boys out there that is trying to make a liveing in the song writing game and most of them starve to death all their life and the first week I am down here I meet a man like Sears and the next thing you know we have turned out a song that will make us a fortune.

Well girlie you asked me to tell you about the girlie up on the Drive that tried to make me and asked me to come and see her again. Well I can assure you you have no reasons to be jealous in that quarter as I have not been back to see her as I figure it is wasteing my time to play round with a dame like she that wants to go out somewheres every night and if you married her she would want a house on 5th ave. with a dozen servants so I have passed her up as that is not my idea of home.

What I want when I get married is a real home where a man can stay home and work and maybe have a few of his friends in once in a wile and entertain them or go to a good musical show once in a wile and have a wife that is in sympathy with you and not nag at you all the wile but be a real help mate. The girlie up on the Drive would run me ragged and have me in the poor house inside of a year even if I was makeing 25 grand out of one song. Besides she wears a make up that you would have to blast to find out what her face looks like. So I have not been back there and don't intend to see her again so what is the use of me telling you about her. And the only other girlie I have met is a sister of Paul Sears who I met up to his house wile we was working on the song but she don't hardly count as she has not got no use for the boys but treats them like dirt and Paul says she is the coldest proposition he ever seen.

Well I don't know no more to write and besides have got a date to go out to Paul's place for dinner and play some of my stuff for him so as he can see if he wants to set words to some more of my melodies. Well don't do nothing I would not do and have as good a time as you can in old Chi and will let you know how we come along with the song.

                                                                CHAS. F. LEWIS.

                                                    Chicago, Ill., Aug. 23

DEAR MR. MAN: I am thrilled to death over the song and think the words awfully pretty and am crazy to hear the music which I know must be great. It must be wonderful to have the gift of writing songs and then hear people play and sing them and just think of making $25,000 in such a short time. My, how rich you will be and I certainly congratulate you though am afraid when you are rich and famous you will have no time for insignificant little me or will you be an exception and remember your "old" friends even when you are up in the world? I sincerely hope so.

Will look forward to receiving a copy of the song and will you be sure and put your name on it? I am all ready very conceited just to think that I know a man that writes songs and makes all that money.

Seriously I wish you success with your next song and I laughed when I read your remark about being busier than a one armed paper hanger. I don't see how you think up all those comparisons and crazy things to say. The next time one of the girls asks me to go out with them I am going to tell them I can't go because I am busier than a one armed paper hanger and then they will think I made it up and say: "The girl is clever."

Seriously I am glad you did not go back to see the girl on the Drive and am also glad you don't like girls who makes themselves up so much as I think it is disgusting and would rather go round looking like a ghost than put artificial color on my face. Fortunately I have a complexion that does not need "fixing" but even if my coloring was not what it is I would never think of lowering myself to "fix" it. But I must tell you a joke that happened just the other day when Edith and I were out at lunch and there was another girl in the restaurant whom Edie knew and she introduced her to me and I noticed how this girl kept staring at me and finally she begged my pardon and asked if she could ask me a personal question and I said yes and she asked me if my complexion was really "mine." I assured her it was and she said: "Well, I thought so because I did not think anybody could put it on so artistically. I certainly envy you." Edie and I both laughed.

Well, if that girl envies me my complexion, why I envy you living in New York. Chicago is rather dirty though I don't let that part of it bother me as I bathe and change my clothing so often that the dirt does not have time to "settle." Edie often says she cannot see how I always keep so clean looking and says I always look like I had just stepped out of a band box. She also calls me a fish (jokingly) because I spend so much time in the water. But seriously I do love to bathe and never feel so happy as when I have just "cleaned up" and put on fresh clothing.

Edie has just gone out to see a picture and was cross at me because I would not go with her. I told her I was going to write a letter and she wanted to know to whom and I told her and she said: "You write to him so often that a person would almost think you was in love with him." I just laughed and turned it off, but she does say the most embarrassing things and I would be angry if it was anybody but she that said them.

Seriously I had much rather sit here and write letters or read or just sit and dream than go out to some crazy old picture show except once in awhile I do like to go to the theater and see a good play and a specially a musical play if the music is catchy. But as a rule I am contented to just stay home and feel cozy and lots of evenings Edie and I sit here without saying hardly a word to each other though she would love to talk but she knows I had rather be quiet and she often says it is just like living with a deaf and dumb mute to live with me because I make so little noise round the apartment. I guess I was born to be a home body as I so seldom care to go "gadding."

Though I do love to have company once in awhile, just a few congenial friends whom I can talk to and feel at home with and play cards

or have some music. My friends love to drop in here, too, as they say
Edie and I always give them such nice things to eat. Though poor Edie
has not much to do with it, I am afraid, as she hates anything connected
with cooking which is one of the things I love best of anything and I
often say that when I begin keeping house in my own home I will insist
on doing most of my own work as I would take so much more interest
in it than a servant, though I would want somebody to help me a little
if I could afford it as I often think a woman that does all her own work
is liable to get so tired that she loses interest in the bigger things of life
like books and music. Though after all what bigger thing is there than
home making a specially for a woman?

I am sitting in the dearest old chair that I bought yesterday at a little
store on the North Side. That is my one extravagance, buying furniture
and things for the house, but I always say it is economy in the long run
as I will always have them and have use for them and when I can pick
them up at a bargain I would be silly not to. Though heaven knows I
will never be "poor" in regards to furniture and rugs and things like
that as mother's house in Toledo is full of lovely things which she
says she is going to give to Sis and myself as soon as we have real
homes of our own. She is going to give me the first choice as I am her
favorite. She has the loveliest old things that you could not buy now
for love or money including lovely old rugs and a piano which Sis
wanted to have a player attachment put on it but I said it would be an
insult to the piano so we did not get one. I am funny about things like
that, a specially old furniture and feel towards them like people whom
I love.

Poor mother, I am afraid she won't live much longer to enjoy her
lovely old things as she has been suffering for years from stomach trouble and the doctor says it has been worse lately instead of better and
her heart is weak besides. I am going home to see her a few days this
fall as it may be the last time. She is very cheerful and always says she
is ready to go now as she has had enough joy out of life and all she
would like would be to see her girls settled down in their own homes
before she goes.

There I go, talking about my domestic affairs again and I will bet
you are bored to death though personly I am never bored when my
friends tell me about themselves. But I won't "rattle on" any longer,
but will say good night and don't forget to write and tell me how you
come out with the song and thanks for sending me the words to it. Will
you write a song about me some time? I would be thrilled to death! But
I am afraid I am not the kind of girl that inspires men to write songs

about them, but am just a quiet "mouse" that loves home and am not giddy enough to be the heroine of a song.

Well, Mr. Man, good night and don't wait so long before writing again to   Yours (?)   MABELLE.

N. Y., Sept. 8

DEAR GIRLIE: Well girlie have not got your last letter with me so cannot answer what was in it as I have forgotten if there was anything I was supposed to answer and besides have only a little time to write as I have a date to go out on a party with the Sears. We are going to the Georgie White show and afterwards somewheres for supper. Sears is the boy who wrote the lyric to my song and it is him and his sister I am going on the party with. The sister is a cold fish that has no use for men but she is show crazy and insists on Paul takeing her to 3 or 4 of them a week.

Paul wants me to give up my room here and come and live with them as they have plenty of room and I am running a little low on money but don't know if I will do it or not as am afraid I would freeze to death in the same house with a girl like the sister as she is ice cold but she don't hang round the house much as she is always takeing trips or going to shows or somewheres.

So far we have not had no luck with the song. All the publishers we have showed it to has went crazy over it but they won't make the right kind of a deal with us and if they don't loosen up and give us a decent royalty rate we are libel to put the song out ourselves and show them up. The man up to Goebel's told us the song was O. K. and he liked it but it was more of a production number than anything else and ought to go in a show like the Follies but they won't be in N. Y. much longer and what we ought to do is hold it till next spring.

Mean wile I am working on some new numbers and also have taken a position with the orchestra at the Wilton and am going to work there starting next week. They pay good money $60 and it will keep me going.

Well girlie that is about all the news. I believe you said your father was sick and hope he is better and also hope you are getting along O. K. and take care of yourself. When you have nothing else to do write to your friend,   CHAS. F. LEWIS.

Chicago, Ill., Sept. 11

DEAR MR. LEWIS: Your short note reached me yesterday and must say I was puzzled when I read it. It sounded like you was mad at me

though I cannot think of any reason why you should be. If there was
something I said in my last letter that offended you I wish you would
tell me what it was and I will ask your pardon though I cannot remember anything I could of said that you could take offense at. But if there
was something, why I assure you, Mr. Lewis, that I did not mean
anything by it. I certainly did not intend to offend you in any way.

Perhaps it is nothing I wrote you, but you are worried on account
of the publishers not treating you fair in regards to your song and that
is why your letter sounded so distant. If that is the case I hope that by
this time matters have rectified themselves and the future looks brighter.
But any way, Mr. Lewis, don't allow yourself to worry over business
cares as they will all come right in the end and I always think it is silly
for people to worry themselves sick over temporary troubles, but the
best way is to "keep smiling" and look for the "silver lining" in the
cloud. That is the way I always do and no matter what happens, I
manage to smile and my girl friend, Edie, calls me Sunny because I
always look on the bright side.

Remember also, Mr. Lewis, that $60 is a salary that a great many
men would like to be getting and are living on less than that and sup-
porting a wife and family on it. I always say that a person can get along
on whatever amount they make if they manage things in the right way.

So if it is business troubles, Mr. Lewis, I say don't worry, but look
on the bright side. But if it is something I wrote in my last letter that
offended you I wish you would tell me what it was so I can apologize
as I assure you I meant nothing and would not say anything to hurt
you for the world.

Please let me hear from you soon as I will not feel comfortable until
I know I am not to blame for the sudden change.

Sincerely,   MABELLE GILLESPIE.

N. Y., Sept. 24

DEAR MISS GILLESPIE: Just a few lines to tell you the big news or at
least it is big news to me. I am engaged to be married to Paul Sears'
sister and we are going to be married early next month and live in
Atlantic City where the orchestra I have been playing with has got an
engagement in one of the big cabarets.

I know this will be a surprise to you as it was even a surprise to me
as I did not think I would ever have the nerve to ask the girlie the big
question as she was always so cold and acted like I was just in the way.
But she said she supposed she would have to marry somebody some
time and she did not dislike me as much as most of the other men her

brother brought round and she would marry me with the understanding that she would not have to be a slave and work round the house and also I would have to take her to a show or somewheres every night and if I could not take her myself she would "run wild" alone. Atlantic City will be O. K. for that as a lot of new shows opens down there and she will be able to see them before they get to the big town. As for her being a slave, I would hate to think of marrying a girl and then have them spend their lives in druggery round the house. We are going to live in a hotel till we find something better but will be in no hurry to start house keeping as we will have to buy all new furniture.

Betsy is some doll when she is all fixed up and believe me she knows how to fix herself up. I don't know what she uses but it is weather proof as I have been out in a rain storm with her and we both got drowned but her face stayed on. I would almost think it was real only she tells me different.

Well girlie I may write to you again once in a wile as Betsy says she don't give a dam if I write to all the girls in the world just so I don't make her read the answers but that is all I can think of to say now except good bye and good luck and may the right man come along soon and he will be a lucky man getting a girl that is such a good cook and got all that furniture etc.

But just let me give you a word of advice before I close and that is don't never speak to strange men who you don't know nothing about as they may get you wrong and think you are trying to make them. It just happened that I knew better so you was lucky in my case but the luck might not last.   Your friend,   CHAS. F. LEWIS.

Chicago, Ill., Sept. 27

MY DEAR MR. LEWIS: Thanks for your advice and also thank your fiance for her generosity in allowing you to continue your correspondence with her "rivals," but personly I have no desire to take advantage of that generosity as I have something better to do than read letters from a man like you, a specially as I have a man friend who is not so generous as Miss Sears and would strongly object to my continuing a correspondence with another man. It is at his request that I am writing this note to tell you not to expect to hear from me again.

Allow me to congratulate you on your engagement to Miss Sears and I am sure she is to be congratulated too, though if I met the lady I would be tempted to ask her to tell me her secret, namely how she is going to "run wild" on $60.   Sincerely,   MABELLE GILLESPIE.